A Private War

A Private War

Perry Cockerell

ISBN- 13: 9781523961153
ISBN- 10: 1523961155

Alliance Publishing LLC
Dallas, Texas

 The story and characters depicted in this book are fiction and are not intended to represent any particular person. The military court- martial in this book is fiction. Some aspects of the book relating to the foreign correspondents serving during World War II are based on fact.

Contents

Some say that the difference between a dream and reality is that there is no truth in a dream. Truth can be theoretical; a concept and about perception. If its right hand is reality, then its left hand is a dream.

A dream is an escape, a longing of desirable places, things, or accomplishments. It is not authentic. It has no borders or limits.

Reality is cold; it leaves no heroes in its wake. It strips what heroes there are of their armor, until they are a myth.

A dream begins at the edge of a desired world, where truth is uncertain. In a dream, heroes awake.

Reality is authentic and can be desirable or rejected because of its truth. It begins at the edge of a dream's end and where life picks back up, settles, or moves on; where what truth that exists is neither black nor white.

PART 1

Andre and Booker

CHAPTER 1

IT WAS A blistering hot day in August of 1930 in Mountain Springs, Alabama. The construction of St. Peter's Catholic Church and School was complete, and the dedication of the church and religious school was set for September 6th. The site would be home to one of the largest Catholic churches and private educational systems in the state. A wealthy family in New York donated the money for its construction. The local children could attend a school exceeding anything available in the nearby public school system.

Father Webster slowly walked the grounds that Sunday morning. He would soon perform his last four homilies at the chapel that had served the daily Mass well for many years.

He noticed that lime from the soil was still spilling from the freshly laid sidewalks. A few of the concrete walkways had fallen leaves imprinted on their surface.

The cathedral stood high and could be seen for miles away; the convent and school were located across the walkway. Such a place was unheard of only a few years ago, during a time when the church depended on every dime from the collection plate. Twenty-five years with the parish, and

Father Webster was finally thinking like a Southern Baptist. He caught himself raising his voice during the homily, and he began to mention the budget and request that members increase their tithes. The Catholics were gaining a foothold in the South among the Baptists and Methodists.

"How are the grounds, Father? Are you inspecting them?" asked Sister Camille as she walked toward the chapel from the convent.

"Indeed, I am," said Father Webster. "Father Sanders is on his way. We want to look around before going in. Do we have a crowd today?"

"We have about thirty inside for the 8 a.m. Mass, Father," said Sister Camille.

"We will have a lot more next Sunday when we dedicate the new cathedral."

"I look forward to that," smiled Sister Camille.

"Is Sister Laurie ready?" asked Father Webster.

"She is. She practiced all day yesterday on the organ."

"She should be ready, then. Ah, look. Here's Father Sanders now," said Father Webster.

"Good morning, Father. Good morning, Sister. I had trouble getting up this morning," explained Father Sanders. "Are you ready, Father?"

"I am. In fact, we are all ready. Sister, have the altar boys meet us at the entrance," said Father Webster.

As the boys and priests gathered at the front of the small church, Sister Camille sang the opening call to worship. She wore a burgundy robe and a black cover over one side of her face. A partition separated her from the congregation, but they could see her through window-like openings. Two angels were carved on the partition that separated the choir in the chapel. The fourteen Stations of the Cross were displayed on the wall. A statue of St. Joseph stood on the left; on the right, a statue of Mother Mary looked down upon the congregation.

Sister Laurie played the organ, accompanying Sister Camille as she sang the opening song. After the song concluded, the congregation stood to sing "Blessed Assurance" as the altar boys entered, carrying the crucifix. The boys led Father Sanders, followed by Father Webster, up to the altar. Father Sanders knelt and Father Webster walked around to the other side of the altar, kissing it before walking to his seat.

Father Webster's reading was taken from Mark 6:22. The congregation stood and the Father put his hand to his head, to his mouth, and to his heart and read:

> *"For when Herod's daughter came in and danced, she pleased Herod and his guests; and the King said to the girl, 'Ask me for whatever you wish, and I will grant it.' And he vowed to her, 'Whatever you ask me, I will give you, even half of my kingdom.' And she went out, and said to her mother, 'What shall I ask?' And she said, 'The head of John the baptizer.' And she came in immediately with haste to the King and said, 'I want you to give me at once the head of John the Baptist on a platter.' And the King was exceedingly sorry; but because of his oaths and his guests he did not want to break his word to her. And*

immediately the king sent a soldier of the guard and gave orders to bring his head. He went and beheaded him in the prison."

"The Word of the Lord."

"The Word of the Lord," the congregation repeated.

Father Webster kissed the Bible and the congregation sat down to hear his last homily. He began: "Some say that because Herod lost his mind, John the Baptist lost his head."

A half mile away, six-year-old Andre Williams walked into his brother's room on the second story of his parents' farm house. It was quite a large home for their family. His father, Kyle Williams, did not own the home. Kyle's family lived in the old house based on an agreement to restore the abandoned and rickety home in exchange for living quarters. If anyone could make the home livable, Kyle could.

Andre was the fourth of five children. His older sister, Deanna, was the quiet one. She was musical and much like her father, the choir director at the First African Baptist Church. Mr. Williams had accepted the position after the prior choir director died. The congregation had no more than fifty people each Sunday, meeting in an old house not far down the street. Mr. Williams was musical himself. He and the organist Mrs. Collins, who was almost seventy years old, took care of the choir on Sundays.

The old reed organ was played by operating foot pedals. Deanna understood music at an early age; she would play around the foot pedals of the organ and reach the keys without raising her head above the level of the keyboard. The organ appeared to play by itself for those who did not realize Deanna was there. She would sometimes skip school to play the organ, but her mother Bertha knew where she was and would retrieve her, sending her back to class.

Bertha was born in St. Martins and was of French descent. Music was an important part of her life as well. Bertha immigrated through New Orleans by ship and never looked back. Once in New Orleans, she traveled to Jackson, Mississippi, looking for a job. It was there that she met Clara Thompson. Clara thought Bertha perfect for her brother George Thompson, who lived in Mountain Springs. George wasn't interested, but his friend Kyle Williams was and Kyle asked Bertha out for a date. Kyle never questioned how Bertha had immigrated to America. But she was quite beautiful, and attracting an American husband came easily to her.

The Williams married in January of 1912. Their first child, Deanna, was born a little over a year later in 1913. Then a second son, Franklin, the next year. Seven years later a daughter LaVonda was born. Another three years later, and Andre made his appearance. Their family was complete one year later with the birth of Ben.

Andre's brother Franklin looked out the window of the second story of their home. His fingers ran up and down guitar, playing a song. Andre approached the door of Franklin's room. Unaware anyone was listening, Franklin sang:

"Please don't look at me that way, I can
hardly say what I have to say,
There is nothing that I haven't told to you,
that I didn't believe you knew.
I am thinking of another time I could feel
you thinking that you were mine,
Now I hold out my hands 'til my arms get
tired and you wait on the other side."

Andre pushed on the door. It opened, hitting the chair that Franklin had placed in that very spot to keep anyone from entering his room.

Franklin, now sixteen years old, stopped. "Andre, what are you doing? Get out of here. Don't come in here while I'm here. I didn't say you could come in."

Andre ran out of the room and Franklin slammed the door behind him. But Andre lurked near the door and listened. Franklin walked back to his guitar. "That idiot," he grumbled.

Franklin put his fingers on the guitar to play the song he had written on a piece of paper. He started singing again:

"You and me, we're both the same,
Don't let me take all the blame,
I promise that I will do all it takes to make up for my mistakes.
So, I'm trying ..."

Andre continued listening nearby in the hall. His head touched the door and it opened once again, hitting the chair and interrupting Franklin.

"Why you ...!" Franklin put down the guitar and lurched toward Andre, who quickly shut the door and ran out of the room.

Franklin stopped and thought for a moment. The kid was only six years old. "Come here," he relented, opening the door.

Andre came into the room.

"Now don't play with this while I'm not here. Put your hand here." Franklin put Andre's small right hand on the arm of the guitar and let him feel the strings. He held the guitar and strummed it.

"Most people strum the guitar using a few chords and they make up a song with those chords," Franklin said. "But I've thought of something. You hear Deanna down there playing the chords on the piano?"

"Yes."

"To play the guitar, I had to learn chords. Then I learned to pick. But then I thought, what if I play a chord for every note? No one does that."

They heard the piano downstairs. Deanna was practicing the song "My Shepherd Will Supply My Need."

"She's playing chords sometimes. That's how I figured it out."

"Can I see?" asked Andre.

"Yes. Here's how you play the C chord." Franklin demonstrated for him, but Andre's fingers could not stretch far enough to make the complete chord.

Deanna's playing continued.

"We have to sing that song in a little while. Now watch me when I play. I'm playing a chord for every note. You don't ever hear that on the guitar," said Franklin.

Andre watched in amazement, but it was too far beyond his understanding. And yet Andre would never forget Franklin's explanation. He looked at his big brother's song, written on a piece of paper and lying on his desk.

"Where is Booker? He's your friend and you should be playing with him." said Franklin.

"He's outside with Ben. He hates music. He says we sing the worst songs he has ever heard."

"I bet his aunt has a say in that," said Franklin.

"We're ready," called Bertha, the mother of five children. She was in the kitchen putting icing on the cake. LaVonda was assisting and Deanna was still playing the piano. Their father and Ben, followed by Booker, were outside putting feed in the barn. Ben was five years old and followed his father everywhere.

Kyle shoveled feed into a compartment in the barn where the cows couldn't reach it. The pigs were in their pen and the chickens were next to the pigs on the side of the barn. Kyle built the chicken pen near the pigs because he didn't think dogs would enter if the pigs were stationed in front of the chickens. Ben assisted by gathering eggs and putting them in a sack. Booker tagged along, also looking for eggs.

"I found five eggs, Daddy!" exclaimed Ben, running to show his father. Kyle put his hand on Ben's shoulder to congratulate him.

"Good job," said Kyle.

"I have two eggs," said Booker.

"Good boy," said Kyle. "Let's go inside now."

"Daddy, do I have to sing?" asked Ben.

"Yes, you have to sing," Kyle smiled.

"I'm not singing," said Booker.

"I don't like singing," said Ben.

"I don't like shoveling feed either on Sunday. It's Sunday, and we didn't go to church just this one time. Besides, it's your brother's birthday."

Kyle was unsure why Bertha didn't want to go to church that Sunday, although he thought it might be due to Andre's birthday celebration. He had to find someone else to direct the choir that day.

"I'm not going to sing if they ask me," said Booker.

"You don't have to sing," said Kyle.

The three were walking towards the house when they saw Clara Thompson approaching. Bertha had invited Clara to the party so that she could take Booker home afterwards.

"There's your Aunt Clara," said Kyle to Booker.

Booker ran to Clara with his arms open wide. "Aunt Clara!" he yelled as he ran to her.

Clara was Booker Thompson's aunt. Booker lost his mother when he was young and never knew his father. Clara had raised him for the past five years.

George Thompson, Clara's brother, worked at a nearby gas station. He disapproved of Clara and he frequently fought with her. He didn't approve of Clara raising Booker, but he had no choice. He wasn't married himself, although many women tried to get him to marry them. There was something about Clara that he didn't like, but he couldn't put it into words.

"Nice to see you, Clara," greeted Kyle as they walked up to the house.

"Hello, Mr. Kyle. How was my precious Booker last night?" she asked.

"Well, we told him we were not going to church and he didn't have to sing at Andre's party, so he was a happy camper all night."

"Which church?" Clara asked.

"What do you mean which church?" said Kyle.

"Nothing," said Clara.

"I forgot something back at the barn. You go in the house and I'll be in there in a minute," said Kyle. "Ben, show Clara to the door."

Kyle went back to the field and picked a flower to give to Bertha.

"How is my precious Ben?" asked Clara as she hugged him.

They walked to the door and Clara knocked.

"You don't have to knock," said Ben.

Bertha and LaVonda were finishing the last bit of icing when they heard the knock.

"Who is it?" asked LaVonda.

"It's Clara," said Bertha. "I invited her."

"You invited Booker's aunt?" asked LaVonda, surprised.

"I did. She can take Booker home after the party." As Clara walked in, Deanna played the piano.

"My, you play good. It's just a matter of time before you are playing up at the church for real," said Clara, walking past Deanna.

"Thank you," Deanna said as she continued playing. "I know I can play that organ. You just have to push the pedal at the right time," she explained.

Clara walked into the kitchen with a large sack. She wasn't going to come to the party without contributing.

"Hello, Clara," said Bertha, placing the knife in the kitchen sink.

"Hello, Bertha, I see that you have your hands full. You all are going to be in a lot of trouble for not going to church this morning."

"I know," said Bertha.

"Here are some party napkins and candles, in case you need some," said Clara.

"Thank you. I do have candles, but thanks."

"So you didn't go up to the new church today?" asked Clara.

"Shush," said Bertha. "I haven't told Kyle about that. I was going to tell him after lunch and see if we could go to the 5:30 service."

"You haven't told him? That's why he looked at me that way out there. He doesn't know what you are up to."

"No. He doesn't know ... yet," said Bertha, touching up the icing on Andre's cake.

"Well, to be honest, I didn't go to church this morning either," said Clara.

"You didn't? Why not? You know Kyle wants you to take over as choir director," said Bertha.

"I know. I went up to the new church, St. Peter's."

"You went to St. Peter's?" exclaimed Bertha.

Deanna stopped playing the piano.

"I did," said Clara in a low tone.

Deanna began playing the piano again.

"The new place is a lot nicer than the old chapel. They let us go in and see it after the service. This was the last Sunday for the old chapel. Next Sunday is the dedication of the new church. You should see it. It is quite a marvelous place and black people can go to it. We can't send our kids to the new school, but we can go to the church on Sundays. I went to the eight o'clock service. I think the Catholics are different than the Baptists. They like to do this thing called the 'Rosary' after the church service. Have you ever heard of that?"

"I have, but I've never done it. You went up there? Why did you do that?" asked Bertha.

"After you told me about it I checked it out. I thought you all would be there this morning. I've tried all kinds of things, even going to Jackson, and nothing works for me," said Clara.

"Does Kyle know you've been going up there? What is he going to do if you don't take over the choir? What will George think about you going up there?" asked Bertha.

"I haven't told Mr. Kyle that I would take over being choir director if he quits. I know he needs me to stay in the choir. And George and I don't talk about anything. George doesn't go to church much and Kyle wants him in the choir. He doesn't approve of anything I do," said Clara.

"Well, we don't have to talk about him right now. I've taken the kids up there a few times and they know about it, but I haven't gotten the nerve to tell Kyle about it. I know he won't like it. I thought this would be a good time to look at other places to go to church," said Bertha.

"The folks are going to be sad to see you go. I've been missing a few Sundays. In fact, I've been going back down to Jackson sometimes. Some friends said to go down there and I wanted to see if that makes any difference."

Bertha ignored Clara's remarks about going to Jackson for the second time. She had a plan for her own kids. "If I go to church up there, then it's just a matter of time before I can get my kids in that school," Bertha confided.

"Black kids going to school there? Do you think they will ever let that happen?" asked Clara.

"You have to start somewhere. I know if we don't do something there won't be much for these kids. All the education they get is from the church. They need a real education to get in college," said Bertha.

LaVonda heard everything. So did Deanna, who stopped playing the piano. Franklin and Andre also listened as they walked down the stairs. They all paused to hear what their mother was saying. They could tell something was happening. Their lives were about to change.

Andre knew about St. Peters. His mother had taken him up there a few times. She was at peace at that church, and so was Andre. She would tell him, "Andre, wouldn't you like to go to school up here?" Andre didn't know what to say, but he understood what she was talking about. School was the last thing on his mind at age six. The kids understood their mother's plan. They would attend the new Catholic church; the church would not discriminate. It was an ingenious plan for 1930 and for her five children. She didn't know what Catholic meant, but she knew she could get her kids educated there.

"My, what a nice cake you have there," Kyle said, walking in the kitchen and handing Bertha the flower he had picked. He kissed her several times as the kids and Clara watched. They saw how their father treated their mother.

"You know, a French girl needs to be kissed ten times," Bertha said.

"And she will be," said her husband as he finished.

"Now, let's go eat," Kyle said as he left for the dining room. Everyone followed.

"Sit here, Booker," said Bertha. "Andre, you can sit next to Booker."

Kyle said the blessing. "Let us be thankful for what we have."

"All right. Just get to it. No big speeches," said Franklin.

"Franklin," reprimanded Bertha.

Andre had worn a tie to the table on his birthday.

"Andre, you look like you are going to a wedding," his father said.

Everyone laughed.

"I'm going to a birthday party," he said. Then he put mashed potatoes on his plate.

There was plenty of food, including fried chicken, mashed potatoes, and gravy.

"Well, are you going to eat 'em or climb 'em?" asked his father.

Everyone laughed.

"He's going to climb 'em," said Ben. "I found five eggs."

"That's great, Ben," said Bertha.

"I found two eggs," said Booker.

"That is great, Booker," said Clara. "How were the boys yesterday? Did they play all day?"

"They tore up my room," said Deanna.

"Booker needs a bath," said LaVonda. "He stinks."

Everyone laughed.

"Booker doesn't stink," said Kyle. "But, if he do stink, it was because he was working around the pig pen and getting eggs."

Kyle turned to Franklin and asked, "What were you doing, Franklin? Playing the guitar? We have work to do and you are up there picking on a guitar. That won't pay you anything while the little kids are working. After this meal is over, I want you and whoever is next to go out and graze the horses. There isn't enough grass on the farm."

"Yes, sir."

"Whose turn is it to graze the horses?" asked Kyle.

"Andre's," said Franklin.

"It's not my turn!" argued Andre.

Kyle looked at Ben.

"It is not my turn! I did it yesterday!" said Ben.

There was a pause.

"Deanna, are you going to play for us?" asked Clara.

"Yes, they are going to play," said Bertha. "They've been practicing. Booker didn't have to practice. We didn't make him do that."

"Booker would like to sing," said Clara.

"No, I wouldn't. I hate to sing. They sing the worst songs I've ever heard," groaned young Booker.

"He doesn't have to sing," said Kyle. "Are you boys and girls ready?"

There were some hems and haws. "Ok. None of that," said Kyle.

They all gathered around the piano while Deanna prepared to play.

LaVonda stood by the side to direct like her father did for the choir on Sundays. "Now, I want to see everyone singing and I don't want to see anyone just mouthing the words."

Then the children sang:

"My Shepherd will supply my need, Jehovah is His name,
In pastures fresh He makes me feed beside the living stream;
He brings my wandering spirit back when I forsake His way,
And leads me for His mercy's sake in paths of truth and grace.
When I walk through the shades of death His presence is my stay,
One word of His supporting grace drives all my fears away;
His hand in sight of all my foes doth still my table spread,
My cup with blessings overflows, His oil anoints my head.
The sure provisions of my God attend me all my days;
Oh, may Thy house be my abode and all my work be praise;
There would I find a settled rest, while others go and come;
No more a stranger nor a guest, but like a child at home."

The proud parents and Clara congratulated them.

But Booker sat with Clara, smiling as if he was laughing at Andre being forced to sing. To Booker, this was the worst song he had ever heard.

"That was so great," said Clara, crying as they finished. "It just breaks my heart. Oh lordy, oh lordy, these kids sing like it was Easter Sunday. I want them to sing that on Easter Sunday next year."

"I love that song. We need to do it more often than just Easter Sunday," said Bertha.

"I agree," said Kyle. "And I have the right person who can direct the choir and do it next. I think Clara can do it. What do you think, Clara?"

"I know what you are up to, Mr. Kyle! I know you want someone else to direct the choir. I have not said yes yet. I can't do it right now. I've missed the last few months of church anyway," said Clara.

"I need you and George up there. That's why I'm nominating you to take over so you will start going to church, and with you we get two in the process. You can get George to start coming. We need another bass in the choir," explained Kyle.

"Is everyone ready for cake?" said Bertha.

"Yes, yes!" the kids yelled.

Deanna, LaVonda, Bertha, and Clara went into the kitchen. A few moments later they came out carrying a cake with candles. They lit the candles and sang, "*Happy Birthday to Andre.*" Andre paused, then blew out the candles.

Franklin gave him toy soldiers from World War I. Bertha gave him a used shirt and pants. Ben gave him a toy plastic horse. And Deanna and LaVonda gave him sheet music that he didn't want.

"This is good," said Kyle. "I'm going to go up and rest a while. I'm tired and just need a nap. Clara, don't leave. I want to talk to you about the choir at the church."

"I was going to go home with Booker. And I'm not sure I can direct the choir," she said to Kyle.

"I bet you can. They need you up there. I know you can sing. We can talk about it later."

"Ok. I'll stay but I'm not saying yes yet," she said, her voice rising as Kyle ascended the stairway to the second floor.

"Good," said Kyle. He closed the door to the master bedroom upstairs.

"I think I'll go up for a while, too," responded Bertha.

The kids went about playing. Franklin walked outside and saddled the horses. Deanna and LaVonda went to their room.

Andre and Booker remained at the table, looking at all the gifts.

"Music? They gave you *music*?" said Booker. "I want *these*," he said, pointing at the toy soldiers.

"Do you want to play war with them?" asked Andre.

"Yes," said Booker. "Do you have an attic?"

"Yes," said Andre.

"Let's go up there," said Booker.

A stairway ran from the kitchen to a door to the attic. The attic was full of old clothes and junk and hiding places for Andre and Booker to play war.

The boys spread the toys out on the attic floor. They pretended to fight in the scary parts of the attic.

After a while, Clara called for Booker.

"Booker, where are you?"

"Is that your aunt?" Andre said.

"It is," said Booker. "I'm up here!"

Clara climbed up to the attic door and opened it. "I thought you might be up here. I can't keep you out of my attic. What are you doing up here?"

"We're just playing," said Booker.

"Well, I better come up there with you," said Clara.

Clara was about to open the door when she looked down and noticed the cake on the table. She went back downstairs to the kitchen table and cut two pieces of the cake for Booker and Andre. Then she walked up the stairs again and looked back, noticing that she had forgotten to pick up the candles. Annoyed, she walked back down to get the candles and matches and then walked back up to the attic. "That should be nice," she thought, walking up the stairs with her hands filled. "Look what I have for you boys!" she called, entering the attic.

Clara put the cake plate on the floor. "I thought you might like another piece of cake," she said.

"Yea!" said Booker.

Clara struck the match but it didn't light. She put the match down near some old clothes that she hadn't noticed were lying on the floor. She struck another match. It did not light either. She put that match down next to the other. The third match worked and Clara lit the candles. She dropped the match on the floor near the others.

"There we go," said Clara as the candles lit.

"Yea!" said Andre.

"Now blow them out," said Clara.

Andre blew out the candles. The boys sat while they ate the cake.

"Are these your war toys?" asked Clara.

"Yes, we are playing up here."

"I can see," said Clara.

"I've killed Booker two times. I won the war," said Andre.

"No, you didn't. I killed you three times," said Booker.

"No. I killed you. You are dead. You stink, Booker," said Andre.

"I don't stink. You stink," said Booker.

"Boys, boys," said Clara.

"Andre, where are you?" called Bertha from downstairs.

"I'm up here, mama," said Andre.

"Come out of that attic. You know I don't want you up there by yourself. Your brother's calling you. You have to go graze the horses."

"I'm up here with them, Bertha. I'm bringing them down now," called Clara.

Andre went to his brother's room and looked out the window. Franklin was putting the saddle on the second horse. Andre didn't want to go out and graze the horses. He looked at the table and noticed the paper on which his brother had written his song. Andre took the paper and put it in his pocket. He didn't know why he did that; he just wanted the song. He looked out the window again. Franklin saw him and was motioning with his arms and saying, "Come down now!"

Andre walked down to the stairs. LaVonda and Deanna were in their rooms, as were his parents. Clara took Booker downstairs.

"Booker, let's go with Andre and see the horses," said Clara.

Clara, Booker, and Andre walked out together.

Franklin was on the horse and the second horse was ready to go.

"Look at that horse," said Clara. "Wouldn't you like to go on a horse ride?"

"Yes!" yelled Booker with excitement, running to the horse.

As Andre climbed on the horse, he looked back and saw smoke coming from the roof. "Franklin, look!" cried Andre, pointing to the roof. Smoke was coming from the wooden shingles with severe intensity. The dry, old wooden house and the incredible heat of the fire caused the home to quickly go up in flames.

Clara screamed as loud as she could. She couldn't believe her eyes.

Franklin jumped off the horse.

"You can't go in there," cried Clara as she tried to stop him. "It's too dangerous!" Franklin fought her off.

"I'm going in," he argued. "Everyone get out of the house!" he screamed as he opened the front door.

It was too late. The house went up in flames with everyone in it.

"Did we do that?" asked Booker to Clara. Clara said nothing.

Andre didn't hear him and remained on the horse, traumatized. Clara screamed. She looked at Booker, ignoring his question.

CHAPTER 2

IT WAS DURING Father Webster's 12:30 p.m. homily when the congregation began to smell the faint scent of smoke permeating through the chapel.

"Herod lost his mind and John the Baptist lost his head," Father Webster said for the fourth time that morning. He sniffed and smelled smoke, but he said nothing.

He began again. "What fascinates me about that passage of the Bible is that the Scriptures say that, when Herod was asked to give his daughter the head of John the Baptist, he was in great distress. Herod knew right from wrong. He had emotions and chose wrong. He made a promise, and he kept it. But when a promise violates the Commandments and is evil, wrong, immoral, or illegal, then it is not a valid promise; it must be ended. You have to break promises that should have never been made, and when you are in a position of power you cannot use that position of power to abuse others, even if it is to be true to your word."

He paused; it was so hot. "You know, this has to be the hottest summer I ever recall here. You would think with a name like Mountain Springs, it would mean a town of cool breezes."

The congregation laughed in agreement.

"I know you must be sweating right now. Next week we will be able to open windows in the new facility."

He returned to his homily.

"Despite the adversity in our personal lives, when people are going through the most difficult time in their life, they reach out and find each other. They become inspired to build, as we did when we built the new cathedral. They become inspired to rebuild by coming back from what has brought them down. It is that strength in spirit that is American. This country has a long history of fierce determination; that no matter what you go through in life, you will find a path to recovery, even when it looks like none is there."

By that time, the smell of smoke was present throughout the chapel. Father Webster proceeded straight to the Eucharist and finished the service. He was the first to exit the chapel and see the burning fire at the Williams's home, as did the rest of the parishioners as they exited the church. Everyone gasped.

"Oh, my God," said Father Sanders. The burning home was only a half mile away and clearly visible. It was a horrific sight.

"Let's go see what we can do," said Father Webster.

Sister Camille, Sister Laurie, Father Webster, and Father Sanders drove to the burning home together.

George Thompson saw the fire and rushed there from his house not far away.

"Jesus Christ," he said, approaching the home. He saw Clara with Booker and Andre. "What happened?" George asked Clara, looking at her suspiciously and glancing back at the burning home. He looked at Clara again and she looked at him.

"What?" asked Clara.

George said nothing. "I don't know anything about the fire. Don't ask me anything," Clara finally responded. Her face turned away to avoid George's eyes as she continued holding Booker.

George knew something wasn't right and Clara was frantic and devastated, clinging to Booker by her side. She turned away from him and grabbed Andre off the horse, ignoring George as he examined the scene. The police and volunteer fire department arrived, but there was not much else they could do. The house was completely destroyed. People gathered around to watch. A reporter from the *Mountain Springs Register* appeared and took photographs.

Sister Camille and Sister Laurie rushed immediately to Clara.

"Thank you, Jesus. Thank you, Jesus," Clara began to say over and over.

"Haven't I seen you up at the church?" asked Sister Laurie to Clara.

"I've been up there a few times," said Clara.

"You've *what*? You haven't been up there," said George. "She doesn't know what she's talking about," he said to Sister Camille.

"Shut up, George," said Clara. The flames were raging so high that it was almost impossible to hear the others speak.

"Let's take the boys with us where they'll be safe for now," offered Sister Camille.

Clara remembered what Bertha had said. *If they let them go to the church, they could go to the school. Maybe if the church took the boys in, they could educate them. She shouldn't mention that she is Booker's aunt. Maybe they will take them together.*

"That would be good," agreed Clara.

"Hold on there, Clara," said George. "You can't just hand them over to these people."

"Do you want *me* to raise them?" said Clara.

"No," said George.

"What else, George? What else, George? What else, George?" repeated Clara, yelling at him.

"Nothing," said George.

"I promise you that we will take care of the boys until we can decide what is best for them," said Father Webster.

"You are right," said George.

Suddenly, Clara changed her mind. She couldn't let Booker go.

"I'm keeping Booker with me. I am his legal guardian. You can take the other boy with you," said Clara.

"The other boy has no parent or legal guardian?" asked Father Webster.

"No. His family was in the house," said George.

"Oh my," said Father Webster. "Sister Camille, take the boy to the convent for now. He can stay with us until we can figure out what to do with him."

"Yes, Father," said Sister Camille.

Sister Camille drove Andre back to the church grounds. Sister Aude was standing outside the convent, watching the fire.

"Sister Aude, this is Andre; his family was lost in the fire," said Sister Camille, whispering to Sister Aude so that Andre could not hear. "Father Webster said that we must not leave him alone. This will be an unbearable tragedy for him. We have no idea what this might do to him, and he is separated from his only friend for the time being. Let's stay with him tonight in our quarters."

Sister Aude led him to an empty room in the abbey; she would stay near him in an adjoining room.

"Are you going to take care of me?" he asked.

"Of course I am. Bless the Lord, O my soul, and never forget all his benefits," she said while washing his face and hands and tucking the bed cover under his chin.

Andre was just a boy; he didn't understand her words.

Sister Aude didn't know how the fire began and never asked. As she got up to leave, she stopped at the end of the bed and turned around, facing Andre.

"Let us know, let us strive to know the Lord as certain as the dawn is coming as his judgment shines forth like the light of day."

Then she walked out of the room.

Andre lay in bed, staring at his rescuer. He did not understand her words, but was grateful to be cleaned and comforted by her. During the day he stayed in the room, sitting on his bed in a state of shock as the sisters cared for him. In the evenings, he cried out in anguish. The only items he possessed after the fire were his clothes and the piece of paper with his brother's song. He would never lose that piece of paper.

Not long after the fire, Clara went back to St. Peter's and told Father Webster that, as the legal guardian of Booker, she needed to take Andre home with her. She had to override Bertha's wishes. Booker missed Andre, and Clara didn't believe that the boys should be separated when they were so young. Father Webster agreed. Without legal guardianship over Andre, Clara was the logical choice to raise both of them. Andre would not attend the school as his mother wished.

"I have to take him back, Father … Mr. Webster … sir."

"I understand. Your home is the right place for the boy now. We will provide you with anything you need at the moment. Sister Camille, take Ms. Thompson to Andre and have his things gathered so she can take him with her."

"Oh, thank you, sir. Thank you, Father," said Clara.

CHAPTER 3

Growing up, Andre and Booker had different memories surrounding the day of the fire.

Andre's memory of the fire had been erased. He couldn't talk about it. Booker never spoke of it, but he remembered it. He remembered Clara's hand on his shoulder, watching the last embers burn. He remembered her comforting words: *Booker, my boy, you are safe. God bless you, my precious nephew. By the grace of God, you are safe.*

Andre did not feel the same sense of comfort in his new house. Although Clara took him into her home and met his basic needs, she never spent time with Andre. He felt rejected, and yet he didn't know why.

But Andre knew one thing: to Aunt Clara, Booker could do no wrong.

And to Andre, Booker could do no right.

Andre felt a connection with St. Peter's, but he did not know why. He would visit the church grounds on occasion. He saw the wealthy privileged white kids attending the school and he wanted to be there. Word of the superior education they offered was talked about around town.

Most black families in the area were Baptists. There was a curiosity with regards to St. Peter's and how it carved out a niche in a traditional Protestant environment. Andre felt his mother's wish and remembered hearing her talk about the church.

Andre and Booker attended Haley County Negro Public School, a segregated school for black children. Over time, Booker proved to be a troublemaker. He was always getting into trouble and drawing Andre in with him as an unwitting co-conspirator. Booker would sometimes pick on Andre, and Andre was afraid of him. After school, the boys would often play in the woods. They could throw rocks in the stream that ran down from St. Peter's. Andre would look up at the church, always wondering what was going on inside. Booker would see Andre stare at the church and he knew that Andre wanted to go to school there. He was annoyed by Andre's curiosity over St. Peter's. He would tell him, "I'm going to kick your butt," and run after him. Andre was faster than Booker and could outrun him; Booker could never find him.

Strong but lacking confidence, Andre could have overpowered Booker in a moment. But Booker had him bluffed. Sometimes Andre hated him.

Once when they were in elementary school, Booker broke his ankle and used crutches to get around. When he saw Andre playing, a jealous Booker took one of the crutches and threw it at Andre like a lance. Andre darted to miss the crutch. Booker constantly challenged Andre to fight; Andre endured and never fought back. Over time, Andre gained strength to defend himself from Booker but it was always a problem between them. Booker believed he was the one in charge.

Booker would often act out during school. Once he put ants in his teacher's chalk tray. Another time, he had the other students move their chairs up a few inches whenever the teacher turned around to write on the chalk board. The teacher figured out what was going on and murmured, "*Horse Feathers!*" after realizing what the children were doing. "Get your chairs back! I know what you are doing."

Booker became sick one day and threw up on the teacher's desk. No one knew whether he was sick or faking it. They hoped he was sick, but they had a feeling he was not truly ill.

Sometimes George would take Booker and Andre to the First African Baptist Church where Andre's family attended before the fire. But the boys were sometimes disruptive, becoming bored and stabbing each other with pencils, disrupting the anthem or the sermon.

As the boys grew older, Booker's behavior was troubling. By the time the boys were thirteen, they were too difficult for Clara. George appeared at her door and told her that he would take the boys to live with him. He had them pack their bags and he moved Andre and Booker to his home. Clara loved Booker and missed him. Without the responsibility of the boys, Clara left for the Jackson, Mississippi, the city she would frequently mention. No one knew what she did in Jackson. She would come and go after that, losing contact with the boys as they grew up. The boys didn't think of her much and after drifting back and forth between Jackson and Mountain Springs, her health and physical appearance changed to the point that she was unrecognizable.

CHAPTER 4

ANDRE AND BOOKER always needed money but they had none. Andre put his mind to getting a real job and thought about it all the time, dreaming and repeating his wish for a job. During the summer of 1938 when he was fourteen years old, that job seemed to come to him. One Saturday, Andre was walking downtown off of Second Street and saw a truck making a delivery on the side of the road. The driver was unloading donations to a used clothing store called the Bargain Barn, which was run by the Women's Junior League. Andre immediately started to help the black lady who was carrying bags into the store. Her name was Ruthie.

"We can't pay you, if that's what you want," she said to Andre as he began unloading the truck.

But Andre continued. Ruthie stopped and watched Andre unload the entire truck.

"You from around here?" she asked him.

"Yeah, I live with some friends."

"Some friends?" she asked. "Where are your parents?"

"They died a long time ago," said Andre.

"Died? I'm sorry to hear that," said Ruthie. "Come on in the back here where we keep all these things rich people donate to the poor. Here, take this home with you to your friends."

Ruthie grabbed a sack of the used clothes that Andre had just unloaded.

"What are you doing?" questioned Mrs. Hoffman, the store manager, in a stern voice.

"He don't mean anything. I just gave him that sack because he unloaded the truck all by himself. We could use him in the store cleaning the floors," said Ruthie.

"Is he any good?" asked Mrs. Hoffman.

"Why, yes. He is a friend of the family," said Ruthie.

Andre looked at her but said nothing.

"Well, in that case, we do need someone to clean and mop the floors on Saturday. He would be cheaper than hiring a company to do that. We'll see how he does," said Mrs. Hoffman. "Young man, I will expect you on Saturday at 9 a.m. If you do well on your first day, you can come back the next Saturday. Ruthie can show you what to do. Is he your nephew?"

Ruthie looked at Andre and said nothing. Andre responded, "Yes, she's my aunt." Ruthie smiled. Mrs. Hoffman didn't realize that she had been misled.

Andre went back each Saturday during the summer and would clean the floors. Getting to know the downtown area and working there was an experience for him. He discovered the Second Street Barbershop across the street and would hang out there before he had to go to work.

Louis and Alvin were the white barbers in the barbershop. Louis owned the shop and Alvin rented a chair from Louis. Saturdays were always their busiest day.

Shorty Miller was the young black shoeshine man in the barbershop. He controlled who came in the door, usually announcing the customer's name as they entered. Carl was a white customer and was the same size as Shorty. When he would enter the barbershop, Shorty would always announce him as "Cousin Carl." Carl would grimace and walk to one of the chairs to wait behind a newspaper for Alvin to cut his hair. He was Alvin's most loyal customer. He never said a word.

Shorty would look out the window and smile and hold up his brush to attract customers. One could see his smile and gold tooth as he grinned, even from far away. His face beamed above the logo "Second Street Barbershop," printed like a rainbow arc over the glass window.

Next door to the barbershop was Betty Lou's Grill, a popular lunch spot. The courthouse was only two blocks away, and the diner was always noisy with excitement. Some days the judge and the jurors would eat together during their break. The waitress would ring a bell, announcing, "The jury is out!" and in would come the jurors, followed by the judge. Lawyers dined at the grill as well, hoping to see someone, pick up a client, or perhaps run into the judge. The grill served peach cobbler in a small bowl for the lunch dessert. Betty Lou's Grill was everyone's favorite restaurant in town. Andre remembered wanting to save enough money to buy his own lunch and eat there, just like everyone else.

On the other side of the barbershop was the Zero Pawn Shop; it was a spooky place with all kinds of strange things to buy.

Andre had been thinking about buying a gift for the girl he liked at school named Sherry. He entered the store one day on a Saturday after work, looking at all the items. The owner, a tall man with thick eyebrows, wore a black tuxedo with a long tail and a top hat. It was a costume, and he looked like a magician. Andre thought he looked like Dracula. The man said, "Good afternoon, young man. Let me know if I can help you."

"Good afternoon," said Andre.

Andre walked around the pawn shop, just looking. He saw an old magazine that had a picture of Django Reinhardt, a French guitar player. He saw old guitars for sale. As soon as he had enough money he would buy a guitar, he told himself.

"And what would you like to buy?" asked the man.

"I was just looking around. I want to buy something for my girlfriend," he said.

"Your girlfriend? You are quite young," said the man.

"She's not my real girlfriend. She doesn't know it yet."

"Ahh, for that kind of girlfriend I have *this*," he said. He pulled out a charm bracelet from underneath the glass counter.

"How much is that?" asked Andre.

"For you, that would be one dollar," he said.

"I don't have that much money," said Andre.

"Then in that case, how about *this*?" asked the man. He showed the boy a ring.

"I don't know her that well and I think she might not understand a ring."

"You are right," said the man. "Then in that case, I have just the right gift for her. How about *these*?" He handed Andre a pair of wrist bands consisting of two circular bands, with one located inside the other. The label on the box said "*Make a Wish*."

"What are those?" asked Andre.

"They are love wrist bands. They are ties that bind. I inscribe your name on one band and the name of your girlfriend on the other. They are joined together and you can wear them together. On the inside is a button that releases the band. See here."

The love wrist bands came apart by pushing a tiny button on the inside under each of the bands.

"When she feels ready, you can give her the other band for her to wear," he said.

"Why does it say '*Make a Wish*' on the outside of the box?"

"Once she puts them on, you can make a wish and your dreams will come true. But only then."

Andre bought the love wrist bands, paying off a small amount of the total price every Saturday until he purchased them. He planned to give one to his girlfriend, Sherry, but she didn't know he liked her.

Leaving the pawn shop, Andre passed by the diner next door called Famous Hamburgers. The restaurant was owned by two Greek men who were always yelling across the diner and flipping burgers. Diners sat on red covered stools placed outside on the sidewalk facing the inside of the grill, watching the cook flip the burgers and lay out the onions. The smoke and smell would rise and one could hear sizzling when the meat landed on the hot open grill. The windows opened and meals were served on outside counters surrounding the grill. A law firm was located above the grill and would close their windows every day around 10:30 a.m. That was when the cooking started; the onion smell would permeate throughout the office.

Second Street in downtown Mountain Springs ran perpendicular to Main Street, which ran straight to the old downtown courthouse. The smoke and smell of onions pervaded the entire downtown. It filled everyone's clothes and the air, even up to the courthouse where the jurors could smell them during a trial. The District Judge of Haley County, sitting at the county seat of Mountain Springs, knew that when the onion smell came into the courthouse it was time to adjourn for lunch.

The jurors either made their way to Betty Lou's Grill or Famous Hamburgers. One time they went to Famous Hamburgers and reported back with the onion smell on their clothes. After that, they went to Betty Lou's Grill for the remainder of their jury service.

People from miles around would talk about how downtown Mountain Springs smelled of onions during the day. At night, the owner would close the windows and the smell would go away. It began again at 11 a.m. the next morning, when the grill started cooking and people began to line up for hamburgers and sit on the red covered stools. Often, just outside the door, a man would stand with a blue umbrella and announce, "Prepare for the coming of Jesus Christ!" And occasionally a man eating a cheeseburger would yell, "Would someone shut him up?"

A block away on Third Street and Commerce, a blind lady sat in a wheelchair every day, begging for money. Her eyes were always closed, her wrinkles deeply embedded; she looked at least 100 years old. The old lady sang in a shrill voice that circulated throughout downtown. And while she sang, she rang the bell in her hand.

No one knew what she was singing, but her voice could stop a train. Each day someone would arrive at 5 p.m. and wheel the lady away, and the next day she would be on the street by noon, beginning her daily routine once again. Her voice and the smell of onions made downtown Mountain Springs quite a scene. The spectacle was often shocking to visitors who were not accustomed to the almost carnival-like atmosphere of people coming and going. As Andre discovered, this was real life and the way things were in Mountain Springs on Saturdays.

CHAPTER 5

ANDRE FINALLY BECAME friends with Sherry. He had been thinking about her for a long time, and he eventually noticed she began to pay attention to him.

Booker had a girlfriend named Mary. She was tough like her father and would take nothing off of Booker. The two would often fight.

Booker asked Andre if he still wanted the wrist bands he had purchased in town. Andre decided to part with them and he gave them to Booker, not knowing what Booker planned to do with them.

One day after Booker and Mary had been fighting, Booker told Mary that he wanted to make up with her and that he had love bands for her. They could go steady. He asked Mary to put her hands around a tree and interlock her fingers. Then he put one of the bands on one hand and one on the other; her hands were now tied together to the tree. Booker had turned the love wrists bands into handcuffs. Mary screamed. A teacher saw them, ran outside, and unhooked Mary from the tree. Booker might have been playing, but his efforts were not taken as a joke. Booker was in trouble.

Andre and Booker were called to the principal's office. The principal had placed the offending wrist bands on his desk. Andre explained that the wrist bands were to be given to a girl if you were going steady with her. He told the principal that he didn't want the bands anymore so he gave them to Booker, who brought them to school and turned them into handcuffs. That was typical of Booker.

The principal told Andre that he had not broken any rules. But Booker had broken the rules by bringing the bands to school and using them like handcuffs, turning love into war. This incident was so serious that Booker would be expelled from school until further notice. The principal called George Thompson to come and pick up Booker. Andre was disappointed about the incident; he could never erase it from his mind. He was responsible for Mary's distress after being handcuffed to the tree; after all, he brought the wrist bands to school, and giving them to Booker had led to trouble.

The other students watched Booker leave school that day. They could hear George yelling incomprehensible words as he led Booker home. Andre felt better now that the trouble-making Booker was gone, at least for the rest of the afternoon. He would see him later that night.

After school, Andre went back to the math teacher's room to get a pencil he had left behind. He noticed the math teacher was sobbing to himself. He realized that the class was cruel to the teacher with their antics; he had never seen a grown man cry.

Booker was soon back at the school, and his punishment was to clean up the classrooms after school. Sometimes Andre would leave something on the floor that he knew Booker would have to clean up.

It didn't take Booker long to return to his old ways.

Booker and another student named Calvin decided to fight behind the school one day, and as the students encircled the boys, yelling and screaming, Booker fought as if he had it out for Calvin. Booker wasn't fighting Calvin. He was fighting his miserable life as an angry teen without a father or mother.

One Saturday after work, Andre found Sister Camille sitting under a tree in the wooded area set aside for the walkways of the Stations of the Cross. He explained to her that he was the boy from the fire in 1930. Sister Camille was overjoyed to see him again after eight years.

Andre had grown up. He was nearsighted, but Uncle George found some money to buy him glasses. Sister Camille would have never recognized him after so much time. They sat together on a bench and talked for hours. He told her that he thought about her for years and wanted to see her again. But he wouldn't talk about the fire. He and Booker avoided that subject.

Andre continued to visit Sister Camille on Saturdays. She took Andre under her wing to teach him and to watch him grow up. She had always wondered what had happened to Andre. She wanted him to attend the church school, and Andre wanted to go to St. Peter's. But neither could figure out a way to make that happen.

Andre liked music. Booker never did. Andre saw a guitar at the pawn shop downtown and the owner with the tuxedo let him pay it out over time as Andre taught himself to play. He showed Sister Camille how he could strum, pick, and play a song that he composed. His family's music continued to run in his head.

"Sister Camille, I want you to hear a song that I wrote."

"Where did you get the guitar?" she asked.

"At Zero Pawn Shop, the place downtown. The one and only place with the guy that looks like Dracula. Cost me two dollars," he said. "Have you been there?"

"No."

"Well, you aren't missing anything. But you should go see him. He looks like he needs to go to church here."

Sister Camille laughed.

Andre strummed the chords, playing a different chord for each note, just like his brother taught him the day of the fire.

"You want to hear a song?"

"Sure," she said.

"Ok. Here it goes. Now don't laugh," he said.

He got ready as he cleared his throat and sang, "*I know you think I've done something wrong.*" Then he started over. "Let me try that again."

"That's ok. Take your time," she said to him.

"Ok. Here we go again," he said. Then he sang:

"I know you think I've done something wrong
I'm only trying to see myself through your eyes
And put myself where I belong
You think I'm hurting, I can't make you see
I can't love you when the person you love isn't me."

"That's a beautiful song Andre, and it sounds so different from what I've heard. I've never seen a hand move so much in a guitar piece. Is that a new popular song?"

"Thank you, Sister. I like to think I can play like Django Reinhardt."

"Who?"

"Django Reinhardt. A French guitar player. I read about him in a magazine at the barbershop. I bought the guitar so I could figure out how to play. My brother taught me to play a chord for every note. Now I'm trying to learn how to pick the guitar and play by ear."

"I think it sounds wonderful," said Sister Camille.

"I'm preparing it for Sherry, but I'm not finished with it. I'm working on a third verse. It's something that I made up, or at least I think I made it up. Actually, I don't know where these thoughts come from. They just come. It reminds me of a song that my brother taught me the day of the fire."

"That was a dreadful day. It looks like you have recovered quite well."

"I erased it from my mind," he said. "I'm going to play this song for my girlfriend."

"Is the girl named Sherry your girlfriend?"

"I think so. But I think she likes Booker."

"She likes your friend Booker? I think if she hears that song, she will like only you," said Sister Camille. "Who taught you how to play the guitar?"

"I taught myself. I used to watch my brother play. But Booker says that my songs are the worst songs he has ever heard."

"That's not nice of Booker to say. I disagree with him on this. I think it is a brilliant song. Very unusual for this time. I've never heard anything like it. How is Booker? He was the other boy at your home the day of the fire?"

"Yes. Just the same Booker. He doesn't want to go to school. He got kicked out for a while. But not me. I want to go to school *here*. We got in trouble at the public school and that was bad," said Andre.

"What did you do?"

"It was my fault."

"What was your fault?" asked a curious Sister Camille.

"I bought some wrist bands with my money from the job downtown. You are supposed to give one to your girlfriend, but Booker brought them to school and used them to tie his girlfriend to a tree."

"Oh, my God. He did that?"

"Yes, but he thought it was a joke and it got out of hand. They come off easy, but his girlfriend screamed and the teachers heard it and rescued her before Booker could do anything," said Andre.

"Why did he do that?"

"I don't know. To be funny I guess. Kids do a lot of mean things as a joke."

"What happened to the wrist bands?"

"The school took them and got rid of them. They kicked him out of school after that for a while."

"You should stay in school," said Sister Camille.

"Booker doesn't want to go back to school. I was wondering if I could come to school up here?" asked Andre.

Sister Camille looked at him, not knowing what to say.

"Andre, I wish you could come here, but they haven't started a school for Negro students yet. They are still raising the money for it. The church does not discriminate so it is just a matter of time before they have the money for a new addition. Someone told me that they occasionally see a Negro boy come up to the school grounds and look into the classroom. That's you, isn't it, Andre?"

"That was me, but I was just looking. I wasn't doing anything," Andre tried to explain to Sister Camille.

"I know, but they don't want you to do that. We are having a nice dance coming up this weekend. The students are dressing up. The school will be closed to the public on Saturday night, so don't come up here. I know I've seen you at times when school is in session. Let me take you to the library and show you some books sometime. I can meet you here and teach you. As far as I am concerned, you will be *my* student here. It will be our pact together."

"I can go to school here?" asked Andre.

"Let's just say that I will teach you here, and I will consider you my student. I have to leave now."

"I will see you next Saturday," Andre said.

"Until then," said Sister Camille.

"*Saturday night*," Andre said quietly to himself.

CHAPTER 6

The next Saturday, Andre went to the tree in the woods to see if Sister Camille was there. She was not. He realized that she would be working at the party that night and something or someone might have needed her attention. He looked up and noticed people standing around the entrance of the church. Figuring it to be the party, he wanted to see what was happening. He walked up to the church and saw people standing in line. It was the 4 p.m. confession. Ever curious, he went in and sat down. He had never been to a confession. Andre took a seat at the end of the front pew and would join in the line when the last person reached the confessional booth. To the right of the booth was a shrine to Jesus and the Mother Mary, with candles on all sides and booklets placed on the altar.

The last person in line entered the booth. Andre watched the red light, realizing he would be next for confession. He was nervous, unsure of what to say. A Hispanic family walked together to the altar and kneeled down to pray. A short time later they rose and walked back down the aisle. The women smiled at Andre as they passed by.

A stream of light shone down the aisle as someone opened the church door behind Andre. An older black woman wearing red glasses and carrying a large purse entered and walked down the aisle. Andre's right arm stuck into the aisle, and the old woman accidentally bumped his elbow as she walked by.

"I'm sorry," she whispered. Andre said nothing in return.

The woman carried a few small candles in a small round wax container in her right hand. She looked at Andre and pointed to the bottom of the Shrine to Mother Mary. "Can I drop the candles here?" she asked him. Andre didn't know what to say, so again he said nothing.

Andre glanced at her hand as the woman put the candles down before the shrine. The long, red fingernails and the unusual gold ring with an eight-pointed star on her third finger caught his eye. He watched her as she lit the candles and kneeled down to pray, "Hail Mary full of grace. The Lord is with thee. Blessed are though among women and blessed is the fruit of thy womb, Jesus. Holy Mary, Mother of God, pray for us sinners, now and at the hour of our death."

Andre thought that the woman seemed familiar, although he didn't know why. He didn't look at her directly; he wanted to remain unnoticed.

The woman rose and walked to the front of Andre's pew, searching the back of the pew for a Bible. Andre watched as she sifted through the booklets. She lowered her head straight down so that Andre had to look at her scalp through her hair.

What an annoyance, he thought. He wanted to get up and walk away. Her head began to rise until she was looking at Andre straight in the eyes. She stared at him through her red glasses for a long time and finally mumbled, "I'm looking for the Old Testament."

Andre said nothing.

She continued, "I've been doing things like Voodoo down in Jackson. Do they have the Old Testament here? I need to see the Old Testament."

Andre said nothing to her.

The woman walked to the altar, continuing her mantra, "I'm looking for the Old Testament," as if she were talking to someone in the church. She passed the statue of Jesus but did not kneel. She continued her mumbling; no one was there to hear her except Andre, who watched her bizarre behavior with curiosity. Andre thought perhaps the woman was one of the homeless who would gather around the entrance of the church before and after Mass.

"What was *that* about?" muttered Andre to himself. He didn't recognize Aunt Clara. She had changed a great deal, but she had not forgotten Andre. She was too embarrassed to announce her presence. She waited to see if Andre realized it was her. The red light went off above the confessional and Andre, nervous as a cat, proceeded to the confessional booth and sat down, unsure of what to do next. He said nothing.

"Is there someone there? I'm sorry I kept you waiting," said Father Webster.

Andre said nothing. He picked up a card and read the written description of his contrition. He didn't understand that he was to state the sin first and then read the contrition.

"That was your contrition. Now what is your sin?" asked Father Webster.

"I want to ..."

There was a pause.

Father Webster asked, "You want to what? What is your sin?" Andre became agitated and exited the booth. The door closed behind him. Andre left the premises of St. Peter's thinking to himself, "*How I wish I was part of this.*" Andre returned home to George's house.

Around 6 p.m., Andre walked back up to the church. He wanted to see the party that Sister Camille had mentioned. Watching from a distance, Andre saw the rich white kids in their suits and ties and girls in long formal gowns. There were Sister Camille, Father Sanders, Father Webster, Sister Laurie, and Sister Aude standing at the entrance as students walked in with their dates and escorts. They were chaperones for the dance. The students had their own band that would play that night.

Andre returned to George's house and went to bed, dreaming what his life would have been like if he had gone to school at St. Peter's as his mother had hoped. He thought: *What if he and Booker were the rich kids in school? What if the nuns and priests were black? What if the white kids were poor and had go to a separate white public school and wanted to go to St. Peter's, just like he did?*

He fell asleep.

CHAPTER 7

WHILE WORKING AT the Bargain Barn during the summer, Andre befriended Shorty Miller, the shoeshine man at Second Street Barbershop. Shorty taught Andre how to shine and clean shoes, apply the polish, and use the brush and the cloth at the end of the shine. For the grand finale, Shorty took out a small plastic tube, smaller than the size of a toothpaste tube, and placed a dab of spit on the shoe. He told Andre that it was his magic potion. It was nothing more than just a used plastic bottle, filled with tap water when the customers were gone.

Alvin and Louis teased Andre and were sometimes cruel to him. One day Andre showed up looking for Shorty, and Louis told Andre that Shorty had died.

"Yeah, Shorty died. Isn't that right Alvin?"

"Yeah, that's right. Shorty died last week," said Alvin.

Andre sat down in shock and disbelief, while Alvin and Louis continued cutting their customers' hair.

Just then Shorty walked into the barbershop, whistling. He had been on an errand. Shorty saw Andre crouched in a chair and yelled, "Skees!" Andre jumped up and hugged

Shorty with all his might; he thought Shorty was dead. Alvin and Louis began laughing at the scene.

"Yeah, he thought you were dead. We told him you were dead, and he began to cry like a little crybaby," said Louis.

Andre said nothing.

"Yeah, he began to cry," said Alvin.

"Skees, you were crying over me?" smiled Shorty.

CHAPTER 8

ANDRE'S JOB AT the Bargain Barn lasted only the summer. He liked downtown and took Sherry there to show her around. The first stop was to show her the Bargain Barn, but he didn't take her inside.

"I was the janitor there on Saturdays last summer. I don't want to stay too long — they might see me and ask me to come to work. The boss lady, Mrs. Hoffman, might see me too, and she's mean. Let's just peek inside, then we'll go across the street to the barbershop. I want you to meet Shorty."

They crossed over to the Second Street Barbershop and stopped in to see Shorty, Louis, and Alvin. Shorty was shining a man's shoes and Alvin and Louis were cutting hair. Cousin Carl was sitting down reading the paper, waiting for Alvin to finish.

"Skees!" said Shorty. "Who is this with you?"

"This is Sherry."

Shorty smiled at Sherry. "You with Skees? I don't believe it. Boss!" he said, yelling at Louis. "Look what we have here! Skees got a girlfriend with him!"

"He doesn't have a girlfriend," said Louis as he continued to cut hair.

"Yes, Boss, he has a girlfriend," said Shorty.

"A girlfriend?" said Alvin, shaving a customer's neck. "He doesn't like girls. Isn't that right, Louis?"

Cousin Carl sat in his chair, looking up over the top of his paper but not saying a word.

"Yes, sir. He doesn't like girls," said Louis. "That's not his girlfriend. He doesn't like girls," said Louis. "Young lady, did you know that Andre doesn't like girls?"

"But he *do*!" said Shorty. "He has one right here!"

"That isn't his girlfriend. Isn't that right, Alvin?" said Louis.

"Yes. You are right Louis, that isn't his girlfriend," said Alvin, shaking his head.

"That's his sister, isn't it Alvin?" said Louis.

"Yes, that's his sister," nodded Alvin.

"He just brought her in here for us to look at her. My, isn't she pretty?" grinned Shorty.

"She is pretty," said Alvin.

"Yes, she is pretty," said Louis.

Andre took Sherry's elbow and began to lead her toward the door.

"Ok, I'm going to go now. Sherry, let's go," said Andre, his face becoming hot.

"Alright, you both take care and don't get into trouble. See you, Skees. How come you're not at work today? Your boss lady sent Ruthie over here looking for you. I told her I hadn't seen Skees."

"She didn't come over here. I don't work there anymore. The summer's over," said Andre.

"Well, she came over here and said you didn't show up for work. She said she thought she saw you with a girl and she wanted to know if we had seen you. Didn't she say that, Boss?" said Shorty to Louis.

"Yes, she came over here looking for Skees. She was going to whip you something good for not showing up for work," said Louis. "Isn't that right, Alvin?"

"Yes, she did," said Alvin. "We told her that you didn't want to go to work and were over here crying like a baby about she was working you too hard."

"Oh yes, she came over here and we told her that you were crying every day like a crybaby," said Louis.

"Ok. I'm leaving," said Andre, rolling his eyes. He knew they were only teasing him, but he was trying to impress Sherry. They were embarrassing him.

"Goodbye," he said, waving without turning around.

"Whew," sighed Andre as he and Sherry walked out.

"Do they always treat you like that?" asked Sherry.

"No. I guess they saw you and decided to put on a show. Here, let's go into the pawn shop."

They walked inside Zero Pawn Shop and Sherry noticed the wrist bands on display in the window.

"Is this where you bought the wrist bands that Booker used on Mary?"

"Oh," Andre said. "Don't bring that up. It still hurts. I don't know why he did that."

"Well, they were just wrist bands. You didn't know he was going to use them like handcuffs," said Sherry.

They left the pawn shop and walked by Famous Hamburgers. The Greek owners were yelling across the diner.

"The smell," said Sherry, turning up her nose. "You had to smell that all the time down here? Did you eat one of those hamburgers? I hate onions."

"You get used to it," said Andre.

They passed the man with the blue umbrella. He stared at Sherry and called, "Prepare for the coming of Jesus Christ." They could hear the blind lady singing and ringing her bell in the background. Downtown somehow seemed different with a girl by Andre's side.

The couple spent all afternoon together in downtown Mountain Springs. Sherry was in love with Andre, and Andre was in love with Sherry by the end of the day.

Sometime later in the fall, Andre went back downtown to see Shorty at the barbershop. Shorty's bench was empty.

"Where's Shorty?" asked Andre.

"He said he got a job shining shoes at the newspaper in Birmingham," said Louis.

"He's been gone a month," said Alvin. "He didn't like the country and wanted to go to the big city."

Andre missed Shorty.

CHAPTER 9

ANDRE AND BOOKER dropped out of public school after the tenth grade.

In 1941, when the boys were seventeen, George decided they needed to enlist in the army. Their life with him ended Saturday, November 29, 1941. He took them to the recruiting station in Mountain Springs after pulling them apart during a fight. It wasn't their first. The boys didn't know why they were fighting. They just did. After dropping out of high school, their future was bleak. George heard that the army was recruiting black soldiers. He decided that he could no longer take care of them and he had no extra money. *The boys are lucky to have a home at all*, he thought.

Now George shook his head.

Enough.

He pulled the boys apart and told Andre and Booker to pack their bags. *If they don't fight once in a while, then they aren't friends or brothers*, thought George.

"This is all I'm gonna take out of you boys. Pack your bags and get 'em in the truck. I have better things to do than put up with both of you. Let's see how you like it now," he grumbled.

After arriving at the recruiting station, George told the boys to wait as he went in to see the recruiter. Andre and Booker were in the front seat of the truck and could see their uncle through the window, talking to the recruiter. It was cold and rainy outside, and they were nervous.

"These are the best young men you will find in Mountain Springs," George told the recruiter. The boys could see his lips moving as they watched them through the rain dripping down the truck's foggy window.

"What do you think he's saying to him?" asked Andre.

"Who knows? Don't make no difference now," said Booker. "What's done is done."

"Why, these boys know how to take care of things. These are good boys. Yes sir, you won't have any trouble with either one of them," he said, turning toward the door. "I'm gonna go get 'em."

George returned to the office with Booker and Andre. The boys stood before the recruiter in dirty overalls, t-shirts, and worn out shoes with holes.

"Just look at this one. Why, he can shoot a squirrel a hundred yards away without a site. I taught him. He's real good. Taught him myself," said George, nodding toward Booker.

"This one, he can shine shoes like no one I've ever seen. Taught by a real shoe shine guy downtown and can he play the guitar! His fingers roll right up the guitar like nothing

I've seen before. No problem pulling a trigger," said George, pointing at Andre.

"Yes siree, you won't be sorry you took these two boys in — these two *men*, that is. They will make the army real proud! Why, if the army didn't need them I'd use them all day long on the farm. Now where do I sign?" asked George.

The recruiter looked both boys over and turned to George.

"Are you their father?"

"Well, no. The one here, Booker, is my nephew. The one here, Andre, he lost his parents, and I took him to raise. Now, where do I sign?"

"Right here. But I will need some kind of guardianship papers. Wait, how old is he?" the recruiter asked.

"He's seventeen."

"You don't have to sign for him. He can sign for himself. In fact, both of them can sign for themselves. They don't need your permission."

"That's ok, just let me sign here in case someone wants a signature. We don't want there to be any mistakes."

The recruiter pulled the paperwork out of the drawer and motioned for the boys to sign the line at the bottom of the page.

"I will be glad to sign this, and the army will sure be glad to take both of these boys off my hands. I mean the army will sure be glad to *have* both of these men. I know what you need, and these two, yes, these two, why — they will ... they will ... yes, they will do you right!"

George stepped outside. The rain was subsiding.

He pulled a cigarette out of the pack in his overalls and lit it. Leaning against the truck as he watched the boys through the office window, he sighed. "*Whew*," he said to himself as he pulled off his hat.

George could hear the recruiter talking to Andre and Booker. He started to smile. It was like sweet revenge, but he didn't want revenge; he wanted someone to take the boys off of his hands. He couldn't take care of them any longer. The army would do that.

The thought of putting Andre and Booker in the army was not something new brought up by Uncle George. Uncle George heard that the army was recruiting black soldiers. Andre thought about joining up and in 1940 had heard that the military was calling for black soldiers. Other kids were joining up in the neighborhood. Word was circulating that the army could provide good jobs for black soldiers. Andre's thoughts of the army and his fight with Booker gave him the excuse he needed to join up. And Uncle George served the purpose of pushing him to enlist.

Andre and Booker came walking out of the office to the truck where George was standing.

"Now take good care of my boys," George told the recruiter.

"We can have them on a bus tomorrow to Fort Bragg, Mr. Thompson. They can stay here tonight," the recruiter said.

"That's good. That's real good," said George. "Thank you."

"Thank *you*, and thank you for sending them to the United States Army."

The recruiter turned to Andre and George, smiling.

"Welcome to the United States Army!" He nodded, shook their hands, and began walking back to the recruiting office.

Both boys looked at George, unsure of what to say next.

"Thanks, Uncle George," said Booker.

Andre was silent.

"Go see the world Booker, and don't get into trouble. And don't come back here after you're finished," he said. "Same for you, Andre. If you get in trouble, they will send you home. Do you want to come back here? No, you don't. This is a new start. Don't let them send you home."

"I won't," said Andre, as he grabbed a duffel bag from the back of the truck. Andre wanted to join the army. Anything was better than living with Booker's uncle. Not that George was bad, but there had to be something else out there for him.

"Take good care of yourself, too," said Booker.

George noticed a tear in Booker's eye.

"Now don't do that. Men don't cry. Give me a hug. You too, Andre. Let's not say anything else."

They stood there while George hugged them both. The recruiter looked out the window, watching the boys as they walked towards the building, side by side.

George got back in his truck and turned the ignition key. As the engine started, he watched Booker and Andre go back into the office, carrying their duffel bags over their shoulders. A tear came to his eye and ran down his face as he drove away.

"Men don't cry," he said to himself, driving away.

CHAPTER 10

The recruiting office had a room for Andre and Booker to sleep in that night. They would leave as soon as they had enough recruits to fill a bus. Andre and Booker were the only ones there. At 10 p.m., Andre decided to leave the recruiting station, slipping out the back window next to his bed.

"Where are you going?" asked Booker.

"Be back in a minute," whispered Andre.

"Are you crazy? What if you get caught? You'll probably get charged for being AWOL! Do you know what that means, Andre? That means *Absent Without Official Leave.* We could both get in trouble!" said Booker.

It was only a half mile to Sherry's house. Andre made his way to her home, crossing through several streets in the alley. He climbed over the back wooden fence and went around to the front of the house. An old guitar that Andre had picked up at the Zero Pawnshop sat on her front porch. Andre bought it one day when he took Sherry downtown. It was so worn out that no one would want to steal it. Andre had pursued Sherry for years.

He grabbed the guitar and went around the back of the house. Andre threw a rock into the open window of Sherry's room, making a small sound. Then another. Nothing. Then Sherry came to the window and looked out.

"What are you doing?" she asked.

"Come around to the front," Andre said.

Sherry came to the front door and pulled the white drapes to the glass window. She looked out and smiled.

"I have a song for you," said Andre.

"What is it?" asked Sherry.

Then Andre sang, strumming the guitar:

"I know you think I've done something wrong,
I'm only trying to see myself through your eyes."

"Be quiet," Sherry said, opening the door. She was wearing a full length white dress. Andre was surprised. She walked over to the porch swing and sat down.

"Is that a new song?" asked Sherry.

"Yes. It's a new one that I made up."

"I hope I like it. Booker says you sing the worst songs."

"Booker doesn't know anything. Why do you bring him up?"

"I didn't mean to bring him up. I'm just telling you what he said," said Sherry.

"Who cares what he says. I don't care what he says. Do you care what he says?"

"No, I don't care what he says."

"Ok then," said Andre.

There was a pause.

"I want to hear your song," said Sherry. "What are you doing here? I can't stay out late. I have school tomorrow. If my father knew you were here, he would run you off."

"I came to see you," said Andre. "I came to look for you from your window — like a frog from the pond. I need you to kiss me to turn me into your knight in shining armor."

"No, I want to keep you as a frog so I can throw you in Murphree Lake. You can see me tomorrow," said Sherry.

"No, you won't."

"What do you mean?"

"You can't," said Andre.

"Why not? And what's that on your head?" asked Sherry.

Andre was wearing an army garrison cap without an insignia that he found at the recruiting station. He wanted to impress Sherry.

"It's an army cover."

"An army cover?" she asked inquisitively. "Why are you wearing an army cover? Did you join the army?"

Andre looked at her and smiled.

"You joined the army!" she said.

"Shush. Yes, I did," said Andre.

"What does Booker think about that?" asked Sherry.

"What do you mean 'what does Booker think about that'? That's the second time you've mentioned him. I think you like Booker."

"Oh, let's not talk about that," said Sherry.

"You went out with Booker."

"I didn't go out with Booker. Did Booker let you join the army?" asked Sherry.

"Booker doesn't have anything to do with 'letting me join the army.' What do you mean 'letting me join' the army? I make my own decisions," said Andre, perturbed by the question.

"What does his Uncle George have to say about you joining the army?"

"Uncle George? He's the one that took us over there and signed us up!" said Andre.

"Your Uncle George took you over to the recruiter and signed you up?" Sherry said in disbelief.

"He did. We signed ourselves up. He caught Booker and me fighting, and he said he had enough of us so he told us to get our bags and dropped us off at the recruiter's office. All he could say were things like 'show me where to sign' or 'let's make it legal' or 'these are good guys' and 'I need them here, but you need them more.' You should've heard him. He sounded like one of those lawyers I used to hear downtown at the barber shop. I didn't believe a word of it, but the recruiter did," Andre told her.

"You don't need to join the army. My father will take you in," said Sherry.

"Your father will take me in? I thought he didn't want me coming around?"

"That's right. He doesn't want you coming around here because you quit high school."

"I don't want to be taken in. I *wanted* to join. I want to go fight," said Andre.

"You want to go fight? Why do you want to fight?" asked Sherry.

"To make a difference," said Andre.

"And where are you going to go fight?"

"I don't know," said Andre.

"You want to go fight somewhere where you don't even know so you can make a difference. And what difference would that be?" asked Sherry.

"A big difference!" Andre said as he rose from the swing. He walked around and then came back to her. "A thought can make a difference. A belief can make a big difference. I think a thought can make the things we imagine happen."

"What was that?" asked Sherry.

"A thought can give you what you want," said Andre.

"What?" asked Sherry.

"A thought gives you what you are asking for."

"And where did you come up with that?" asked Sherry in a perturbed manner. "From that church you are always visiting?"

"I don't know. Actually, I do know. It was in some book I read. Some lady named Behrend. Genevieve Behrend was her name. She was born in Paris."

'Ok," said Sherry reluctantly. "And why were you reading a book by Genevieve Behrend, who was born in Paris?"

"I don't know. I'm so poor I was trying to read up on how to make some money. Thoughts come to me and I don't know where they come from. I think things happen if you think about them and want them enough and keep asking for them. I try visualizing them and it's like they appear later."

"You are strange, Andre. Sometimes I think you are off this planet. You are a dreamer. You've always been a dreamer," said Sherry.

"Well, you are always showing me where to go. You are a window for me. I've always looked into a window, looking for you."

"Yes, and you like to throw rocks at my window. I see. I'm a window and you're a dreamer," said Sherry.

Andre looked out and saw the full moon. Then he looked at Sherry.

"Beautiful," he said.

Sherry looked out and saw the full moon.

"What is beautiful?"

"The moon is. The moon is beautiful," said Andre, looking at the moon and then at her. "People are always asking where God is."

"Where God is? Who is asking where God is? I'm not asking where God is," said Sherry.

"You see the moon and the stars and so I figure God must be the black part that fills up everything else. Some kind of electrical force — that must be who we are talking to when we pray. God must be the part we aren't looking at because we are looking at the stars."

"Ok, this is getting too deep for me. I'm going to go in now," said Sherry, getting up from the porch swing.

"No, don't go. I have something for you. Do you want to hear my song?" he asked.

"What?"

"A song I made up. Sit down. Don't go. I will play you a song."

"Ok. One song and then I have to go in," she said.

"Ok. Let me see here." Andre grabbed the guitar on the porch and began moving his fingers up the guitar, playing the chords to practice. He sang:

"I know you think I've done something wrong,
I'm only trying to see myself through your eyes
And put myself where I belong.
You think I'm hurting, I can't make you see
I can't love you when the person you love isn't me.

I can't stop feeling, my heart still feels like before.
How can I tell you to make you see what I mean?
I couldn't mean it anymore.
If I could see you, I'd try to explain
You're my heart's life, it can't take the pain.
I'm alive - keep me alive."

He finished. Andre strummed his guitar, playing a chord for each word of the song, just like his brother taught him the day of the fire.

"I added a third verse. Here it is..."

"I'm not the guy that you think I'll turn out to be.
You knew somebody with love too easy to say.
But girl, you know that isn't me.
It's not that easy to say I'm in love,
'Til it's something we both are sure of.
If you want me to say I'm in love,
Make it something we both are sure of."

"That's beautiful, Andre. It almost brings me to tears. Where did you get that song? Don't tell me. It just came to you?"

"Yes. It did just come to me, but I don't know where it came from."

"Why did you sing that I'm in love with someone else? I'm not in love with someone else."

"You are not in love with Booker?" asked Andre.

"I'm not in love with Booker. I already said I didn't like Booker. I *don't* like Booker. I like only you," Sherry said proudly.

Andre waited. He put the guitar down.

"I love you, Sherry."

"I love you, Andre."

He kissed her and they embraced. Andre's glassed fogged up.

"I have to go."

"Don't go," said Sherry.

"I'm probably AWOL."

"You make sure you come back here, and don't do anything foolish over there."

"I will and I won't," said Andre.

He walked away.

"Andre," Sherry said. "You will need this." She threw his garrison cap at him. He caught it and smiled. Andre made it back to the recruiting station without notice. Only Booker knew he had left.

CHAPTER 11

AFTER A FEW days, Andre and Booker processed in and boarded a bus with other recruits. It was a cold and rainy December day and a long, uncomfortable ride to Fort Bragg, North Carolina. The boys were assigned to the 9th Infantry Division.

The bus drove through downtown Mountain Springs. Andre looked out the window as they drove up busy Main Street. Now seventeen, he remembered his summer job at the Bargain Barn three years ago. He stared at the barbershop as they drove by. Shorty's face appeared, looking out the window. Andre flinched and his eyes widened. Then Shorty disappeared. He was not there; Andre was daydreaming again. He was visualizing things as if they were happening or visualizing things as he wanted them to be.

The bus headed out of downtown into the countryside. Andre remembered growing up and hunting with Booker and the difficulties of living in Alabama in the 1930s. Their short pathetic life together with George was spent throwing rocks, fishing, hunting, fighting, getting into trouble, getting into arguments, and dealing with George, who could be brutal. Times were difficult for three grown men in one household, but it made them strong. Clara was long gone to Jackson, Mississippi, most of that time, except those periods when she returned. Andre had forgotten her.

Andre and Booker were silent for most of the trip to Fort Bragg. Andre decided to read a book that he brought with him.

"I want the window after an hour. I can't stand it sitting here," said Booker.

"Ok," said Andre as he read.

"What is that you're reading?" asked Booker, taking the book away from Andre.

"Hey," said Andre. "Give that back to me."

"*Andrew* ..." Booker read from the cover. Then he kept reading, "*Andrew* ... *Johnson* it says. And who the heck is Andrew Johnson?" Booker asked Andre, disgusted by the thought of Andre reading a book. "And what the heck are you doing reading a book about Andrew Johnson when you are on your way to the army? You probably got this book because you liked the first name."

"Let me have that," said Andre, taking the book back from Booker.

"There are no pictures in it. Forget it. I would never read a book without pictures," said Booker, returning the book. "You won't need that. Andrew Johnson won't be able to help you now," said Booker.

The bus continued on while Andre read the book with curiosity.

Booker was bored with nothing to do, so he started up the conversation again with Andre. "So who was Andrew Johnson? Did you get that from that church? They will want it back. They'll send one of those nuns up here to whip your butt in the army and take it back. You don't steal from a church. I bet the army would never get in the way of one of those nuns."

"Funny. I didn't steal it," said Andre as he continued to read.

"So who was he?" asked Booker.

"He was one of the presidents."

"You mean like Roosevelt?" asked Booker.

"Yes, like Roosevelt."

"So what about him?"

"He was the only one impeached," said Andre.

"Impeached? What the heck are you talking about? Impeached. I'm going to impeach your butt! What are you talking about impeached?" said Booker impatiently.

"Knock it off," said the guy in front of them.

"Ok, ok," said Booker.

"He got in trouble but was still president after his trial," said Andre in a low tone.

"He was tried and nothing happened to him?" said Booker.

"Yeah," said Andre.

"Hmmph. That don't sound like much of a trial to me. If they tried him then he was guilty," said Booker.

"He was found not guilty," said Andre.

"That don't matter. Did he do it?" asked Booker.

Andre didn't respond.

"He was probably lucky. Someone saved him," said Booker.

"How did you know that?" asked Andre.

The bus drove for a while and then Andre put down the book.

"What do you think it will be like?" asked Andre.

"What do you mean 'what do I think it will be like?' Who knows? Probably kicking our butt for the next two months, for all I know," said Booker. "Where did you go last night?"

"I went to see Sherry to say goodbye."

"Sherry? She doesn't want you. She wants me. She likes me. She doesn't like you anymore."

"Yes, she does," said Andre.

"No, she don't. She told me she doesn't like you anymore. She loves me."

"Shut up. She doesn't even like you," said Andre.

"All right. Touchy. Didn't mean to step on your lady," said Booker.

The bus drove on for a while.

"I don't know if this will beat Mountain Springs," said Andre.

"Mountain Springs? Anything beats Mountain Springs. We had nothing. We have nothing now. Might as well make the best of it. At least I know how to shoot," said Booker.

"You taught me that well. I remember that time we were hunting and we came across a rabbit. I remember getting up closer and shooting it and his entire head came off. That made me sick. That was the first time I saw the death of an animal. I couldn't do that again," said Andre.

"Yeah, that hurt. But we didn't kill it for no reason. It was supper. That's the way it goes. You were just a scared kid," said Booker.

"I wasn't a scared kid. I was the same age as you," said Andre.

"Well, you acted scared."

"I didn't either."

The bus drove on for a while and passed over a small creek.

"You remember fishing for crawdads at the creek?" asked Andre.

"Yeah, we stole bacon from the house for bait and those crawdads came running out of the water and we didn't have to do anything but watch 'em climb up the line."

"Yeah, that was fun. We had to make sure that Uncle George didn't find out we was stealing the bacon, or he would have kicked our butts good," said Andre.

"He would have," said Booker.

"I wonder where they will send us?" said Andre.

"Probably send us to be a cook on a ship somewhere, for all I know," said Booker.

"We aren't going to be a bunch of cooks. That will be one sick army if they make us cooks."

"They will be, if they eat what *you* cook," said Booker.

"You know, a while back I was looking out the window and seeing downtown Mountain Springs and the stores downtown. I could still smell the onions."

"I never smelled them. I never went downtown," said Booker.

"I wondered what I was leaving behind."

"What do you mean you wondered what you were leaving behind? You were wondering what you were leaving behind? Are you crazy? You don't have nothing. You never had nothing. So you couldn't leave nothing behind!" exclaimed Booker.

"I know Uncle George wanted to put us in the army, but I wanted to join up," said Andre.

"You wanted to join up?"

"Yes," said Andre.

Booker paused and looked at him.

"You did, didn't you?" said Booker, looking at Andre. "Well, there wasn't anything else for us to do. We don't have college or nothing, not even a high school education. We can't get a job."

"We could have gone to college," said Andre.

"Is that why you kept going up to that church school, to get into college? They weren't going to take you. You had to be white and have money to go that school up there," said Booker.

"I don't know what they required. I liked going up there."

"Yeah you did, and we could never find you. Uncle George was always looking for you on Saturdays, and you would always disappear for a few hours. I knew where you was going, but I said you were off hunting or fishing or something," said Booker.

"I thought I could find some help and see if there was something I could do up there. I somehow think there is something else out there for me," said Andre.

"Who told you that? That sounds like something someone put in your head. That crazy head of yours. You are always dreaming about something," said Booker as he reached over and grabbed Andre's head. He put his fist in Andre's hair and began to rub it.

Andre pushed off his hand, and it appeared as if they were going to fight. But then another new recruit in front of the boys turned around. "Knock it off. Do you want to get us in trouble?"

Booker took his hands off of Andre.

The bus drove on.

A few miles down the road, Andre looked at Booker. "I wanted to get a job and do something. Make some money," he said, lowering his voice so no one would hear them.

"Nobody's going to hire you, you crazy fool, unless you can do something. You have to be able to do something," responded Booker.

"What are you going to do?" asked Andre in disgust.

"Me? I'm going to do this for now. I'm not thinking about nothing else right now. Just this," said Booker.

The bus drove on and they said nothing else. The bus was quiet with the new recruits, unsure of their future.

Fort Bragg, North Carolina, was their new home.

"Here it begins," said Booker.

Booker and Andre had one thing in common: they were determined to have no problems in boot camp and to not get into trouble. They were not going to get kicked out and be forced to go back to Mountain Springs. Booker would be a fierce fighter. Andre would keep his boots shined. They both could shoot a firearm. George's timing was perfect. Andre and Booker arrived at Fort Bragg, North Carolina, on Friday, December 5, 1941. If Booker thought they were going to be cooks, he was mistaken.

A drill instructor came into the bus and told them to get out and stand in formation. They were intimidated at first, stepping off the bus and then realizing they were so far away from home — they *were* only seventeen years old. They stood in formation with the other black recruits.

The drill instructor stood in front of the group and said, "We want good men to serve in the army and be proud of it. As the newest recruits of the United States Army, you are the lowest of all ranks and will conduct yourself accordingly. You will use proper military courtesy. When spoken to by a superior you will also use the words 'Yes, sir' and 'No, sir.' Anytime you want to talk to a drill sergeant, you will bring yourself to proper attention like you are now, and get yourself into position and say, 'Sir' and 'Private,' whatever your last name is, and then request permission to speak. You will speak when spoken to and not before. As soon as I give you the word, I want you to turn your pockets inside out, take your wallet out, all your pictures and papers, and lay 'em up on the table. You got forty-five seconds to get it done. Move it out."

The new soldiers were assigned to barracks. Tomorrow would be their first day.

The next day they were up early at reveille and went out for a mile run and exercise, followed by their first chow. Later they received a haircut and were issued boots and uniforms. After that, they were processed through medical and administration and received a multitude of shots.

Each day was harder than the one before. They took many tests, studied maps, trained and fired their weapons many times at the shooting range, learned hand-to-hand combat and how to use gas masks. They were intimidated by the drill instructors during training, especially since the drill instructors could recognize and call the soldiers by name once they began wearing their uniforms. The instructors had the new soldiers constantly on the run with endless lines. They had chow together three times a day and met other GIs from different walks of life. They told each other their stories and over time would became friends for life. They became battle buddies.

Boot camp was thirteen weeks of pure hell for Andre and Booker, but they felt prepared. After graduation ceremonies, they learned that they would travel to London and then to North Africa aboard a British ship.

PART 2

The Press

CHAPTER 1

Oliver Smith was born in 1906 and grew up in Birmingham, Alabama. His father was Bruce Smith, a former preacher who became the president of the Southern Baptist College in Alabama, a school founded in 1900 to educate children of freed slaves. His mother, Maryellen, always stressed the importance of education. Oliver's college experience and middle class background gave him the means and ambition that so many others did not possess at that time.

After earning his degree in journalism from the University of Tennessee, Oliver's first job was as a travel writer for the *Birmingham Defender*. Before joining the paper, he freelanced and sold articles to magazines. One article earned him $500 — quite a sum in the 1940s. He befriended the editor of the *Birmingham Defender*, Ed Nelms, who was impressed with his writing.

Nelms allowed Oliver to tour Latin America and write about his experiences. Smith traveled to Chile where he wrote of his impressions of the racial conditions at that time. In Cuba, he wrote about eager youngsters hoping to find U.S. baseball recruiters. In Trinidad, he wrote about the hot weather. His articles thrust him into the limelight of black journalists; he was becoming a rising star. Oliver's reporting was exotic and forward-looking. He couldn't sit still in Alabama; Smith longed for travel that would take him to far corners of the world. He continually pushed the envelope and used his writing pen to fill it. Sometimes his themes were political, and in 1940 he moved from news to editorial writing and endorsed Norman Thomas of the Socialist Party of America for president. That was a mistake he would always regret. He would never switch from news reporting to the editorial staff or abandon Roosevelt again.

Washington faced a dilemma as the United States entered World War II. It needed the support of patriotic African Americans, but many of these men resented the discrimination they experienced. The War Department announced that African Americans would serve in the war, but American troops would remain segregated. The FBI, particularly J. Edgar Hoover, was concerned that black journalists sent into the war zone might become disgruntled and write stories exploiting these soldiers' conditions. There was talk of reigning in black newspapers that wrote negative stories about race relations during time of war. The War Department decided it would not go after journalists for printing negative stories, but would instead seek the reporters' cooperation.

Americans were hungry for any news of the war. They were accustomed to Ed Murrow's nightly radio reports from

London during the Blitz, where he began with his opening "*This* is London" and ended it with "Good night, and good luck." Murrow established his *Murrow's Boys* and celebrity status. He returned to Washington, D.C., to be honored on December 2, 1941, at a dinner with over 1,000 guests in attendance.

In January of 1940, Howard K. Smith, a Murrow's Boy, reported from Berlin. He interviewed Hitler and other S.S. leaders, but would never allow Nazi propaganda to enter into his reports. On December 6, 1941, the Nazis seized his material and ejected him from Germany. Smith left for Switzerland to continue his reporting.

Eric Sevareid, another Murrow's Boy, was the first to report on the fall of France and the French surrender to Nazi Germany in 1940. He worked with Murrow from July to October 1940, covering the Battle of Britain.

On December 7, 1941, the Japanese bombed Pearl Harbor. The world changed for the United States; no longer could it sit and watch Europe at war with the Axis — Germany, Italy, and Japan. Newspapers soon began clamoring to send journalists overseas to cover the war. Nelms could see the power of war reporting to the public through broadcast journalism, but he could also see that Murrow's Boys were garnering the bulk of the reports. Nelms needed to capitalize on this opportunity through print media, and he needed reporters on the ground to cover the story of the black soldier.

CHAPTER 2

On December 8, 1941, the War Department hosted a conference attended by journalists across the nation to determine the process for accrediting war correspondents. Although now in his seventies, Nelms covered World War I as the only credentialed black journalist. He sent Oliver to the conference, hoping to have Smith approved to cover the current war. There was just one problem: Oliver wrote an opinion article endorsing a socialist opponent over Roosevelt in the 1940 election. Would this hurt his chances of being selected? Would politics enter the decision to select him?

Only two black journalists attended the conference. Besides Smith, the other black attendee was Andrew Phillips, the owner and editor of the *African-American Statesman* in Chicago, the largest black-owned newspaper in the country.

Oliver entered a large room with tables arranged in a square, the chairs facing each other. Some attendees were standing near the coffee pot at the registration table, but no one was there to sign him in yet. Oliver walked around the conference area, perusing the room and place cards at each table. He found his name and sat down in his designated chair. He opened his briefcase and withdrew papers to thumb through while waiting for the conference to begin.

Before long the attendees arrived. Many knew each other and were shaking hands and patting each other on the back. Andrew Phillips walked in the room, looking distinguished in his suit, tie, and cuff links. He had a handkerchief in his pocket and a U.S. flag pin on his suit. Phillips was friendly and outgoing, shaking hands with everyone. He was well-known and looked and acted like a United States senator rather than a newspaper publisher. Oliver realized he should have been circulating with the other reporters, but he was impressed watching Phillips work the crowd. Phillips, the publisher of a paper with a circulation of over 500,000, sat down next to Oliver.

"Hello, I'm Andrew Phillips," he said as he offered his hand.

"Oliver Smith, *Birmingham Defender*. Looks like we are here for the same reason."

"Yes, we are," said Phillips, taking his seat. "Have you seen the agenda for today?"

"I was just reviewing the materials. Looks like a lot of discussion and several speakers," said Oliver.

"Are you sending someone to cover the war, or are you going yourself?" asked Phillips.

"We haven't decided, but I'm going to pitch myself for the job."

"That's good. Isn't your editor David Nelms?"

"Yes."

"I know Nelms — he's a good guy. We worked together at the same newspaper in New York awhile back. I heard he bought the newspaper in Alabama. What's the circulation of the paper?"

"It's 235,000. I'm not going to ask what yours is. I think I already know."

"It's ok. I didn't mean to imply that we were competing. I just wanted to see if circulation was trending up."

"Are you going to cover the war?" asked Oliver.

"No. I'm too old to do that. But my daughter wants to go over there."

"Your daughter?"

"Yes. Her name is Tatiana. She is going to be the first black journalist to cover the war in Europe, once she gets some training under her belt. She needs more experience before I send her out as a foreign correspondent. You know, she's about your age. You might end up meeting her eventually if she goes. Here's her photo," he said, pulling the snapshot out of his wallet and showing it off as a proud father would show off a baby picture.

"She's beautiful," said Oliver.

"Yes, she is. You know, the clamor for war reporting is not just coming from men who want to go over there. Women journalists want to be credentialed too. They want to join the military, not just stay behind with desk jobs. I'm sure you're going to see many female journalists credentialed to cover the war. Do you have any family?"

"No. Just me. Well, I have my parents. My father and mother still live in Birmingham."

More people began to enter the room, looking for their seats as the conference was about to begin.

"We'll talk after the session," said Phillips.

They didn't talk afterwards, but Oliver did not forget Tatiana's picture.

CHAPTER 3

Shortly after the bombing of Pearl Harbor, President Roosevelt held a news conference in the Oval Office to discuss the war and answer questions. Security was tight at the White House following the attack, and the reporters were coming in one by one after going through heavy screening and frisking by the Secret Service. While the president was talking and joking with the reporters in the office prior to the news conference, Harry McClain walked into the Oval Office after being frisked and cleared. He worked for the National Negro Association and *Atlanta Daily World.* He was the first black journalist to attend the White House press conference.

President Roosevelt looked up at him and smiled. The other reporters watched in amazement, seeing history being made. McClain walked around the president's desk and the president extended his hand.

"Harry, I'm glad to have you here," said the president.

"Thank you, Mr. President," he said.

"Did you get frisked?" asked the president.

"I did."

"Security is tight these days," said the president.

May Craig, a political journalist working for the Gannett news organization as their Washington correspondent, walked into the room. She had her own column called *Inside Washington* and worked with the Women's National Press Club and Eleanor Roosevelt's Press Conference Association supporting women in journalism. She reported from London and wanted to cover the war in Europe.

The president finished greeting McClain and the men looked over to see Craig walk in. She appeared disheveled and was fixing her dress. She looked up and saw the president and the other reporters looking at her.

"You too?" asked the president. "Did you get frisked?"

"I did. You've got a new system out there," she said to the president.[1]

"I will have to hire a female Secret Service agent around here to do the frisking," said the president.

The reporters laughed.

The president began talking while the reporters continued to arrive: "I wanted to tell you that occasionally I have a few people in to dinner, and generally in the middle of dinner some — some 'sweet young thing' says, 'Mr. President, couldn't you tell us about so and so?'"

"Sweet young thing?" queried May Craig.

"I know she isn't — it isn't an individual, it's just a generic term," said the president to May.

"Really," said May.

The reporters in the room laughed.

"Really," said the president. "Well, the other night this 'sweet young thing' in the middle of supper said, 'Mr. President, couldn't you tell us about the bombing? Where did those planes start from and go to?'"

"What did you say to the sweet young thing, Mr. President?" asked May.

"Now May, I don't think that is nice," said the president jokingly.

The reporters laughed.

"But anyway, I said, 'Yes. I think the time has now come to tell you. They came from our new secret base at *Shangri La*!'"

The reporters broke out with laughter.

"And she believed it!" said the president.

There was more laughter.

Miss Craig asked the president, "Mr. President, is this *sweet young thing* a young lady?"

The reporters in the room laughed and interrupted her.

"No, May, not at all." said the president. "*Sweet young thing* is a generic term. It happens to be a woman."

More laughter.

"Is it always feminine?" she asked him.

Laughter again.

"What was that, Miss Craig?" asked the president.

"Is this 'sweet young thing' always feminine?" she repeated.

This time there was loud laughter in the room.

"Now May. I call it a 'sweet young thing.' Now when I talk about manpower, that includes the women; and when I talk about a 'sweet young thing,' that includes young men."

There was even louder laughter to the president's response. Then Roosevelt became serious. "When I say manpower, I am talking about men and women and from all races. I was just kidding with May and that is off the record," said the president.

The reporters became quiet.

"Before we start with the questions, I want to announce that I have established an Office of War Information that will be coordinating with the news media during the war. The War Department will credential news journalists to travel to the theaters to report the war. This will include the Negro journalists and women journalists who will be allowed to report in theater."

The reporters clapped and praised the president's remarks. May smiled, as did Harry. They were pleased by the president's announcement. There were many more questions. The president was handling the war and the journalists.

May looked down at her purse. The president did not realize that she had just recorded the first presidential press conference. The nature of presidential press conferences would forever change after that, as would the reporting of the war.

CHAPTER 4

THERE WAS NOT much that Oliver needed to do to convince Nelms to let him apply for certification from the War Department to cover the war in Europe. He knew that was what Oliver wanted and he wanted it too.

"Go ahead. That's why I sent you to the conference," Nelms told Oliver from his office desk, sipping his morning's coffee and looking at the newly published morning newspaper.

"I figured you did and you knew I wanted to go. It fits in with all the travel writing you used to do," said Oliver.

"I did. Besides, there isn't anyone else to send at the paper. All the other papers are sending journalists. I can't let Phillips take all the glory. Is he sending his daughter?"

"He is," said Oliver.

"How do you know?"

"I met him. He showed me her picture," said Oliver.

"He showed you her picture at the conference?" asked Nelms.

"He did."

"They say she is quite a gal. Nice looking."

"She is. She certainly is."

"I understand now why you want to go."

"That's not the reason. He said she wouldn't be going over there for a while; she still has a lot to learn here before being a foreign correspondent," said Oliver.

"Yes, she is young. You will be America's first credentialed black journalist to cover the war. When she goes she will be America's first credentialed black *female* journalist to cover the war. Phillips and I talked about it. I told him to find you at the conference. If she goes over there she will need to have some support. It could be difficult over there for both of you."

"That's good. I'll make sure that happens," said Oliver.

"You can do what I did in World War I. You wear an army uniform and travel under their orders, give them your reports, and work with a public relations officer. You submit your stories to them for approval. We wrote stories in a room with the censors so that they could make sure nothing was transmitted without their approval. Then you go on to covering the next story. There is no time to rest. It's a lot more difficult than working here," warned Nelms.

"I'm ready for it."

"There is just one problem — or at least I hope this isn't a problem. You wrote an opinion piece endorsing Roosevelt's socialist opponent."

"That was a mistake," admitted Oliver.

"Hell of a mistake. I can't believe I let that get out of here," said Nelms.

"I know."

"How can someone not endorse Roosevelt?" asked Nelms.

"Let's not talk about it. I've been through that."

"The War Department might not credential you if they think you are going to write something that might undermine the war effort," said Nelms.

"I'm not going to do that," said Oliver.

"I know you won't. I will make sure of it. The War Department wants to send journalists over there, but they don't want stories coming back that could affect the war — such as reporting about discrimination of the black soldier. The censors will make sure that doesn't go to print."

"Understood," said Oliver.

"Just focus on the individual black soldier or soldiers or platoons. That's what the readers want to read about anyway. Not some political stuff about how the government should do this or not do that."

"Roger that, sir," said Oliver.

"And Oliver," Nelms said as Oliver began to leave.

"What?"

"Get a haircut. You're in the army now."

Oliver smiled. Nelms resumed drinking his coffee and looking over the newspaper as Oliver closed the door behind him.

Nelms attended college and worked his way up through the *Birmingham Defender*, acquiring the paper and eventually becoming editor. He was much like Oliver when he was young and covering the American black soldiers serving in World War I; untamed, impulsive at times, longing for adventure. Now Nelms was grounded and stable.

During the First World War, Nelms covered the 369th Infantry, formally known as the 15th Regiment New York Guard or the "Harlem Hell Fighters." Under the command of Commander William Hayward, they fought at Château - Thierry and Belleau Wood and spent 191 days in combat, longer than any American unit in the war. Nelms reported Colonel Hayward's famous line: *My men never retire; they go forward or they die.*[2]

Twenty-six years later, Nelms was editor of the largest black newspaper in Alabama and second largest in circulation next to the *African-American Statesman* — a feat he accomplished in his seventies. In 1940, the circulation of the *Birmingham Defender* was 105,000. By 1944 it had grown to 235,000. Nelms wanted his paper to grow to 500,000, the circulation that his competitor, the *African-American Statesman*, had already achieved.

Nelms was not worried about J. Edgar Hoover monitoring the newspaper. He knew that his readers wanted to know about the war. Lacking access to the *Associated Press*, *United Press International News Service*, and *Reuters*, he needed a reporter in Europe to provide news stories about the black soldier. There was no other way to get the stories he needed.

More stories meant more papers, and more papers meant greater advertising … and that meant more revenue. Oliver would be key to that growth.

While waiting for his credentials, Nelms assigned Oliver to cover stories at home, sending him to military bases where black soldiers were trained. Oliver toured the training camps of what would become the first Red Tails of the Tuskegee Airmen. He visited a desert camp in Arizona, a number of bases in the South, and even camps on the Canadian border. The bases were all segregated.

Oliver wrote in one of his stories:

> *The White House in 1940 said that black soldiers would be in the war but would remain segregated.*

It took six months for the army to approve Oliver's application, and he soon learned that London would be his first stop. The Allies had invaded North Africa. Oliver suspected he would go to France, but the country was still occupied and the War Department was silent. To be credentialed, he needed a press pass issued by the War Department and a U.S. passport. Only reporters employed by legitimate publications could receive a press pass. He signed a written agreement to submit all his copy for military review.

Oliver told Nelms the good news, and Nelms told him to start packing. The story, *War Department Selects African American Writer to Cover Troops*, ran the next morning in the newspaper.

CHAPTER 5

MARYELLEN SMITH, OLIVER's mother, went outside on a cool morning in Birmingham and picked up the newspaper. Still in her white robe after making coffee, she glanced down at the headlines on her way back to their southern row house. She sat down on the porch swing to read the paper as coffee smells permeated the air. This was the best part of her day; going outside in her robe, picking up the paper, and reading it with a cup of coffee. Those quiet moments were like prayer time to her. She could think and clear her mind as she sat in the stillness of the morning. She would look at the newspaper to see if her son had a by-line and listen to the sounds of Birmingham as it awoke for the morning and work began.

Maryellen opened the paper and read: *War Department Selects* ... She read further and saw her son's name in print. Oliver was going to war.

"My goodness! Bruce, Bruce, come here! Oliver's going to London!" she excitedly called to her husband.

Bruce came down the stairs, already dressed in a work shirt and work pants. His days started early — he had been up for more than an hour. After pouring his coffee, he walked outside to the porch.

"What is it?"

"Oliver is going to London!"

"What? Let me see that," he said as he carefully took the paper from her hands and sat down next to her on the swing. He read the headline out loud, *"War Department Selects African American Writer to Cover Troops."* Then he read the short article.

Bruce handed the paper back to Maryellen.

"You know that's all that he's interested in, don't you? He doesn't want to stay around here."

"What do you mean, that's all he's interested in?" said Maryellen.

"Interested in getting away, that's what."

"Getting away from what?" she asked.

"Getting away from here, I guess. Heck, I don't know. Look around here and see what this city is becoming. It's becoming a big city. But he doesn't want to have anything to do with it. He always wants to leave."

"No he doesn't, Bruce. He doesn't always want to be leaving and taking off."

He looked at her and smiled.

"You're right. But who knows what goes on in his mind. He's always got to take a trip here, take a trip there, and take a trip to … you know, as Jesus said …"

"Bruce, this is not Sunday morning," said Maryellen, interrupting him and drinking her coffee. "On another subject, do you think he will ever settle down?"

Bruce looked at her, his eyes wide with amazement.

"Settle down? Oliver? Settle down here? Who knows? Who with? Sure, he'll settle down, but it won't be here. He's always looking for something new, some new place to go to. It will have to be one strong lady to tame him and get him to settle down in one place."

"I wonder who that lady will be. I've always wondered that."

"Me too," he said.

"At least he's not going to the Pacific. That could be dangerous. There must be something planned going on in Europe, otherwise they wouldn't send him over there. I was hoping that he would stay here and settle down, find a local girl and give us grandkids," said Maryellen.

Bruce looked over and put his arm around Maryellen. With sympathy he told her, "I'd like to have grandkids too, but it's not going to happen with him anytime soon. Especially with the way things are out there and with his lifestyle. How can anybody afford anything during this depression? We're lucky we have what we have. Most folks have nothing."

"He told me that this might be his last trip. Maybe he will settle down when he returns," she said.

"I hope so. But all he wants to do is go off someplace like South America and write stories. Now he wants to go to Europe and write stories. Who knows what's next?"

CHAPTER 6

SHORTY'S REAL NAME was Lee Roy Miller. Lee Roy was different from Oliver. He had no formal education, but he had an education of his own, working around a barbershop and listening to all kinds of stories going on in town. There were always stacks of newspapers on the barbers' chairs that he would throw out at the end of the week. But before he threw the papers away, Shorty always read the front pages. He wanted to move up in the world.

Shorty Miller left Second Street Barber Shop and Mountain Springs without telling Andre of his move to Birmingham. One day in 1939, he decided to move his shoeshine business to the *Birmingham Defender*.

Alvin and Louis were sad that he was gone, but they would never let on. They weren't paying him anything to shine shoes in the barbershop. Even the curmudgeon Cousin Carl was disappointed, but he would never admit it either. Shorty left and said his goodbyes, walking down Second Street in front of Zero Pawn Shop and Famous Hamburgers, getting the onion smell all over his clothes as he went to catch the bus to Birmingham. Alvin, Louis, and Carl stood at the door watching Shorty walk away, unable to tell him that they didn't want him to go. Shorty's name was never mentioned again in the barbershop.

Shorty set up his new shoeshine stand near the front entry elevators on the first floor of the *Birmingham Defender*. There he could catch the employees and anyone off the street who might walk by and need a shine. People passing by could see his stand through the window. Nelms would get his shoes shined once a week on his way to work in the morning. One day, while shining Nelm's shoes, Shorty asked him for a job.

"Yes sir, Mr. Nelms. I would like to work for the paper one day."

Nelms looked up from the paper he was reading.

"You would, would you?" Nelms said.

"Yes, I would," Shorty said with confidence as he took the towel out to complete the finish on the shine. He pulled out his plastic tube that contained nothing but water and finished the final shimmering.

Nelms lowered the paper; he looked at Shorty and smiled. He had a job for Shorty. Shorty looked at Nelms and realized something had happened. Nelms took him seriously. Shorty had been promoted.

Nelms respected Shorty for his courage and told him to give up shining shoes. Shorty would now be working with the delivery routes during the day.

"Leave the shoeshine booth behind," Nelms advised. "Your name is Cub now. Report to me on Monday on the eighth floor."

Nelms paid for the shine and stood up.

"Thank you, sir!" Shorty looked up and watched the old man with white hair walk out the door with the beginning of a slight limp.

"Don't call me *sir*," Nelms retorted as he left the building.

The next Monday, Nelms told the newly named "Cub" that he would be working in the delivery department to learn how the paper was delivered. He told him to start reading up on the English language. Nelms gave Cub books on proper writing styles and told his protégé to practice writing in preparation for the night shift as a proofreader. If Cub could proofread the next day's newspaper stories the night before they went to press, and the paper came out the next morning with no errors, Cub would receive an extra $5.00 per day beyond his normal paycheck.

Over a year later in 1940, Nelms gave Cub his first assignment to cover a story. He wanted to see if — and how well — Cub could write.

"Start with a strong lead in sentence ... get a quote ... check out the story ...," he would say as Cub left his office.

"Yes, Boss." Cub was scrambling and as happy as anyone could be to be on a real assignment. He longed to see his name in print with a by-line.

"Don't call me *Boss*!" Nelms yelled as Cub dashed out of his office.

Nelms watched over Cub and encouraged him to write every day, forcing him to learn proper English. Cub worked at the paper for three years before any of his articles were printed with a by-line, and that was only after heavy editing. But Cub was satisfied. His name was in print. He was finally a reporter.

In June 1942, Cub submitted a story to Nelms. It regarded Admiral Nimitz and his pinning of the Navy Cross on Doris Miller, the first African American recipient of that particular honor. Miller was awarded the Navy Cross for his actions during the attack on Pearl Harbor. Miller manned an anti-aircraft gun and fired at the attacking Japanese planes, despite having no prior training in weapons' use.

Nelms sat in his office and read the article. He couldn't believe it. He got up out of his chair and went to Cub's desk. It was after 7 p.m. and the night crew was working, but Cub was still busy at his typewriter. He was already working a double shift.

"Cub, come with me," commanded Nelms.

Cub grabbed his coat and hat and followed Nelms to his office. Nelms reached for his hat and coat and motioned to his protégé.

"Let's go to the club."

Nelms drove them to the Tower Club, a restaurant with a beautiful view overlooking downtown Birmingham. Cub was amazed at the invitation.

The men sat down and looked out at the sparkling lights of the city.

"You know Cub, it doesn't get any better than this. I'm lucky, because my father started this newspaper. His vision became my vision. You look out there and see this city."

"I do, Boss. It's quite a site," said Cub.

"This newspaper tells stories that are not told by other newspapers. My paper tells it like it is. We don't get involved in politics, and we don't endorse politicians. I don't do endorsements anymore. That was a mistake. We want to be better than the other newspapers, and I want to write stories that are healthy for today. I'm seventy-three years old and have had many experiences. I always try to relate those experiences to what is happening today."

"Yes, Boss," said Cub.

"You don't have to call me *Boss*. Where did you get that?" asked Nelms.

"Yes, sir," said Cub.

"And not *sir*, either," said Nelms. "We are not in the military. Oliver might think he's in the military going to London. We are not in the military."

"Yes, Mr. Nelms."

Nelms smiled and leaned back in his chair, looking directly at Cub.

"I was just thinking ... I still can't believe I let Oliver move over to the editorial board and write an opinion piece endorsing that candidate in the socialist party over Roosevelt. I agreed to move him from newswriting to editorial, and the first thing he does is endorse a socialist candidate. I lost ground in circulation for that. My paper — endorsing a socialist candidate? I'm not going to let that happen again."

"No, sir," said Cub.

"I just received news that Oliver has been cleared to travel to Europe to cover the war as a correspondent. He's the first black journalist approved to cover the war over there."

"Does Oliver know yet?" asked Cub.

"He will tomorrow. I just got the word today."

"I'm happy for him. But I'm also just happy that I can show up and have this job," said Cub.

"That's good. You are doing a good job, Cub. And I'm glad Oliver got picked to go to Europe. He can help us elevate the level of debate. We can't get the story of the black soldier here — we have to get it over there where it is happening. We have to send someone there to get into the thick of it. They have to get into the foxhole with the soldier. That's the way it's done. That's how I did it in World War I. Our job as journalists is to give food for thought. At least, that's how I was taught," said Nelms.

Cub nodded. "My father taught me how to shine shoes. One day I told him I was going to work for the newspaper and he asked me, 'Why would you go into a business where you can't get a job?' When my first story came out and I got my first by-line, my mother showed it to him and he said, 'By golly, his name is in the paper, and he didn't kill nobody.'[3] My, how things have changed."

The waitress came and set their drinks on the table. Nelms and Cub raised their glasses.

"Here's to change," said Nelms.

They drank and looked out the window at the nightlife of Birmingham.

"Cub, I don't believe it. Actually, I *do* believe it. I couldn't find anything wrong with your story today. No errors. No corrections. I want to congratulate you. You are a real journalist," Nelms toasted Cub.

"Thank you, Mr. Nelms." Cub raised his glass again to toast with Nelms.

"You know, you should return to school and get a degree. Over time you will be interviewing more and more people. More sophisticated and important people. There is so much more to learn out there. I will give you some of my rules. When you start doing interviews with significant people, the first thing you do is read whatever you can about the person publicly. Nothing irritates someone more than to be asked facts, which everyone already knows is in the public domain. Find out what you can, get the person comfortable, and ask that they amplify on a subject. They will do that."

"Yes, Mr. Nelms," said Cub.

"First thing next semester, I want you to enroll in college. The paper will cover the cost of your education. If you are going to write for this paper, I want you to have the credentials. I'll make some calls and get you in. I know the head of the school. I shouldn't have let you work these past few years without requiring you to continue your education."

"Work *and* go to school?"

"Yes. You will have two jobs. Take it or leave it."

"I'll take it."

"I thought you would. We'd better go. We need to get back to the paper. As they say, show up early, do what you have to do to get the story done, and don't go home until tomorrow."

"That's what they say?" said Cub.

"Or, if you keep your nose to the grindstone it will eventually become horribly disfigured."[4]

"What was that?" asked Cub.

"Let's go," chuckled Nelms as he stood to leave.

CHAPTER 7

The War Department assigned credentials to 558 print and radio correspondents to cover World War II. Of these, 127 were women. It was their responsibility as journalists to get the story, no matter what it took. Many did so under extreme circumstances and even in violation of the law.

Margaret "Maggie" Bourke-White was the first woman to be credentialed by the War Department and the first to work in a combat zone. She had been the associate editor and staff photographer of *Fortune* magazine and the first female photojournalist for *Life* magazine. In 1930, she was the first western photographer to take photographs of the Soviet Union. In 1941, she traveled to the Soviet Union just as Germany invaded. She took refuge in the U.S. Embassy, capturing the invasion on her camera. In 1942, she headed to North Africa, attached to the U.S. Army Air Force.

Nelms told Oliver that he was the first of many black journalists to be credentialed by the War Department to cover the American troops. Other black journalists were sent to the British Isles, the Mediterranean, North Africa, Italy, the Pacific, Alaska, China, Burma, and India.

Oliver had one day to pack before he headed to London on June 8th. The United States had been at war for six months. On June 7th, the Battle of Midway ended three days after it began with a decisive victory for the U.S. and the Pacific fleet. Only six months after Pearl Harbor, the U.S. decisively struck a blow to the Imperial Japanese Navy by sinking four Japanese carriers.

The British were fighting both the Germans and Italians in Gazala in North Africa, near the port of Tobruk in Libya. The Axis was commanded by "Desert Fox" Colonel-General Erwin Rommel. The Allied forces of the Eighth Army were commanded by Lieutenant-General Neil Ritchie and were under supervision of the Commander-in-Chief Middle East, General Sir Claude Auchinleck.

In the European arena, the United States declared war on Bulgaria, Hungary, and Romania. In the Pacific arena, the Japanese invaded the islands of Attu and Kiska in the Aleution Islands, and one of their submarines shelled Sydney, Australia.

Oliver was treated as a celebrity during this time. Word of his selection added to his rising-star status and circulated through the journalism profession and the military Public Affairs offices. Instead of waiting to be sent to Europe on a troopship from the states, Oliver was given a ticket to fly directly to London at government expense on a Pan-American Airways Clipper flight.

Maryellen looked at her son with tears in her eyes as Oliver prepared to board the plane to London. "Be safe and make sure you come back," she said softly.

"I will, mama. I will be safe," Oliver assured her.

"You know how dangerous it is being in war, no matter what they say. Now listen to your mama and listen good," she said to her son, who was in his thirties. "I understand that there have been lots of battles over there. No matter what they might ask of you, don't volunteer or do anything that would put you in danger," she said.

"Ok, mama. I'm not going to war. I'm going to *cover* the war. There is a difference," he said to his mother with a smile, expecting to hear the caution from his mother.

Bruce put his hand on Oliver's shoulder. "Son, be safe. Your mother and I are hoping that after this is over you will come back and settle down and get married and have some kids. You know she's been looking forward to that day," said Bruce.

"I know, Dad. I don't know when I'm going to do that, but I need to do this now."

"I know you do. I just want you to make your mother happy and proud of you. You know how she wants grandkids and you are getting into your thirties now. You don't want to get too old to do that."

"That day will come, I'm sure."

"I'm proud of you. I hope you make her happy. And I want you to be happy, too."

Oliver hugged his parents and boarded the plane, waving to them once more as he walked toward the door. Maryellen and Bruce waved back to their son, so handsome in his army-issued military trench coat with an arm patch emblazoned with the correspondent's "C" and an army hat that displayed his equivalent rank of major.

Maryellen cried. *All mothers cry,* thought Oliver as he turned and walked onto the plane. The door closed behind him.

Maryellen and Bruce stood looking through the window, watching the plane take off and head toward the horizon until it could no longer be seen.

CHAPTER 8

The next morning, Nelms ran a story with a picture of Oliver boarding the plane in his uniform. With his assigned rank of major, Oliver could go wherever he wanted and enjoy more freedom of movement than the regular military. The military's only real check on the press was the ability to censor the articles for sensitive information that could affect the ongoing operation of the war. They were the "free press" reporting on the war.

Arriving in London, Oliver spent his first night at a hotel by himself. He carried a bar of chocolate that he planned to eat the next morning, setting it on a nearby table before he went to sleep. When Oliver awoke, he noticed a rat eating his chocolate bar. After a week of becoming familiar with London, he sent his first dispatch:

> *I woke up to a rat on the dresser in the hotel eating the only chocolate bar I brought with me. There are a lot of differences here. In America you get big bulky Sunday papers. Here, you get eight pages. In America you buy all the clothes you can pay for. Here, you hoard coupons until*

you must have a shirt. In America you can have bacon and eggs every morning, with butter and plenty of sugar. Here, you are lucky to get an egg.[5]

London had been under siege since 1940 and many reporters were in the city covering the Blitz. Once situated, Oliver checked in with the Military Public Affairs Office to learn of his orders. The room was filled with reporters, each awaiting verification of his credentials. Major Jonah Lee checked him in and verified his identity and credentials.

"You are with the *Birmingham Defender*?" Lee asked.

"Yes, I am," answered Oliver.

"Congratulations on achieving your credentials," said Lee.

"Thank you," Oliver nodded.

Colonel Walter Dixon walked into the room. Oliver was surprised to see him; Dixon was the first black colonel he had ever seen. The colonel called the room of reporters to order:

"You gentlemen will be given a chance to go to war. Each of you will be assigned a ship to take you to a location that will be determined later. You will be spread out among the convoy. Some of you will be carried in British ships that will also carry American troops."

The room became noisy with excitement, filled with shouts of "Yeah!" and "About time!"

Col. Dixon smiled at the response.

"You can't tell us where we are going?" asked one of the reporters.

"I cannot. We do not report ship movements. You know that," said Dixon.

"Once we are in the theater, can we report?" asked one of the reporters.

"You can report once you are able to transmit, but all written reports have to be cleared through the military censors. You should have all signed the formal agreements by now. We are making sure that the reports would not interfere or undermine the military operations."

"Where do you see the war in Europe heading?" asked another reporter.

"It's a matter of time before the free French are converted to the Allies and the Third Reich is removed from North Africa and Europe, is my own guess," said the colonel.

North Africa, Oliver thought to himself. *That must be where we are heading. We must not be going to France.*

After the questioning, Maj. Lee handed Oliver an envelope that contained his orders. His instructions were to report to a train station at a certain location later that night in London. There were many last-minute things to do: get his laundry, buy extra socks and underwear. The army picked up his bedroll and took it away for convoy labeling. Oliver packed everything else in his only canvas bag.

Maj. Lee drove Oliver and a few of the other reporters across London to the train station. The journalists walked up and down the station platform to keep warm that night; it was too cold to sleep. Lee failed to mention that the train would not arrive until the next morning. When it finally arrived, the reporters boarded and began their journey, tired and exhausted. The train came to a stop and pulled in alongside a British ship. The men checked in at an army desk, gathered their baggage, and climbed aboard. The good news was that it would be two days before the ship would leave.[6]

Oliver checked into his room on the ship and rested for the next three hours. There was nothing they could do except wait as time dragged on. Oliver walked to the deck and stood at the rails of the ship as he watched troops marching aboard in the rain, heavily laden with steel helmets, overcoats, rifles, and huge packs on their backs. It was a thrilling site, watching ships load the British and American soldiers. Oliver returned to his room and lay on his bed on the top bunk, writing notes from the day.

CHAPTER 9

Oliver was relaxing on his bed when the door opened and an older man entered the room. Alexander MacGowan of the *London Times* came in with his duffel bag. He was sixty years old, a heavy smoker, and appeared unfit for the trip.

"Looks like I'll be bunking with you, Yank."

Oliver sat up to greet his new roommate.

"Oliver Smith."

"I know who you are. You are the first Negro journalist from America to cover World War II. I read the papers."

"I've read your work, too. Aren't you the oldest journalist going into combat?"

"Yes, I am. I also covered World War I."

MacGowan put his duffel bag on his bunk and lay down. He pulled out a cigarette.

"Want one?" He offered the box to his new roommate.

"No, thanks," said Oliver.

Both were quiet for a few minutes. Oliver asked, "So how is it, covering stories during a war?"

"It's simple. The key is to get away from the command and visit the troops, one by one, in the foxhole. You go look for them, going from foxhole to foxhole, and find out what their story is. Find out who they are, where they're from, who their friends are, where they live in the city, what their feelings are ... point is to make *them* the story and keep yourself out of the story."

Oliver nodded. "I do write from personal experiences. I write what I see."

"Write what you see, of course. Write what you see *and* write what the soldier sees. That's what prints."

The reporters talked further. MacGowan finally said that he was going to sleep, and the men said their goodnights.

It was quiet in the room and both thought that the other was asleep. Oliver heard MacGowan's voice coming through the bedspring on the top bunk.

"So why are you doing this?"

"Doing what?" asked Oliver.

"You know. Coming here to cover the war?"

"My paper needs the story. We don't have access to Reuters or the other newspaper services," said Oliver.

"That makes sense. But what I was wondering was whether you were doing this for yourself or for the newspaper?"

"Both, I guess. After Pearl Harbor, I went to the conference in Washington to argue for black reporters' acceptance to cover the war," said Oliver.

"But I want to know if you are doing this for your own ego or to serve others? Is this a calling of your own making, or is someone else calling you to do it?" asked a curious MacGowan.

Oliver was nervous about the question and the depth of the conversation with someone he had just met.

"You must be a philosopher," Oliver said.

"I guess I am."

"I don't know the answer to that. I've always thought that what I do is was what I was called to do," said Oliver.

"If that is the case, then you have achieved what most others have not been able to achieve," said MacGowan.

"What is that?" asked Oliver.

"The ability to combine one's life work with what you were intended to do in the first place. That source out there, whatever you call it — God, Jesus — something out there pulling at you to head in a certain direction. Many people haven't figured that out, and they go about doing the same job over and over again, hoping they are going to be happy at the end and finding out they were miserable the whole time ... and that achievement, money, power, or position never bring happiness."[7]

"What *does* bring happiness?" asked Oliver.

"Oh, for me, doing what I'm doing. I have no wife, no family, so I can go about doing what I'm doing. I know what I want, what I was intended to do, and what I'm here for. When I get up in the morning, when I think a thought, when I write down what comes to me, I know it is not me but something else driving me. I'm lucky in that regard."

"You are lucky. I think I'm still searching," said Oliver.

"Sooner or later you come to the realization that it's not a job, power, position, achievement, or the accumulation of wealth that makes a person who they are. It is service to others."[8]

"Man, this is deep. Are you always this deep on the first date?" asked Oliver.

"Not always, Yank. But I sensed that you have a gift, and that you were sent here to use it and make the best of it," said MacGowan.

"Thank you."

"I guess I will go to sleep now. Good night."

"Good night," said Oliver.

Wow, Oliver thought to himself as he turned over. He was amazed how profound this first conversation was with the elder British journalist; he wondered why their worlds had intersected.

CHAPTER 10

On their first morning out to sea, the ship's gunner's mate tested their fire. The guns boomed, releasing an incredible display of power. A few days outside of London, the ships arranged in formation and came together like a floating puzzle, all pieced together to form a picture. The ships began to roll and the men became sick.[9]

On board the ship, Oliver was given a tour to meet the American GIs. Here he could employ his interview techniques by asking where the soldiers were from and whether or not they knew a particular person. Did they live in a certain part of town? His goal was to show interest in each individual by asking specific questions.

Master Sergeant Billy Gentry, a black soldier from New Orleans, took Oliver to the galley where the enlisted men were waiting to talk to him. Gentry led him through the winding halls, stepping through the ship compartments and passing other soldiers and sailors coming and going. The ship was busy and the galley was noisy with clanging pots and pans. The enlisted men were either standing or sitting at the tables. Some were playing cards, others were reading.

The soldiers stood up when Oliver and Gentry came into the room.

Gentry shouted.

"Now you see this man here? This 'C' on his arm means 'Correspondent'."

Gentry felt the material for the "C" and said, "Hey, that's nice," referring to the quality of the material.

The men laughed. Oliver also laughed, but he put his hand on Gentry's, gently removing his hand from his arm.

Gentry continued. "He might want to ask you some questions. You can answer them IF YOU WANT TO," the master sergeant yelled loudly. "You don't have to talk to him. You don't have answer his questions. BUT YOU CAN IF YOU WANT TO!"

More troops entered the room from the back doors in the galley. Word spread that a black reporter was on the ship interviewing the troops. Soon the entire room was filled mostly with black soldiers. They were amazed to see a black journalist wearing an army uniform.

Oliver pulled out his pencil and notebook and smiled at the young soldier standing in front of him.

"What's your name?"

"Private Buford Trigg."

"Where are you from?"

"Mississippi."

"Did you go to school there?"

"Yes."

Each soldier was different. Oliver made them feel important by asking their individual stories, their background and home.

"Hello, I'm Oliver Smith. What's your name?"

"Private Booker Thompson."

"Where are you from?"

"Mountain Springs, Alabama."

"I'm from Birmingham. Have you heard of the *Birmingham Defender*?" asked Oliver.

"No," said Booker.

"I have," said Private Andre Williams, as he stepped from behind Booker. "I had a friend from Mountain Springs who shined shoes and he took his shine business to that newspaper."

"Really? What's his name?" asked Oliver.

"Shorty. He shined shoes at the barber shop in downtown Mountain Springs."

Oliver took notes as the soldiers answered his questions. He didn't realize that Andre had just mentioned Cub Miller, the reporter. Oliver didn't know that Cub started out shining shoes at the newspaper. He missed an opportunity to engage Andre further about Shorty.

"Good. What's your name?"

"Private Andre Williams."

"Where you from?" asked Oliver.

"From Mountain Springs, Alabama, the same place where Shorty had his business."

"How did you and Private Thompson find each other?"

"We grew up together. The army let us go to boot camp together."

"Where did you go to school?"

Andre was about to answer the question when another group of soldiers came into the room, so noisy it disrupted the interview.

"I'm sorry, I didn't get that," said Oliver.

"I was about to say …," said Andre.

The room became even louder. Master Sgt. Gentry interrupted and said, "Hold on everybody, you will get your turn with the reporter. If you would get behind here and wait your turn, he will get to everyone. Now quiet down so we can hear."

"It's good to meet you," said Oliver, turning his attention back to the other soldiers who were waiting to talk with Oliver. Oliver went from soldier to soldier, shaking hands and asking similar questions. It was a full day of moving about the ship, interviewing any soldier willing to talk.

CHAPTER 11

Oliver retired to his room where MacGowan was resting.

"Long day?"

"Yes. I must have talked to a hundred soldiers. I couldn't get all the names," said Oliver.

"I did, too. This ship is mostly Brits, since this is a British ship. I asked them where they are going, and not all know the ship is heading to North Africa. I'm going to rest a bit before dinner."

"Me too," said Oliver.

Oliver climbed into his bunk under MacGowan and looked up at the bed springs above. A few minutes later he heard MacGowan begin to snore.

By 1700, Oliver could smell the food from the galley. MacGowan climbed out of the top bunk and both cleaned up and walked to the galley through the winding corridors of the ship.

MacGowan and Oliver made their way through the buffet line and turned to find a seat at one of the green cloth-covered tables. The ship was swaying and they had to kept their balance to keep their food from falling off the plate.

"Here's a place," said MacGowan.

"All right," said Oliver.

Ernie Pyle, one of the world's most well-known reporters, entered the galley and joined the other soldiers in the buffet line.

"That's Ernie Pyle over there," said MacGowan, nudging Oliver.

"Where?"

"Getting in line. See over there?"

"That *is* him. I don't know him personally, but I do know of his reputation," said Oliver.

"I know him quite well," said MacGowan.

Pyle was busy shaking hands and greeting the soldiers at tables along the buffet line. He wore a silver identification bracelet that read *Ernie Pyle, War Correspondent.* His face was thin and he was bald, except for sandy red hair around the sides that was turning gray.

McGowan continued to watch Pyle and turned to Oliver. "He was a traveling news journalist like you in the thirties. He was too young to join up in World War I and joined the Navy Reserve, hoping to see action. But the war ended. He has the same aspiration as we all do. We all aspire to be journalists."

"I think I'm like him. I have to go where the action is," said Oliver.

MacGowan nodded and sipped his water. "He's more comfortable with the individual soldier than he is with the military brass or even with his own colleagues. He's a lone ranger and likes to work by himself."

Pyle made his way over to the table and recognized MacGowan.

"Come over here, Pyle," said MacGowan, motioning to him. "How is my good friend?"

Pyle smiled. "Alexander MacGowan, my old friend. Where have you been all this time? I'm not surprised I would find you on a British ship."

"I didn't see you at Public Affairs. I wondered if you were covering this war," said MacGowan.

"Oh, yes," said Pyle confidently.

"Pyle, meet Oliver Smith. He's with the *Birmingham Defender*."

"Oliver Smith," said Oliver, reaching his hand across the table.

"Ernie Pyle. So you got credentialed with the government?" he asked Oliver.

"Yes. It took six months, but it came through."

"Are you the first Negro reporter?" asked Pyle.

"I am the first in Europe. There are five others being sent around the world to cover other parts of the war."

"That's good. Stick with MacGowan and he will show you the ropes. He's been doing this a long time. I don't think you'll have any problem."

"Thank you."

"I hear there are 800 ships on this convoy to Africa. Submarines are waiting at Gibraltar for us," said Pyle.

"There are?" asked Oliver, surprised.

"Yes. It's about time the U.S. joined the war. The fight has been going on in Africa for the last two years in the Tunisia Campaign. The Brits can't do it by themselves, can they MacGowan?"

"Of course we can," sniffed MacGowan. "We've only asked the Americans to lend a helping hand."

"Right. Once this war really gets started, we will be in France. I suppose it makes sense to start the battle in Africa," said Pyle.

"Why is Roosevelt doing that?" asked Oliver.

"He's taking the fight to the enemy. Diverting resources. Fighting the enemy at the edges and draining his supplies. Freeing up the Mediterranean. Any number of reasons," said Pyle.

"I see," said Oliver.

They sat together at a table eating their lunch, saying nothing. Then Pyle said, "See those boys over there? Whether they know it or not, and they probably do, they are about to go into harm's way into North Africa. They are young boys. Just seventeen to twenty-one in some cases. Young men taking on the most difficult job in America, having no idea what they will encounter. No one realizes the stress they must be in. The Germans are waiting to attack the convoy, I assume before we get there. We will see if Hitler will start this war in the Mediterranean. These boys are just waiting this out. There can't be a greater service you can do than to go into battle for your country. I respect them."

CHAPTER 12

MacGowan, Oliver, and Pyle met every night for dinner at the same place and exchanged stories. After a few days at sea, the enlisted men performed a variety show. There was an accordionist, saxophonist, trumpet player, violinist, guitar player, and cowboy singer. Andre couldn't help but join in after a call was made for musicians. The white troops welcomed him when they heard that he could play the guitar borrowed from the ship's company.

"If you play that song you made up, I'm walking out. That is the worst song I've ever heard," said Booker, yelling at him as he left the table.

"I wouldn't dream of it," said Andre, walking to the front of the room with the rest of the men.

One enlisted corporal performed a Gypsy Rose Lee-style striptease burlesque. He twirled and stripped, twirled and stripped, swung in front of the stage, lifted his veil, and kissed the top of Ernie Pyle's head. The crowd went wild as the music played.

The troops enjoyed their free time at sea, but they knew that the war was on. They heard there were enemy submarines waiting for the convoy, but the ship went through the Straits of Gibraltar without an attack. Oliver recorded this in his journal.

The next day, their ship arrived in Oran. Troops went ashore with rations carried on their back, many sharing with the pitiful looking Arab children. Soon the troops found themselves without food. The soldiers began to eat discarded oranges that they found on the ground. Some ate so many that they got diarrhea and broke out with rashes on the first day of the landing.[10]

The streets and sidewalks of Oran were lined with palm trees. There were restaurants, apartments, and elevators, along with garbage in the gutters and dogs roaming the streets. Horse carts outnumbered autos, and the Arabs were dressed in rags made from sheets. Most of the women showed their faces.[11]

The American troops were welcomed by the French and Arab people. When an American tank pulled up and stopped in the city square, a soldier popped his head out of the tank. The crowd recognized his accent and began to cheer as he climbed out. A woman kissed him, and the crowd circled the tank and carried him off, lipstick all over his face.[12]

Booker and Andre were with the 39th Infantry Regiment and part of the 9th Infantry Division known as the "Fighting Hawks." They were the first of the United States troops to set foot on foreign soil when they stormed the beaches of Oran. Their regiment would patrol the Spanish Moroccan border. The boys participated in fighting on their first day in Africa and experienced the sight of death, the booms, and the chilling noises of war.

Oliver, Alexander, and Pyle were permitted to go ashore to follow the troops. They found a four-room hut that would serve as press headquarters. It was cold, and the only light they had came from candles or flashlights.

Pyle went off on his own, hitching a ride in a jeep. Oliver and Alexander took a walk and surveyed the immediate area. They were not alone. Charles Collingwood, one of "Murrow's Boys," was there as a broadcast journalist. He was young and green and was about to prove his reporting abilities.

Margaret Bourke-White, or "Maggie" as she was called, arrived on the scene. Traveling to Africa, the ship she was on was torpedoed, and she and the other survivors spent a day at sea in a lifeboat before being rescued.

Helen Kirkpatrick with the *Chicago Daily News* accompanied the U.S. Army to Algeria after covering the London Blitz since 1940. Her first job was with the *Chicago Daily News* in 1939. She secured that position by telling the proprietor, Frank Knox, that she couldn't change her sex, but that he could change his policy of not hiring women. Knox hired her immediately.

Other journalists included Hal Boyle, with the *Associated Press*; Jack Thompson, with the *Chicago Tribune;* Eliot Elisofon, a photographer with *Life;* Graham Hovey, with the International News Service; Bill White, with the New

York *Herald Tribune;* and Frank Kluckhohn, with the *New York Times.*

Oliver came across Booker and Andre one day. They were naked, washing their mess kits and clothing in gasoline cans heated over an open fire. Other soldiers worked alongside them; some were taking sponge baths in the heat of the day.

Oliver recognized the boys and discovered one of his first stories.

"You guys doing ok?"

"Yes," said Booker.

"I am," said Andre.

"Aren't you the two guys from Alabama?" asked Oliver.

"We are," said Booker.

"How is it going so far?"

"We've experienced our first action. It's definitely different than boot camp, but we haven't been here long yet."

"You guys are infantry soldiers, aren't you?"

"We are," said Booker.

"I haven't run across many black infantry soldiers. When I do, it's rare."

"They're here," said Andre. "Our basic training was all black."

"Why did you want to come here?"

"I didn't know where we were going. I just wanted to do anything to get out of where I was," said Andre. "But I still wanted to fight. This is our war, too."

"Right you are," agreed Oliver. "What is that?" he added, referring to a picture that was lying on a rock in front of Andre. "Is that your girl?"

"Sure is," said Andre. "I have something to go home to. She is my window to the future. She says I'm a dreamer, and I say she is my window."

"Your girl is a window?" asked Oliver.

"She's my window to the future," explained Andre.

"That's funny. Nice looking gal," said Oliver. "Look, I'll be checking in on you periodically. You don't mind that, do you?"

"No," said Booker, digging his foxhole.

"I don't," said Andre.

Oliver moved on to interview some of the other soldiers, but he made a special note to revisit his Alabama friends.

CHAPTER 13

Oliver and MacGowan not only ate their meals with the troops, but they also dug their own foxholes in the trench with the soldiers. Oliver followed MacGowan's instructions, moving from foxhole to foxhole, looking for soldiers to interview. The journalists usually went their own separate ways during the day.

While digging alongside Oliver one day, MacGowan asked, "Any luck finding the colored units, Yank?"

Oliver stopped to wipe dirt from his eyes. "I did run into two of the soldiers I met on the ship. I'm finding mostly supply maintenance and engineering units. Finding colored units — or any unit — while under fire is almost impossible."

"I don't know where you're going to find the colored units," said MacGowan. "No one keeps that kind of information. Just keep looking and you will find them. They are out there."

"I'll bet if I find them in a forward area, it will be by accident," said Oliver.

MacGowan finished his foxhole and sat down to relax. He pulled out a cigarette, a precious commodity in the war zone.

"You never know. They're here. Roosevelt called them up four years ago. You know, what I *did* find was an astonishing number of German sympathizers among the French in North Africa."

"You did? Why are they sympathizers?" asked Oliver.

"They're probably not really sympathizers, but the Nazis bring supplies. People are loyal to those who feed them," said MacGowan.

Lighting his cigarette, MacGowan leaned back and rested against the side of the foxhole. "I'll bet you can tell the American Negro story in a way that no other can," said MacGowan.

"Yes, I suppose I can," said Oliver. "You have another cigarette?"

"Need a light?" asked MacGowan, pulling the lighter from his pocket.

Oliver lit the cigarette and rested on the ground, the nicotine relaxing his entire body. The night winds of the Mediterranean were cold; the men had no blankets and no hot water.

"Today I watched our men fight honorably with the enemy. I am proud of how our men are serving," said Oliver to MacGowan.

"Me too," agreed MacGowan.

"They are covering themselves in honor," Oliver said. "I need to write that down. Yes, that is what I'm going to write — *our men are covering themselves in honor.*"

"That sounds good. I think you are a real journalist," said MacGowan jokingly.

"That did sound good. If I don't write things down, I forget them. I hate it when I come up with a thought and don't write it down. I can never say it the same way the second time."

MacGowan laughed. "That is true. You are getting into combat journalism."

"Yes, I am."

"What are you writing down now?" asked MacGowan.

"I'm writing, *this story cannot be written in a way to give it the justice it deserves*," said Oliver.

He continued to write. Oliver was still wearing his army helmet, the straps undone and hanging to his chin. He would only sleep a few hours that night before getting up.

The next morning, Oliver returned to the hut where the other journalists were working. He typed his first story to send to Nelms. Back in the United States, Cub read the story in amazement. He wanted to be sent to cover the war.

They entitled the feature: "*Our First Battle of the War.*"

CHAPTER 14

Oliver and MacGowan traveled hundreds of miles along the North African front finding troops. Many times Oliver would watch the black troops man the large artillery guns. Then BOOM! The mountain shook and Oliver's ears roared every time a barrage was let loose. Oliver would frequently journal how proud he was of the black soldiers who served during the campaign.

The reporters traveled continuously, moving from camp to camp every few days, eating and sleeping outside. Their days lasted from dawn till midnight or later; they felt grimy at all times. They stood on the sidelines, watching bravery and death on the battlefield.

In October 1942, Rommel was defeated in Egypt. Rommel disobeyed Hitler's orders and retreated to Tunisia; he couldn't risk the destruction of his entire army. Rommel and his troops would fight again.

Oliver looked for Andre and Booker but never found them again. "*They left no forwarding address*," he wrote in his journal. He wondered where they might have gone. In fact, the boys were sent to protect Tunis and assigned to Kasserine

Pass, a two-mile stretch of land near Tunisia in an area called the Dorsal Mountain Range. Little did they know they were being reassigned to the place where Rommel would conduct a surprise attack.

"Now listen up," said the army major. "As I call your name say 'here' and stand over there in line. The names I'm going to call are being reassigned to Kasserine Pass."

"Kasserine Pass?" said Booker. "Never heard of it."

"Me neither," said Andre.

"Thompson."

"Here."

"Trimmer."

"Here."

"Kirkpatrick."

"Here."

"Ellis."

"Here."

"Hawkins."

"Here."

"Williams."

"Here."

"Saller."

"Here."

"Adkerson."

"Here."

"Ok. You are to take the next transport to Tunis. There is a lift going there tonight," said the major, who had been ordered to send additional support.

"Kirkpatrick, you are the most senior. Take this list and make sure your men make it to Kasserine Pass."

"Yes, sir."

"They got us. Let's get our stuff and head out," said Booker.

Two days later, Andre and Booker and the others were in Kasserine Pass. They pulled their bags from the jeep and dropped them to the ground. The boys were among the additional soldiers being deployed to protect Tunis. Their commanding officer was Colonel Alexander Stark, who commanded a brigade made up of French and U.S. units.

"Man, this is going to be something," said Booker.

"Do you think we're in trouble?" asked Andre.

"I hope not. Let's make the best of it," said Booker.

A journalist covering the movement was there as the troops arrived and asked to take the soldiers' photograph.

"Smile," he said. The camera flashed. "I can get a copy to you later if I see you again." The soldiers picked up their duffel bags and went to their next assignment.

In January 1943, the press learned there would be a conference in Casablanca and that Roosevelt and Churchill would be in attendance. Oliver and MacGowan caught a transport from Oran to Casablanca. Oliver was assigned to cover the event.

Pyle wasn't going to the conference; he didn't care about the brass. Instead, went to an airfield at Biskra. He wasn't allowed to write the actual name of the city in his stories. As a substitute, the censors had him write "*A Forward Airdrome in French North Africa.*" There, the American bombers were flying daily flights over the Mediterranean ports of Bizerte, Tunis, and Tripoli. Pyle was a pilot himself and had over 1,500 flying hours. He interviewed pilots and mechanics and tracked their daily flights. Shortly after he arrived, the Germans bombed the field and Pyle found himself in real danger for the first time during the war.[13]

One evening, it was reported that a Flying Fortress bomber named Thunderbird was missing. The plane lost both engines following an attack by the Germans. All the Fortresses except one Thunderbird made it home. Two hours after the other planes landed, a black speck appeared and then a red flare streaked across the horizon; an officer on the ground fired a return green flare. That low speck in the sky turned out to be the last Fortress, limping home. The bomber landed as the pounding hearts of a thousand men ran toward the approaching plane to help bring the crew, thought to be dead, back to life.[14]

Being a pilot himself, Pyle was at home with the flying men in the field. He could not imagine leaving the field to cover a political conference in Casablanca. The action was here, with the troops, and that was where he belonged. It was a good feeling for him.

CHAPTER 15

Once in Casablanca, Oliver found the troops housed in office buildings, hotels, and garages. Some were camping in parks and vacant lots on the edge of town. Some were in tents or slept on the ground. Oliver and McGowan found a room at the Lamounia Hotel in Casablanca, a former palace within the gates of the old imperial city of Marrakesh. At dinner with MacGowan, a waiter tipped Oliver as to the presence of a woman of interest.

"There is a mysterious woman in the hotel who is just like you."

"What do you mean?" asked Oliver.

"She's of your race. She is a black American."

Oliver wasted no time and finished his dinner. "You should take this one, Yank. It might be something," suggested MacGowan.

Oliver paid his bill and attempted to bribe the waiter to give him the woman's room number.

"I can't do that, Monsieur."

"Of course, you can't do that. I would never ask you to do that," said Oliver.

"Of course, I would not do that, and I would not tell you with my own words, as Allah is my god," said the waiter.

"And I would never hear you if they came from your words either, as Jesus Christ is my God," said Oliver.

The waiter grinned and handed him the dinner bill. Oliver tipped the waiter, and as he walked away, he opened the receipt. On the back of the receipt in neat, squared print was a room number. Oliver turned and looked back at MacGowan, who knowingly smiled in return.

Oliver found the hotel room number and knocked on the door. No one answered; he thought perhaps he had been scammed by the waiter. He heard sounds of a piano and horn drifting through the hall from downstairs. He walked back to the elevator and pressed "1" for the first floor. He followed the music down the hall, leading him to the hotel nightclub. Oliver opened the door to a smoke-filled room, the audience watching the stage in anticipation. He found an empty seat and sat down. A waiter came and took his order.

Finally, the stage lights came on and out stepped a gorgeous woman. Oliver immediately recognized her. She was Josephine Baker, a 36-year-old black actress from St. Louis, Missouri. Although an American citizen, she moved overseas and became a citizen of France in 1937.

Applause erupted from the crowd. Smoke filled the room as the piano began to play the song's introduction. Josephine, wearing a formal low-cut white dress, started to sing and move across the stage. The audience cheered in delight as she sang the song, "*Don't Touch Me Tomato.*"

Oliver smiled and watched her as the song continued and Josephine danced across the stage. Unfortunately, it was her last song of the evening. The lights dimmed and the crowd applauded.

Oliver decided that this was his chance. He finished his drink, knowing that Baker needed time to get to her room. He left the club, found her room again, and knocked. A man opened the door — Oliver hoped that the waiter had given him the correct room number.

"Excuse me, but I am Oliver Smith and I was wondering if I could have a word with Ms. Baker."

A voice inside the room called out, "Who is it, François?"

"It's a gentleman who is asking to have a word with you."

"Where is he from?" she inquired.

Oliver decided to take control of the situation. "I'm from the United States. I'm a reporter," he responded loudly in his most professional voice.

"The gentleman is a reporter, Mademoiselle."

Josephine rose from the couch, tightening the sash on her white silk robe.

"And he wants to talk to me?" she asked.

"Oui, Mademoiselle," said François.

"It's okay, let me take this." Josephine walked to the door. "So, you're the gentleman looking for me?"

"Yes, Miss Baker. My name is Oliver Smith, and I am with the *Birmingham Defender*. I'd like to ask you some questions, if you will allow me."

"Oh, of course. Why not."

Josephine returned to the couch and leaned against a large red pillow. Oliver followed her, pulling up a chair by her side.

"So what brings you to Casablanca? Did you come to see my show?" she asked.

"Yes, I did. I'm covering the war. I learned that you were here, so I thought I would come see you in person. As a matter fact, I'm embarrassed to say that I thought you were dead."

"There has been a slight error. I'm much too busy to die," she said.

Oliver chuckled. "That's funny. And that was a nice number you did down there."

"Thank you. I've been recovering from pneumonia, but I'm better now. I'm glad that I was able to perform tonight."

"Pneumonia? That sounds serious," Oliver said, concern in his voice.

"I had to go to the hospital, but I'm fine now. I'm recovering in my room. I'm not contagious, and the doctor gave me permission to perform tonight."

Oliver sat back in his chair. "So you like to stay active?" he said.

"You know me; I dance a lot, sweat a lot. Anything to make me sleep," she said. "I have to stay fit for the movies."

"I heard about your movie, *Zouzou*."

"You did? That was a French movie. Did you see it?"

"No, I didn't see it actually. I heard a few guys on the boat over here talk about it. I understand that you were also in *Moulin Rouge*?"

"Yes. That was my last film."

"Tell me — how did you get into show business?"

Josephine hesitated. "I didn't ask, but would you care for a drink? Francoise, bring Mr. Oliver a glass of champagne, and I will have one as well." She continued, "Now, you were saying something like 'how did I get into show business?' Let's see … my father taught me how to sing and dance. They tell me he used to carry me on stage during the finale."

"You are from St. Louis? Did you attend school there?"

"Yes, but I dropped out of school. I went to New York and finally found some success on Broadway."

"What brought you to Paris?"

"I wanted to go to the Theatre des Champs-Elysées."

"I understand you have been entertaining the French troops in the Middle East?"

"I was a vagabond of the road in the service of France, preaching the word of de Gaulle. I've had several close calls in enemy air raids, and sometimes I'm bone tired; sometimes I don't feel well, but whenever I'm tempted to chuck it all, I tie myself off to some quiet nook. I remember France, my race, and my resolve, and I gain fresh strength to carry on."[15]

The conversation continued until Oliver completed his interview. After thanking Miss Baker for the scoop, Francoise politely escorted Oliver to the hall. Back in his room, Oliver prepared his story to cable it out the next morning. He felt confident that the military censors wouldn't edit his article. He wrote:

> *Baker told this author that 'there has been a slight error, I'm much too busy to die' with a gay smile and French accent. Her face was uplifted toward the eternal snows of the nearby Atlas peaks.*[16]

Nelms received the story, impressed with his journalist's success. "My gosh, he hasn't even been in Casablanca one day and he's already chasing skirts. I guess he has forgotten the word Roosevelt."

"What was that?" said Cub.

"Nothing. Oliver's in Casablanca to cover the conference and he's chasing skirts. But this *is* a story. I guess he had to do this one," chuckled Nelms.

The next morning, Maryellen Smith sat on her porch swing with her coffee and newspaper. She immediately noticed the headline: "*Reporter Interviews Josephine Baker: She's Too Busy to Die.*"

"Bruce, come quick and look at this story. Oliver interviewed Josephine Baker!"

"Let me see that," said Bruce, as he stepped onto the front porch, taking the paper from Maryellen's hands. "*Reporter interviews Josephine Baker,*" he read aloud.

"Do you think he will bring her back home?"

"No way," said Bruce, continuing to peruse the article.

"Who is Josephine Baker?" asked Maryellen.

"I don't know. It says here that she is some exotic dancer from St. Louis who immigrated to France. He can't bring a woman like that to Birmingham. She would never come here and never stay put here. She has to be abroad, like him. He was probably lucky to get that story. He was sent to cover the war, and he covers her. At least he has his mind in the right place."

CHAPTER 16

THE CASABLANCA CONFERENCE would not take place for a few days and Oliver had time on his hands. One evening, an army counterintelligence officer found Oliver at dinner. The officer was unable to find a reporter who would publish a story that he wanted to see on the front page of the newspapers. He couldn't get other journalists in Casablanca to undertake the story, so he thought he might attempt to convince Oliver to take it on.

"I have a story that will be of great interest to everyone," said Major Dowler.

"What is it?" asked Oliver.

"It's not a story about race, if that's what you are looking for. It's not about color either. Are you still interested?"

"Yes, but it depends on what it is."

"It's about the French collaboration. Some believe that the Americans are all welcome over here. But in fact, there are French who are collaborating with the Germans. We need someone to blow this story worldwide, so we can convert the French forces fighting in North Africa to fight for us instead of Germany."

"But not all French forces are allied with Germany," said Oliver.

"I know that. But it's the others that we want to convert. The Germans promise all kinds of things to them as inducements. If you could write a story about this, it could turn the tide of the war in North Africa to our favor."

Oliver thought about it and realized that this kind of story was far beyond anything his newspaper had written. After listening to the officer, he went back to his room to ponder the story.

He decided: *If anyone is going to write this story, it might as well be me.*

Working on the article most of the night, Oliver finally went to sleep at 0500. He got up at 0700 and delivered it to the army censors in their staff office.

"Here's the story for you," he said, handing the report to the major who greeted him as he entered the room. Oliver assumed the censor would finish reading it by the time he grabbed a cup of coffee from a pot in the back of the room. He speculated that the censors were on the same page as the major who had shared the information with him.

Oliver walked over to the coffee pot and began to pour a cup. He heard a yell across the room.

'Some might be *pro-Nazi*?" yelled the major with whom he'd just handed the report. "Are you kidding me? Where did you get *that*?"

The loud voice startled him and Oliver poured coffee all over his hand. "Ouch," he murmured to himself.

Oliver was stunned but continued pouring his coffee. He turned around as if nothing had happened. All typing stopped in the room, and everyone turned in their chairs, watching the reporter cross the room. All eyes were on Oliver. Oliver calmly walked over to the officer while the heads of everyone in the room moved, watching him and waiting for his response. The room was completely quiet.

With a cool head, he approached the major. "Yes. That is true."

The major waited a few seconds, although it seemed like a full minute to Oliver. He responded, "Hmphh. Very well."

Everyone went back to work. The room became noisy again with typing.

"I'm cutting that out of the story," said the major, striking through the paragraph with his red pen bleeding across the paper.

The officer read further: "*The French are not all like that …*"

"What?" he said loudly. "Nope, we can't write that either. I'm striking it." His pen marked through another line. "I can only allow you to print something like this if you can prove to me that it has been printed somewhere else," he said.

The major continued to study the article, mumbling aloud as he read. Oliver watched him, cringing as his work was being proofread. It was as if he were submitting his first story at deadline to an upset night editor and waiting for his reaction.

"No. I can't do this story. I admire your zeal, but we can't go with this. This might be true, but it could also be dangerous. Why don't you do another story, like the one you did on Josephine Baker? I liked that one."

"Thank you," said Oliver, deciding it would be best for him to leave.

"You can take this to the colonel if you don't agree with me," said the major loudly.

"No thanks," said Oliver, exiting the building.

Oliver walked out of the building, realizing that he might have been set up. Or perhaps the officer thought Oliver was naïve enough to run with the story. Why had the officer come to him? The story was obvious, but why wouldn't anyone else touch it?

Never again would he run with a questionable article without checking with MacGowan or a more experienced journalist. This was a hard lesson, and it was his second mistake. His first mistake was not endorsing Roosevelt when he moved from news writing to opinion writing. *I should have stuck with covering the individual black soldier instead of going off into a completely different direction*, he thought to himself. This could have been a costly mistake, not only for his career but for the Allies as well. He cringed, thinking that this story might have actually been published with his name on it. He realized that he was glad there were army censors to check his work. As a member of the press, he never thought that he would believe that.

Oliver wrote back to Nelms, describing the incident. He needed to journal his experience to get it off his chest. Nelms read the letter at his desk while sipping a cup of coffee. He smiled; he had been there before. He penned a letter back to Oliver:

O,

Looks like you learned a hard lesson. Stick with black soldier. Be accurate. If it isn't accurate then it can't be printed. And not everything accurate can be printed.

Cub wants to go over there. I can't spare two reporters abroad for long. Come home so I can send him over there.

Regards,

N

CHAPTER 17

Oliver and what seemed to be hundreds of other reporters from across the world were in Casablanca to cover the conference on the first day. Roosevelt was the first U.S. president to travel by airplane, leaving Miami on January 10, 1943. He traveled to Morocco to meet Prime Minister Winston Churchill. Churchill flew in as well, with MacGowan covering his arrival. On the day that Churchill landed in Casablanca, Hitler declared "Total War."

Oliver was amazed to see these great leaders and what he knew was history in the making. He and MacGowan went to the Anfa Hotel where the leaders would pose for photographs. Roosevelt and Churchill were sitting down. Churchill was wearing a three-piece black suit, a hat, and a bow tie. A watch chain hung from his vest. There was a lapel on his jacket and a handkerchief in his suit pocket.

Oliver and MacGowan watched as the cameramen and photographers preserved the occasion for posterity. Roosevelt was smoking a cigarette. The leaders of the Free French forces, Henri Giraud and General Charles de Gaulle, stood up to shake hands in front of Roosevelt and

Churchill. The cameras were rolling. Oliver could sense the tension between them. Giraud and de Gaulle were asked to stand up a second time to repeat their handshake because the cameramen complained that it had occurred too quickly the first time.

In a final photograph taken on January 24, 1943, Roosevelt and Churchill were seated together behind military generals and admirals representing the Allies. Churchill had a cane and a hat on his lap. Roosevelt was seated with his back straight and his legs crossed. Oliver watched in amazement, so close to the U.S. president. It was one thing to write opinion stories in Birmingham about Roosevelt, whom he had never seen in person before; it was another thing to be in Casablanca, seeing him as the Commander in Chief of the United States. He felt he was part of the military.

The reporters in attendance had a chance to walk by and shake hands with the heads of state. The line was long, and Oliver ruminated over the editorial he had written two years before, feeling like a hypocrite waiting to shake the president's hand. *How could I have written that story?* he thought to himself.

Christ, I can't believe I did that. Why didn't I have good judgment and why didn't someone stop me? He wanted to blame Nelms for not objecting to his opinion piece. But Nelms let Oliver run when he was on the editorial side of the paper. Oliver's brief foray into editorial news was a short-lived infatuation. He knew he was no editorial writer. He had only himself to blame. He had to learn to hold himself accountable and would never again stray from news reporting.

"Good afternoon, Mr. President," said Oliver to President Roosevelt.

"Thank you. And who are you?" asked the president.

The line stopped as Roosevelt paused to talk to Oliver, the only black journalist in the queue.

"Oliver Smith, *Birmingham Defender*." Oliver cringed, hoping the president didn't recognize his name.

"Oliver Smith. Oliver Smith. That name sounds familiar to me. Where have I heard that?" asked the president.

"You probably haven't, Mr. President. I'm sure you have better things to do than read the *Birmingham Defender*."

"But I don't! I always enjoy reading the papers when I can. I do love reading a good opinion piece now and then," said the president, smiling at Oliver.

Oliver looked at the president and shook his hand. His smile was guarded; he felt caught.

"I appreciate your paper and your being here, covering the war. We want journalists like you covering this campaign."

"Thank you, Mr. President, for allowing me to be selected to come here."

"You are welcome. By the way, say hello to your editor, Mr. Nelms. That is his name, isn't it?"

"Yes," said Oliver.

"I met him once at a reception when I was governor of New York. He probably doesn't remember."

"I'm sure he remembers, Mr. President. How could he forget something like that?"

The line pushed forward and Oliver couldn't hold it up any longer. *That was great*, he thought to himself. *Maybe he didn't remember that I did not endorse him in 1940 after all.* Oliver had just met the President of the United States. Meeting someone face to face, he now had personal knowledge of that person. It would affect how he covered them the next time. He would be more careful with his stories in the future.

Oliver shook hands with Winston Churchill. He never expected to meet him either.

CHAPTER 18

Oliver and MacGowan remained in Tunisia and drove hundreds of miles along the African front. Sometimes they sat in silence for long stretches as they gazed at the landscape. It was cold and rainy; mud caked the car's tires and fender. The reporters continued through scattered towns, but none appeared interesting enough for a stop. Many Americans imagined a hot desert, but they would have been surprised that the weather was no different than England.

Often the journalists' days were spent at headquarters, where they were briefed by intelligence officers regarding the day's action. The reporters would ride shotgun with army drivers and go to the location to ask questions, get quotes and names, return to attend press conferences, type their stories, submit them to the censors, and finally send the report to their news organization. Many reporters wanted to spend more time in the field but were obligated to spend a large percentage of their time writing. Editors needed the day's news. There was no time to waste.

While driving one day, Oliver and MacGowan observed men and equipment on both sides along the road. There were black soldiers and white soldiers working side by side.

"See there?" Oliver motioned. MacGowan looked over and saw soldiers of all colors, working as one. "The enemy and harsh conditions of battle bring the troops together."

"In war, there is no black or white soldier," said MacGowan.

"You're right. War seems to remove the narrow minds that once existed," said Oliver.

"Now *you* are the philosopher," said MacGowan.

"Like you? I remember what you told me back in London on the first night on the ship," said Oliver. "But I guess I am getting that way. When I drive along here, I see no color. There are no color lines in foxholes or when a landing barge is being shelled."

"That can be your lead sentence," said MacGowan.

Nelms penned Oliver's stories under the headline: *"Oliver Smith Tells What It's Like in African Big Push."*

CHAPTER 19

Tatiana Phillips was one of five children born to Andrew and Ethyl Phillips. She was educated in Chicago public schools. From the time she was six, Tatiana loved to play the piano. She loved it so much that her mother had to physically remove her from the piano so that her daughter would complete her homework.

Tatiana wanted a career in journalism, just like her father. On Saturdays, Andrew would take Tatiana to the newspaper and she would play in his office while he worked. Tatiana was his daughter, and she was a daddy's girl. The two had a real bond.

On January 14, 1943, the same day that Oliver was covering the Casablanca conference, Tatiana's father brought her into his office and showed her a photograph.

"Tatiana, take a look at this," he said, handing her the photo.

"Are they in the army?" she said.

"Not exactly. They are war correspondents. They cover the war and they wear the U.S. Army uniform while covering the war. These women are in London. They are (reading from the back of the photo) Mary Welsh, Dixie Tighe, Kathleen Harriman, Helen Kirkpatrick, Lee Miller, and Tania Long."

The ladies were all sitting on a concrete slab wearing army uniforms. They wore beige skirts, brown jackets, belts, and hats. It was cold that day and gloves covered their hands.

"Let me see that," said Tatiana, reaching for the photograph.

"Does it interest you?" asked her father.

"Sure does. Are you asking if I want to join the army?"

"You could if you wanted to, but you would never get to the war in time. The time is *now* to cover the war. There are plenty of other journalists and broadcasters covering the war already. London is where the war stories are, if that's something that interests you. There are reporters and photographers all over the globe. Margaret Bourke-White was in Moscow in 1941 when the Germans attacked," he said.

"What do I have to do?" she asked.

"First, we have to get you some experience."

"Ok."

"There's a journalist named Oliver Smith from the *Birmingham Defender* who has been covering the war in Europe for a couple of years. You two could meet up in London. I met him briefly in Washington, D.C., after one of the conferences they had after the bombing of Pearl Harbor. I know the editor of the *Defender* and we talked about our papers pooling resources."

"I *am* interested. It sounds dangerous. What did Margaret Bourke-White do after the attack?"

"She took refuge in the U.S. Embassy and captured what she could on camera. I need to send you out to cover something like a foreign correspondent would do. You need to become accustomed to the travel and difficulty that goes along with the job. You have to live in difficult situations. Why don't you start by going up to Washington, D.C., and find something to write about?"

"How about covering a day in the life of Eleanor Roosevelt?" suggested Tatiana.

"That sounds good," Andrew said, picking up that day's newspaper. "You know she runs a column of her daily schedule, but it's published after the fact. How would I figure out where she is on a given day?"

"The White House Press Secretary's office?"

"Correct. Contact them — she has her own press secretary. They should be able to give you her schedule. Do you know what day you'd like to go up there?"

"January 14th would be good."

"Is that a special day?" he asked.

"No, but I read that the Pentagon is going to open on the 15th. That might help me better understand the war. I can do both of these at the same time."

"Now, that is a good idea. The Pentagon. I hear it is supposed to be a huge building in D.C. Get some photos of that."

Tatiana caught a train from Chicago to Washington on her first assignment outside the paper. It would be a tough two days. The First Lady was scheduled first to be in West Virginia. Tatiana took the midnight train to Arthurdale and was on the same train as the First Lady, although she didn't realize it. The purpose of the visit was to meet with the members of the Arthurdale Advisory Committee.

The First Lady was having breakfast with the manager of the project in a house on top of a hill overlooking the woods. The reporters were not allowed in close proximity, so Tatiana waited to see where the First Lady's entourage would take her after the meeting.

"Follow those cars," she told the taxi driver. The driver stayed close behind the line of cars until they pulled into a community center in Scotts Run.

"I wonder — why are we stopping here?" said Tatiana.

"There was a mine disaster here recently," said the taxi driver.

The First Lady's car stopped. Her Secret Service security detail got out and walked into the center. Tatiana opened her door. "Let me out here, but don't leave," she told the driver.

Tatiana followed the group, hoping for an opportunity to talk to Mrs. Roosevelt. As a reporter without clearance, she didn't know if she would even be admitted into the center at all. She would have to take her chances. Tatiana walked toward the First Lady's car. The Secret Service followed Mrs. Roosevelt into the building. Tatiana caught a glimpse of her face and was amazed. The First Lady was taller than she had imagined, with light brown hair and blue eyes.

Tatiana waited outside until the entourage entered the building. She walked confidently inside the doors and down the hall, peering into the room where it appeared the group was meeting. It was a closed meeting but the door was not locked. The First Lady was talking to a group of ladies seated in rows. Tatiana opened the door without making a sound. She decided to take a chance and walk in, pretending to be a late arrival. *Maybe no one will recognize me*, she thought. As soon as she stepped inside the room, the First Lady stopped talking. Tatiana cringed.

"Thank you for coming," said First Lady Eleanor Roosevelt, smiling kindly at Tatiana.

Tatiana smiled back but didn't say a word. She was mortified. She was the only black woman in the room and she was walking in after the event started — crashing an event with the First Lady of the United States. Everyone in the room looked at her as she walked in to take her seat. But she didn't have a choice; once inside, she was already committed. The room was quiet, and she could hear the sound of her own footsteps tapping along the floor as she found a seat at the end of the row on the third aisle.

Tatiana thought to herself, *Please Mrs. Roosevelt, don't ask me who I am*, as she approached the seat and sat down. She cringed inside. *What am I doing crashing this event and walking in late? What will I say if the First Lady asks me who I am? What will I tell her? I can't lie if I am asked.* She was about to die. But she was going to get the story, no matter what it took.

After Tatiana sat down, the First Lady resumed her talk.

"Thank you for allowing me to visit here. I am so happy to come to Scotts Run and see what has happened with the improvements that are being made after the mining disaster. That was so unfortunate. I've talked with several women who lost their husbands."

The group gave her a quiet applause of gratitude.

She continued, "One woman, Mrs. Quinn, has reason to be proud of her man, who was a foreman. He escaped and went back to save, if he could, the thirteenth man who happened to turn toward the fire instead of away from it. Unfortunately, he was trapped in the fire and died. I hope there is some way to obtain recognition for a civilian hero who dies for his fellow men."[17]

Tatiana pulled out her notepad and wrote everything down. The meeting went on for an hour, concluding with a question and answer session with the First Lady.

After the meeting, the women stood up as Mrs. Roosevelt was leaving. They gave her a round of applause. She walked by each row, shaking hands and thanking each attendee. She came to the third row where Tatiana sat and said, "Thank you, my dear, for coming to this today."

"Thank *you*, Mrs. Roosevelt," said Tatiana.

"Was your husband working in the mine?" she asked.

Tatiana was caught and she realized she couldn't lie to the First Lady. "No, ma'am. I am with the *African-American Statesman*."

"You are? That's Andrew Phillips's paper, isn't it?"

"Yes, it is. He's my father."

"Well, what a surprise. So this visit is not a coincidence?" asked Mrs. Roosevelt.

"No, it's not. Actually, I was on the same train as you last night. My father sent me on an assignment to help prepare me for a trip to London as a foreign correspondent. I'm going overseas to cover the black soldiers participating in the war. I want to be the first black female journalist to cover the war."

The First Lady looked surprised. "Really? You want to go to the war zone? That is wonderful. A wind is rising throughout the world of free men everywhere and they will not be kept in bondage."

A Secret Service agent interrupted and said, "We need to run now, Mrs. Roosevelt."

Tatiana stood there in a daze, taking in what the First Lady had just said. This whole scene was surreal. Mrs. Roosevelt's words to her were as deep as anything she had ever heard in her life. Tatiana followed the First Lady until she slid into the car and waved goodbye to the excited crowd.

Tatiana found her taxi waiting. "Follow the First Lady's car," she told the taxi driver as she entered the cab. The taxi joined the parade of cars and headed toward the train station. The First Lady boarded the train to New York City; her next stop was a speaking engagement at Columbia University's Institute of Arts and Sciences. Tatiana purchased a ticket and found her seat in an adjoining car. As Tatiana felt the train pull away from the station, she pondered the First Lady's statement to her. She realized how satisfying it was to be a reporter, covering stories and writing about notable people. Something about meeting these new people, being on the move, and recording her thoughts on paper and seeing her articles in print brought her great depths of satisfaction. Now she understood why her father was a newspaper man. He must have experienced the same thing when he was her age.

Upon arriving in New York City, Tatiana hailed another taxi and followed the First Lady to the school, but she was not admitted to hear the speech. It was a private event and Tatiana was not registered. Following the program, the First Lady and her entourage took the train back to Washington.

Tatiana studied Mrs. Roosevelt's schedule and purchased a ticket for the same train. Hungry, she made her way to the dining car and ordered steak and a glass of wine. Tatiana mulled through her notes, outlining her report.

A black woman on the other side of the car was dining alone and noticed Tatiana. They glanced at each other. The lady was wearing a flowered hat with white gloves and a dotted low cut dress. After finishing her meal, she got up and walked over to Tatiana.

"Hello," she said a bit hesitantly.

"Hello," said Tatiana.

"I couldn't help but notice you. Are you a reporter?"

"Yes, I am. How did you know?"

"I presumed as much. I noticed you were writing something on your notepad."

"What's your name?" asked Tatiana.

"I'm Alice."

"It is nice to meet you, Alice. What do you do?"

"Right now, I work for the Department of Labor. I was a teacher and a reporter in Louisville for awhile, and I did some writing in Kentucky. A few years ago I got a job with the Department of Labor. I don't know how long I will have this job. My real passion is journalism."

"Me too," said Tatiana. "I grew up in the business. My father is the editor of a newspaper."

"What paper?"

"The *African-American Statesman* in Chicago."

"That is something to be proud of! What are you doing here?"

"I'm covering a day in the life of Eleanor Roosevelt."

"That sounds fascinating. I would like to be a White House Correspondent. You know that the First Lady has a weekly women's-only White House press conference?"

"No, I didn't know that."

"She does. It means that a lot of newspapers had to hire women journalists to cover her conferences. Some of the women are going on to become war correspondents."

"That's what I want to do," said Tatiana.

"It's happening more than you think. Margaret Bourke-White covered London and Russia after Pearl Harbor. I want to be the first female African American reporter to receive White House accreditation," said Alice.

"That's great! It's funny you mention Bourke-White's name. My father recently told me about her being in Russia when the Germans attacked. He showed me a photograph of women military correspondents. I want to be the first African American reporter to cover the war in Europe," said Tatiana.

"You keep up what you are doing and you will." The woman held out her hand. "I'd better leave. It was nice meeting you. Oh, here is my card if you ever need to contact me." She reached in her purse and pulled out a business card.

"Wonderful meeting you, too," said Tatiana. She realized she had not caught the woman's last name. She had mentioned that her name was Alice. Who was she? Tatiana looked at the card; it said Alice Allison Dunnigan.

I'll bet she becomes someone important someday, Tatiana thought to herself, impressed with her new friend.

Tatiana did not realize that the lady she had just met would become the first African American female correspondent to receive White House credentials.

CHAPTER 20

TATIANA'S TRAIN WOULD not arrive in Washington, D.C., until 3 a.m. the next morning on January 15, 1943. She awoke after only a few hours of sleep and decided to review the notes from her trip. *Did I really just meet the First Lady?* she thought to herself. The sound of the train's engine vibrated in her ears as she mulled over the day's events. She knew she had to find a hotel in Washington to spend the rest of the night before continuing her journey following the First Lady. A taxi took her to an available hotel where she checked in and slept soundly until ten in the morning.

Tatiana woke up but still felt exhausted. According to her schedule, Mrs. Roosevelt was heading to New Jersey for a visit to Marlboro Hospital, lunch at the USO Club, and finally to the Monmouth County Social Service annual meeting. *I'm not going to follow her today,* Tatiana said to herself after the long trip from West Virginia to Washington, D.C. *I'm going to stay in Washington and cover the Pentagon instead,* she decided. Tatiana looked out the window as she sipped a cup of coffee.

Tatiana called her father from her hotel room.

"Did you get anything on the First Lady?" he asked.

"I did, father! I couldn't believe it. I walked into the meeting late and everyone noticed me as I entered the room. The only vacant seat was on the third row at the end. I was the only black person in the room. Mrs. Roosevelt even stopped speaking until I took my seat. You could hear my heels click with each step. I thought I was going to die. Tears were coming from my eyes. I wanted to cover the event so I just went into the room, deciding that I would ask for forgiveness rather than permission. I couldn't help myself. I don't know why I did it."

Andrew laughed, "You did it because you are a reporter. You do what it takes to get the story. It's in your blood. That's why you did it."

"I hope so. I even talked to her after the event. It went by so fast, though. She said she knew you, and said to tell you hello."

"Oh, yes. She knows who runs the newspapers. I did meet her once."

Tatiana continued, "Mrs. Roosevelt traveled from Washington to West Virginia, then New York City. Now she's going to New Jersey. This lady travels non-stop and works all the time. I can't keep up with her."

"That's ok," her father chuckled.

"I'm going to stay here and cover the Pentagon instead. It opens today."

"That's good. At least you saw a side of Washington that we haven't seen before. You see now how difficult it can be to get stories. But I'm the editor calling for the copy. You have to produce something every day to earn your keep."

"I know."

"Send something back about what the First Lady said. I imagine there's something you can write about."

"Ok. See you, father. Love you, but don't print anything about me crashing her event."

"I won't. See you, Tatiana. Love you, too."

Tatiana took a taxi to the Pentagon, looking forward to viewing the opening of what appeared to be an important new government entity. She learned from her research that construction began on September 11, 1941, a few months prior to Pearl Harbor. She had done her homework.

Returning to her hotel room after the opening, Tatiana began her report:

> *The dedication of the world's largest office building was today in Washington, D.C. Construction began on September 11, 1941, with a cost of $3.1 million. Shaped like a pentagon due to a shortage of steel, the height was limited and the location was selected so that it would not obstruct the view of Washington, D.C. Originally constructed with separate dining facilities in June 1941, President Roosevelt ordered the end to discrimination and the removal of "Whites Only" signage.*

CHAPTER 21

Rommel attacked Tunis on February 19, 1943, catching the Allies by surprise. Rommel saw Tunis as a strategic goal for the Axis and the Allies, as well as a place to rebound after being driven out of Egypt. This began the Battle of Kasserine Pass, where Booker and Andre experienced their most brutal fighting in the war.

The first strike was repulsed with tank reinforcements, but the fighting continued with devastating casualties to U.S. forces.

The sound of the booms was overwhelming. Andre saw a German approach Booker; he pulled his rifle up and shot the German. The bullet flew by Booker's head, startling him. The German fell dead, shot between the eyes. Booker was amazed. But Andre and Booker were familiar with weapons, even before joining the army.

"Thank you, my friend," Booker said before returning to fight.

"No problem," said Andre.

The Germans advanced, and both Booker and Andre were out of ammunition. They resorted to hand-to-hand fighting, taking Germans down to the ground and stabbing them with their bayonets. They killed many Germans and were bloodied all over.

The troops were ordered to higher ground in order to overtake and eliminate the German artillery. They were reinforced by an armored battalion, but Rommel broke through by February 20th. They escaped, but more than 1,000 American soldiers were killed during the battle.

Before they left Mountain Springs, Andre and Booker believed they were going to war. Now, they *were* in war. They never thought it would be this difficult and under such demanding conditions. The hand-to-hand combat was far more strenuous than anything they experienced in Oran. They were just two boys from Alabama, killing Germans in a war across a world from their own. They wondered how they got there.

CHAPTER 22

By March 1943, command of the U.S. II Corps passed to General George S. Patton, with Omar Bradley assigned to the role of Assistant Corps Commander.

On March 28, 1943, Booker and Andre's regiment attacked in southern Tunisia. The soldiers fought their way north into the city of Bizerte, where they began clearing the town.

On April 2, 1943, the 99th Pursuit Squadron of the Tuskegee Airmen was deployed overseas to North Africa, the first black flying squadron to be sent during the war. Cub covered the squadron shipping out from Alabama; the soldiers would join the 33rd Fighter Group when they arrived. Nelms sent word to Oliver to expect them.

The Allies had by now conquered North Africa, chased the Germans and Italians out, and converted what was left of the French resistance. After Rommel was recalled back to Germany, word began to spread that the journalists would be heading to Sicily. The Allies were taking a methodical approach to eliminating the Axis, piece by piece. They would attack the perimeters of Africa and move through Sicily, Italy, France, and into Germany. In the north, they would do the same by pushing the Germans from Russia and onward through the Balkans and surrounding Germany, until the enemy was vanquished through ground forces and relentless air bombing campaigns. They would finally crush the enemy in Berlin.

CHAPTER 23

"Oliver, I'm not heading to Sicily," said MacGowan, dropping his duffel bag.

"You're not? Why not?" said Oliver.

"I'm going north to cover the war. The Brits will be heading towards France and Germany. I want to be there when it happens — it will be a different war over there. A ship is leaving today, and I plan to be on it. I enjoyed our time together in Africa," said MacGowan.

"I did, too," said Oliver. "I hope you get another shipmate on your trip back and share with him all the knowledge you have imparted to me. I'll see you in Paris."

"That you will," said MacGowan. The two men shook hands.

They had become real friends. Oliver watched MacGowan walk off with his duffel bag toward the sunset, smiling as he thanked the elder gentleman for befriending him.

CHAPTER 24

In May 1943, Cub took a trip to Camp Hood, Texas, to write an article about the 761st Tank Battalion, known as the 761st. Major Paul Bates, a white officer, assumed command of the battalion of the black soldiers' training for over a year. They had been relocated from Camp Claiborne in Louisiana. There were over 100,000 soldiers stationed at Camp Hood, preparing for war.

Cub reported:

Bates ordered a battalion dress formation after taking command. He stood on the hood of a jeep so that everyone could hear him, as seven hundred black soldiers listened to their new white commander. Then he said to them, "Gentlemen, I've always lived with the point of view that the rest of my life is the most important thing in the world. I don't give a damn about what happened before. Let's go from here. And, if you're gonna go from here, if you're gonna make it, we got to do it together." [18]

The major continued, "Make damn sure you are cleaner than anybody else you ever saw in your life,

> *particularly all those white bastards out there. I want your uniforms to look better, cleaner than theirs do. I want your shoes and boots to shine better, cleaner than theirs do. I want you to be better. Because gentlemen, you must get ready. This battalion is going to war!"*
>
> *Major Bates says that he always stays with his troops during training, reminding them that they are really going to war.*
>
> *This reporter observed on a forced march one dusty evening Bates yelling to the sweaty soldiers decked in full packs and fatigues: 'One mile, two miles, can't quit … three miles, four miles, won't quit … you stay alive in battle … because you're better trained and tougher than the other poor sonsofbitches. You win because you're good. And by God, you're gonna be good, or we'll all die on the way to being good.'*
>
> *The black soldiers believe in Bates; they believe in him because he believes in them.*

During their training, the soldiers learned how to identify each other's position, how to drive the vehicles, how to load the main gun, how to be a bow gunner, and how to shoot every weapon in the arms room. They went to the range every week to shoot.45 Colts, .50 caliber and .30 caliber machine guns, Carbines, grease guns, and Thompsons. Maj. Bates was with them at all times.

They were ready to be deployed.[19]

CHAPTER 25

In preparation for *Operation Husky*, the invasion of Sicily, on June 2, 1943, the 99th Fighter Squadron of the Tuskegee Airmen flew its first combat mission, attacking enemy units on the volcanic island of Pantelleria in the Mediterranean. This would clear the sea lanes to prepare for the Allied invasion of Italy.

On June 9, 1943, a flight led by Lt. Charles Dryden was attacked by enemy aircraft. Lieutenants Willie Ashley, Sidney P. Brooks, Lee Rayford, Leon Roberts, and Spann Watson engaged the German fighter planes, forcing the enemy to retreat. A garrison of 11,121 Italians and 78 Germans surrendered. Later, Lt. Charles B. Hall scored the first aerial victory by a Tuskegee Airman by downing a Focke-Wulf 190.

Oliver reported:

> *These brave men were being awarded the Distinguished Unit Citation for their performance in combat. I interviewed their commander, Lieutenant Colonel Benjamin Davis, near Fez, French Morocco. Toni Frissell,*

the American photographer known for her fashion photography, captured the moment on film. Frissell became the official photographer for the Tuskegee Airmen.

Oliver and Pyle were told to report to a Navy ship for the invasion of Sicily. *Operation Husky*, the mission to liberate Sicily, would begin on July 30, 1943, with a combined British-Canadian-American invasion with amphibious and airborne landings at the Gulf of Gela.

Ninety thousand troops from the Seventh United States Army supported Bernard Montgomery's British Eighth Army landings on Sicily. Once in Sicily, Oliver was stunned with its beauty; however, many homes had been ransacked by the Italians, removing anything that could have been of use to the Allies.

The fighting was brutal on both sides. The 200,000-man Seventh Army suffered 7,500 casualties and killed or captured 113,000 Axis troops. After two years of fighting in Africa, word began to spread that some in the troops were suffering from fatigue or battle stress.

After serving at Kasserine Pass, Andre and Booker were transferred to the 3rd Infantry Division and sailed to Sicily from Tunisia where the division made an assault landing at Licata and fought to Palermo and to Messina. Their colonel gave his regiment this slogan: *Anything, Anywhere, Anytime — Bar Nothing.* He also said, "The enemy who sees our regiment in combat, if they live through the battle, will know to run the next time they see us coming."

On July 31, 1943, while attached to the 1st Infantry Division, the 39th Regiment suffered its first serious reverse at the Battle of Troina, where entrenched and heavily armed German forces repelled an assault by the 39th Infantry Regiment with heavy casualties.

General Patton asked for a status report from Major General Clarence R. Huebner, the commander of the U.S. 1st Infantry Division.

"The front lines appear to be thinning out. There seems to be a large number of soldiers ill at the hospital with no symptoms other than the stress of battle," he told the general.

"I don't believe it," said Patton.

CHAPTER 26

ON AUGUST 2, journalist Eric Sevareid, one of "Murrow's Boys," was on board a Curtiss-Wright C-46 Commando. While flying over Burma on an airlift mission, the plane developed engine trouble. Sevareid parachuted out of the plane to safety, but not before grabbing a bottle of Carew gin on his way out. He landed behind enemy lines, but fortunately a U.S. Army Air Force rescue team recovered the party and carried them to safety.

On that same day, General Patton arrived at the 15th Evacuation Hospital near Nicosia, Sicily, for an inspection. Private Charles H. Kuhl of L. Company, U.S. 26th Infantry Regiment, happened to report to the infirmary that day as well. The general approached the wounded in the hospital and praised them for their service. He saw Private Kuhl sitting on a stool midway through the tent ward.

"How were you injured, soldier? Where are you wounded?" asked the general.

"I'm nervous. I guess I can't take it," said Private Kuhl.

The general flared up and slapped Kuhl across the face and grabbed him by the collar. Patton then dragged Kuhl to the tent entrance and shoved him out with a kick to his backside.

"Don't admit that, you son-of-a-bitch. You hear me, you gutless bastard? You're going back to the front." The general turned and stormed back into the tent ward.

Medical corpsmen picked up the private and took him back inside the tent. He had a temperature of 102.2 degrees and was later diagnosed with malarial parasites.

The general recorded in his diary that night:

> *I met the only errant coward I have ever seen in this army. Companies should deal with such men, and if they shirk their duty, they should be tried for cowardice and shot.*

On August 5, 1943, the general issued a directive:

> *It has come to my attention that a very small number of soldiers are going to the hospital on the pretext that they are nervously incapable of combat. Such men are cowards and bring discredit on the army and disgrace to their comrades, whom they heartlessly leave to endure the dangers of battle while they, themselves, use the hospital as a means of escape. You will take measures to see that such cases are not sent to the hospital but dealt within their units. Those who are not willing to fight will be tried by court-martial for cowardice in the face of the enemy.*

On August 10, 1943, Private Paul G. Bennett, 21 years of age and of the C. Battery, U.S. 17th Field Artillery Regiment, 1st

Infantry Division was reported AWOL and showed up at the 93rd Evacuation Hospital. He had signs of fever and dehydration, fatigue, and confusion. He requested to go back to his unit but his request was denied. He could not have picked a worse day to show up. General Patton decided to visit the tent and noticed Bennett, huddled and shivering.

"What's the trouble?" the general asked.

"It's my nerves," Bennett responded. "I can't stand the shelling anymore."

Patton became enraged and slapped him across the face, yelling, "Your nerves, hell, you are just a goddamned coward! Shut up that goddamned crying. I won't have these brave men who have been shot at seeing this yellow bastard sitting here crying."

Patton slapped him again, knocking off the soldier's helmet.

"You're going back to the front lines, and you may get shot and killed, but you're going to fight. If you don't, I'll stand you up against a wall and have a firing squad kill you on purpose. In fact, I ought to shoot you myself, you goddamned whimpering coward."

The general drew his pistol threateningly, but hospital Colonel Donald E. Currier physically separated the two. Patton left, demanding that the medical officers send Bennett back to the front lines. The general turned and confessed to Currier, "I can't help it, but it makes my blood boil to think of a yellow bastard being babied, and I won't have those cowardly bastards hanging around our hospitals. We'll probably have to shoot them sometime anyway or we'll raise a bunch of morons."

A nurse at the hospital witnessed the event and told the story of the confrontation to her boyfriend, a captain in the Seventh Army Public Affairs detachment. Press covering the invasion, including the Saturday Evening Post, NBC News, Newsweek, and CBS News, heard of the incident. One of the journalists, Demaree Best of the *Saturday Evening Post*, left Sicily and went to Algiers. Best gave a summary of the slapping incident to Eisenhower's Chief of Staff, Major General Walter Oliver. Eisenhower asked the media to suppress the story for fear of backlash and concern that it would undermine the war effort, and he could not afford to lose Patton.

Patton reported to General Eisenhower, wearing his helmet liner painted red with big stars. He knew what was coming from the general.

"Sit down," said Eisenhower.

"I prefer to stand," said Patton.

"Well, at least stand at ease," said Eisenhower.

Eisenhower explained why he was in trouble. Tears began welling in Patton's eyes. Eisenhower was about to order him back home when he realized that he couldn't do it; he needed Patton too much. Eisenhower bit the bullet and said to himself, "*Dammit, I'll just take the licks if I have to on this one.*"

Eisenhower rose and walked around to Patton's side. "George, despite all that, I'm going to give you another chance."

Patton put his head on Eisenhower's shoulder. His helmet liner came off and clattered across the floor. Eisenhower laughed.

Patton pushed Eisenhower away and said, "Thank you for that and I'll stay, you son of a bitch." Patton stamped out of the room.[20]

Patton had Private Kuhl and Private Bennett summoned to his office on separate days and apologized to them. It was something he loathed doing.

The fighting to liberate Sicily lasted through August 16, 1943.

CHAPTER 27

OLIVER HEARD OF the events surrounding Patton, as did the other journalists. He wasn't interested in the story, and he was not going to make the mistake of covering a story like that, especially after striking out in Africa over the French collaboration story. It was too far from his objective of covering the black soldier. He remembered Nelms' advice: *Focus on the black soldier.* He would not lose sight of his mission again.

Oliver never heard of the battle stress or fatigue that Patton's men suffered, but he understood what it meant. He felt it himself but never considered that it was a real illness.

Pyle also chose not to cover the Patton story. He wrote about the individual soldier and never felt comfortable around the brass anyway. He made it a point to never mention Patton in his stories.

After the Battle of Sicily ended, Eisenhower ordered Patton's Seventh Army broken up, with a few units garrisoned in Sicily. The majority of the forces were transferred to the Fifth Army under Lieutenant General Mark W. Clark. This was a blow to Patton; he was ready to move on to Italy and Germany with a passion.

On August 29, 1943, Eisenhower came to Sicily and awarded the Legion of Merit to Field Marshall Montgomery.

In September 1943, the Allies invaded Italy with three invasions that would attack both sides of the mainland. It would take more than a year to liberate Italy.

Operation Baytown began on September 3, 1943, by the British XIII Corps, part of the British Eighth Army under General Montgomery. The XIII Corps crossed the Straits of Messina from Sicily to Reggio di Calabria under heavy artillery barrage from Sicily. The objective was to tie the German forces in an area so the Allies could gain a foothold in Italy. The Germans did not believe that it was the main invasion, and their engagement consisted of leaving a regiment to defend the coast. The Italians offered no resistance after being massively bombarded.

Operation Slapstick took place on September 9, 1943, at the Italian port of Taranto by the British 1st Airborne Division. The division was transported by Royal Navy ship across the Mediterranean. The landing was unopposed. The ports of Taranto and Brindisi on the Adriatic coast were captured.

Operation Avalanche also began on September 9th. The U.S. Fifth Army was composed of the U.S. VI Corps, the British X Corps, and the U.S. 82nd Airborne Division. The operation took Salerno. Booker and Andre fought at Salerno and saw intense action through to the Volturno River and then to Cassion. They would fight through October 1943 before they would rest.

Oliver saw death, destruction, and hunger in Italy wherever he reported and wherever the enemy departed.

> *I look at hundreds of hungry people who are without homes, cold, and nothing left. I see bombed beaches and bridges destroyed by the enemy.*

He wrote about the uniformed services that had brought the forces together, even though they were segregated:

> *Our army is separated by racial lines, but every man in uniform has been brought together by their job. Freedom for all is our aim, and even the most rabid hater of different races has been forced to admit that to gain victory and freedom for himself, he has to share same with every comrade in arms.*

He wrote how black and white soldiers shared their food and lives:

> *Hungry white soldiers gladly take mess kits at colored chow lines and vice versa. Men who had never eaten, slept, or drunk with a different race now share the same battle bottle of wine with a different race, use fingers in the same rations, and bunk in the same ditch or tent. Now no one can deny credit to colored men in all branches of service*

> *over here. Every landing and invasion has groups doing various jobs and no one is disrupted by advanced treachery or by inefficiency.*

In one story he looked towards the future:

> *Many lives will be lost before the final victory is achieved, but already our men are looking ahead toward their part in the postwar world. While statesmen study maps in anticipation of global control, these boys lie on the ground and swat flies and sweat on rocks to make this control possible, and all they want to know is will they be allowed to enjoy what they have fought for.*

Nelms sent Cub to Italy to relieve Oliver in December 1943. He recognized Oliver's need for a reprieve. Oliver chose to go to London to recuperate.

CHAPTER 28

On January 22, 1944, the 3rd Division was part of the amphibious landing at Anzio in Italy under the VI Corps of British and American units. Booker and Andre fought against German counterattacks for the next four months. The division fought off an attack by three German divisions. In one day it suffered over 900 casualties, the most of any U.S. division in one day.

The Battle of Monte Cassino, also known as the *Battle for Rome*, lasted for five months, with multiple assaults by Allied troops.

Cub reported that the 99th Fighter Squadron members were crack pilots, succeeding in air attacks against the Germans. The squadron ran their scoreboard to twelve Nazi planes destroyed, two probably destroyed, and four damaged during two days of fighting:

> *... a record for the current invasion of Anzio and Nettuno Beaches, south of Rome. Like football players bursting into a dining room after a triumph in the season's classic, war-weary pilots were jubilant in their description*

of victories over the Luftwaffe, giving vivid recollections of how they poured hot lead into enemy aircraft.

Cub drove thirty miles to a hospital to find and interview Second Lieutenant George McCrimby from Fort Worth, Texas. McCrimby was suspended by one foot, the result of diving a plane at 350 miles an hour and parachuting the remaining 1,000 feet to safety near Anzio Beach, Italy. He was recuperating from minor bruises sustained in the grueling ordeal. He related the story to Cub:

"Something hit underneath the ship and then another burst cracked the side of my cockpit, plunging the plane to dive at 4,000 feet. I tried to pull out, but had no control. The elevators had been knocked out. I had no alternative but to jump. I tried the left side but the slip stream knocked me back. Then I tried the right side and got half way out when again the slip stream threw me against the fuselage. I struggled until all but my right foot was free and dangled from the diving plane until the wind turned the ship at about 1000 feet and shook me loose. I reached for the rip-cord six times before finding it, but my parachute opened immediately, landing me safely in the cow pasture." [21]

Cub reported that Staff Sergeant Joe Louis, the world's heavyweight champion, visited the troops and made frequent appearances at hospitals, camps, and theaters. Cub wrote:

The Mustang fighter group's base was not listed on Joe's regular slate in August, and it would have been necessary for the soldiers to travel 50 miles to see the champion in action, so Joe took his day off to come to the flat, dusty airbase to mingle with the boys.

Accompanied by S/Sgt. Jimmy Edgar, Detroit, and Sergeant Jackie (California) Wilson, Los Angeles, the champion arrived just in time to see the pilots, led by their daily long-range missions deep into enemy territory.

"These fellows sure can fly," Joe opined as he sat beside First Lt. William C. Wyatt, group special service officer, in a jeep, watching the sleek, silver Mustangs zoom in one after the other for neat landings on the metal-stripped runway.

Joe met the colonel, sipped a cool lemonade with him, then strolled over to the group's briefing room, where Col. Davis happily pointed out all the places the group has flown on the giant wall map.

Joe glanced proudly at the white-washed wall of the group, on which is listed sixty-three victories. He enjoyed the rare privilege of sitting in on the mission's critique and addressed the fliers at it conclusion.

Revealing no sign of his much-discussed reticence, the champion declared, "I am glad to see you fellows. I've been keeping up with you in the papers. I have visited many airfields and have spoken to a lot of pilots; they all speak well of you and give you lots of credit."[22]

In May 1944, the war-weary troops enjoyed watching Marlene Dietrich sit on top of a piano as she and her accompanist performed especially for the soldiers. Andre and Booker were now in Italy and saw the most glamorous woman in the world singing "Falling in Love Again" from her 1930 movie, *The Blue Angel.* Dietrich wore a long white dress with gold angels sewn into the pattern.

Dietrich became a U.S. citizen in 1939, and as a staunch anti-Nazi, was one of the first celebrities to actively support the Allied war effort. A month following this particular performance, Dietrich — dressed in the U.S. Army Air Force uniform —would entertain the troops in France following the Normandy invasion.

Booker and Andre would go to France but it wouldn't be through Normandy; it instead would be through *Operation Dragoon*, the southern invasion of France.

PART 3

The Liberation of France

CHAPTER 1

By May 1944, many journalists were heading to London. Something was going to happen. New reporters were arriving to replace those who were leaving. Oliver didn't know what was going on, but he heard it was going to be big, whatever it was.

Nelms sent word to Oliver that Cub was on his way. Cub and Oliver met at the Cumberland Hotel in London, where Oliver had a room.

"Glad to see you," said Cub.

"Likewise. How was Italy? Is Nelms already missing you?" asked Oliver.

"Probably not. I'm to replace you here after this. You've been gone a long time. We read about you every day," he said with excitement.

"I've watched your reporting as well," said Oliver. "I'm going to be permanent in Paris after the war. Did he tell you?"

"No, but I think everyone suspects that you want to stay over here. But not me. I eventually want to get back to Birmingham. Someday I'd like to be editor of the paper."

Just then a beautiful black woman carrying a briefcase strolled past Oliver and Cub.

"I hope you men are ready for this," she said as she walked past them toward the front desk.

"Who was *that*?" asked Cub.

"*That* is Tatiana Phillips," said Oliver.

"Do you know her?"

"No, but I know her father."

"Who is she?"

"She is the daughter of the publisher of the *African-American Statesman*, the most important black newspaper in America."

"The *African-American Statesman*?" asked Cub.

"Yes."

"Her father's the editor?"

"Yep," said Oliver. "That paper is our biggest competitor. Looks like the game is on."

"I'll bet her father wants to give her some experience before she takes over his paper," said Cub.

"He does. He told me at a conference in Washington, D.C., on the day after Pearl Harbor, that she was going to cover the war in Europe."

As Tatiana approached the elevator, she turned around and noticed Oliver watching her. He saw the touch of a smile play across her lips. Oliver's eyes widened as the elevator door closed and Tatiana disappeared.

Cub and Oliver picked up their bags and waited to catch the next elevator.

"She'll be the country's first black female war correspondent in Europe," said Oliver.

Cub wasn't paying attention to Oliver; he was busy toying with the idea of becoming editor of a major newspaper. "Just think … if that happens, I will have gone from a shoeshine boy to editor of a newspaper."

"Yeah, I'll bet Nelms is grooming you to be editor someday," said Oliver. Then he stopped. "Did you say you shined shoes?"

"Yes. You didn't know?"

"Know what?" asked Oliver.

"I set up my shoeshine station at the newspaper and asked Nelms for a job."

"I didn't know that. That must have been before I came to the paper. How long ago?"

"Five years ago, in 1939."

"Where did you live before you came to Birmingham?" asked Oliver.

"Mountain Springs."

Oliver paused. "You know, I met two soldiers from Mountain Springs. One said that he knew a man who shined shoes and went to work for the paper in Birmingham."

"That was me. Did he mention the name Shorty Miller?"

"I don't remember. If he did, I didn't pick up on that. I'll have to listen more carefully next time."

CHAPTER 2

After settling in their rooms, Oliver and Cub decided to take a cab to the War Information Office in London.

"Let's see if Public Affairs has any information about our schedule. All I know is that we're leaving on a British ship tomorrow," said Oliver. "I've already done that once before, two years ago."

"Good idea. I have the names of a couple of soldiers from Alabama. Nelms promised their mothers that I would check on them," said Cub.

The reporters walked down to the lobby and found a taxi outside the hotel. The car door was already open, so Oliver peered in. He was surprised to find Tatiana Phillips sitting next to the window in the backseat.

"Well, hello! Do you mind if we ride with you?" said Oliver.

"Not at all," smiled Tatiana.

"I'm Oliver Smith."

"And I'm Cub Miller," introduced the other, sliding in next to Tatiana.

"Tatiana Phillips. Glad that you boys could make it. I thought we were going to have to leave you and you'd have to take the next taxi."

The three passengers were quiet as the taxi pulled away from the curb. After a few minutes, Oliver decided to strike up a conversation.

"So Tatiana, what brings you to London?" asked Oliver.

"The war, of course. What brings you? I thought you were a travel writer. Tell me, has it been difficult for you to transition from travel writing to combat journalism?"

"Not at all. I'm used to war," said Oliver. "I've been over here for the last two years."

"That's right. I did hear that. I'm sorry," she said.

"I'm used to *peace*," said Cub. "I know how to be *real* friendly." Cub grinned and gave Tatiana a little nudge with his elbow.

Tatiana looked at Cub and smiled, uninterested in taking the bait. Cub was 5'7" and Tatiana was quite tall at 5'10". Oliver was 6'2", slender, and in excellent physical condition. He looked handsome and professional in his perfectly tailored suit, tie, and cufflinks.

Tatiana turned to Oliver, a serious look on her face. "And you, Mr. Smith. Are you interested in peace?"

"Call me Oliver, please."

"Yes, Oliver. You did a great job on your Josephine Baker story. Actually, I'm afraid that I thought she was dead."

"Me too, but I'm glad to report that she's alive and well."

"How did it happen that your paper sent you to cover the war in Africa, and your first story was an interview with Josephine Baker?" asked Tatiana.

"It wasn't actually my first story over there."

"I'm sorry, that one sticks out in my mind for some reason. I find your stories very interesting. Or rather, should I say, I find what *interests* you to be very interesting. Do you have a good story you are pursuing now?" asked Tatiana.

"Not really. I have to search for them, just like you," said Oliver.

"I don't have to find my stories," she said. "I have too much to do already. I'm sure I'll be up all night writing one of the stories that my father needs tomorrow. I'll be up all night ... by myself."

"How is your father?" asked Oliver.

"You know my father? You know the editor of the *African- American Statesman*?"

Tatiana was being coy. Her father had mentioned Oliver after the conference in Washington in 1941, and she began to follow Oliver's stories in his paper. Their paper subscribed to the *Birmingham Defender* and Tatiana saved clippings from many of his stories. She knew she would be meeting up with Oliver at some point. She wondered if Oliver knew much about her. She knew that Ed Nelms and her father had discussed the possibility of them working together in Europe.

Oliver nodded. "I met your father the day after Pearl Harbor. We were attending the conference in D.C. about the credentialing of war reporters. I think everyone has heard of him."

"Dad's fine. Thank you for asking. I forgot to ask — what is the name of the small paper that you and Cub work for?"

"The *Birmingham Defender*," Oliver and Cub said together in unison.

"I know that paper. It has a circulation of about 100,000?" said Tatiana.

"Actually, about 235,000," said Oliver.

"Our paper's is 500,000 but my father hopes that it will be over a million one day. That is why he wants me over here reporting. I'll be the first African American female reporter covering the war."

"You know, I think I've heard that before," smiled Oliver.

"Heard what?" said Tatiana.

"That you are going to be the first female black military correspondent in Europe covering the war," said Oliver.

"For one thing, I'll get my introduction into combat journalism," said Tatiana.

"You certainly will. I wish you and your father well. War is pretty tough," said Oliver.

"I don't," said Cub, glaring at Oliver.

"You don't what?" asked Oliver.

"I don't wish them well. Why do we wish them well? They are the enemy … the competition."

The taxi driver was listening and smiled at the conversation in the back seat.

"No, *there* is the enemy," he said as they passed a fake body of Hitler hung in effigy.

The driver slowed the taxi and pulled to the curb.

CHAPTER 3

The three reporters arrived at the United States Office of War Information that the president had referred to in his interview in 1941. The purpose of the office was to deliver propaganda during the war, but that objective was kept hush. The office was not classified, but the military monitored its visitors. After waiting only a few moments, Major Jonah Lee joined the reporters to answer their questions.

"How can I help you, gentlemen and lady?" asked Lee. "Nice to see you again, Oliver. Been a while since our trip to Africa."

"Nice to see you as well, Major Lee," said Oliver.

Cub inquired about the 761st and wondered if it was true that General Patton had called for them. Tatiana asked when they would be allowed to follow the invasion into Normandy. Oliver asked if the Allies would come ashore in the South of France.

"I can't answer these questions," said Lee. "Let me find the colonel who can."

Colonel Dixon entered to the room; Oliver had not seen him since 1942.

"Who wants to know about General Patton?" asked Col. Dixon.

"That's me," said Cub.

Dixon turned to Cub. "We don't reveal the general's schedule. You can write about the war, but we approve all that is submitted back to the states. We will provide transportation to you while in the theater, but we are not a taxi service for the *Birmingham Daily Observer*," said Dixon.

"Understood," said Cub.

"I'm sure it's just a matter of time before the 761st Tank Battalion arrives. You shouldn't even know that — I'm curious where you heard that information," queried Dixon.

"It's our job to keep up with the black soldier," answered Cub.

"Do you have any news regarding the Allies' advance into France?" said Oliver.

"Do I look like I work for the *Alabama Daily Observer*? It's not my job to give you information like that. Why would I tell you that? So you can announce it on the front page of your paper? Who are you kidding?"

"Actually, it's the *Birmingham Defender*. I've already been covering the war for two years," said Oliver.

"Whatever. The *Birmingham Daily*, the *Alabama Observer*, whatever you call yourself today — you're just lucky to be here at all. I don't know why we allow news media types running around here, trying to drum up news stories."

"Are the Allies going to invade France?" asked Tatiana.

"Well, hello there, Miss Phillips. I'm glad to see that you made it to London," welcomed Dixon.

"Thank you, Colonel," said Tatiana.

"And how is your father?"

"He's doing well and looks forward to the stories I'm going to send. He also sends his good wishes to you and thanks you for allowing me to come here and report as the first female black journalist to cover the war."

"You are welcome, and congratulations on your accomplishment. Your father and I talked about that."

Oliver grimaced as he listened to Tatiana throw her femininity and her father's connections around.

"Come *on*," said Oliver underneath his breath.

"Give him my best," said the colonel. Turning back to look at Oliver, he said, "Now, you were saying something about invading Southern France?"

"Yes, I would also like to know about that," said Cub.

"You are asking me about an invasion? Now, why would we tell the press about our invasion plans? So you can print it in advance of the invasion?"

"So there *is* an invasion?" said Cub.

"As I said before, it's not my job to give stories to the *Birmingham Observer* and there had better not be any stories about how horrible things are for the black soldier, or how we failed to do this or we failed to do that. If I receive a story like that, I will turn it over to Hoover to see if it could be considered sedition."

"We are not going to do that, Colonel," said Tatiana. "I'm sure I can speak for all three of us when I say that we are here to only report about our fighting men and women in action."

The colonel turned to Tatiana, his harsh face melting into a smile. "I'm sure you will Tatiana. I'm not concerned about your reports. I look forward to reading your stories when you get over there."

"Thank you, Colonel," Tatiana smiled at him.

"Once we have information to share, we will do that. The government is allowing reporters to cover the war, but it's on your honor to respect the tradition of the press during times of war. We are not going to censor the press, but we will have to approve every story before it can go to print," said the colonel. Oliver already knew this.

The reporters offered their thanks, and Col. Dixon left the room, followed by Maj. Lee.

"You were pretty hard on them, weren't you, sir?" asked Lee.

"Not really. Oliver has made a hero of himself reporting the war for the last two years. I just wanted to bring him down a notch."

Dixon didn't have it out for Oliver. But he had read Oliver's stories and was well aware of how the journalist was enjoying celebrity status. The colonel also knew about Oliver's opinion piece endorsing Roosevelt's opponent.

"Understood, sir."

"And I want them to work for their stories. It's not up to us to give them stories. They have to work for them like everyone else."

"Understood, sir," said Lee.

CHAPTER 4

Two DAYS LATER, Tatiana became ill and was hospitalized in London. She developed neuralgia of the left arm and leg, which rendered both semi-useless. It would take a month to recover and she would be unable to travel to France. She was quite upset about her plight. Hoping for a possible romance in Paris with Tatiana, Oliver saw that particular dream go down in flames.

Oliver and Cub went to the hospital to visit her.

"Sorry you won't be making the trip, Tatiana," said Oliver in an attempt to comfort her.

"I'll bet you're sorry. I did not come 3,000 miles for nothing. I'm going to report the war from here," she said.

Oliver raised his eyebrows, surprised at her determination.

"We'll bring you back something when we see you next," said Cub.

"Thanks, Cub."

"You take care," said Oliver, touching her shoulder.

"I'm sure we'll see each other again," said Cub.

"I'm sure we will. You boys take care. I only wish I could be there with you. I was going to be the first female black journalist covering the war."

Oliver grinned, having heard that line a hundred times by now. "I didn't realize that," said Oliver, coyly. "But you will. Something will happen and you'll get your break. You will make it over there."

CHAPTER 5

Colonel Dixon heard that Tatiana was in the hospital and decided to visit her.

"Sorry to see you're laid up," he told her.

"Thank you Colonel; my left arm gave out on me. They say it is neuralgia. I didn't come 3,000 miles to write about the war in a hospital bed. Now I can't even write. You've got to do something to get me over there."

"Hmm. Did they say when you will get out?"

"The doctor didn't say," she said.

"It's clear that you can't travel with the convoy. And I'm not sure they would've let you go anyway, even if you were healthy. It's too dangerous at first. You can go after the beaches are cleared. We are not sending all credentialed reporters anyway. Once you are credentialed, you'll wear the uniform and have the equivalent rank of major."

"I see. Thank you again," she said.

"You could write about the Women's Army Auxiliary Corps. The 6888th Central Postal Battalion will be moving to Birmingham later this year. They have the first commissioned African American majors, Charity Adams and Harriett West Waddy. That could get you started."

"I will, Colonel. By the way, I met a lady named Alice Allison Dunnigan in D.C. Do you know of her?" asked Tatiana.

"Is she a journalist in Kentucky?" said Dixon.

"She works for the Department of Labor."

"She'll go a long way, I'm sure," said the colonel. "On another issue, be careful. It's dangerous out there. There are journalists all over the world covering the invasion, and the competition is unbelievable for stories. Some will do anything to get the story. Everyone will be watching you. You are a journalist first, so you can't fight in the war just because you wear a uniform. Just be careful and don't do anything illegal to get the story or violate the rules of engagement. Journalists cannot do that. That military uniform requires you to follow the rules. Besides, you can get killed out there even if you *are* careful and following the rules. It can happen to the best of us."

"I will be careful, Colonel. By the way, have you heard from my father? How is he?" she asked.

"He's fine. Take good care, Tatiana."

He gave her a quick hug and left.

CHAPTER 6

After Tatiana was released from the hospital, Colonel Dixon made sure that she received a military uniform. Now she could travel under official orders and join Oliver and Cub in the official ranks of being an accredited military correspondent. Col. Dixon discussed the possibility of joining the army, but Tatiana couldn't imagine taking time to return to the United States for training. It was important that she be able to move around with the same freedom as Oliver, Cub, and the other correspondents and to be in the war *now*, while it was happening.

Tatiana dressed in her uniform and looked at herself in the mirror. Then she pulled on white gloves. She turned around to see how the uniform fit, turning her head to see her backside. Then she put on her cover.

"Not bad," she said into the mirror. "I think I can do this."

She returned to Public Affairs to work with Col. Dixon until she could find a way to get to Paris.

"Ready to write about the Women's Army Auxiliary Corps, assuming your paper doesn't have anything else for you?" asked Dixon.

"Of course," said Tatiana.

"Ok. Here is what I have on the WAAC," said Dixon, handing her a stack of papers.

The WAAC, created in 1942, was segregated and had over 6,500 black women in its ranks. The WAAC director was Col. Oveta Culp Hobby, the wife of former Texas Governor William P. Hobby. Majors Harriet West Waddy and Charity Adams joined the WAAC in 1942 and attended officer candidate school at Fort Des Moines. They were the only two black women to attain the rank of major in the WAAC during World War II. Harriet West Waddy was the first black officer promoted to major and was named an aide to the WAAC director.

Tatiana read that Maj. Waddy had been given the assignment of visiting different installations across the United States to gather information from African American WAACs about their treatment in the army. Her report was eventually sent to First Lady Eleanor Roosevelt.

"My gosh," Tatiana said, reading that Waddy's report made it to Mrs. Roosevelt. "I hope she didn't crash a talk given by the First Lady like I did," she thought to herself.

Tatiana tracked down Maj. Waddy in Des Moines for a brief interview over the phone. She asked Waddy about her integration of the WAAC.

Waddy said, "As an African American woman, there is not a single door in Washington, D.C., that I can walk through; but as a major in the WAAC, there is not a door I *cannot* walk through."

Tatiana was impressed.

Tatiana asked Waddy about a radio broadcast that she made in April 1943, as First Officer Harriet West, on behalf of the army, urging black women to get into uniform.

"What prompted you to make the radio address?" asked Tatiana.

"I didn't believe that joining a segregated military and accepting a situation which does not represent an ideal of democracy was a 'retreat from our fight,' but was instead our contribution to its realization."

"That is great," said Tatiana.

"In my view, service in the wartime military will help blacks gain acceptance. Military service will give black women a chance to show their abilities and be of future benefit to the whole race."

Tatiana had her story.

CHAPTER 7

D-Day took place June 6, 1944, and would last for the next two months. Oliver and Cub made it to shore several hours after the troops landed.

Charles Collingwood of CBS arrived at Utah Beach hours after the first wave of soldiers hit the beaches. Collingwood, a Rhodes Scholar at Oxford University, was from Three Rivers, Michigan. He was recruited by Ed Murrow and was an eloquent on-air journalist. His report was broadcast two days later.

Bill Downs and Larry Lesser, "Murrow's Boys" with CBS, were not able to deliver their reports due to trouble with their transmitters. Downs had been introduced to Murrow by Collingwood. Downs, a wire reporter stationed in London, had worked the cable desk in New York for the United Press.

Lesser was hired by Murrow in 1939 when he approached him for a job. He was working for the United Press, reporting on the London Blitz. In 1941, he was assigned to Moscow.

Lesser could have been the first reporter to broadcast from the American beachhead with the American 4th Infantry Division, but his audio cables were lost by Navy couriers en route to London. Richard C. Hottelet witnessed the seaborne invasion of Normandy by air in a bomber that attacked Utah Beach six minutes before the invasion began. Hottelet had been hired by Murrow in January 1944. Three years earlier, he had been held by German police on suspicion of espionage and was released.

Ernest Hemingway was aboard one of the ships, but the invasion was too dangerous and his ship was not allowed to go ashore. The landing craft he was on was within sight of Omaha Beach when it came under enemy fire and turned back. Hemingway was returned to the *USS Dorothea L. Dix* (AP-67). He recorded that day:

> *... the first, second, third, fourth and fifth waves of [landing troops] lay where they had fallen, looking like so many heavily laden bundles on the flat pebbly stretch between the sea and first cover.*[23]

Martha Gellhorn successfully argued her right to report the war in a letter to the U.S. War Department:

> *It is necessary that I report on this war. I do not feel there is any need to beg as a favour for the right to serve as the eyes for millions of people in America who are desperately in need of seeing, but cannot see for themselves.*[24]

Gellhorn first experienced war reporting in the 1930s in Spain. It was there that she covered the Spanish Civil War and met Ernest Hemingway, her future husband. Hemingway reportedly asked Gellhorn why she wasn't writing about the war. Her response was, "I don't know about weapons and battles." His response was, "Write about what you *do* know, and that is people."

In 1944, Gellhorn was the first woman to report the invasion of Normandy by locking herself in a toilet room on a hospital ship. She wrote of the landing:

> *When night came, the water ambulances were still churning into the beach, looking for the wounded. We waded ashore in the water to our waist.*[25]

Helen Kirkpatrick made it ashore in France. She was attached to the Free French Forces, and the first war correspondent to be so assigned.

Oliver and Cub made it ashore by landing craft once it was clear. Oliver found an apple tree where he could record in his journal as he watched the ongoing landings and men transporting supplies. *That must have been quite an invasion,* he thought. It had cleared out by now, but he could see evidence of the initial phase of the assault. Many men had died coming ashore. *What a sacrifice,* he pondered.

"Look over there," Oliver said to Cub, pointing to the beach. "That's Martha Gellhorn. Tatiana is going to be jealous when she hears that other women made it to shore. She was so determined to make it to France."

"You know these people," said Cub. "I'll bet she will be upset. If there is a story out there, a real journalist will do whatever it takes to get it."

In spite of the war-torn area, cattle were grazing nearby as if nothing had happened. They were actually a peaceful sight. Oliver wrote in his journal, sitting under the tree:

> *... the first black troops set foot on the shores of France in the war ...*

The sound of artillery pounded up the road.

Later that night he and Cub stayed in a tent with the other soldiers. Oliver wrote in his journal:

> *I'm with CPT James East of New York. In the next tent is Warrant Officer Clary Andre of New Jersey. The outfit already has four Purple Hearts. Cpl. John Carey of Klein Bluff, Arkansas, shot down a German plane on D-Day while landing under fire. Everywhere I go are tales of our men coming ashore in water up to their necks to take part of the assault on the Jerry. 'Jerry' is slang for German soldier.*
>
> *The primary objective of the blimp is to keep enemy planes high where automatic weapons could hit them. They had the proud distinction of being the only barrage balloon outfit used by the allies in the invasion. German defenders were 300 yards away and fighting like hell when these men began stringing up their silver sausage to protect the hordes of Americans that were to follow them. And so good*

> *was their defense that not once has any beachhead sprouting their balloons been strafed by German planes.*[26]
>
> *On D-Day, Pfc. Israel of Middleton, Ohio, helped capture 11 Germans a few hundred miles from the beach. He and a white soldier found them cut off from the main body of Germans and rented them up.*
>
> *Cpl. Jesse Muslin of Fruitdale, Alabama, was on guard on D-Day when he saw a German crouching. He fired and the Nazi threw up his hands and came forward to surrender.*[27]

By June 14th, "Murrow's Boy" Bill Downs made the first live broadcast from Normandy to the United States.

After reporting the invasion, Martha Gellhorn made her way back on a hospital ship headed to London and turned in her story. The army arrested her for violating rules of engagement, revoked her credentials, and sent her to a location outside of London where she would stay with a military nurse. But she found a way out and convinced a British military pilot to fly her to Italy. She would cover the war from there. Gellhorn would not be stopped, even by the Allies or the rules of engagement.

CHAPTER 8

Oliver and Cub traveled with Maj. Lee in his jeep onward toward the liberation of Paris. The goal was to take Paris in the next few months and let General de Gaulle restore the government in France, ousting the Germans from their occupation of the past four years.

The reporters would follow the convoy with General de Gaulle to Paris and cover his entrance into the city. That would be news back home. They were witnesses to history.

The fighting continued as the Allies advanced to Paris. The reporters were kept far enough away from the fighting that they could only cover what happened after the area ahead was clear.

Once they reached the Seine River south of Paris, the reporters were unable to proceed after they lost their escort. Their advance would have to wait while the Allies cleared out the last pockets of German resistance. On the first night of their wait, the reporters found an abandoned chateau on the side of the road after the convoy came to a halt. They spread out, looking for food and provisions. Fortunately, neighboring French families were willing to give them a chicken. Oliver was even given a bottle of sweet wine. They had a feast on their first night.

Down the road, the Allies were clearing the area and shelling the Nazis. Two hundred German soldiers, shelled into a daze, surrendered.

Oliver started a fire in the fireplace. They had their first French dinner on French soil.

"You know you are not supposed to have sweet wine with chicken. We are in France, and we are already violating all the French rules of engagement during our first few weeks here," said Maj. Lee.

"And we have no appetizers or champagne," shrugged Oliver.

"Or dessert or digestif," said Lee.

"What's a digestif?" asked Cub.

"It's an after dinner drink," said Lee. "It's big over here. You guys can drink. I can't."

The men cooked dinner and sat around a wooden table on musty chairs covered with cobwebs. Inside, the chateau looked like a haunted house.

"So who wants to say grace?" asked Oliver.

"I will," said Lee. "Bless us, Oh Lord, and these thy gifts, which we are about to receive, from thy bounty through Christ Our Lord. Amen."

"Amen," said Oliver.

"Amen," said Cub.

Lee carved the chicken and they savored the meat. It was the first home-cooked meal they had since they left

Birmingham. It was far different from the rations that had become part of their daily routine.

"Man, that's good," said Lee.

"Sure is," said Cub.

"So, what do you think it's going to be like when we reach Paris?" said Oliver to Lee.

"I imagine de Gaulle will proceed down to Notre Dame, make a big speech, and go back to the Hundred Years' War with England," said Lee.

"Too funny. But England came to the defense of France while France was divided in half. I hope all the streets are cleared and the Germans are gone. This country has been occupied too long by the Germans," said Oliver.

"I think once Paris is liberated, it's onward to Germany," said Cub.

"This has been going on two years now. It's amazing how they pulled this together," said Oliver. "When you look at how they accomplished this, it truly is unbelievable."

"What do you mean?" asked Cub.

"The Allies first went into North Africa. I remember landing at Oran in '42. I was on a convoy with 800 ships. We thought we were going to be sunk by submarines after coming around the Straits of Gibraltar."

"You did?" said Cub.

"Yes. It was tense. The Allies went into North Africa and cleared out Rommel. We went to Sicily and cleared the Germans and Italians there. Then on to Italy and cleared the Germans again. The Allies bombed Germany on a daily basis from the air. The Russians fought on the Eastern Front to reach Berlin. The Allies invaded Normandy and pushed all the way to Paris. From there, it's onward to Germany. Straight to Berlin; straight to Hitler," said Oliver.

"I don't think they will go to Berlin after Paris. I think they have to free Southern France before they go to Germany. They have to finish off France," said Lee.

"What was that?" asked Oliver.

"I think the Allies have to invade from the south of France," repeated Lee, reaching to pour another glass of wine.

"Another invasion in the southern part of France?" said Oliver.

"There has to be. It would make sense. There are still over 50,000 Germans in southern France. If you go straight to Berlin, you will fight the enemy coming out," Lee explained.

"The Allies have to do a left hook into northern France, then a right hook into southern France. Then they meet up somewhere in the middle and go to Germany. Then from France and Italy and bomb the hell out of them from the air from London on a daily basis. The Russians have been assaulting Germany from the eastern side to get through to Berlin for some time. It will be an assault on Germany from all sides," said Lee.

"I can see how complicated this war is," said Oliver.

"At least, that's what I think. I think the Russians want to claim the entire Eastern Front for themselves. They are marching forward to Germany while we fight from the west. They want everything along their path for themselves," said Lee.

"I guess it looks like you and I are going to southern France," said Oliver to Cub.

Cub was listening in amazement. They continued their conversation, hoping that one bottle of wine might be enough to remove any fears they had of going into Paris. For a short while, they were free from the intensity of the moment.

"I propose a toast," said Lee.

"To the Marines," he cheered, as he held up his glass.

Cub and Oliver repeated, "To the Marines."

"To the Commander-in-Chief."

Cub and Oliver repeated, "To the Commander-in-Chief."

"To the United States Navy."

Cub and Oliver repeated, "To the United States Navy."

Finally, "To the United States Army," they said in unison.

"What did we just do?" asked Cub.

"*That* was a dining in. Now I'm going to sleep," said Lee. "Hooohaaa!"

Oliver and Cub looked at each other. They *were* in the army, they thought. The two reporters found a spot to lie down and went to sleep. They spent the next three days and nights at the chateau, waiting for the Allies to advance to Paris.

CHAPTER 9

In Washington, D.C., journalist May Craig with the Gannett newspapers stood before the Women's National Press Corp and took the microphone to say, "There are 127 accredited American female war correspondents bringing written descriptions of conflict back to the civilians at home. The war has given women a chance to show what they can do in the news world, and they have done well. This follows the tradition of prior women journalists Jane Swiss Helm who covered the Civil War, Anna Benjamin who covered the Spanish American War, and Peggy Hull who covered World War I. We have come a long way since a woman named Jose Glover from Cambridge, Massachusetts, owned the first printing press in the colonies."

The crowd cheered.

"These are difficult times for America with what is going on in our country. We need to make certain that there is work out there for the women journalists and that jobs are not lost. We are thankful to the First Lady, who has instituted the Women Only press conference. This has caused news organizations to employ female journalists. Some of the correspondents covering the press conferences have gone on to be war correspondents."

The crowd clapped in response.

"I want to thank some of our war correspondents who are out there now and have been for some time. Margaret Bourke-White has covered the Blitz in London and was the first female correspondent to cover the African campaign. She was in Russia when the Germans attacked. We all remember how she reported that event."

"And Georgette Chappelle, we know her as 'Dickey,' has been covering the war for *Look Magazine*."

The crowd cheered.

"Marguerite Higgins has been covering the Seventh Army for the *New York Herald Tribune*. You never know. She might enter Berlin with the troops when we get there. And we *will* get there."

The crowd went wild with applause at the mention of winning the war.

It would not just be left up to men to report World War II.

CHAPTER 10

In July 1944, Ernest Hemingway attached himself to the 22nd Infantry Regiment commanded by Col. Charles 'Buck' Lanham, the unit that participated in the assault of Utah Beach on D-Day as part of the VII Corps.

Hemingway was in Rambouillet and found a small band of village militia. He rented ten rooms at the Grand Veneur Hotel, and some of the rooms were stacked with weapons. Many with the press made their way to the hotel by August 22 in anticipation of the liberation of Paris. Rumors were flying that Hemingway was actually engaging in war with his militia instead of merely reporting the war. There was Gellhorn, violating the rules of engagement to make it to Normandy. Then there was Hemingway, moving from the pen to the sword. Had they violated the rules of engagement?

Colonel Dixon gave a press a briefing about the imminent Allied movement into Paris. Many reporters had no place to sleep. They spread straw over the floor of the hotel dining room. Ernie Pyle made it to the hotel as did Andy Rooney, an army journalist covering the war for the *Stars and Stripes.* Bruce Grant, the city editor with the *Chicago Sun*

Times, was looking for a room and found Hemingway. He heard that Hemingway had rooms tied up in his name.

Grant found Hemingway in the dining room. Hemingway was hosting correspondents who were listening to him speak when Grant approached him for a room. An argument ensued and Hemingway, in his uniform and carrying a .45 caliber weapon, told him to "get the hell out of here."

Ernie Pyle was lying on his straw bed and came up to a sitting position to see what was happening. Andy Rooney was in the room watching as well.

Hemingway raised his fists. But before the fight began, Harry Harris, an AP photographer, braced himself between the two men. With one hand on Hemingway's chest and the other on Grant, Harris tried to shove them apart. Hemingway left and went outside to a small garden.

Hemingway soon returned to the room and threw open the door, saying to Grant, "Well, are you coming out to fight?"[28]

CHAPTER 11

In August 1944, Lee Miller, a female photographer and fashion model in the 1920s, traveled to Saint-Malo, France, after she was told the fighting had ceased. She hitched a ride in a jeep, carrying only her camera and a blanket roll. When she caught up to the troops on the outskirts of Saint-Malo, the Eighty-third Division was fighting door-to-door, rooting out the Nazis. She was pinned down in a narrow street with German gunfire overhead. She wrote:

> *I sheltered in a Kraut dugout, squatting under the ramparts. My heel ground into a dead detached hand, and I cursed the Germans for the sordid ugly destruction they had conjured up in the once beautiful town. A hand was thrown at me, and I picked up the hand and threw it back the way I had come and ran back, bruising my feet and crashing into the unsteady piles of stone and slipping in the blood. Christ it was awful.*[29]

The fighting continued onward through France to Paris, and into southern France and onward into Germany.

CHAPTER 12

On August 1, 1944, fifty-six days after the Allied landings at Normandy, the Third Army became operational in Southern France under the command of General Patton. After being sidelined for a year, Patton was given a second chance; a rare feat when even congressmen were demanding his removal.

Patton asked for more tankers. The army reported that the 761st Tank Battalion at Camp Hood, Texas, was available.

"Who asked for color?" Patton said, "I asked for tankers."[30]

LTC Bates, the white commanding officer of the 761st Tank Battalion, told the troops that Patton asked personally for them; he would only take the finest and best. The 761st would finally receive orders to deploy to Europe. The men were waiting for the chance — now it was their turn. Activated in April 1942, the battalion endured a two-year wait. Many soldiers wondered if they would ever be called to duty. The battalion consisted of over 700 black soldiers from all walks of life and from all over the country. Ruben Rivers walked in the rain to Tecumseh, Oklahoma, to catch a bus to Fort Knox in March 1941.

Ruben met E. G. McConnell, who was sixteen when his mother dropped him off at the recruiter in New York. She lied about his age and said, "Take good care of my son." It was E.G.'s first time away from home. In all, over ninety black soldiers enlisted at Fort Knox, Kentucky, to learn tank operations and mechanics.

Captain John Roosevelt "Jackie" Robinson, who commanded a tank platoon, would not go to Europe. He was sidelined due to a charge brought up by court- martial.

LTC Bates summoned him to his office. Lt. Robinson reported with a crisp salute. Bates stood up from behind his desk and smiled to shake hands.

"Robinson, I want to commend you and your outfit on your work down here," he said. "You have the best record of all the outfits at the camp, and I'm singling you out for a special mention," Bates told him.

"Sir, I didn't know anything about tanks when I got here. I owe it to my platoon sergeant. I put him in command, and he's done a wonderful job of explaining things to me. I learned as I went along," said Robinson. [31]

"I don't care how you accomplished what you did," Bates continued. "The fact of the matter is, you found a way to make your outfit tops, and that's all I ask."

Bates informed him of the charges that the army was bringing against him. "This isn't right," Bates said.

"I don't reckon I'll be going overseas with you, sir," said Robinson.

"Jackie, this should never have happened," said Bates.

"Sir, take care of the guys when you get over there. They need you."

Bates remained until the court-martial ended. Robinson was acquitted, but he was not sent with the 761st Tank Battalion. He was reassigned to another unit.

Before leaving Camp Hood, Brigadier General Ernest A. Dawley, commander of the Tank Destroyer Center at Camp Hood, delivered a speech to the 761st. He concluded, "When you get there, put in an extra round of ammunition and fire it for General Dawley." [32]

On August 9, 1944, the 761st Tank Battalion, equipped with Sherman tanks and M5 General Stuart tanks, departed for Camp Kilmer. Their emblem, a black panther superimposed on a silver shield, was emblazoned with the battalion's motto:

"Come Out Fighting"

CHAPTER 13

War-torn and weary after two years in North Africa, Sicily, and Italy, Booker and Andre left Italy by Navy transport ship LST 281 to St. Raphael, France. They had already endured the most challenging times of their lives. They were on their way home, but to get home they would have to fight through France and Germany until the war ended. By this time, they were tired, worn out, two years older, and fatigued. They were taking part in *Operation Dragoon* to free southern France.

On August 12, 1944, days before Operation Dragoon began, Lt. Alexander Jefferson with the 301st Fighter Squadron, 332nd Fighter Group, 15th Air Force was flying his nineteenth mission to knock out radar stations at Toulon Harbor on the southern coast of France. The goal was to prevent the Germans from detecting the Allied ships, scheduled to land between Marseilles and Nice as part of *Operation Dragoon.* Sixteen P51s flew over the coast in four flights of four each. The first three sets of four hit their targets at low level and flew out to sea. Jefferson was the "Tail End Charlie," meaning the last plane to go in. Anti-air fire knocked out the plane flown by Bob Daniels, who landed in the sea before he was picked up by the Germans. Jefferson was hit and ejected. He fell through trees, landed on his feet, and rolled over.[33]

A German placed the muzzle of his Mauser against Jefferson and said, "Ja, Ja, Herr Leutnant. Fur Sie ist der Krieg vorbei." (*Ah, yes, Captain. For you the war is over.*) Jefferson was taken to a Luftwaffe field north of Toulon, along with Daniels. On August 14, Jefferson and Daniels were placed aboard a train to Orange. They were taken to a barn where they came across Richard Macon, who had also been shot down on the same mission near Montpellier. They were then taken to Oberusel, Germany, outside Frankfurt and later to Dulag Luft, where they were interrogated. The men were kept in solitary confinement. [34]

Operation Dragoon began on August 15, 1944. Churchill initially objected to the invasion but finally agreed to it. Its name originated from Churchill's belief that he had been "dragooned" into it.

The 3rd Infantry Division was shifted to the operation in southern France after fighting in North Africa, Sicily, and Italy. The invasion occurred between Toulon and Cannes with three American and one free French armored divisions. Support came from American, British, and French commando and airborne formations and French and American battleships, Allied escort carriers, cruisers, and destroyers.

Over 94,000 Allied troops and 11,000 vehicles landed on the first day of the invasion. German resistance was weak because many of their forces had been left to fight the Allies in northern France. The chief objective of the operation was the capture of the ports in Marseille and Toulon.

On the morning of the invasion, the ships of the Western Naval Task Force approached under the cover of darkness and were in position at dawn. The first of 1300 Allied bombers from Italy, Sardinia, and Corsica begin aerial bombardment shortly before 0600. Bombing was continuous until 0730, when battleships and cruisers spotting aircraft began firing on targets. The most serious fighting was near St. Raphael, where the LST 281 landed. A bombing run of 90 Allied B-24 bombers were used against German strong points.

The U.S. ships were coming closer for the invasion. Booker, Andre, and other army personnel were carried on the Navy ships because all ships were needed to carry troops ashore.

The commanding officer of LST 281 looked at his watch; it showed 1700.

"Ask for orders," the Commanding Officer said to his communications officer.

"Yes, sir."

Control Vessel PC-130 flashed its orders.

"Did you get it?"

The communications officer scribbled notes on a small pad.

"Yes. It says, 'Stand it', sir."

"Thank you."

Three hours and twenty minutes went by and the CO looked at his watch. It was now 2020. The control ship began to flash.

"Decode the message," the Skipper said calmly.

"Proceed to beach immediately."

"All right. We're on. Let's go."

LST 281 passed by the control vessel that was still flashing orders.

"Did you get it?" asked the Skipper.

"Yes, sir. It said, 'Expedite.'"

Below deck, 280 Navy personnel were cramped in their compartments along with army personnel assigned to the ship; the other ships were full. All ships had been used to transport troops.

CHAPTER 14

By 2100, the ship was 200 yards from shore. A German Bomber Do-217, one mile away, headed toward the LST. The Skipper ordered anti-aircraft fire, but the bomber reached the ship and dropped a radio controlled bomb, a Henschel HS 293, before it could be brought down. The LST continued firing anti-aircraft guns but to no avail. The bomb dropped, landing mid-ship, and the destruction began. Sailors were blown off the ship, and those below escaped to the beach on their own. The bomb killed forty men in all.

Andre and Booker found themselves in the water, gasping for air while trying to grasp their equipment and weapons. From the water they could see the bombing of their ship as it continued ashore ahead of them. Andre's glasses were still intact on his face; fortunately, the strap behind his neck was not broken.

Alabama felt very far away.

Andre spotted Booker in the water. He had made it to the surface and was attempting to swim ashore.

"Is that you, Booker?"

"Yes. I'm glad they gave us these belts. I never thought I would need it."

The two swam ashore, miraculously still gripping their weapons. Hundreds of other men appeared to be making their way to the beach as well. The night was dark, and they could see the anti-aircraft shoot through the sky like comets. On shore, they observed Germans advancing to combat the invasion. Andre, Booker, and the rest of the troops coming ashore were swimming directly into the fight. They had to make land as soon as possible to find cover.

By 2200, many of the men reached the beach, helping and rescuing others on the way. Once on land, their company was forced to climb fifty-foot cliffs to begin the fight forward. They fought for the next six days. The German 11th Panzer division attacked the Aixen Provence to prevent the Allies from advancing.

The bombing continued and Andre and Booker, along with their platoon, advanced further into a wooded area. Andre and Booker became separated from their platoon. They knew they couldn't be too far away; it was only a matter of time before they would reconnect with their troops. They had nothing to eat that night — food was the last thing on their minds. But their adrenaline was flowing and they observed the attacks throughout the night as the invasion continued.

"Where do we go from here?" asked Andre.

"We move forward. We should connect up with the Allies in no time. This is just temporary," said Booker.

Booker and Andre continued walking through the wooded area. There was no visible trail, but they could still see the invasion proceeding in the distance.

"We just need to get back to the Allies. You doing okay, Andre?"

"I'm fine."

He didn't notice blood dripping from the back of Andre's leg.

CHAPTER 15

ANDRE AND BOOKER made their way toward a house that appeared to have been partially bombed, hoping to find food and water. Andre limped, unaware that he had been injured. Booker entered the house to clear it, as they had been taught in boot camp. Two French women came out, one still wearing an apron and the other brandishing a rake, uncertain if there were Germans outside the house. It was pitch black outside, with little visibility. The women didn't realize that Booker and Andre were Allies. Booker motioned to the women to move closer to the trees. The women objected, and one began to beat Booker with the rake. Andre watched from a distance as Booker pushed the woman wearing an apron closer to the tree with the butt of his gun, attempting to clear them away from the home.

The bombing continued and the women began screaming. Andre thought he saw Germans in the trees not far behind Booker and the women. He pointed his weapon to shoot when another bomb exploded, knocking his aim off-target. His glasses fell off as he fired his weapon. The bomb landed near the home and destroyed it. Andre's misaimed shot hit Booker in the back and Booker fell to the ground. The women froze as they watched Booker collapse; they hadn't realized another soldier stood waiting nearby. The ladies scattered after realizing that Booker and Andre were Americans, not Germans. They disappeared into the dark forest with no home to seek refuge. Thanks to Booker, the women had successfully been cleared from the home prior to it being destroyed, saving them in the process.

Andre pulled himself to his feet and found his glasses. The strap had come off from behind his neck. He ran to Booker; his friend was still alive and shaking.

"Booker, I can't believe it. I thought I saw Germans coming toward us from the woods." Andre looked again but wasn't sure if he saw anyone. There was a great deal of commotion at that point; bombing raids continued and it was dark.

"Are you ok?"

"I don't know," Booker moaned.

Andre tried to help Booker into a comfortable position.

"Let me look at your back," said Andre, shaken. "Jesus," he breathed, looking at the wound on Booker's back. Andre was scared now. The wound was serious.

"Is it all right?" asked Booker.

"I think so. God, I'm sorry about this," said Andre, helping Booker lie back down. "Does that hurt to lie down on your back?"

"No. I think I can handle it," said Booker.

"Stay here, my friend. I have some sulfonamide in my pack. Let me get it." Andre found the first aid supplies, ripped Booker's shirt apart in the back, and applied the sulfonamide to Booker's wound.

Andre then placed his jacket under Booker's head.

"Here. Take this." Andre put a cigarette in his mouth, lit it, and handed it to his friend. The nicotine seemed to have an immediate calming effect on Booker as he drew in the smoke.

The two rested, listening to the sounds of the night in the forest.

"Feeling better?" asked Andre.

"I guess," said Booker. He turned his head toward Andre.

"You had to clear the house out for their own protection," said Andre.

"Yeah, I did."

"You saved their lives."

"Yeah," said Booker.

It was quiet. Andre decided to keep the conversation going. "Reminds me of my brother trying to go into the house to clear everyone out during the fire, but he couldn't."

"What?" asked Booker.

"You saved the women. If you hadn't gone in and cleared out the home, they would be dead by now," said Andre, making Booker's legs more comfortable.

Booker didn't say anything in response.

"Yeah, he went in the house and that was it," recalled Andre.

Booker again said nothing. A few moments passed and Booker asked, "What did you say a minute ago?"

"You mean the Germans? There were Germans in the woods. I thought I saw Germans in the woods. I was thinking they would be everywhere and I thought I saw some appear," said Andre.

"Did they get away?" asked Booker.

"I think so. I don't see any now," said Andre.

Booker grimaced as he tried to get comfortable. "I guess the women left," he said, squinting in the dark.

"Yeah, they ran away into the woods. Do you want to sit up?" asked Andre. Booker nodded, so Andre pulled him into a sitting position and helped him lean against a tree. He began combing the ground, looking for wood to put under Booker's legs.

"You will get over this soon and we will be back in battle," said Andre.

"I don't know," said Booker.

Andre tried to make Booker laugh, "Sure, you will. We will have some good times again, just like we used to."

Booker lay still with his eyes closed. "What did you say earlier?" he asked.

"About what?" asked Andre.

"Something about women," said Booker.

"I said you went in and cleared them out of the home. You saved their lives," said Andre.

"Right," said Booker.

Then it was quiet again.

Andre wanted to keep Booker awake and engaged. "You know, when you were at the trees with the women, it reminded me of when you tied Mary to the tree back in the eighth grade with those wrist bands. Remember that? That was stupid. It's funny looking back now."

"Yeah, that was stupid," said Booker with a small laugh, groaning with pain. "Ooh, that hurts." He paused for a minute and then asked, "Why did you bring that up?"

"I don't know why that came up. I guess I thought it might make you laugh. It just came to me," said Andre. "A lot of stuff in the past comes up during this war."

It was quiet for a while. Booker soon was in a state of shock and could no longer understand Andre. "You brought up Mary. I heard you. What about her? Why were you thinking about Mary?"

Booker had at first laughed about the incident. Andre realized now that Booker was becoming delirious and was no longer laughing.

"I wasn't thinking of her. It's nothing. Forget about it," said Andre. "I was just talking. Trying to keep you awake, trying to make you talk. Trying to keep you comfortable."

Andre realized it was a stupid mistake to mention Mary to his friend at such a difficult time. Why did he do that?

"Were you talking about when I tied her to the tree with those bands?" asked Booker.

"Yeah, there was no reason for that. Just forget it," said Andre.

Booker was sinking further into a state of shock.

Then Booker asked, "What are you talking about? Mary and the woods ... you mean the time I tied her hands behind the tree in the eighth grade? I did that as a joke with those bands you bought at that pawnshop. I wasn't trying to harm her. Why are you bringing that up now? I was just trying to move the women out of the house and closer to the woods. Their house was bombed. I wasn't going to do anything to them. I was trying to protect them," Booker said, raising his voice to Andre.

"I know that. Don't worry about it, Booker. It doesn't mean anything," said Andre.

"What did you say about clearing out the house?"

"You cleared out the house and saved the women," said Andre.

"No, you said something else."

Andre paused as he attempted to make Booker comfortable.

"It's nothing," said Andre.

"No, it's something. You said something about your brother going in the home. What was that about? Why did you bring that up?" asked Booker.

"I didn't say anything. Forget about it," said Andre.

"I'm not going to forget about it. Were you talking about when your house burned down, and your brother went in to get everyone out? Is that what you were talking about? I was there. I saw it just like you did. What are you thinking?" asked Booker.

Andre said nothing.

"You think I started the fire at your home. You've always thought that," said Booker.

"I don't think that. I would never think something like that, much less right now," said Andre, surprised.

"I didn't start the fire in the house. You did. You've always thought I did it. I know you do. You started the fire. I know you did."

"Shut up," said Andre loudly. Then he stopped himself. "I don't think that," he said, getting up and walking away.

"You started the fire!" said Booker, yelling at Andre as he walked away. "You started the fire! Hey you, soldier. I'm talking to you! You started that fire!"

"Shut up!" yelled Andre as he continued walked away.

Another air raid came and bombing shook the ground. Andre fell into a leafy sink hole from the blast, covering him with leaves. He was out.

The next morning, U.S. soldiers searching the area came across an unconscious Booker. The women had disappeared and Andre was still unresponsive, hidden in the darkness and leaves of the forest. As far as they knew, Booker was the only casualty in the area.

"He's still alive. Let's evacuate him immediately," said the young medic. The soldiers placed Booker on a makeshift stretcher and dragged him through the woods, loading him on a truck with the other wounded. They took Booker and the others directly to an evacuation unit.

Andre finally came around. He was covered with leaves and his leg injury was on its second day. His wound was dirty with soil and leaves, and he knew he risked an infection if he didn't get medical attention soon. He pulled himself up and walked toward the battered home. He remembered the women and Booker ... but they were gone.

He was alone.

Andre left the woods and walked toward the road. He thought to himself: *If I can find a way out down the road, maybe I can find the Allies.* Andre saw a car approaching on the road ahead and flagged it down. The driver motioned for him to get in the car and Andre entered on the passenger side. The man was with the French Resistance.

"I can take you up the road. There are Allies ahead," the Frenchman said in broken English. They only drove a few hundred feet when Germans hiding across the woods fired on them. There *were* Germans in the area, just as Andre thought last night.

"Jesus Christ!" said Andre, ducking. The Frenchman was shot and the car slowed to a stop. Andre opened the door, rolled out of the car, and crawled back to the woods. Positioned on the other side of the road, the Germans were unaware that Andre made it out and into the thick cover of trees.

The Germans approached the car and inspected inside as Andre watched from the woods. As one of the soldiers leaned in to turn the car off, his partner walked around to the other side of the car and noticed the open door. He immediately turned around and scanned the wooded area, pointing his weapon toward the trees. He knew someone had escaped.

Without warning, the sound of bombs once again shook the ground. "We have no more time. We must leave now," said one of the Germans. The men disappeared, leaving Andre gasping with relief as he leaned against the rough bark of the tree that had protected him from certain death.

Once the bombers were out of sight, Andre crept out of the woods and crawled back to the car. He looked inside; the Frenchman was dead, the cigarette still hanging between his fingers. The small ash that extended from the cigarette had not yet fallen.

Andre pulled the Frenchman over to the passenger seat. He turned the key and began to drive northward out of St. Raphael, knowing that his leg injury required immediate help.

Andre had no trouble driving down the road; none of the cars passing by suspected anything unusual. Before long, he noticed a car behind him, two uniformed Germans in the front seat.

"*My God, I'm done now*," he whispered, sweat beginning to appear on his eyebrows.

Andre took a deep breath. He would not panic, but would continue on as if nothing was wrong. He would not speed up or slow down or move to the side so that the car could pass. About a mile down the road, Andre decided to make a right turn. He pressed the blinker and turned, hoping that the Germans would not follow him. He breathed a sigh of relief when the car continued straight ahead. He was safe.

Andre got back on the road, traveling north and thinking of St. Peter's Church back in Mountain Springs. Under pressure, he was resorting to the only sense of security he possessed. Then only a short distance ahead, Andre saw a church sitting atop a hill on the outskirts of town that reminded him of St. Peter's. *Maybe that is a sign or maybe it could be headquarters for the Allies*, he thought. He heard that the Germans would sometimes seize churches, but perhaps the Allies had already reclaimed this church. He prayed for the latter; he would seek help there for his injury.

Andre pulled into the dusty driveway and drove to the back of the church, leaving the dead French Resistance fighter in the car. He went to the door where the priest resided and collapsed.

The Allies continued to fight during *Operation Dragoon* for the next seven days as they removed the Germans, fighting from camouflaged pill boxes. The towns of St. Raphael, Marseille, and Toulon were being liberated by the Allies and French with pockets of resistance.

PART 4

The Dream

CHAPTER 1

"Oh, Mon Dieu!" cried Sister Martine as she watched Andre collapse on the doorstep. She looked at Andre briefly and ran to find Father Patrick. Father Patrick's basset hound, Choupinou, heard the noise and ran to the door barking.

"Father, come! A man fainted at the door!" said Sister Martine. "It's a soldier."

Father Patrick was in his study and followed Sister Martine. The sound of bombs exploding in the distance echoed in their ears. "Choupinou assis!" said Father Patrick as he walked to the door. Choupinou stopped barking.

Father saw a soldier in military uniform lying on the ground. Fumbling for the man's dog tags, he read aloud, "*Private Andre Williams.*" The priest looked up at Sister Martine. "This is an American soldier. What is he doing here? He is injured — we need to move him inside now."

They pulled the unconscious Andre further into the church. Across the street in a French café, Vichy Lt. Kestler sat looking through the window, drinking his coffee. Kestler, a French gendarme, was the only guest at the time — the bombing caused most of the city's residents to seek shelter. Kestler flinched at the sight and sound of bombing in the distance.

Father and Sister Martine moved Andre to a spot near a bed, hoping to help him up to a more comfortable place once he awoke. Father said, "He's breathing and his pulse seem fine. Maybe he will gain consciousness soon and tell us what this is all about."

"I will go make some coffee. Perhaps the smell will wake him up."

In the kitchen, Sister Martine looked out the window and noticed Lt. Kestler walking across the street toward the church. She poured coffee into the cup and ran to the room, placing the cup under Andre's nose. Sounds of the invasion and bombings echoed through the building.

"Father, the Vichy police are coming," she said anxiously.

"Let them come," said Father Patrick.

They heard a knock at the door. Then another knock.

"Help me, Sister," groaned Father Patrick, grasping Andre under his arms and pulling him onto the bed.

There was another knock at the door.

"It appears he is not going to go away," said Sister Martine.

"Apparently not," said Father Patrick as he walked to the front door and opened it.

"Bonjour, Father. Excusez-moi, but I was wondering if you need any assistance?" offered the gendarme, tipping his hat.

Lt. Kestler opened his identification and showed it to Father Patrick. "So, you have a gentleman with you?" he inquired.

Father Patrick said nothing in response.

"You will find that I can be of excellent assistance in these kinds of matters."

"Merci." Father Patrick smiled and began to close the door.

"By the way, Father, you know the city is under attack by the enemy. I'm just checking to make sure there are no wounded soldiers in the church."

Father Patrick paused and asked cautiously, "Is there anything else?"

"No. I suppose not."

"Merci."

Father had almost closed the door when he felt the pressure of Lt. Kestler's gentle push, leaving only a few inches between the priest and the gendarme.

"Just one more thing, Father, in case you have information that might be helpful. Here is my card. Please take it."

"In case of what?" asked Father Patrick.

Lt. Kestler smiled at him as if Father Patrick were caught in a lie. "In case the man you have inside with you now is an American soldier."

Father Patrick paused, with no change in his expression. "Then I will keep your card just in case the man inside is an American soldier."

Father Patrick closed the door with a sigh of relief. He knew that the Vichy police would be back if they suspected that Allies were in the church. The south of France was not yet liberated.

Sister Martine peered through the window. “Father, the policeman is walking back to the café. I believe we are going to be watched.”

“It’s only a matter of time before he comes back with others,” said Father Patrick.

CHAPTER 2

ANDRE FELL ASLEEP in the bed, not knowing where he was or who sat by his side. Being there reminded him of home. He began to dream the story he imagined years ago ... a dream that he and Booker were rich kids attending the wealthy St. Peter's Catholic School. He dreamed that the other poor black kids in Mountain Springs were also rich and attended the same private school. All the wealthy white kids in Mountain Springs who, in reality, went to the St. Peter's Catholic school, were now poor and forced to attend a separate white public school system established just for them. He imagined Father Webster, Father Smith, Sister Camille, Sister Laurie, and Sister Aude as black priests and nuns.

"Andre is your name? What kind of name is that? Who names their kid Andre?" demanded the young Booker Thompson, a fellow student at St. Matthias Catholic School. Booker was neatly dressed in his uniform of beige pants, white shirt, blue coat, and black tie. The symbol of St. Matthias Catholic School appeared in gold stitching on the front pocket of his coat.

Andre looked at himself, dressed similarly. Where was he? He was dreaming and at this moment he was attending the wealthy Catholic school up on the hill that he remembered as St. Peter's. The old chapel was there. The large cathedral was there. There was a convent and a school, and he could see the other kids walking through the school doors on their way to class, carrying their books. The girls wore checkered dresses, white shirts underneath, and oxford shoes and socks.

Looking around, Andre couldn't believe where he was. He saw Booker and responded, "Hi, Booker."

"How do you know my name?" asked Booker.

"You wouldn't believe me if I told you," answered Andre, shaking his head. "My mother gave me the name Andre. She was from St. Martins. Her family was French and she thought it sounded good." They walked into class.

This was quite a different Booker from the one he knew in real life, Andre thought to himself. Andre realized that he was in a dream, but he could go in and out of his dream and control the dream at will. The name of the school and church in his dream was St. Matthias rather than St. Peter's.

"Well then, nice to meet you, Andre. My name's Booker Thompson."

"Nice to meet you, too," said Andre, smiling at Booker. How strange to meet a boy he had actually known all his life.

The students attended school and Mass each day and were taught by the nuns and priests. It was only a short period of time before Andre learned that the dream Booker was the same trouble-maker as the Booker of reality. Once again, Booker began to pick on Andre and enjoyed intimidating his new friend. Andre relived Booker's taunts and aggression, including the instance when Booker threw his crutch at Andre.

During Mass, when Father Webster was giving his homily, Booker pulled a pencil from the pew and stuck Andre in the back of his neck with the sharp tip. Andre turned around, and with no surprise found that the source of the attack was Booker. Andre reached for a pencil and returned the stab to Booker's thigh. Father Sanders turned around and looked at them sternly.

Father Webster continued: "In the first chapters of John, Jesus performs miraculous signs in the village of Cana. The first, of course, is his changing of water into wine at the wedding celebration. The second story relates the story of Jesus delivering a royal official's son who is on the brink of death. Both stories show that when Jesus performs a miracle, it is an invitation to belief, an opening for deeper faith."

Andre and Booker were not listening; the homily was above their heads. Only the words, and not their meaning, flowed into the boys' ears.

Father Webster continued: "Jesus said that whoever serves me must follow me. You might wonder whether Jesus was ignoring the Greeks who wanted to talk to him but could not understand him. Jesus's response is that unless a grain of wheat falls to the ground and dies, it remains just a grain of wheat; but if it dies, it produces much fruit."

Booker was drawing on a small piece of paper with his chosen weapon of the day. He didn't mind going to Mass, because he could just doodle or daydream while sitting in the pew. After the Mass concluded, Booker asked Andre, "What are Greeks?"

Booker was unkind to Father Sanders, the math teacher. Father Sanders was old and grumpy and was sometimes mean to the students himself. When the children couldn't answer his questions, he would grumble, "*Horse feathers*!" The students could hear his angry yelling through the walls of the classroom next door. The Sisters said nothing, but they knew that something was wrong and that Father Sanders was too old to continue teaching.

Once Booker placed ants in the chalk tray under the chalkboard. When Father Sanders reached for the chalk, ants crawled on to his fingers and began biting his hands.

Another time, Booker encouraged the students in the class to scoot their chairs up each time Father Sanders turned his back to write on the chalkboard.

"Let's move our chairs up every time he turns around and writes on the chalkboard," he told them. Even the girls joined in the prank. And so during math class the next day, each time Father Sanders turned around to write on the chalkboard, the class slowly moved their chairs toward the teacher.

"When you multiply 25 by 27, you multiply the bottom number by the top number..."

The class moved their chairs forward a few inches.

Father Sanders heard the noise and turned around. The class was silent and still. No one said a word. He was unaware that the students had moved.

He went back to the chalkboard and continued, "Take this number ..."

The class moved up again and the Father Sanders turned around. There was total silence. The chairs had moved up and no one said a word.

This continued as the class slowly moved their chairs up in unison, inch by inch. The first row of chairs was almost all the way up to the front of the room. Father Sanders had no space to maneuver and realized what had occurred.

He yelled, "Get your chairs back! I know what you are doing! What's wrong with you?"

Dreaming, Andre recalled the week Father Sanders died; the students were required to attend his funeral Mass. Sister Laurie gathered the eighth grade students in preparation to sing "My Shepherd Will Supply My Need."

In reality, Andre remembered his family singing this song on the day of the fire. Now the song had become mixed into his dream.

Sister Laurie looked at Andre. "Andre, you're going to have to sing the words. I don't want you up there mouthing the song," she said sternly to him.

He remembered his sister LaVonda saying the same thing on the day of the fire. His memory of the fire, when he was young, was being interspersed in his dream.

The students looked neat and clean in their uniforms. Sister Laurie smiled as they rehearsed, while the singers continued their practice until each note was correct.

Just before the Homily, Sister Laurie made her way to the piano and played the introduction. Sister Camille directed the students as they sang:

"My Shepherd will supply my need,
Jehovah is his name.
In pastures fresh he makes me feed,
Beside the living stream.
He brings my wandering spirit back
When I forsake his ways,
And leads me, for his mercy's sake,
In paths of truth and grace."

The choir of students continued singing the second and third verses while tears streamed down their faces. The students felt remorse for their treatment of Father Sanders and were fearful that Father Webster might say something about their disrespectful behavior in his homily. The nuns were not impressed. They knew how the students treated Father Sanders.

Preaching from the new St. Matthias Cathedral, Father Webster began: "Here was a man that lived his life as intended by Jesus Christ. A man who was honest, caring, charitable, cared for the poor, worked hard, had little to show for it in the end — except what he had given to Christ. He ended his life like Christ, unappreciated and rejected. He was not missed until he was gone. We do not realize how valuable a person is in our lives until they are gone. We always remember how he treated us and how we treated him. May he live his life in Heaven and in peace."

Andre, Booker, Sherry, Mary, and the other students sat in silence during the homily. They knew that Father Webster was talking directly to them; they would always regret their treatment of Father Sanders.

Afterwards, Father Webster spoke with Andre. "You will be glad you came to St. Matthias, Andre."

"I will?"

"Yes, you will. You have been given a great opportunity. You can do what you like after this."

They walked together in silence for a few steps, and then Father Webster said, "Don't worry about Father Sanders. God has taken him now. You were just kids, but that does not excuse you."

"But we knew we were wrong in the way we treated him," said Andre.

"Ask for forgiveness the next time you go to confession. Remember to give thanks in all circumstances, because that is the will of God for you. Test everything and retain what is good; refrain from all that is evil," advised Father Webster.

"I will. Father, what will you do this weekend?"

"Oh, probably travel south about fifty miles. I spend one weekend going from home to home, taking the ministry to as many families as I can. There aren't many black priests in Alabama; they are always surprised to see me. They expect to see a Baptist Minister. I have to keep up with the competition."

Andre looked up at Father Webster and smiled. "I would like to come back and work here at the school someday."

"Andre, you will probably have another life. I see you doing something else. It's not easy in the South. I see you spreading the word in some way. I'm not sure what it is, but God will lead you in the right path."

Andre's dream continued. He remembered the dance that Sister Camille mentioned that Saturday afternoon when he returned to look for her after working at the Bargain Barn.

He remembered the day he was to meet her. She wasn't there and he saw the wealthy white kids walking into the school where the dance was to be held. But this time, in his dream, he attended the school — and he and Booker were the wealthy kids. He visualized Booker as sophisticated and mild-mannered, but still with his trouble-making tendencies.

The boys wore their best suits and the girls wore their best dresses. Booker was dressed in a black suit with a white tie. Andre wore a white suit with a black tie; all the other boys were similarly dressed. The music came from a phonograph playing old music from the 1930s. Father Webster, Sister Camille, Sister Laurie, and Sister Aude chaperoned the dance.

"Isn't this wonderful?" said Sherry, perusing the room full of kids.

A new song began to play on the phonograph, and Sherry and Andre began to dance. "I sure am glad they made all the boys practice our dancing last night," said Andre. "I've never been to a dance before."

"We are high society now," said Sherry.

Over Sherry's shoulder, Andre saw Booker remove a flower from a vase and walk it over to Mary. Andre and Sherry were close enough to eavesdrop on their conversation.

"Why, thank you," Mary cooed. "I'm sure you thought about this all night."

They danced a few steps and Mary said, "My father wants to know if you'd like to come over for dinner when the school year ends."

"You told him about me?" said Booker.

"I did."

They danced a few more steps. Booker was the best dancer of the evening. His feet flowed across the dance floor with ease; it was as if he had been dancing all of his short life.

Mary looked at the floor. "I actually made that up. I want you to meet my parents," she confessed.

"Okay. I accept. What did you tell him?"

"That you are romantic, smart, intelligent, and sometimes a trouble-maker."

"So you told him the truth?" said Booker.

She touched his shoulder lightly with her hand. "Of course, I told him the truth."

Andre and Sherry danced their version of a waltz, the center of attention in the room. "I guess your parents are rich?" Sherry asked. Andre imagined the entire crowd looking at them in the middle of the dance floor.

"I don't have any parents. They're dead," said Andre.

"I'm sorry I brought that up."

"That's ok," said Andre.

"Sometimes I feel guilty being in a private school, especially when there are so many others out there who can't go to a school like this with the depression going on. I feel sorry for all those white kids who have to go to their own white public school. It's unfair the way they are treated. We get to attend this rich exclusive private school, just for us. You know they aren't getting the same kind of education we have here," said Sherry.

"I know they aren't getting the same education as we are, but I'm not sure how that is fixed. I was just lucky that we had the money to send me to this school, I guess. You know, I don't even know why I'm here. But I figure there must be a reason why I am," said Andre.

"There is a reason," said Sherry.

"*There is a reason, but I don't know what it is,*" said Andre to himself.

"What was that?" asked Sherry.

"Nothing. Sometimes I think this is a dream," said Andre.

"Andre, you know better than that. I can assure you that this is no dream," said Sherry.

Andre smiled at her. "*If only you knew*," he said to himself in a low tone.

"What was that?" asked Sherry.

"Nothing. You are right. This is not a dream," he said.

After the dance, Andre saw Booker motion to him to come up to the stage. "Stay here, Sherry. You haven't seen the second act."

Andre continued to play the guitar as he grew up, and sometimes he could get Booker to play with him. But Booker always disliked music. He endured it to satisfy Andre. Andre considered music an escape from reality.

Even in Andre's dream, the sophisticated version of Booker was disgusted that he was forced to sing with Andre — or that Andre even liked singing. Booker hated music and singing. Apparently some things do not change, even in dreams.

Andre walked over to Sister Camille and announced, "I'm going to play my song."

"You are? Wonderful!" beamed Sister Camille. Andre and Booker climbed to the stage and picked up the guitars leaning against the back wall.

Booker whispered to Andre as they were walking up to the stage, "Just tell me you're not going to play that new song you wrote that you keep playing, '*If That's How You Feel*,' or something like that. If you do, I'm going to walk off the stage. That is the worst song I've ever heard," said Booker.

Booker stepped forward on the stage as Andre strapped on his guitar. Booker grabbed the microphone, announcing,

"We'd like to play you a song that Andre Williams made up. He's always running off and playing his guitar, and no one can find him after school. He doesn't have anything else to do but play the guitar, I guess."

There was laughter.

Booker continued, "Andre wrote a song. I think you should hear it. I think it is the worst song I've ever heard."

"Booker!" fussed Sister Laurie.

The crowd laughed, and some of the kids booed.

"I'm just kidding, Sister Laurie," he said, trying to recover. But he wasn't kidding. Then he announced, "Here is Andre Williams and his new song."

"Ok. We won't do that one," Andre said, grabbing the microphone. "We are not going to do that song. Let's do '*Take the Hand*.'"

"Ok. I *will* do that one. That one's ok," said Booker in a soft voice.

"What did I hear you just say?" asked Andre into the microphone. "Did you all hear that?" Andre asked the crowd.

Someone yelled, "We did."

"I didn't say anything," said Booker. He took the microphone from Andre and said to the crowd, "Ok, we are going to do another one of Andre's songs. It's called '*Take the Hand*.'"

The crowd clapped.

Then there was a pause and Booker grabbed the microphone to pipe in, "That is his second worst song."

"Booker!" Sister Laurie rebuked him again.

The crowd laughed.

"You are impossible," said Sister Laurie, shaking her head.

The crowd laughed again.

"Just kidding again, Sister Laurie," said Booker.

Then they sang:

"There's a hand that reaches
Reaches from a heart
One that isn't able
One that doesn't know just where to start.
So it starts with the hands the one sure to tremble
Gives itself away
Strains to find a gesture
Something that the heart could easily say.

Take the hand
It would mean so much to the heart to touch you.
Play the part
Would you hold the hand and warm the heart?
And take the hand that's waiting
Open it and find
There's a heart that's reaching
There's a heart that's reaching from inside.

Take the hand that's waiting
Open it and find
There's a heart that's reaching

There's a heart that's reaching
There's a heart that's reaching
From inside."

In Andre's dream, he imagined Booker singing and dancing. But Booker would and could have done neither. His dream gave Booker talent, even when he didn't actually possess it. The students cheered, impressed with their performance. They had no idea that Booker could sing.

"That was a nice song," said Father Webster.

"Yes, it was," said Sister Laurie.

"It truly was," said Sister Aude. "You should sing that again next week in class."

"That's a good idea, Sister Aude. Andre and Booker, can you both sing that again in music class next week?" asked Sister Laurie.

"No way. I'm not singing that again. I can't believe I even got up there and sang that with Andre. I don't know how he gets me to sing with him. I think that was the worst song I have ever heard!" said Booker, walking off.

"I guess he doesn't like singing," said Father Webster.

"I would have never imagined that," said Sister Laurie as they watched Booker walk away.

After the dance Booker, Mary, Andre, and Sherry decided to walk out into the fields surrounding the campus, enjoying their success at the party. No one realized they had left the building. Andre brought his guitar with him.

"Hey," Booker said to Mary.

"Hey what?" said Mary.

"Would you like to go listen to the cotton grow?"

"Do what"?

"You know. Listen to the cotton grow?" said Booker, pointing towards the cotton fields.

"I've never done that," said Mary.

"You've never done that? I don't believe it. You'll like it," said Booker.

Mary shrugged and turned to her best friend. "Ok. Sherry, I'm going with Booker. He's taking me to hear the cotton grow, whatever that is."

Andre and Sherry walked together while they watched Booker and Mary run off into the cotton fields, laughing and talking. They could hear the couple's conversation and see Mary's long dress flying in the wind.

"Can you really hear the cotton grow? I've never heard of that before. What is it?" asked Sherry to Andre.

Andre shook his head, smiling to himself. "I can't believe he is going to do that to her."

"Do what to her?"

"Tell her to listen to the cotton grow. You can't hear cotton grow."

"What? You don't hear anything?" Sherry asked.

"Of course not. There's no such thing. You can't hear the cotton grow," said Andre.

"Well I thought it was strange, but you never know. I'd never heard of it before," Sherry said.

"He's just trying to get her alone out there. Watch, in a few minutes you'll see her get up and slap him, and then she will run off," said Andre.

"I hope he doesn't have those wrist bands with him," said Sherry.

"Oh, that hurts," said Andre, laughing.

"That was bad," said Sherry. "I can't believe he brought those up to the school and tied her to a tree. Mary fell for it. I thought she was going to kill him after that."

"What *is* bad is that I bought the love wrist bands."

"You did?"

"You didn't know that? I thought everyone knew that. I didn't get in trouble because I didn't bring them to school. Booker did," said Andre.

"You mean they were supposed to be love wrist bands to give to your girlfriend like a bracelet?" said Sherry.

"Yes. They are not to be used the way Booker used them."

"Why did you buy them?"

"I bought them for you."

"For me?"

"Yes, before you knew I liked you," said Andre. "The man at the pawn shop downtown who looks like Dracula said that you use those when you are going steady."

"So why didn't you give them to me? Why did you give them to Booker?"

"I thought you liked Booker, so I had no more use for them."

"So Booker kept them together and used them like they were handcuffs? That's just like Booker. I want to strangle him sometimes," said Sherry.

Andre and Sherry talked to each other as they walked into the field, watching Booker and Mary running up ahead. Booker and Mary disappeared into the cotton.

Booker said, "Ok, Mary, now get down on the ground and put your ear right here." He demonstrated and she obeyed.

"I don't hear anything?"

"Keep listening."

"I still don't hear anything," said Mary.

Booker gave Mary a long kiss. "That is the sound of cotton growing," said Booker seriously.

"I never understood how cotton grew until tonight." Then she paused and looked at Booker.

Mary got up and brushed the dirt off of her dress. She looked at Booker and said, "Well, I think the cotton has gotten a little taller. I'm going back to the campus. I don't want to be seen with you. The nuns will start to ask questions."

Mary left, leaving Booker alone … listening to the cotton grow. She was going to get back to the school before curfew.

Booker looked at her as she ran off.

"Wha'd I do?" he yelled. Mary looked back at him and smiled as she ran across the cotton field, her long white gown flowing in the wind.

Booker smiled as he watched Mary run back to the school. It would take a lot more than watching the cotton grow for him to get Mary.

Andre and Sherry continued to walk. Andre's guitar was behind his back, hanging by a shoulder strap.

Booker and Mary were far in the distance. They watched Mary get up and run back to the school. "See there? Just like I predicted," said Andre.

"Now that's funny," said Sherry.

"Sherry, look over there," Andre said, pointing to a cleared piece of land ahead. "That's where my parents' home was."

"The one that burned down?" she asked reluctantly.

"Yes, there isn't anything left," said Andre.

"Booker said you accidentally started the fire in the attic," said Sherry.

"What?" said Andre, stopping in his tracks.

"That's what he said."

"He said that? That idiot. I did *not* start the fire in the house. He started it."

"We don't have to talk about it. I shouldn't have said that. He told me not to tell you. I guess I wanted to know what the truth was."

"I didn't start the fire," said Andre. He was upset.

Bringing up the fire at that moment was like piercing his heart with a knife. That was the worst thing Booker could have said. Nothing was more off limits than that. Sherry had no idea how devastating such a suggestion was to him.

"Do you want to go over there? I will if you will, but don't feel like you have to," she said.

"Let's go over there," Andre said.

"Ok," said Sherry.

As they got closer to the area, Andre was hurting. They reached the area where the house had been located, and there was nothing left. Andre recalled the day of the fire to Sherry with agonizing difficulty.

"Let's go back," he said.

After walking a short distance, Andre said, "I just thought of something. Listen to this."

Andre pulled his guitar around and began to strum the chords to the song that his brother taught him on the day of the fire. He never finished the entire song, but Andre kept the original sheet of paper with the words and chords on it from the day his life changed forever. It was the only thing he had left from inside the home. He knew the song by heart. He played and sang the song to Sherry:

"Please don't look at me that way, I can
hardly say what I have to say,
There is nothing that I haven't told to you
that I didn't believe you knew.
I am thinking of another time I could feel
you thinking that you were mine.
Now I hold out my hands 'til my arms get
tired and you wait on the other side.
You and me, we're both the same, don't let me take all the blame,
I promise that I will do all it takes to make up for my mistakes.
So, I'm trying hard to be the man and it's
not a hard thing to understand,

For I think that my being would cease to
be if you didn't believe in me,
If you didn't believe in me."

"That's beautiful," said Sherry. "Did you write that?"

"It was my brother's. He was singing it the day of the fire. I can hear bells in the last line, like the ones they use at church."

They walked back to the school.

"You are trying to make up for your mistakes. What mistakes are those?" asked Sherry.

"I have plenty of mistakes, I guess," said Andre.

"You want me to believe in you?"

Andre stopped and looked at her. "Yes, I need you to believe in me. I need a window to the future, so I can move on."

"I believe you," said Sherry. "I can be your window to the future. You can be my dreamer."

Andre kissed Sherry.

Andre's dream was quite a fantasy for the 1930s.

CHAPTER 3

Sister Martine came in to check on Andre. She looked at him resting. He seemed to be smiling while he was asleep.

"Whoever he is, this man must be important to them," she said.

Father Patrick scratched his chin. "We don't know that. If Vichy knew something about him, they would have already taken him. For all they know, he is just another lost parishioner."

Father Patrick returned to his study while Sister Martine kept watch. Andre awoke an hour later. "Bonjour," said Sister Martine, still sitting by his side.

"Who are you? Where am I?" asked Andre. "I must have been dreaming."

"You are at the Church of the Immaculate Conception in St. Raphael. Shouldn't you be with your forces?" asked Sister Martine.

"I've been separated from my platoon for a almost a week. I came in the south of France with the invasion, and our ship was attacked. We had to swim ashore. Some of the troops were reunited, and some of the others were told to go another direction."

"What happened to them?"

"They were shot. I made it up here with the help of the French Resistance."

"Why did you come to our church?" asked Sister Martine curiously.

"To seek help. I need to get back to my platoon."

"Where are you from?" she asked gently.

"Alabama," he answered. "I like this place. It reminds me of where I grew up. I knew a Sister there who reminds me of you. I just woke up, but in my dream I was attending the school there — it was a school I always wanted to attend. In my dream, all the black kids were wealthy and the white kids were poor."

"What was the name of the school?"

"I called it 'St. Matthias Catholic School' when I was dreaming about it. That wasn't its real name. It was actually for the rich white kids."

Sister Martine, not being fluent in English, misunderstood what Andre said to her. She thought Andre said that he had attended a school for wealthy black students called St. Matthias Catholic School.

Sister Martine was somewhat familiar with the South in the United States. She had heard of the segregation that prevailed in the South, and the poverty and poor conditions suffered by both black and white citizens following a major depression. She was surprised to hear there was a private Catholic school for black students. It seemed very unusual for the time, especially in the United States. In her confusion, she misunderstood that Andre was only relaying a dream.

Sister Martine opened the door to Father Patrick's study and closed the door behind her. She breathed a sigh of exasperation as she sat in the chair facing his desk.

"Father, I spoke to the Negro American soldier. He didn't say much except something about attending a rich school for black Catholic students in Alabama."

Father Patrick looked surprised. "I didn't realize there were many Negro Catholics in Alabama. That's quite curious. What did he say was the name of the school?"

"He said St. Matthias," repeated Sister Martine.

"I can tell you that there's no church by that name. That's a dead giveaway," said Father Patrick. "They aren't going to name a church after the thirteenth apostle before naming the first twelve apostles."

Father Patrick began thumbing through some material to see if he could find a church by that name in the United States. He drummed his fingers on the desk. "St. Matthias, St. Matthias ... I doubt there's a school there by that name, but you never know."

The priest checked his watch. "It's almost eleven forty. Let's see if he's well enough to go to Mass."

"Do you think anyone will attend Mass with the invasion in progress?" asked Sister Martine.

"Who knows? Life goes on," said Father Patrick.

Sister Martine found Andre sitting on his bed. "Private, we would like to invite you to Mass, if you feel well enough."

"I would like to go. Do you think the Father will take my confession?"

"Of course, he will. The confession will follow Mass."

Father Patrick performed the noon Mass for the twenty faithful in the pews. Andre was physically unable to make the walk down the aisle for the Eucharist, so Father came to Andre's pew and offered the bread to Andre.

"The Body of Christ."

Andre took the bread and said, "Amen."

Lt. Kestler was not one to be sidetracked. Still curious about the presence of the mysterious soldier, he decided to walk around the perimeter of the church during Mass. As he walked toward the back of the church, an unfamiliar parked car with a man sitting in the passenger seat caught his attention. Kestler tapped on the window, and when the man did not respond, opened the door. The Frenchman's body tumbled to the ground, his body was covered with bullet wounds and dried blood. Kestler checked his pulse — nothing. Immediately the gendarme knew that the man was with the French Resistance, and the church was hiding an Allied soldier.

Now with the backup of additional Vichy police, Kestler returned to the church and entered through the main doors. Andre was sitting in a pew at the back of the church where Father Patrick was talking to him. The gendarme wrapped his fingers around Andre's upper arm.

"Thank you for your assistance, Father. We will be taking custody of him now," said Kestler. Father Patrick watched with surprise and concern as the police grabbed Andre and took him out of the church.

It was only a matter of time before the Allies captured St. Raphael. Andre was released and transported back to a ship off the coast for medical treatment. Paris was finally being liberated, and the Allies would operate in Paris through the end of the war. Andre was sent to Paris to recover, while Army Judge Advocate General (JAG) began an investigation into the shooting of Booker, as well as Andre's capture.

CHAPTER 4

THE ALLIES RACED towards central France, imprisoning thousands of German captives during its march to Paris. Meanwhile, General Montgomery held the Germans immobile in the northeastern front of France. And on August 25, 1944, von Cholititz, the German garrison and military governor of Paris, surrendered at the Hotel Meurice, new headquarters of General Leclerc.

Maj. Lee, Oliver, and Cub followed in their jeep behind the convoy bringing de Gaulle into Paris. Other reporters rode in the convoy, including journalist Helen Kirkpatrick, who was riding with the tanks of General Leclerc's 2nd Armored Division. Thousands of dignitaries and journalists were converging on Paris.

De Gaulle was escorted into Paris, where he made a rousing speech at the Hotel de Ville:

> "*Why do you wish us to hide the emotion which seizes us all, men and women, who are here at home, in Paris that stood up to liberate itself and that succeeded in doing this with its own hands? No! We will not hide this deep*

> *and sacred emotion. These are minutes which go beyond each of our poor lives. Paris! Paris outraged! Paris broken! Paris martyred! But Paris liberated! Liberated by itself, liberated by its people with the help of French armies, with the support and the help of all France, of the France that fights, of the only France, of the real France, of the eternal France!*"

Following the speech, a thanksgiving Mass was to be held at Notre Dame Cathedral to honor the resistance fighters. De Gaulle would be in attendance. Helen Kirkpatrick was determined to cover de Gaulle's entrance into the church. She climbed the surrounding fence and made her way into the cathedral behind the police following de Gaulle. The police held the crowds back so that de Gaulle could enter the church. As soon as de Gaulle entered the cathedral, bullets peppered the pavement behind him and Kirkpatrick and others were shoved into the church. It was dark inside Notre Dame, and she was only a few feet behind de Gaulle when machine gun fire erupted, killing the man next to her and hitting the stone pillar to her left. The French police fired back and apprehended the man. The people were chanting, "*Vive la France! Vive les Etats-Unis!*" Gun fire could still be heard in the distance, either in celebration or response from the last remaining pockets of resistance.

CHAPTER 5

Maj. Lee drove Oliver and Cub to the Avenue de Fontainebleau, where they saw overturned vehicles as well as makeshift barricades of sandbags and cars. Dummy Germans were hanging in effigy. The reporters noted that the Parisians had already begun making repairs in some areas; all signs of organized resistance had ended, and the Americans and armored vehicles were in control of certain areas. The fighting French of the Interior had taken charge of the other areas.

"You will like Paris after we get it cleared," said Maj. Lee, driving them through the streets outside the city. The sky over Paris was hazy and gray; small rain drops peppered their jackets. The wind was blowing hard. Oliver sat in the front seat, and Cub was crammed in the back among all the bags. They held on to their hats as Lee whisked them through the city.

"I'm going to stop here. I think it's safe," said Lee. "You can walk around safely and mingle with the crowds. They are very appreciative."

Oliver and Cub were barely out of the jeep when French women began to surround and kiss them on both cheeks, as if *they* were the liberators. Oliver felt as though he was being given credit for the entire U.S. military liberation of Paris. The French women did not care who these men actually were; they were grateful, happy, and relieved. Loud cheers from the crowd gave the area a parade-like atmosphere.

"I wonder if Nelms would suspect what we are doing now? I think I'm going to like this assignment," laughed Cub.

Ernie Pyle entered Paris in a jeep with Henry Gorrell of the United Press, Capt. Carl Pergler of Washington, D.C., and Corp. Alexander Belon of Amherst, Massachusetts. They were kissed until they were red in the face. Pyle wrote:

> *Once when the jeep was simply swamped in human traffic and had to stop, we were swarmed over and hugged and kissed and torn at. Everybody, even beautiful girls, insisted on kissing you on both cheeks. Somehow I got started kissing babies that were held up by their parents, and for a while I looked like a baby-kissing politician going down the street. The fact that I hadn't shaved for days, and was gray-bearded as well as bald-headed, made no difference. Once we came to a stop, some Frenchman told us there were still snipers shooting, so we put our steel helmets back on.*[35]

As Oliver and Cub walked down the sidewalk, more and more French citizens streamed out of the buildings to kiss them. Lee watched, smiling and taking advantage of the boondoggle he had received in his assignment to drive two journalists around Paris.

Lee drove the reporters to the Hotel Scribe, headquarters of the Allied Press. The censors were present but were not currently in business, and the Western Union office was not yet up and running. There were a dozen or more reporters waiting to send stories — with or without a censor's stamp.

The men watched the commotion through the window as throngs of people continued cheering through the streets.

"Can you believe we are here and covering this story?" Oliver asked, not quite believing the scene himself.

"I have never been kissed so much in my life!" said Cub.

"Me neither," said Oliver. "I think I might move here!"

The men heard more commotion, but all they could see were people running into the street, still cheering. They had no idea what was going on.

"Let's get you back into the vehicle. I'm going to take you to your hotel," Lee said.

"Can you drive us around to other parts of the city?" Oliver inquired.

"Ok, but not too far."

Lee took them further into Paris, where things were not so calm. As they reached an intersection, machine gun fire sprayed across the jeep. Lee stopped the vehicle. The men ducked when they heard gunfire coming from another direction.

"Get out and get behind the vehicle!" Lee shouted as he pulled his weapon. Oliver and Cub complied, bending down as low as possible. The firing stopped, and it became quiet. Sheets of paper floated in the wind down the middle of the street. The rain had stopped.

After a moment, Lee told them: "I can't take you any further. I can't be responsible for you this far out. It looks like the city is still not secure in some areas."

They waited a few more minutes, then more gunfire shot across the intersection. Lee remained calm and did not return fire; there was no target. In the background they could hear a baby crying, followed by more rifle and pistol firings. A grenade exploded nearby. It was quiet afterwards.

"We've gone in so deep, I might not be able to get you out. We need to go. Get in the jeep — we are turning around," ordered Lee.

After passing through a check point, Lee drove them to the Scribe Hotel, where the press set up their headquarters. Lee helped the reporters get their bags out of the jeep. "I hope you don't think that I surrendered back there by not taking you any further into Paris," he said. "If you had been injured, it would be my hide."

"Thanks," said Oliver. "We understand. Major, where are you from? I'd like to mention you in the newspaper."

"I'm from Virginia, but I don't think I'm the right color to be included in your reports on the black soldiers over here. You sure you want to include me?"

"Sure I do, Maj. Jonah Lee. I will, however, note that you are white guy," teased Oliver.

Lee smiled.

"Thank you, Major," said Cub. "I feel like we are army buddies."

"We are. You are welcome. You two take care," said Lee.

Oliver checked into his room and looked out the window. The people were still on the streets, celebrating noisily. He lay down on his bed and wrote in his journal, recording his trip through France to Paris:

> *The first time I saw Paris her heart was old, and she was not very well fed, but oh, how gay! The heart of France, in fact, was mad with joy, because Americans had arrived. I met the first American soldiers to enter the city of Paris. They were members of the company of drivers, who were especially chosen on this occasion to drive Gen. de Gaulle's party into the liberated French capital. Our arrival concluded three days and nights of camping on the outskirts of the city, waiting the mopping up the last pockets of German resistance. Along the broad boulevards, we saw many vehicles overturned and sandbagged, which the enemy had used as barricades in their last stand, but in a few places where road blocks had been, we saw workmen already making repairs.*
>
> *Dummy Germans were hanged in effigy in two places, but all signs of organized resistance had disappeared. Americans in armored vehicles were in control of certain areas, in others FFI (Fighting French of the Interior) were in charge. Beautiful women dashed into the streets to kiss dusty GI lads, to throw flowers and to offer wine and fruit.*

> *I have never been kissed so much in all my life. Almost every woman I meet on the street stops and kisses me on both cheeks. It is a beautiful custom. At least a dozen women brought their babies and children up to us to be kissed. I felt like a small-time politician running for Congress — and if I ever run for any office, I will be rather experienced in this kissing business. Thousands of bicycles filled the boulevards, and crowds lined the streets to wave and shout welcome.*[36]

Paris was liberated. Free. And the city was finally quiet.

CHAPTER 6

ONCE PARIS WAS safe, Mary Welsh convinced the *Times* to let her travel by plane to a military base at Argentan. From there, she found a reluctant army major who drove her to Paris in a jeep. He was unfamiliar with the maps, but Welsh could speak French and was more accustomed to the country's roads. On the drive to Paris, Welsh frequently reminded the major to drive on the right side of the road. Finally, she convinced him to let her take the wheel. Stopping at a café along the way, she and the uniformed major were greeted by the restaurant owner with, "*Liberte, egalite, fraternite*!" and presented with many wet kisses.[37]

In Paris, Welsh found Hemingway at the Hotel Ritz. Wearing her uniform and white gloves, Welsh was directed to Room 31 by the concierge. Mary knocked on the door and was greeted by Private First Class Archie Pelkey.

"Is Mr. Hemingway here?" she asked.

"Papa, there's a dame here," he yelled into the room.

Hemingway came to the door, welcoming Welsh with a merry-go-round bear hug, her feet nearly crashing into the walls. "Oh, my pickle!" he said as he twirled her around.

"Did you receive my letter?" she said, her arms around his neck.

"Yes I did, and I read it every day until I lost it," he said.

As he put her down, Mary glanced around the room. Members of the French underground militia whom Hemingway had befriended in Rambouillet were sitting on the floor, barefoot and cleaning their weapons. A tray of champagne rested on a table in front of the French windows, a sign of celebration. After cleaning his weapon, one of the men lay down on one of the twin beds; his war-torn boots were carelessly plopped on the pink satin coverlet.

Welsh and Hemingway spent the next week together in the hotel and traveling around Paris.

One morning Hemingway's friend Marlene Dietrich, who was also staying in the hotel, came to visit Hemingway. They had been friends since the 1930s when they met on a ship heading to America. He was like a father to her and she was like a daughter to him, yet he was only three years older than she.

"Ah, my little Kraut. You are getting so beautiful they will have to make passport pictures of you nine feet tall."[38]

"Oh Papa, I never know what you will say or write. That's what fascinates me about you. I love you, but we could never be lovers."

"And I love you, too. Let me take your overcoat."

Hemingway noticed that Marlene was dressed in a white tuxedo with a black tie.

"You are out of uniform. But you are always so well dressed."

"I dress for myself. Not for the image, not for the public, not for the fashion, not for men,"[39] she said as Hemingway carried her coat to the closet.

"I'm about to shave, if you don't mind. Mary is still asleep."

"I don't mind. I will follow you."

Entering the bathroom, Hemingway resumed shaving and Dietrich confirmed the bathroom's cleanliness before sitting on the edge of the bathtub.

"You know I like everything clean. I'm a freak about that," she said.

Hemingway hummed to himself while Dietrich took in the moment, realizing she was with one of the most famous American writers. Her bond with him was like no other. Then she began to sing:

"Falling in love again ..."

"Are you doing that number on the USO tours?" Hemingway asked, interrupting her before she could finish the song.

"Yes. I've been through Algeria, Italy, Britain, and now France. I sat on a piano in Italy, singing it while the pianist accompanied me for the troops."

"It reminds me of *The Blue Angel.* What happened after that? Were you offered a contract?" asked Hemingway.

"I did have a contract. There was an option but the option was not picked up."[40]

"Did that bother you?" he asked.

"No," she said. "How could it bother me?"

"When did you learn that *The Blue Angel* was a success? Right afterwards?" he asked. He paused and turned to look at her curiously.

"No, no. I was on the ship going to America. Why are you asking me these questions?"

"I'm still a journalist. It's my business."

"I received cables and they said that I had a big success. I never thought I would have. You know I was a star in the film, you know that. Well, you don't know that."

"I do know that."

"You don't know that. I was a star in the film. It said: *Emil Jannings in The Blue Angel*, and then came all the names of all the actors and I was on the bottom of the list. And now everyone thinks I was a star in the film, but I wasn't."

"You *were* the star in the film." Hemingway turned around to look at her. "You have been praised by the greatest of those in the arts, by presidents, international leaders, and critics. But it was the troops here whom you have touched that matter the most. You have graced the lives of soldiers whose pain and anguish are relieved for those brief moments because of your presence and glamour. Their despair has been uplifted. You stand for beauty, sensitivity, and justice."[41]

Marlene looked at him with amazement. "I do love you, Ernest."

Mary awoke and padded to the bathroom. "Well, good morning. I thought I heard singing."

"Yes, I was falling in love again," said Marlene.

"Love has always been your game," said Mary. "Marlene, did you know that Ernest can sing? He can sing '*I Don't Know Why, I Love You Like I Do*,' even though he is a bit off-key sometimes."

"Anything you say, my pickle," said Ernest, turning back to shave.

"His favorite song is '*Aupres de ma blond, qu'il fait beau, fait beau, fait beau*,'" said Mary.

"Yes, I know Papa can sing," said Marlene.

"Can you sing that?" asked Mary to Ernest.

"I don't think you want to hear me sing," he said, putting the razor under the tap to wash it off.

"Sure, I do. Sure, *we* do. I will sing with you," said Mary.

"You want to hear me sing?" said Ernest. "I've been known to belt out a song."

Then, with Mary singing alto harmony, Ernest performed with gusto his version of the old French song:

"Apres la guerre finie.
Tous les soldats partis,
Mademoiselle a une souvenir
Apres la guerre finie." [42]

CHAPTER 7

On August 27, 1944, hundreds of young soldiers stood on the stern deck of the *H.M.S. Esperance Bay*, a British transport ship leaving New York City. The troops took their last look at the Statue of Liberty and watched her head disappear behind the New York skyline as they departed. The men were embarking on the greatest adventure of a lifetime.

Nelms reported the story, but he needed Oliver to return; the reporter had been gone over two years. Cub was sent to replace him, but Oliver wouldn't leave just yet. With Tatiana in Paris now, Oliver decided he would stay in France a little longer. He would rather stay in Paris than go back to the paper — the war wasn't over yet.

Cub heard that the 761st would enter the theater at some point. They would be the first black mechanized soldiers to fight for the United States. He would cover them if they came to the theater in France.

On August 31st, the Third Army's advance across Southern France came to a halt when it ran out of gas. They had raced two hundred miles westward at Avranches to the port of Brest, a feat accomplished in only six days. Patton hoped to reach Germany in September before the Germans could regroup. By now, the Allies had liberated more than fifty thousand square miles of territory.

The *H.M.S. Esperance Bay* ported in England on September 8, 1944. The 761st would spend another month training and being issued new Sherman tanks with 76mm guns before crossing the English Channel to France. They would follow the invasion into France and Germany as the Allies headed towards Berlin.

In the same month, "Murrow's Boys" Bill Downs and Walter Cronkite were stranded near the front lines in the Netherlands during the *Battle of Arnhem*, which lasted from September 17 through September 26, 1944, in the towns of Arnhem, Oosterbeek, Wolfheze, and Driel, as well as the countryside. After the reporters became separated in the dense forest, Cronkite concluded Downs was dead and made his way back to Allied territory in Brussels, where he happily discovered Downs at the Hotel Metropole.

"Why didn't you search for me before returning to Brussels?" asked Cronkite angrily.

"Are you nuts?" said Downs. "Going through those woods shouting 'Cronkite, Cronkite' — I'd have ended up in a Berlin hospital."

"Why?" asked Cronkite.

"The word 'Cronkite' sounds like the German word for 'sickness'. I didn't want to be taken to a Berlin hospital," explained Downs.

Cronkite laughed.[43]

CHAPTER 8

At the JAG headquarters in Paris, Army Colonel David Martins was settling into his newly assigned office, where the army JAG offices would locate through the end of the war. Colonel Martins was well respected; everyone knew he would make brigadier. It was just a matter of time.

"Captain," Martins said, looking at Capt. Jesse Weinstein, "I want you to check the story of a Private Williams coming off of *Operation Dragoon.* He turned up wounded at a Catholic church in St. Raphael with a dead member of the French Resistance. He was captured by Vichy police and was recaptured after St. Raphael was liberated. I want you to find out why the soldier was at the church, and why he was not with his platoon. He was in medical in Paris but has been released. We need to decide whether he can be sent back to the front. If not, you will represent him if he needs it. We can't spare a single man."

"Yes, sir," said Weinstein.

"Capt. Thomas, a Private Thompson was found by our troops in the woods, not far from St. Raphael. He was also part of *Operation Dragoon.* He was shot in the back and admitted to the hospital here. They removed the bullet, and it appears to be from an American weapon. Find out why he was shot in the back by one of our weapons. It was probably friendly fire," said Col. Martins. "His injury is too severe, so he will be sent home as soon as he is able."

"Yes, sir," said Thomas.

"Both of the soldiers came off of the same ship — the LST 281 that was attacked during *Operation Dragoon.* They were probably separated from their platoon," said Martins.

"Yes, sir," said Thomas.

Army Captains John Thomas and Jesse Weinstein would soon find themselves on opposite sides. They were Army Reserve Judge Advocate General officers (JAG), activated during the war in 1942. They had worked together in the same office for the past six months. They were not friends, but the men tolerated each other. They were from very different backgrounds.

Thomas was a JAG attorney, licensed in New York and California. He was competitive and wanted to rise professionally after the war by using his service as a springboard to something better. Perhaps a federal position after the war, he thought. He was raised in Lumley County, Alabama, one county over from Haley County where Booker and Andrew grew up. He knew the country well, having grown up in Alabama. He was familiar with Mountain Springs and had been there many times. He was also familiar with St. Peter's Catholic Church and its origin. After graduating from Montgomery Law School in 1933, Thomas took a job with the Department of Justice and spent time in New York and

California, obtaining licensure in both states. He considered himself important; Thomas was known to be arrogant and unable to admit a mistake. He always had an excuse for his behavior.

Thomas wasn't adept with administrative tasks. After leaving New York for California, he wanted to keep his licenses current in both states but forgot to pay his New York bar dues for several consecutive years. Shortly before being recalled to the war, he found himself in an embarrassing situation. His name was posted in the New York Bar Journal, on notice of his suspension from practicing law in that state. He was reinstated only after an investigation. The attorney for the New York Bar recommended that Thomas not be required to re-take the New York bar exam and that he had "good cause" due to his recall into the service. It was an embarrassment for his name to be listed in the bar journal of that state. This information inevitably made its way through to those in the Justice Department who read the publication. Some thought it was humorous that Thomas found himself in this situation. The man who always had an excuse couldn't wiggle his way out of this one, but he managed to land on his feet as he always did. For a while he was the butt of jokes, but interest in the mishap eventually died down.

Capt. Weinstein knew of this story, having read it in a bar journal that someone left in the JAG offices. Weinstein came to loathe Thomas at times. He particularly disliked Thomas's elitist attitude. Thomas behaved as if DOJ attorneys were somehow superior to state prosecutors.

Weinstein grew up in Lee County, Illinois, on a farm not far from the city of Dixon. He was from a devout Jewish family. Weinstein earned his law degree in 1940 from the College of Law at the University of Northern Illinois. After law school, he took a job as an assistant district attorney in Lee County to be close to home. He married a girl from Dixon during law school. They wanted to live and start a family where they grew up.

During law school, Weinstein joined the JAG Corp for extra pay. He spent six months on active duty after law school and reported to a reserve unit in Chicago. Then he was activated after the war began. He spent only a year and a half as a prosecutor, handling misdemeanor cases before being recalled. He had never tried a felony case.

During his short stint with the Lee County DA's office, Weinstein learned that state criminal trial law was not what he wanted to do for the rest of his career. But he appreciated the trial experience the DA's office gave him, and he enjoyed his work with the JAG Corp better than the DA's office. After the war, he decided he would look for a job with a private law firm and keep his reserve commission active.

Weinstein was not competitive like Thomas, but he was more creative and marched to the beat of his own drum, working in his own world. Not being from the deep South, working on the case involving Andre and Booker was something new for him.

CHAPTER 9

Oliver went to see Maj. Lee in the new spaces for Public Affairs.

"Lee, how are things here in your new offices?"

"Working out fine. How is the reporting on the black soldier coming along, now that you are in France? Not quite as difficult now, is it?" said Lee.

"It isn't. Cub is waiting for the 761st tank battalion to arrive in theater. They will be the first black mechanized battalion in battle. I was wondering if you possibly have any information on any soldiers we might be able to interview," asked Oliver.

"As a matter of fact, I do," said Lee. "There is a Private Booker Thompson in a medical facility here now. He just came off of *Operation Dragoon* and was injured near St. Raphael."

"That sounds like the soldier I met on the ship in London and in Africa. Where is he from?" asked Oliver.

"Says here, Alabama. Mountain Springs, Alabama," said Lee, reading from his file.

"That's him. I'm on my way," said Oliver.

Oliver went to the medical facility set up for the Allies in Paris. He stopped at the front desk to ask permission.

"I'm Oliver Smith, with the press. I'd like to interview the soldiers for stories back home. I promise not to talk to them if they don't want to talk."

"That's fine. You have press credentials." The private waved Oliver through.

Oliver spoke to each soldier and inquired of each about their injuries. Finally he ran across Private Thompson, who agreed to talk with him. Oliver recognized Booker immediately and sat down in the chair next to his bed. "Private Thompson, do you remember me? Oliver Smith, *Birmingham Defender*. We met in London and in Africa. How are you doing?"

"I'm ok."

"What happened to you?"

"It was nothing."

"What do you mean nothing? You were shot in the back. I want to write a story about you."

"No. Don't write anything."

"Why?"

"Because it's not worth it," said Booker.

"You've been fighting for over two years. What do you mean it's not worth it? Of course it's worth it."

"No, it's not. It's not worth destroying another man's life."

"What's not worth destroying another man's life?"

"I wasn't injured by the Germans."

"I'm sorry. Was it friendly fire?"

Booker paused. "Yes, it was friendly fire. That's how to report it. Report it as friendly fire." Thompson explained that he and Private Williams were separated from their platoon during the fighting in *Operation Dragoon* and had made their way north on foot. He remembered seeing a home with two women. He told Oliver that he asked the women for help, when one of the ladies started screaming wildly at him. The other had a rake and began to beat him with it. Booker was trying to calm her down and subdue her and pushed her toward a tree when the bombing happened. A shot rang out, and a bullet hit him in the back.

Booker stared at the wall and stopped speaking.

"You say that you were shot, but it was not by the Germans?" asked Oliver.

"Yes. It was an accident. My friend Andre Williams accidentally shot me while shooting at some Germans."

"That's unfortunate." Oliver wrote down Booker's account of the incident in his notebook. "I'm sorry about your injury. You have served your country honorably and will be rewarded greatly for it."

CHAPTER 10

Oliver went back to JAG headquarters to see Maj. Lee.

"Major, I just came back from the medical facility. I visited with Private Booker Thompson. Do you remember him?"

"I don't," said Lee.

"He was on the same ship we were on in June of '42. He served in North Africa, Sicily, Italy, and was injured in St. Raphael during *Operation Dragoon*. Do you have any information that you can give me for a press release?"

"I was going to tell you that you can write about his experience here, but nothing else," said Lee.

"What do you mean?" asked Oliver.

"I can't talk about pending cases. His case is under investigation."

Oliver paused. "What are you talking about, pending cases? I just went over there to interview him about his war service for a press release about his service back home. He's from Alabama."

"Did he tell you how he was injured?" asked Lee.

"Yes. He says he wasn't injured by the enemy. He was shot by another American soldier by accident."

"I know," said Lee. "He was found alone under a tree. Looks like someone was taking care of him. He had a bullet in his back. It turned out to be an American bullet from his battle buddy, Private Andre Williams."

"I know Private Williams," said Oliver. "He and Thompson were in boot camp together. They grew up together."

"Thompson was up for a Purple Heart until medical discovered that piece of information. We were just checking to make sure he is eligible for a Purple Heart, and whether the wound is from friendly fire. His award is on hold for now until we clear up what happened to him. We can't write up an award if we don't know the circumstances. He's been injured in other ways as well from the operation, but it won't take much time to clear this up. We are hoping we can get him well enough to travel home."

"Where is the other soldier? Private Williams?" asked Oliver.

"He was in medical for injuries as well, but he's probably out by now. And I have something else for you," said Lee.

"What's that?" asked Oliver.

"A few Tuskegee Airmen were shot down prior to *Operation Dragoon* when they attacked Toulon Harbor. Says here that a Maj. Alexander Jefferson from Detroit, Michigan, was captured. We don't know what happened. Another plane was shot down and the pilot landed his plane at sea. We think they were captured by the Germans and are headed to some German prison camp. There was no sign of them afterwards," said Lee.

"Thanks, I will look into the story," said Oliver. "This will be a first about a captured Tuskegee Airmen, prisoner of war. Let me know if you find out anything else about him," said Oliver.

"Roger that," said Lee.

CHAPTER 11

Colonel Dixon had Tatiana assigned to the Canadian Army; she would follow them into Rouen, France. The Canadians liberated Rouen by August 30, 1944. The city was heavily damaged by bombings and a fire that the Germans would not allow the French to extinguish. Tatiana was shocked by the extent of the damage. It seemed a strange coincidence that this was the city where Joan of Arc died, burning at the stake.

From Rouen, Tatiana traveled to Paris, escorted in a jeep by an army major to the Scribe Hotel. There, she would meet up with the other journalists. Oliver and Cub happened to be coming down to the front desk as she was checking in. She was standing at the front desk in her brown army uniform and white gloves.

"Tatiana!" said Oliver, pleasantly surprised. "How did you get here? You look great in the uniform." Oliver gave her a hug. "Let me look at you. You look wonderful."

"Long story, but Colonel Dixon got me credentialed, and I was able to follow the Canadian Army to Rouen. Well, hello Cub!" she greeted the other journalist.

"Hi, Major Phillips. Nice uniform," said Cub.

Tatiana put her arms around both men. "We need to meet up to compare notes. Let's dine together after we settle in," said Tatiana. "Did you boys have a rough time getting here?"

"We had a few interesting nights together on the way to Paris," said Cub.

Oliver looked Tatiana over. "I see you've recovered from your illness," he said.

"Yes. It was just a matter of days before I was out of the hospital, but I was not allowed to travel to France with the invasion. I've been reporting from London. I think Colonel Dixon and Public Affairs were glad to get rid of me. I was making their lives miserable."

Oliver looked at his watch. "There are morning briefings at 7 a.m. — we were just on our way. If you hurry, you can make it. You can come with us. It's just about a fifteen-minute walk. Everyone walks everywhere in Paris," he said.

"I'm so exhausted," sighed Tatiana.

"Just leave your bags here at the front desk and come with us. You can pick them up when you come back," suggested Oliver.

"Oh, ok. I'm ready now," she said.

It was an enjoyable walk to the Public Affairs Office. The streets were busy and people were outside cleaning the sidewalks, opening their stores. The trio could see the Eiffel Tower in the background; they walked past Notre Dame and crossed over the Seine River on their way to Public Affairs. Looking to their right, they saw 27 rue de Fleures.

"Oliver, I meant to tell you that I enjoyed your story about Josephine Baker in Casablanca. Was she over there recovering? What made you write about her?" asked Tatiana.

"I heard about her while I was there," he said.

"What angle were you covering?" asked Tatiana.

"Just that she was a famous celebrity from America," said Oliver.

"That's interesting. Some people say that she was there to help the Allies. That she was a spy. I assumed that's why you were covering the story."

Oliver was stunned but didn't say anything. That *did* make sense. Baker must have been in Casablanca supporting the Allies. She agreed to meet with the press to make the story appear that her presence there was nothing more than just about being a performer. While Oliver thought he landed a great story, Baker had used him to give her cover. Now he realized that he needed to probe his interviews better to find the purpose of the article. Anyone can write a story, but what is important is the *purpose* of the story. What makes a story a story? What makes it relevant as opposed to just words on a paper, printed to read? *Keep pushing and you will get the real story*, he told himself.

"You are right. She was there for some reason," said Oliver.

"I liked what you wrote. '*With a gay smile and a French accent ... her face uplifted toward the eternal snows of the nearby Atlas peaks.*' How romantic," Tatiana said.

Oliver stopped, smiled, and pointed ahead. "This is where it started. You should have seen the entrance of de Gaulle into Paris. The crowd was overwhelming. The women were kissing us all over the place," said Oliver.

"I can only imagine," grinned Tatiana.

Oliver smiled back at her.

CHAPTER 12

Tatiana, Cub, and Oliver walked into the Public Affairs Office. Although crowded with reporters, they were quick to spot Ernie Pyle.

"Ernie, nice to see you again," said Oliver, greeting Pyle.

"Likewise," he returned. "That was a *great* story you did on Josephine Baker." Oliver smirked. "Just kidding. You did a great job covering the Africa and Italy campaigns. You really got down with the troops along with MacGowan. I told you he would show you the ropes. I respect that. Did you hear about MacGowan?"

"No, the last I saw him was in Africa," said Oliver. "What about him?"

"The front page of the paper said he was captured by the Germans but managed to escape from a train in Germany."

"Really? I spent a lot of time with him in Africa. He said to find the story and not be the story. Good for him." said Oliver. "Ernie, this is Tatiana Phillips."

"Yes, I know Tatiana. How is your father?" nodded Pyle.

"He's doing fine. Thank you for asking."

"Cub Miller. Nice to meet you. I've heard a lot about you," said Cub, extending his hand.

"Thank you. Are you with Tatiana or Oliver?"

"I'm with Oliver and the *Birmingham Defender*."

"Great," acknowledged Pyle.

The room was smoke-filled and the commotion ongoing. They knew that there was going to be an important announcement. The door opened and Maj. Lee entered the room.

"Colonel Dixon will be out in a few moments to answer your questions."

The noise continued and a few moments later the door opened again. The press stood up as if they were military, standing at attention for a general.

"Thank you. Take your seats. You don't need to do that. You are not in the military, although some of you look like you are," he said.

And thus began the first of many military briefings in Paris. Later, the public affairs officers would provide briefings at the Scribe Hotel.

CHAPTER 13

BACK AT THE hotel, Oliver was dressing for dinner while Cub sat at the desk typing a story.

"I'll be going to dinner with Tatiana tonight," said Oliver.

"Oh, no. I think she wants to go out with me," said Cub.

"I don't think so, Cub. Believe me, I'll be taking this one."

"If you say so," said Cub, continuing to type.

Oliver met Tatiana in the lobby. She looked strikingly beautiful in her uniform. She was wearing a brown coat, a beige skirt with a belt, a garrison cap, and white gloves.

"You look very nice," said Oliver, wearing his uniform as well.

"Thank you," said Tatiana. "You look nice yourself." The two walked to La Coupole Restaurant and were escorted to their seats by the waiter. Oliver sat down and looked across the dinner table at the most beautiful woman he had ever seen.

"Have you been here before?" Tatiana asked.

"No, I haven't," admitted Oliver. "But I've heard about it and wanted to come."

The waiter appeared. "Bonjour, puis-je vous offrir un aperitif?"

"He is asking if he can offer us drinks," Oliver translated to his date. "Oui. Deux coupes de champagne," he told the waiter.

"Very nice. I'm impressed," said Tatiana, smiling. "It looks like you were busy in North Africa."

"You read my stories?" said Oliver.

"Of course. As I mentioned earlier, you did a good job with the Josephine Baker piece."

"Is that the only one you read? I wrote that two years ago."

"No. I read others. That was the only one I remember, though."

"Ouch. I felt that one," said Oliver.

Tatiana smiled.

"So tell me. How did Colonel Dixon get you smuggled into France?" asked Oliver.

"Two months after the invasion, when Normandy was clear, I came through Rouen with the Canadian Army. Colonel Dixon got me attached to them."

"Yeah, that is the key to this. Get yourself attached to an army unit and follow them."

The waiter arrived with two flutes of champagne. "Would you like an appetizer?" asked the waiter.

"Merci, I would like oysters with a glass of wine," she said.

"A dozen or half-dozen?" asked Oliver.

"Half-dozen," said Tatiana.

Oliver repeated the order in French, "Six huitres avec un verre de Muscadet Sèvre et Maine s'il vous plait," said Oliver to the waiter. Then he looked at Tatiana, "You always pair wine with the region."

"Very good. I *am* impressed," said Tatiana. Oliver smiled. He had hoped to impress her with his French. "I wonder if they even have oysters with this war going on?" she asked.

"I think they still have them. I don't think they ever stopped. The Muscadet is a white French wine made in the Loire Valley near the Atlantic coast. It will go well with any seafood."

"So how well do you speak French?" asked Tatiana. "I just know a few words."

"I'm learning more each day," said Oliver.

"I'm studying Russian. I think it is going to be important for Americans to understand the Russians now that we are fighting with them. Somehow, I think they will be the ones that we'll need to watch when this war is over," predicted Tatiana.

"I think you are right," said Oliver.

"My father showed me a picture of a few women correspondents covering the war in London. I read up on one of them named Kathleen Harriman. She went to Moscow and decided to spend a lot of time learning Russian so she could understand the Russians."

"You really know this stuff," said Oliver.

"I looked at the names of the journalists. One was Tania Long, whose real name was Tatiana — the same as mine. Her mother was a Russian named Tatiana Mouravieff. That really got me interested."

The waiter brought the wine and poured it.

Oliver lifted his wine glass and said, "Santé, Prospérité, Bonheur." *Good health, prosperity, happiness.*

Tatiana responded in Russian, "Nas darouje." *Cheers.*

"That was good," said Oliver, drinking his wine. "So tell me, what did you write about back in the states?"

"Oh, nothing as exciting as your stories. To get ready for this trip my father sent me on a mission to D.C. to cover a day in the life of Eleanor Roosevelt. I stayed over and reported on the opening of the Pentagon."

"Eleanor Roosevelt. I've never seen her in person. I've never seen the Pentagon either."

"I followed the First Lady to Virginia and back to Washington. I ended up crashing one of her talks at a local women's club. I walked in late and the only seat available was on the third row. I was the only black woman in the group and they all saw me walk in late. The First Lady stopped her talk and waited for me to take a seat. I thought I was going to die when I walked in late."

Oliver laughed, "Wow."

"But I kept walking to take my chair, hoping no one would notice me. I will never do that again. Then Mrs. Roosevelt even talked to me afterwards," said Tatiana.

Oliver laughed. "You crashed a presentation by the First Lady? If you can do that, you won't have any trouble over here in the war."

"I did. My father taught me a long time ago that when it comes to getting the story, it is better to ask for forgiveness than for permission," said Tatiana.

"He's right. But that can be dangerous over here. You could get killed in this job, and you don't want to be violating the rules of engagement for reporters," said Oliver.

"I won't do that," said Tatiana.

"You're much too glamourous to be violating any rules," said Oliver.

"Well, look at you," she said. "I'll bet you don't violate the rules."

They smiled and drank their wine, looking at each other.

Oliver put his glass down. "So you covered the Pentagon opening? I'll bet that was something to see," he said.

"It was large and impressive. They let us walk around in part of it. I couldn't believe how big the place was — I can't imagine how anyone finds their way around in it. The walking must be incredible to get from one place to the other with all the stairs. I wouldn't wear heels in that place if I worked there."

"I forgot to ask. Was today your first in Paris?" asked Oliver.

"Yes, I was literally just checking in at the Scribe when I saw you in the lobby."

"And you were in Rouen the entire time before coming to Paris?"

"Yes. I learned a lot about the city while I was there. Do you know the story behind the city?"

"No. What is it?"

"That's the city where Joan of Arc was burned at the stake."

"I didn't know that."

"The city was terribly damaged from bombing. I was stunned to see how much of it was burned. The Germans wouldn't let the French put the fire out in their own city."

"I didn't realize that. An interesting history lesson on being burned at the stake and being made a saint five hundred years later."

Tatiana continued: "It is. There was a church in the downtown area of Rouen that had no stained glass in it. One of the residents said that they took the stained glass windows out of the church and stored them somewhere so the Nazis wouldn't find them and so that they wouldn't be damaged. The Canadians were the ones who liberated the city. That was a good story to send back to Chicago since many of our readers are from Canada."

"We came in through Normandy on D-Day after it was cleared. Then it was onward to Paris. Lee, Cub, and I were delayed a few days outside of Paris because we didn't have an escort into the city. The Allies were still clearing out the Germans. We ended up camping out in an old abandoned chaillot, finding whatever we could to eat after the rations ran out," said Oliver.

"That sounds like a lot of male bonding."

"It was," said Oliver. "I can see how some journalists can get caught up in the war and lose sight of what they are doing. They start wanting to be a part of the campaign. It gets in your blood and I would imagine that sometimes they can't help themselves."

"So what are you and Cub working on now?"

Oliver sat back in the booth. "Let's see. Cub has been asking about the 761st Tank Battalion. He also reported on the Buffalo Soldiers when he was in Italy."

"What is the 761st Tank Battalion?" asked Tatiana.

"They are the black tank drivers. Their symbol is the black panther. They were trained in Camp Claiborne in Louisiana and then at Camp Hood in Texas. They were called by General Patton and sent to New York City and then London before coming to France. They are to arrive sometime we understand, but we aren't supposed to know that."

"That sounds interesting. I would like to cover them," said Tatiana, taking a notepad from her purse.

"There is an officer named Lieutenant Colonel Paul Bates from Los Angeles who leads them," said Oliver. "Cub can give you more information about them. He's been waiting to cover them when they arrive in France."

"Thank you," she said as she wrote. "What are the Buffalo Soldiers?"

"They are the 92nd Buffalo Division. They are 4,000 black soldiers, mostly from the South. They were sent to Arno in Italy to break through what is called the Gothic Line."

"It appears you and Cub have been covering the black soldiers," said Tatiana.

"Yes. I started out with the troops in North Africa. Then the Tuskegee Airmen in 1943. Then I covered them through Sicily and then to Italy. So we have the Tuskegee Airmen, the 761st Tank Battalion, and the Buffalo Soldiers. There are also countless black soldiers working in infantry divisions in fighting and supply and logistics roles. I've searched through the entire North African forces looking for individual stories to send back." said Oliver.

"Well, it looks like I have a lot to learn during my time here."

"It won't take long. In about two months you'll have it down and know where to go, who to trust, who not to trust."

"I hope I can cover some good stories over here while the war is still going on," said Tatiana. "My father is going to require that I send him something daily to justify the cost of the trip over here."

"We all have the same requirements. I'm sure you'll find some good stories. Daily stories can be tough because you have to find something new and get it written, cleared, and transmitted. If you want something in depth, it is going to take a lot of time to do that. I write both – I complete daily reports and then I try to work on something significant that I can send back. Make it good because there is a cost to transmit. Every word counts. I've learned to shorten the words to cut down on the transmission cost."

There was a pause. Then Oliver asked, "You remember our meeting with Colonel Dixon back in London when we asked him about the 761st?"

"Yes, I remember that meeting. I think he intentionally gave you a hard time. He probably liked your Josephine Baker story," teased Tatiana.

"Thanks. I get kidded a lot about that one. I have a story I'm working on about some Tuskegee airmen shot down prior to *Operation Dragoon*. I'm also looking into a story about a soldier I visited from Alabama who was injured in St. Raphael. He claims it was caused by friendly fire. I hadn't seen that before. I'm not sure how I'm going to cover that story."

"You mean the friendly fire story?"

"Yes."

"Did they find the pilots that were shot down?"

"Not yet. They think they were captured and sent to German prison camps," said Oliver.

"What about the friendly fire story? How did that happen?" asked a curious Tatiana.

"Not sure. I interviewed the soldier but he didn't want the incident reported. Turns out that I met him for a few minutes on the ship that took us to Oran in '42. He and his battle buddy were sent somewhere else. I never got an address for them. They are from Alabama, and I always write about servicemen from Alabama. It gets great press. Nelms, my editor, wants stories like that," said Oliver.

"How are you going to report friendly fire?" asked Tatiana.

"I'm not going to report that one," said Oliver reluctantly.

"But it happened. Why wouldn't you want to report it?" asked Tatiana curiously.

"I don't report everything that happens."

"Why not?"

"After two years I've learned that some stories could undermine what we are doing over here. I learned my lesson once in Oran when I submitted a story about the French Resistance. Some army major tipped me off about it, or at least I thought it was a tip. Turned out that it was turned down by all the other reporters and he came to me looking to see if I would submit it. I should have realized I was being set up. I won't make that mistake again."

"That doesn't sound like a set up. That sounds like a political hot potato that no one was going to jump on. It might have done some good if the higher ups would have printed it," said Tatiana.

"Maybe," said Oliver.

"So the friendly fire story … in what way will the friendly fire story undermine the war?" Tatiana began to wonder about what Oliver was suggesting.

"They traced the bullet in his back to his battle buddy's gun."

"*What*?" she asked.

"The bullet came from his buddy's gun."

"Well, it was a mistake. Mistakes happen. It *has* to be a mistake. There must be an explanation for that," Tatiana said, now understanding Oliver's concern.

"There is. I just hate to see that happen to anyone. I'm sure that it is hard on the soldier who shot him accidentally. They were friends," said Oliver.

"Which is all the more reason to assume it was an accident," said Tatiana. "The story will have a human side to it. Everyone knows these kinds of things are going to happen. Maybe you can write it in a way that it won't be harmful to anyone. You are just reporting reality."

They talked for hours through dinner, dessert, and coffee. Finally, they returned to the hotel.

Riding the elevator up to their rooms, Oliver reached behind Tatiana's back and pulled her close. She returned the embrace and the two began to kiss. The elevator door opened and there was Cub, holding an ice bucket.

"Excuse me," said Cub. "I was going down to get ice for the room. But it looks like I might need the ice here."

"Nice, Cub," grinned Oliver.

"Hello, Cub," said Tatiana nonchalantly, as they exited the elevator and walked down the hall.

"I guess I'll see you back in the room, right Oliver?"

"Of course you will," winked Oliver.

When they reached her room, Tatiana unlocked the door. "Are you coming in?"

The door closed behind them.

CHAPTER 14

On September 16, 1944, the *Battle of Hurtgen Forest* began near the Belgian-German border. It was a brutal trench war between fortified towns, tank traps, and minefields. It was followed by *Operation Market Garden*, the largest airborne operation up to that time. Field Marshall Montgomery wanted to enter Germany over the Lower Rhine. He thought that a bold airborne invasion from the Lower Rhine into Germany could end the war by December 1944. That would not happen.

In October, the *Battle of Aachen* began to retake the first German city. Most of the civilian population had been evacuated and a large part of the city was destroyed. On the same day, the Canadian First Army consisting of Canadian, British, and Polish formations initiated the *Battle of Scheidt* to open up the Port of Antwerp, so that it could be used to supply the Allies in northwest Europe.

In early October 1944, several reporters complained that Ernest Hemingway had violated the Geneva Convention governing the conduct of newsmen in war. The Inspector

General Third Army summoned him to a hearing at its headquarters in Nancy.

A British army colonel was assigned to handle the investigation of the complaints against Hemingway. The colonel told him, "The specific charges against you, Mr. Hemingway, are that you removed your correspondent's insignia from your uniform and assumed command of Free French partisans, who began to address you as Captain or Colonel."

Mr. Hemingway, defending himself, said nothing to the charge.

At the hearing, several reporters testified that they had seen hand grenades, land mines, bazookas, rifles, and small arms in Hemingway's room at the hotel in Rambouillet. They testified that he had set up and maintained a map room and that a full colonel had, in effect, served as his chief of staff.

Hemingway listened to the charges and took his own defense.

"Do you promise to tell the truth and nothing but the truth, so help you God?" the colonel asked him.

"I do," said Mr. Hemingway, wearing his uniform. The trial had the appearance of a court-martial, with Hemingway on trial and professional colleagues as his accusers. The accusers were ready to burn him at the stake.

"Mr. Hemingway, the complaint being made against you is that you removed your correspondent's insignia. Is that true?"

"I did remove my tunic and insignia on occasion."

"And why was it necessary for you to do that?"

"Because the August weather had been hot and humid."

"I see. Another complaint is that you assumed command of a French Resistance group outside of Rambouillet. Did you assume command of any resistance group?"

"I did not."

"Well then, were you ever asked to assume command of a resistance group?"

"Yes. I was so asked."

"And what was your response to that request?"

"I repeatedly spurned any pleas to assume command of them."

"I see. Well then, Mr. Hemingway, do you know a U.S. Army major by the name of Major James W. Thornton?"

"I do."

"Did he ever ask you your advice about disposing troops around the edges of the town of Rambouillet?"

"He did."

"Did you give him advice?"

"I did."

"And why did you give him your advice?"

"Because he asked for it," stormed Ernest Hemingway.

The room began to laugh.

"Thank you for that," said the colonel. "Then let me ask you this: did you assist the troops in the defense of the town of Rambouillet?"

"I did not."

"Let me understand this: your testimony is that the major asked you for advice about the disposing of troops around Rambouillet, to which you gave advice to the major. But you did not take part in the defense of Rambouillet with the major's troops?"

"That is correct."

"Mr. Hemingway, did any of the resistance fighters refer to you as Captain?"

"What was that?"

"Let me repeat the question in case you did not understand it: did any of the resistance fighters refer to you as Captain?"

"Like a ship's captain? Well, if they did, it was out of affection only," said Mr. Hemingway.

"So you spent a lot of time with them and got to know them."

"Of course I did. That was my job. I was covering the resistance groups. What better place to cover the war than to cover it from the French who were fighting to regain their country."

"Your intention was to report the war and not to fight or assist in fighting the war? Correct Mr. Hemingway?"

"That's correct."

"Well then, can you explain this to me? It was reported that you had weapons and ammunition stacked in hotel rooms in Rambouillet that were rented in your name."

"Yes."

"In fact, it was reported that a fight nearly broke out at the hotel between you and another reporter because there were not enough rooms for the reporters, and some had to sleep on the floor in the hotel lobby since all the rooms were taken."

"And your question is?" said Hemingway.

"It has been reported that you and another reporter nearly got into a fight over the rooms and that you challenged him to go outside and fight."

"Yes."

"Is that true?"

"Is what true?"

"That you rented rooms that were full of ammunition and supplies for the resistance fighter and that you challenged a reporter to go outside and fight?"

"Both are true."

"Thank you. Now, did you go on patrols with the resistance group conducting intelligence?"

"No."

"Then why were you seen with the resistance groups when they were on patrol?"

"Because I was with them in my capacity as a newspaperman looking for a good story for professional use."

"It was reported that you had a colonel with you who was with the French Resistance and served as your chief of staff."

"That's not true."

"He did not?"

"No, he did not."

"Then why was he seen on many occasions reporting to you for information?"

"He wasn't reporting to me for information. The colonel's French was so poor that he had needed help in communicating with the partisans. I was translating for him."[44]

Hemingway was his own best witness and lawyer. Some reported that the allegations were true and that Hemingway should have been removed from France, but the hearing ended with no action being taken against him. And why would the army want to remove him? Although the allegations could have proved to be the end of Hemingway's time in France, the army would not serve as Pontius Pilate for some prosecutorial journalists. Even in journalism, war could be hell.

Hemingway left to cover the *Battle of Hurtgen Forest.* He stayed there for two weeks, but was forced to return to Paris with pneumonia.

CHAPTER 15

Cub left Paris to cover the crossing of the 761st Tank Battalion from Britain into Normandy. The day finally arrived. The battalion consisted of 760 black and white men who reached Omaha beach on October 10th, four months after D-Day. By that time the beach looked like a working ant hill with thirty thousand troops a day pouring in with food, tanks armored card, guns, vehicles, and cargo. These were the first armored black soldiers on foreign soil, equipped with M4 Sherman tanks armed with 76mm guns.

By October, the Allies surrounded Germany on all sides. Germany was being invaded by the U.S. and British forces. For the next six days, the 761st moved for hundreds of miles, from Normandy to Metz. This area was referred to as "The Gauntlet."

By October 28th, the 761st reached Saint Nicholas de Port east of Nancy. LTC Bates called a battalion formation. Soon quarter-ton jeeps, loaded with MPs and .50 caliber machine guns, rolled in and took strategic defensive positions. A single jeep and an armored scout moved to the head of the formation and stopped next to Bates.

Cub watched a three-star general step out of the jeep, receive Colonel Bates' salute, and take a stand on the hood of the jeep. The general stood with his feet apart and fists on his hips, stationed above two ivory-handled pistols in an Eisenhower jacket. It was General George Patton. He was the most dashing figure that Cub had ever seen. He recorded the general's speech:

> *"Men, you are the first Negro tankers to ever fight in the American army ... I have nothing but the best in my army. I don't care what color you are, so long as you go up there and kill the Kraut son-of-a-bitches. Everyone has their eyes on you and is expecting great things of you. Most of all, your race is looking forward to your success. Don't let them down, and don't let me down. They say it is patriotic to die for your country. Well, let's see how many patriots we can make out of those German son-of-a-bitches."*

The soldiers cheered. Cub couldn't believe General Patton's speech and couldn't wait to get back to Paris to write about it.

CHAPTER 16

Back at the hotel in Paris by train in one day, Oliver found Cub at his desk with a typewriter, preparing his story about the general's speech.

"Did you find anything?" asked Oliver.

"About what? You mean the 761st?" said Cub.

"No. The soldier," said Oliver.

"I'm working on a story about General Patton's speech to the 761st. They are heading towards Germany. You won't believe what he told them."

"What did he say?" asked Oliver.

"Something to the effect of making patriots out of the enemy by making them die for their country. Can you believe he said that?" said Cub.

"That *is* good. And he said that to the 761st?"

"Sure did. What about the soldier from Alabama?" asked Cub.

"I found him. He's Private Booker Thompson. He says he was trying to subdue two French women after their home was bombed and was shot in the back. That is all that he remembered. Now he is up for an award."

"That's good," said Cub, typing.

"Except that the military has postponed the award, because it ends up that the bullet in his back turned out to be American-made. The Germans didn't shoot him. Private Williams, his friend, did."

"Private Williams?" said Cub.

"Yes. Why? Do you know him?"

"What's his first name?"

"Andre."

"What's his last name?" asked Cub.

"Williams."

"Where is he from?"

"Mountain Springs, Alabama," said Oliver.

"I know Andre Williams," said Cub. His typing stopped.

"You do?"

"Yes. That's Skees! He's probably the same boy that was in Mountain Springs when I was shining shoes back at the good old Second Street Barbershop with Louis and Alvin. He would come visit me every Saturday one summer. I looked forward to it."

Oliver sat down on the bed. "I met him on the transit to Oran in '42. Just briefly. That means he had been fighting for over two years in North Africa, Sicily, Italy, and France. No break whatsoever. These guys are probably fried by now," said Oliver.

Cub continued reminiscing. "I can still smell the onions. And there was this crippled lady in a wheelchair begging for money and ringing a bell. Whew, man — she could sing, and that voice would knock gloves off of any boxer. I bet she could kill a 100 Jerries if we brought her over here and put her on the front lines and told her to start ringing that bell. Why, the Jerries would turn around and run back to Berlin."

"Cub, did you hear a word I just said?"

"Yes, I did. I heard every word. I know Skees. At least, I knew him that summer. If he has been over here that long, then these guys have endured something no one else can imagine."

"What do you know of him?"

"He would show up on Saturday mornings. He lived with a man that he called his uncle, but he wasn't really his uncle. There was another kid that he mentioned. He didn't say much about him, but the other kid sounded like a troublemaker. It seemed like Skees got that job to get away from home. Tell you what, I'm going to take over the story about Skees, if it really is Skees. If it isn't, you can cover the story."

"Oh, I'm going to cover this one," said Oliver. "I was in Sicily when Patton went off on the two soldiers over there. This war has been going on for over three years. There is a battle stress syndrome or fatigue being reported. I've been in the trenches. I know what they are going through. Maybe not exactly, but close to it."

"Then let me work on this one, too. I have a personal interest in the story," said Cub.

"That's fine with me. We need to see if we can talk to him."

"I'll know in a second if it is him," said Cub.

CHAPTER 17

Colonel Martins was in a good mood that day. Capt. Thomas came into his office while Martins was getting coffee.

"What have you found out, Captain?" Col. Martins asked.

"Well sir, I visited Private Thompson. He says that he and Private Williams were in St. Raphael and found the home where the women were. He said that he believes it was Private Williams who shot him by accident. He doesn't remember much after that, except soon after he was shot, there was a bombing that knocked them all over."

"Have you found Private Williams?" asked Martins.

"He was not at the scene when they rescued Private Thompson," said Thomas.

"That's in the file I gave to Capt. Weinstein. You two need to get together to sort this out. Looks like these two files are related. These are the two that were missing from the LST that was attacked," said Martins.

"There is one other issue, Colonel. The bullet in Private Thompson's back was from an American rifle," said Thomas.

"Probably friendly fire," said Martins.

Capt. Thomas was not convinced. Being familiar with the conditions where Williams grew up, he saw no reason for the shooting. He planned to teach the young Private Williams a lesson he would never forget. No one shoots another American soldier and gets away with it. This was no accident. The private pointed his weapon at another U.S. soldier. He was lucky that Thompson didn't kill him, thought Thomas. He thought Williams had no place being recruited into the service.

CHAPTER 18

THE 761ST ENTERED combat on November 8, 1944, fighting in the towns of Moyenvic, Vic-sur-Seille, and Morville-les-Vic. They were leading the edge of the advance when the Germans launched their offensive against the Allies in the Battle of the Bulge. The 761st was on the high ground south of Chateau-Salins and through Moncourt Woods to northwest of Bezange-la-Petite, opposed by the German 11th and 13th Panzer Divisions. It was a quiet morning, but the entire valley along the front would soon experience fire, death, and destruction.

Before long, the Germans fired and LTC Bates led the 761st into battle. The artillery fire began with explosions beyond anything the young men had heard before.

German snipers were seen running into a haystack, where they began picking off infantry. Corporal Coleman Simmons charged the haystack with his tank and pointed the gun directly into the haystack. The Germans jumped out yelling, "Kameraden! Kameraden!" TC Johnny Holmes cracked the turret hatch and noticed that one of the Germans looked like a kid.

"Yeah, great. Okay, you Kraut bastards, drop your gear. Understand? Drop everything," he ordered.

Private Clifford Adams was the first Black Panther to die during that battle. He was an aidman with a medical detachment and was rendering aid to a wounded soldier when a shell landed nearby.

LTC Bates continued to move the 761st forward, but a French drover with a herd of cows temporarily blocked the road. *A possible collaborator sent by the Germans,* LTC Bates thought. Bates went down and arrested him.

Bates moved his command post to higher ground and stood atop his jeep to survey the area and his tanks. Submachine gunfire hit the jeep and Bates jumped into the driver's seat. A bullet hit him and knocked him out of the air like a bird. The white man whom the 761st trusted for over two years was now injured and immediately evacuated. The 761st was stunned. The Panthers were growing as a team and suffering as a team, while American and German bodies were scattered all across the landscape. LTC Bates' leg was shattered, but he was expected to survive.

Cub reported on LTC Bates' injury, the 761st's first day in battle, and the young soldier's death. Cub learned the deceased soldier was from Texas, but did not mention his name.

CHAPTER 19

BATES WAS SENT to Paris to recover. Tatiana interviewed him at his hospital bed; he was surprised to see her in her military uniform.

"Hello," she said to him.

"Hello," he said. "I haven't seen a black female correspondent before."

"I'm the first," she said. "My name is Tatiana Phillips, and I work for the *African-American Statesman* in Chicago. Do you mind if I ask you a few questions?"

"Not at all," he said. "Why the interest in me?"

"Well for one, you commanded the 761st — the black tank battalion into battle."

"Yes, I did."

"Our paper would like to know about your experience leading a black fighting unit."

"Ok. I can do that."

"Let's start from the beginning. So tell me where were you born, Colonel?"

"Los Angeles."

"Where did you go to college?"

"Rutgers University."

"Were you drafted?"

"No. I enlisted."

"Really? That's great."

"I was granted a commission as a First Lieutenant. I was trained by General George S. Patton himself."

"I heard what he said to the battalion. One of my reporter friends got that story. It went world-wide after that."

"The one where he said to see how many Kraut son-of-a-bitches can die for their country?"

"Yes. That one. He said it so eloquently," said Tatiana.

Bates laughed. "Indeed, he did. I still remember, when we were in training, he said something like '...you go to treat a platoon of tanks like a piece of spaghetti. If you want to go somewhere, you can't get there pushing it. You got to get in front and pull it.'"

Tatiana smiled.

CHAPTER 20

It was December 16, 1944, when the press was called again to a briefing at Public Affairs. Tatiana, Cub, and Oliver attended just as before, taking their seats in the same place. All the journalists were taking notes of the unclassified information presented to the room.

Colonel Dixon entered the briefing room, followed by Maj. Lee and other public affairs officers. It was the same protocol. The colonel would say a few words, followed by Public Affairs officers briefing certain aspects of the status of the war.

"A German Counter-Offensive has begun as of December 16, 1944," said the colonel. "Hitler counter-attacked the Allies. He is hoping to end the war without the Allies advancing further. He's employed the same tactic of all losers: when you are not winning, counterattack, even if your generals disagree. We believe that the attack is contained."

He said that General Eisenhower ordered Patton to command the VIII Corps and attack toward the north in order to stop the German penetration.

Patton moved the Third Army north with nearly twelve thousand vehicles. The 761st Tank Battalion located near Saarbrucken and Zweiburcken was ordered to the Ardennes. Dixon reported that General Eisenhower sent his *Order of the Day* to all troops: "Let everyone hold before him a single thought, to destroy the enemy on the ground, in the air, everywhere to destroy him."

The press referred to the counter-offensive as the *Battle of the Bulge.* The battle took place in the densely forested Ardennes region of Wallonia in Belgium, France, and Luxembourg.

CHAPTER 21

Maj. Lee provided Oliver with more details about the shooting of Private Thompson after Oliver quizzed him. "You didn't hear this from me," he told Oliver.

"Is there any way I can talk with him?" said Oliver.

"You'll have to talk to his attorney," said Lee.

"Do you know where Private Williams is now?" asked Oliver.

"He's here. We have to decide whether to send him back to the front or send him home. He's already been in the war for over two years, so he either gets sent back, or he is here for the duration. It won't take long to figure that out."

"Who is his attorney?" asked Oliver.

"Let me see," said Lee. "It's Capt. Weinstein. You can find him at JAG. Oliver, come back to my office. I want to show you something else that might interest you."

"Ok."

Lee took Oliver to his cubicle, a desk between two sectional panels that divided the cubicle offices. A pile of papers was stacked haphazardly on his desk.

"Oliver, take a look at this," he said, picking up a report from the top of the pile.

"A black lieutenant named Lt. John Fox with the Buffalo Soldiers, the 366th Infantry Regiment, was killed after calling in artillery fire. He had to adjust the position so that the fire would land on his position in order to kill the advancing enemy."

"Wow, that is really something," said Oliver.

"Another soldier named Rothacker Smith, was injured and taken prisoner."

Oliver didn't know what to say. "Thanks, Major. This is something we need to know about. We need to find someone else who can cover the Buffalo Soldiers in Italy. I've already been there. Maybe our paper can send another reporter."

Oliver researched Lt. Fox and found that he was born May 18, 1915, in Cincinnati, Ohio. Fox attended Wilberforce University and graduated as a second lieutenant from ROTC in 1940.

CHAPTER 22

Oliver went back to his hotel room; Cub was typing away.

"Private Williams is still in Paris. You should see if you can find him," said Oliver.

"Do you know where?" asked Cub.

"I don't know, but check and see if Maj. Lee will tell you. I squeezed some other information out of him today."

"What information?" asked Cub.

"He told me that Williams was found at a Catholic church in St. Raphael."

"What was he doing there?" asked Cub.

"He could have been driven there by a member of the French Resistance, whom they found dead in a car outside the church. Williams was injured. You should go see the private since you already know him. I'll go visit the church in St. Raphael," said Oliver.

"I'll find Williams. It will be so different seeing him now. He'll be so grown up, I imagine. He was just a kid coming in the barbershop. He probably won't even recognize me. I'm completely different now. I don't like looking back, and this is going to mean going back to a time that I don't really want to remember," said Cub.

Oliver got ready and left to take Tatiana to dinner. Cub didn't ask questions; he knew where Oliver was going. Cub could see that the romance between Oliver and Tatiana was growing stronger and he was the odd man out.

On Christmas Eve they all dined together, but Oliver and Tatiana spent time alone afterwards. They strolled hand in hand to the Eiffel Tower, marveling at the war-torn City of Lights at midnight.

CHAPTER 23

Oliver traveled to St. Immanuel Catholic Church in St. Raphael by train from Paris. Civilian transportation by train to southern France had been restored.

Oliver found Father Patrick outside, repairing a hinge on the church door.

"Hello, Father. My name is Oliver Smith, with the *Birmingham Defender.* I wonder if I could ask you a few questions about the American soldier who recently found refuge at your church, but was taken away by the Vichy police."

Father didn't say anything, but motioned for him to follow. Once inside, the Father's basset hound Choupinou began to bark at Oliver.

"Choupinou, arretes!"

Sister Martine brought coffee to the priest's study, and the Father and Oliver began to talk. Choupinou lay down on the floor to sleep.

"It was the strangest thing — the young man," Father said.

"What was he doing here?" asked Oliver.

"I'm not sure. He was an American soldier."

"Can you tell me what he told you? Why he was here?"

"I don't believe I'm at liberty to say. I must respect his confidence."

"I understand. Can you at least tell me what happened to him?"

"The Vichy police took him. I don't know what happened to him after that."

"I thank you for your time," said Oliver.

"You are welcome," said Father Patrick.

Sister Martine offered to walk Oliver to the train station. On the way, she said that the soldier was only there briefly and did not say much to them. But she did remember that Andre talked about attending a wealthy black school by the name of St. Matthias. She told Oliver that he said that he had lost his family in a fire when he was young. Not realizing that Andre was only telling her a dream — and intended only as a dream —she inadvertently led Oliver down a false trail. Oliver was surprised by what Sister Martine told him. He would become obsessed with trying to understand why Andre mentioned the name of that church and where the church was located.

As he sat back on the return train and began scribbling notes for his report, Oliver wondered how to approach the story. Most of his other reports were general stories about the war and snippets about individual soldiers. This particular tale had the potential of becoming a story of its own.

Every day for a week, Oliver checked with the Military Public Affairs office. They would release no comment on Private Thompson or Private Williams. Nelms called his reporter in Paris.

"I need a story, Oliver. We are paying you top dollar to deliver news here, not to travel around in France on vacation," chided Nelms.

"I'm on to something here and need more time. I need you to check out some information in Alabama for me."

"What's that?" asked Nelms.

"Would you send a reporter to Mountain Springs? Let me know if there is a church school there by the name of St. Matthias."

"Sounds like a Catholic church," said Nelms. "What does that have to do with your story?"

"A soldier was injured during *Operation Dragoon* and collapsed at a Catholic church here. He told the priest and sister that he went to a school in Mountain Springs by that name. The nun said she didn't believe the story. I need to know if he really attended that school."

"Ok. I'll drive down there over the weekend myself. I have to be down in that area anyway to check on my mother. I don't have anyone to send down there on a boondoggle."

"Also, can you check to see if there is a report about a house burning down in Mountain Springs during the time when this soldier would have been a young boy?"

"I'll bet the local paper has an article going back that far," said Nelms.

"It would have to be around ...," Oliver thought for a moment. "I don't know the date. I would say around 1930."

"I will see what I can find out," promised Nelms.

"Thanks Ed. You won't regret this. I think I have a story here," said Oliver.

Nelms made his way down to Mountain Springs and decided to stop in town for gas. Before leaving, he stepped inside the garage, where an old man was tinkering under the hood of an older model car.

"Excuse me, but is there a church in the city of Mountain Springs called St. Matthias?"

"Saint who?" asked the old man, dabbing his brow with a dirty rag.

"St. Matthias," said Nelms.

"Who the hell was that?" said the old man, wiping his greasy hands.

"One of the saints. The thirteenth apostle. The one that replaced Judas," said Nelms.

"There ain't no St. Matthias around here. I never heard of one. There *is* a St. Peter's up the road. That's where them rich white folk send their kids. Why? Are they building another one of them Catholic churches again?"

"No, I just had the name wrong. I'm looking for St. Peter's" said Nelms.

"Just down the road on the edge of town. You will see it on the side on the right," said the old man as he returned to looking under the hood of the car.

"Thank you. Have a good day," said Nelms.

Nelms made his way up the road. The old man was right — a huge cathedral stood on a hill, almost the size of the castle. As he pulled into the parking lot, Nelms noticed a white picket fence on either side of the church with a metal gate entrance.

Getting out of his truck, Nelms walked up to the front and peered toward the cross that stood atop of the main sanctuary. There were four doors across the front of the building, two in the center. Above the doors were stained glassed windows designed with eight circles. Other buildings and a tall bell tower were attached to the main structure; a statue of the Divine Child was prominently displayed in the square in front of the buildings.

Nelms walked inside the front doors and observed the pews and altar up front behind tall, golden framed panels. There were candles along the front of the stained-glass windows and white marble columns along either side of the interior.

"Whew," thought Nelms to himself. "This is majestic. Is this how they worship?"

Sister Camille was busy rearranging hymnals among the pews. She noticed Nelms at the entrance of the church, looking lost. "Can I help you?" she asked as she walked towards him.

"I had no idea about this place. I had heard about the church but I've never driven up here. I had no idea what I was missing. Is there a school here?"

"Yes, this there is also a school," said Sister Camille.

"Who goes to school here?"

"Children of the parishioners or others in the community."

"Does it accept all children?"

"Regretfully, not yet," said Sister Camille.

"Do you have any Negro children here?"

"Regretfully, we do not. Are you interested in attending our Mass sometime?" asked Sister Camille.

"Yes, I am interested," said Nelms.

"Where are you from?" asked Sister Camille.

"I'm Ed Nelms, editor of the *Birmingham Defender*. I was thinking about writing a story about this church."

"Bless you. Would you like for me to show you around?"

"No. That's fine, Sister. I should be going. I have a newspaper to take care of."

"Thank you for coming," smiled Sister Camille.

Father Webster walked into the sanctuary as Nelms exited the front doors.

"Who was that?" asked Father Webster.

"He said he was editor of the *Birmingham Defender*, Father," said Sister Camille.

"I don't *know* him, but I've heard of his paper. Did he say why he was here? Is he interested in coming to Mass?" asked Father Webster.

"He said he was interested in writing a story about the church; he said he'd heard about the church, but has never been here. He also wanted to know if we accept students of all races in our school. I said that we do not."

"I was afraid that might be what he was here about," said Father Webster. "He could be writing a story about whether Negro students can be admitted here. This is a church, and we need to accept *all* students. Let me know the next time he comes. I would like to talk with him."

Nelms made a trip to downtown Mountain Springs. He found the town newspaper called the *Mountain Spring Register*. With some help from the editor, he located a clipping about the fire from 1930. The editor remembered it. The story was entitled "Cause of Fire Unknown" with the subtitle "Sole Survivor Taken to New Catholic Facility." There were Clara and George standing in front of the burned home; Father Webster, Sister Camille, and Sister Laurie could be seen in the background with two small children standing by their sides. Nelms sent the article to Oliver.

CHAPTER 24

Maj. Lee told Cub where he could find Private Williams; he would be at one of the facilities set up by the Allies for wounded soldiers. Williams had been sent there with his leg injury.

Cub found Andre in the recreation room where other soldiers were playing cards or table tennis. He was sitting on a couch with his injured leg resting on the coffee table in front of him.

Cub walked over to him and touched his shoulder. Andre's eyes were closed, as if he was sleeping or dreaming.

"Andre?" said Cub.

Andre just sat, unresponsive.

"Andre. Are you Andre Williams?" said Cub.

Andre's eyes opened wide when he looked at Cub. "Is that Shorty?" he asked in disbelief.

"It's me, Skees. Shorty Miller."

Andre wobbled as he stood up. He was so happy to see Shorty that he could barely control himself. Other than Booker, he had not seen anyone from home in over two years.

"What are you doing here? Are you visiting? Are you still back at the barbershop? Are Louis and Alvin still there?

I went to the barbershop before I left, and they said you took a job in Birmingham."

"I did. I worked my way up to news reporter."

"Ah, Shorty, I've been through hell these past two years."

The two sat down on the couch and Andre told Cub about the recruiter and boot camp. He told him about going to North Africa, Sicily, and Italy, where it seemed like they stayed forever. He told Cub how he and Booker found a way home by taking the LST to the operation in Southern France.

In return, Cub told Andre all about his new job, mentioning that he wanted to do a story about him for the paper.

"You know, I never knew much about your background when you were coming up to the barbershop. Where did you live?"

"I lived with a friend named Booker and his Uncle George."

"I remember you mentioning those names. Where did you go to school?"

"At the public school. Only a few years of high school." He paused. "Except that I used to go up to the library at the church sometimes."

"You mean up to St. Peter's school?"

"Yes."

"What about your parents and the rest of your family?"

"They died in a fire when I was six years old."

"I remember that now. It's all coming back to me," said Cub.

The men talked for hours, it seemed. Cub promised he would come back to visit Andre soon. "Just hang tight here, and everything will be ok. I hear you have a good lawyer."

Cub left.

Andre walked over and sat down at a window where he could see the Eiffel Tower in the distance. He had nothing else to cling to but his memories of Sherry. He dreamed of seeing Sherry at the top of the Eiffel Tower. And as he was coming closer to her as he sang:

"You are my window, you cast my shadow
All in the light is you
All I ever saw in the love light was you
All I knew.
You are my prism, you are my reason
You're where I want to be
You are everything that I want you to be.
You're my key
Set me free
Open up my mind
Make me be the soul you hope to find.
Keep me in line
We know I'm not all I should be feeling
Don't make me fake it, I'm not all love sense.
Not all, always, not all, free and
Not all, me and not all you are, you are
You are, you are, you are, you are my window."

Each time he sang "*You are,*" he saw himself advancing closer to her until they were finally together at the top of the Eiffel Tower by the end of the song. They could see for miles around from the top of Paris. Yet he had never actually been to the Eiffel Tower.

CHAPTER 25

"Did you find Private Williams?" asked Oliver as Cub plopped down on the bed.

"I did. He's at a facility for wounded soldiers in Paris."

"Did you ask him about Private Thompson?"

"I didn't. I couldn't bring myself to ask him about it. We had so much ground to cover."

"I guess you did," said Oliver. "Did you happen to ask him where he went to school?"

"He told me that he had a few years of high school and said something about going to a library up at the church."

"What was the name of the church?"

"He was referring to St. Peter's," said Cub.

"Interesting. When I visited the church in St. Raphael, the nun told me that he said he went to a Catholic school in Mountain Springs for wealthy black kids. She didn't believe the story — I don't either."

"He didn't go to a Catholic school in Mountain Springs for wealthy black kids. There isn't one. He went a few years to the public high school. But he did mention that he would go up to St. Peter's. St. Peter's is a private school for wealthy white kids. I can tell you that for sure," said Cub. "What was the name of the church he gave to the nun?"

"She said it was St. Matthias," said Oliver.

"The thirteenth apostle. The replacement. How interesting. He replaced St. Peter's with St. Matthias. He goes from the first apostle to the thirteenth. Probably some symbolism going on there. Who knows? As I said, St. Peter's is for rich white folk, and he says that St. Matthias is for rich black kids. He made that up. Andre wanted to go to school up there for some reason. Who knows why? I remember him mentioning the name one time in the barbershop. He was sitting in one of the customer's chairs, reading from a stack of papers. One of the pieces of paper was a brochure about that school when it opened. I remember he told me he went up there one time to see it."

Oliver sat back in the chair, folding his arms. "He probably said that from the stress of war, or she misunderstood him."

"Oh, I think he's always wanted to go to school up there. He probably spent time going up to the school, watching, being jealous of the rich white kids attending, wishing he could go to school there. Who wouldn't during the Depression?" said Cub.

"What about this kid that he grew up with? What do you know about him?" asked Oliver.

"Not much, but I think he was a troublemaker. I believe Skees went to work downtown so he could get away from their place on the weekends."

"Why was he living with them? Where was his family?" asked Oliver.

"He said that his family was dead — they died in a fire," said Cub.

"Do you know what caused the fire?" asked Oliver.

"I never asked him," said Cub.

"Ed found a newspaper clipping about the fire and sent it to me. Look at this article. It shows the two boys with nuns in front of the home."

"Really? That probably explains it. The church was his new home, I suppose. At least in his mind," said Cub.

"He grew up with the other kid?" asked Oliver.

"He did," said Cub.

"Now he accidentally shoots his friend in the back. That must be a terrible thing to endure for him now. No family, no home, and then he shot his best friend," said Oliver.

"So it ends up that the soldier who is shot in the back — Private Thompson — is the same kid Private Williams lived with and was in the house when his family died. They've served together for two years in North Africa. This is some war-torn kid," said Cub.

"Maj. Lee mentioned that Andre's lawyer is a Capt. Weinstein. I think I'll see if he will talk to me about his case, off the record. That might help us clear up some of our questions." Oliver continued to wonder about the house fire involving both of the privates, but said nothing.

"Is Weinstein his lawyer? I told him he had a good lawyer, but I just said that to him to make him feel better."

"Let's hope he doesn't really need one," said Oliver.

CHAPTER 26

AT THE HOSPITAL, Capt. Thomas and another JAG officer, Lt. Benson, visited Private Thompson in his bed.

"Private, my name is Capt. Thomas, and I'm investigating the injury you received. After examination of the wound it appears that the bullet pulled from your back was from an American rifle and not a German bullet. Do you have any explanation of this?"

"Yes."

"What is it?"

"My friend Andre accidentally shot me. We got lost after our ship was attacked and ended up at a house in the woods. I was trying to clear the house out. The home was bombed and I cleared the women out. We came under attack — I remember the house being bombed and the women screaming."

"Anything else?" asked Capt. Thomas.

"He said he thought he saw Germans in the woods; that's what he told me. He came over to check on me."

"Who came to check on you?" said Capt. Thomas.

"Private Williams."

"What happened after that?" asked Capt. Thomas.

"We talked. Just talked about nothing. He mentioned Mary."

"Who is she? Why did he mention that name?"

"Probably just to make me laugh. Keep me talking, sir."

"I see. Was she a friend?" asked Capt. Thomas.

"Just a girlfriend, sir."

"He mentioned your girlfriend?"

"Yes sir, he said it reminded him of a time when we were in school. He would bring up the past sometimes. He was always doing that. He didn't mean anything by it. He said something like ... he saw a German. He said something about the women near the tree reminded him of the eighth grade."

"Did you see any Germans?" asked Capt. Thomas.

"I didn't, but I wasn't looking in the woods. It was dark. He killed a German in Africa at Kasserine Pass, sir," said Booker.

"Ok. What did he mean by women near a tree and the eighth grade?" asked Thomas.

"That was nothing. She was just a girl in school. I know what he was referring to. Something way back. It's nothing. Just forget about it, sir."

"Forget what?" asked Thomas.

"Forget what he said. It's nothing, sir."

"I need to know what that has to do with your injury, if anything," said Capt. Thomas.

"Sir, it's nothing. He was just talking to keep me alive."

"All right," said Thomas. He looked at Booker and a few seconds passed. Then Booker explained; he didn't want to bring it up, but he thought the captain might move on after that.

"Sir, he was referring to the time he gave me some wrist bands that he bought at a pawn shop in downtown Mountain Springs. I was playing with them at school and accidentally tied my girlfriend to a tree with them. I didn't mean to do it — I was playing with her, but it turned out to be bad because I couldn't get her unlocked. She screamed and we got in trouble and I got kicked out of school for a while. He's never forgiven me for that. He always brings that up when we talk about Mary. He was just trying to make me laugh. Keep me awake."

"Private, none of this makes sense. Why would he bring up something like that from so long ago?"

"I don't know sir, he was just crazy talking; trying to make me laugh while I was hurting, I guess. He didn't mean anything by it, sir," said Booker.

"Doesn't it seem strange to be bringing it up at that particular time?" asked Thomas.

"He didn't mean anything by it. He wouldn't do anything to hurt me on purpose. Sometimes he would just say things for no reason. We talked about a lot of things. He was trying to keep me alive. I guess he thought if I went to sleep I would not wake up. So he talked about anything he could think of to make me laugh."

"Did you talk about anything else?" asked Thomas.

"He said I would get through it. He told me I saved the women's lives by clearing them out of the house and how that reminded him of his brother trying to get his family out of the fire when his house burned down," said Booker.

"What was that?" asked Thomas.

"Nothing sir. That happened a long time ago. It has nothing to do with this," said Booker.

"I guess I'm not following you. You said he talked about you tying a girl around a tree. He brought up something about his home being burned down when he was young?" said Thomas.

"Yes, sir. We were young. I was there when it happened. His home burned down and his family was killed. I guess he brought it up because he thought I started the fire," said Booker.

"What was that?" said Thomas.

"Nothing, it has nothing to do with this, sir" said Booker.

"Did you just say that you were in his home when you were young, when it burned down, and he thought you did it?" asked Thomas.

"No, sir, I didn't mean that. He doesn't think that. I just said that. I didn't know if I was going to live or not and whether we would talk about it. Things just went through my mind," said Booker.

Booker realized he had made a mistake. He implied something to Capt. Thomas that he did not mean. Or at least he wasn't sure what Andre really thought about the fire. That was a subject they would never discuss.

Capt. Thomas looked at Private Thompson and was curious about the two incidents being recalled at the same time after Thompson was shot. He would look into them further.

"So is it your testimony that your friend shot you in the back?"

"He did, sir, by accident. He said he was shooting at Germans," said Booker.

"Ok. Would you mind signing a statement regarding your memory of the incident? This states that this was your testimony to me. Lt. Benson here will witness your signature."

"Ok," said Booker.

"And for your information, the statement says that Private Williams admitted to discharging his weapon, and that a shot from his weapon hit you in the back. You remember him saying that he was attempting to shoot Germans as a defense to you and the women. You talked about how he cleared the women from their house prior to the bombing of the home. It says that he mentioned the name Mary, who was a girl in the eighth grade, after he discharged his weapon. Both of you discussed the fire that occurred at Andre's home when you were young. That is basically what this says. You can add to it whatever you wish," explained Thomas.

"Yes, sir," he nodded.

Booker signed the statement.

CHAPTER 27

Capt. Thomas informed Colonel Martins about the statement given by Private Thompson. Capt. Weinstein received a copy of the statement as well. The question became whether the statement implied criminal behavior and whether it was admissible. It was hearsay, but it provided some information regarding the circumstances of the shooting and supported self-defense and defense of third persons. But the statements about the girl named Mary and the incident about the fire at Private Williams's home were troubling to Capt. Thomas.

Weinstein would interview his client after receiving the statement. In his mind there was nothing to prosecute. Private Williams had done his job and deserved recognition for his service.

"Why did you shoot him?" Weinstein asked his client.

"I thought I saw Germans in the woods."

"You were defending your fellow soldier," said Weinstein.

"There wasn't one there, sir," said Andre with some remorse.

"What?"

"I didn't see the Germans afterwards."

"You say you saw Germans, but they were not there?" asked Weinstein.

"Yes, I thought I saw some and I aimed to shoot at one," said Andre. "We were bombed and the house was bombed and my aim was off. I didn't see them after the shooting, but I did later when I was coming out of the woods."

"Ok. Unless your mind is playing tricks on you, you were defending a fellow soldier. That is defense of a third person and self-defense. The only reason this incident is even being investigated by JAG is because one of the JAG officers is raising questions about the two incidents that you and Private Thompson talked about after the shooting. There was some talk about an incident with the girl named Mary that is in the statement that Private Thompson signed. Tell me again what this lady named Mary has to do with this so I can better understand it."

"It doesn't have anything to do with this," said Andre. "I was just talking to him afterwards to keep him talking and awake. He was getting worse, and I thought it might keep him awake. I was referring to a time when he tied his girlfriend to a tree in the eighth grade, and how she yelled at him like the French women. Just reminded me of that. There's so much that goes on in your head when you are out there. Things just come across your mind. It seems like everything reminds me of something in the past. That had nothing to do with me shooting my weapon."

"Did you just say that you shot because something reminded you of Private Thompson when he tied his girlfriend to a tree?"

"No sir. I shot because I thought I saw Germans."

"What happened after that?"

"A bomb blast knocked me off balance at the same time that I shot. My aim was off and the bullet hit Booker," said Andre.

"You didn't intend to shoot your weapon at Private Thompson?"

"No, sir, of course not."

"And the bullet hit him because your aim was off due to the attack?"

"Yes, sir."

"The other issue that the JAG is going to raise is that there was some talk about clearing out the home and how that reminded you of the fire at your home when you were young. What does that have to do with this?" asked Weinstein.

"It doesn't have anything to do with this. We were just talking about some things in the past. I was trying to keep him talking," said Andre.

"The fire has nothing to do with this, Private?" asked Weinstein.

"No, sir."

Weinstein was busy writing notes, saying nothing.

Andre asked, "So what do you think of the case they have against me?"

Weinstein stopped writing and put his pen down.

"Private, I can't see how this will be seen as anything other than an accident and self-defense. I don't think there is anything to investigate further. You thought you were shooting at a German, and you had already shot a German in Africa prior to this. The other thoughts that came across your mind, like the wrist bands — those are just thoughts. Those are not evidence of your intent. The prosecution has to show some culpable negligence, criminal in nature, such as your causing the death of Private Thompson by involuntary manslaughter if he were to die. I can't even believe they would consider that."

"I wasn't trying to harm him," said Andre.

"Of course you weren't. In this case, you were reacting to an event. You were probably more than generous in revealing your inner thoughts, which was not helpful to you in this situation. In my opinion, the court should dismiss the case. There's no culpable negligence. There is no criminal behavior here. This is self-defense. Anyone can see that. You were even defending the French women from the Germans. I think what is driving this are those two statements about the incident around the tree and the house burning — the fire that burned your family. Those two incidents that were discussed after the shooting has one particular JAG officer speculating that you might have shot Private Thompson to get back at him. Those recollections are raising some questions in his mind. Anyone else besides him would not think twice about this."

"I never thought that. That is ridiculous. How long will this take?" asked Andre.

"If I can't get it worked out, probably about three days. JAG wants to hold the trial in Paris so that if you are cleared, we can send you back to your company or platoon or you can be reassigned. I don't think they would throw the book at you after your service for the past two years," said Weinstein.

"I want this over with as soon as possible. I don't want this hanging over my head for very long. I'm sorry about Booker — we grew up together. We were more than friends. When I go back to Alabama, the only home I have is with him and his uncle."

"I understand," said Weinstein. "I'll see what I can do to expedite this case so we can move on. I think you have told me everything I need to get this case ready."

"Thank you, sir."

CHAPTER 28

WITH THE ARTICLE that Nelms found at the *Mountain Springs Daily Register*, Oliver began to speculate that this case could center on the fire at Andre's home back in 1930. *Why else would the soldier bring up such an incident with his friend?* he thought to himself. Oliver was determined to find the young Private Williams and dig up more information about the ongoing investigation. He was now working on a story that he did *not* want to report, but he wanted to better understand the situation. He arranged a private meeting through Andre's attorney.

Capt. Weinstein was a maverick. He was military, and he loved the military, but he was also a jokester with many idiosyncrasies. He was brilliant but lacked military bearing at times. He could win cases that no one else could win. His colleagues knew he was essential, but he would never rise high in the military.

Oliver found Weinstein in his cubicle office, his feet propped up on the desk. Oliver was going to talk to Weinstein about Andre's strange story at the Catholic church, which he assumed Weinstein knew nothing about.

On his desk stood a framed photograph of what appeared to be the attorney and his young wife, toasting champagne. Weinstein kept himself well-groomed, and what was left of his hair was receding in both the back and the front of his head. It was clear that the lawyer kept himself in good shape, probably through lifting weights and jogging, guessed Oliver.

"So what brings you here, Mr. Smith?" asked Weinstein.

Oliver pulled up a chair. "I think I can help with your defense."

"In what way?"

"First, I don't want to report this kind of story, because I know how badly it will go over back home. But, it *is* a story, and if it's going to be told, I want to be the one to tell it."

"Ok. That doesn't help me," said Weinstein.

"Second, I need to know why Andre shot the other soldier, Private Thompson," said Oliver.

"Really? You want to know that?" said Weinstein.

"If you can tell me."

"My client has given me consent to talk to you, but nothing I say can be printed. If you understand that, I can discuss public information that is not subject to attorney-client privilege. But tell me — is it you or the press in general that is interested in this case?"

"I wouldn't say the press is interested in the story. *I'm* interested in it. I've been covering black soldiers since '42 in Africa. I don't want to see the black soldier maligned by this story, nor do I want to see Private Williams's career destroyed."

"It's just one incident — nobody's going to blame anyone else for what happened."

"What will his defense be?" said Oliver.

"The entire thing was an accident, self-defense and defense of third parties. There was no culpable negligence, and the case can be handled administratively. Both were injured and under the heat of battle. There is no case here. Williams fired his weapon at what he thought were Germans. He slipped when the area was bombed and his aim was off. End of story."

"The prosecutor found and interviewed the two women and Thompson. They all say that the shot came from Andre's weapon," said Oliver.

"It did, but that doesn't mean he deliberately attempted to shoot his friend. These things happen. People get hurt at the gun range like this."

"What are they going to charge him with?" asked Oliver.

"Probably some kind of culpable negligence, I would guess," said Weinstein.

"I'm no lawyer, but does this really look like a case that needs to be prosecuted? It seems like these guys were practically brothers. I doubt the private had any intention of harming his friend," said Oliver.

"That's what I think, and had this been any other case this would have never gone anywhere."

"What do you mean?" asked Oliver.

"It has something to do with some things that were ... no, I can't get into that. I'm sorry. Let's just say that this prosecutor doesn't believe Private Williams's story. He thinks there are other things involved," said Weinstein.

"I've done some investigation of Private Williams, and there are some unusual things about his past."

"Like what?" asked Weinstein.

"Well, for example, did he tell you where he went to school?"

"No, and I didn't ask."

"Would you check his military records, and let me know what they say?" asked Oliver.

Weinstein pulled Andre's file and looked at his enlistment record.

"It says here that he attended a public high school for two years."

"Did he ever mention the name 'St. Matthias'?"

"No, but again, I didn't ask. Why does it matter where he went to school?"

"I don't know for sure if it does, but after he collapsed, he told a nun down in St. Raphael a story about a school he attended."

"Ok. How did you find that out?"

"I went to the church in St. Raphael and talked with the nun there. She asked me to check the school he attended. She thought that might explain a few things."

"Really? I can't even get JAG to let me go investigate outside the city. You reporters can go where you want any time of day, and we in the military can't go anywhere without security advance travel orders. You should see what it takes to get an order through the chain of command. Maybe I should hire you as an investigator on some of my other cases." Capt. Weinstein began to wonder about Private Williams.

"The nun said that Andre told her that he went to a Catholic school for privileged black kids in Alabama."

"What?"

"Some expensive private school for Negro kids," said Oliver.

"That's interesting. What does that have to do with his shooting of Private Thompson?"

"Private Williams didn't go to a privileged Catholic school for Negro children. He went to public school in Alabama. This is 1944 — there are no such schools there like that. They hardly have public education for the black kids."

"What do you make of it? How does this relate to the shooting of Private Thompson?"

"I checked on his past. He and the other soldier grew up together. He has no parents, no brothers, no sisters, no one. They were all killed in a fire when he was young. The Catholic school that he is talking about was up on a hill outside of Mountain Springs. It's called St. Peter's Catholic Day School. Admission is only open to privileged white kids who can afford for it. Andre saw that school all the time, and he wanted to be there. I think he dreamed up this story that he and Booker Thompson were taken to St. Matthias — the name he gave for what really is St. Peter's — after the fire.

There isn't a St. Matthias school. He had to have dreamed the whole thing up."

Oliver's theory and explanation were of course true, because Sister Martine had simply misunderstood Andre when he told her about his dream. Oliver suggested that Weinstein find the truth behind why Williams would tell such a story to the nun at the Catholic church.

"Sounds interesting, but how does that help his case here? Are you saying he is insane? That's not a legal defense, and the judge will think *I'm* crazy. So he wanted to go to a private school with rich white kids. He's black. Who could blame him? How is that relevant now?"

"I think the kid who did burn down his home was Private Thompson," said Oliver.

There was a pause.

"What did you just say?" asked Weinstein.

"I'm not sure why I just said that. I'm actually not sure about it yet."

"Do you have proof that Private Thompson burned down Private Williams's home?"

"No, I don't, but I can show you an article back in 1930 that my editor sent to me the day after the fire," said Oliver, pulling the article from his briefcase.

"Ok, so it shows that the private's home burned down in 1930," said Weinstein, looking at the article. "What does that have to do with this trial, and why do you think the soldier at age six burned down his friend's home?"

Oliver paused and said, "Reporter's instinct?"

Weinstein looked at him, not sure whether to react.

"All that sounds interesting, and you can print whatever you like — you are not subject to rules of evidence. I can't just go into court making wild accusations, and even if I did, what difference does it make?" asked Weinstein.

"I'm speculating. They were young, so they wouldn't have understood the consequences of what they were doing. I believe Private Thompson accidentally burned down the home and never admitted it. Andre thinks *he* burned the home down and created this whole fantasy about his life growing up in a Catholic school — maybe to find a way to get himself forgiven. I think Andre has been searching for a way to forgive himself his entire life. Why did he go to a Catholic church after the shooting — to confess? And is he angry at Private Thompson?"

"I guess he felt like he needed forgiveness," theorized Weinstein. "I don't know about that process in the Catholic church. I'm Jewish."

Oliver smiled and groaned, "Hmmph. I think the way to handle this case is to first prove who burned down the home during the trial, and see if you can shock Williams into reality. He is experiencing some kind of impaired judgment. He isn't insane, but he has erased this whole fire incident from his mind. After two years fighting in Africa, no telling what is going on with him. You heard about what Patton did in Italy?" asked Oliver.

"Yes, I read the story broken by Drew Pearson. Let me see if I understand this. You want me to go into a court-martial, put my client on the stand so I can shock him into reality, so we can figure out who burned his home down when he was six years old? Is that what you want me to do?"

"Why not?" said Oliver.

Weinstein was about to tell Oliver he was off his rocker, but he decided to play it cool. "Well, for one reason, this is a court-martial. This is the army. I don't do shock therapy in criminal cases when I defend the accused. I defend soldiers against criminal charges. We have chaplains for this kind of thing. I'm not a priest."

Oliver said nothing in response. He realized how ridiculous he sounded. His suggestion was preposterous. He wanted Weinstein to use the witness stand to find the truth behind Andre's dream, which Andre intended only as a dream in the first place. It would have no place in a criminal trial.

Oliver was a journalist, not a JAG officer. He was trying to discover Andre's true story. And Weinstein was defending his client from criminal charges based on reality. He wasn't going to delve into something that happened years ago, even if it could benefit his client psychologically.

Weinstein explained logically why Oliver's idea did not make sense.

"I don't mean to throw everything you say aside," said Weinstein, "but let's look at what you are asking me to do. To do what you suggest, I'd have to put him on the stand. Your theory means that he probably *did* shoot Private Thompson deliberately, because he was angry at Private

Thompson and thought he accidentally burned his home down with his family in it, and he has been carrying this grudge with him his entire life. And so during the war he accidentally shoots his friend. If I put Andre on the stand, I could end up letting the prosecution prove his case when they cross examine him. That's insane. We run the risk of the private possibly breaking down and revealing that this was no accident, but something else — like it was attempted murder instead."

"I hadn't thought of it that way," said Oliver.

"The prosecution says that right after he shot Private Thompson, Private Williams said something referring to another childhood friend named Mary and an incident in the eighth grade. He says that he thought he saw a German, but there was no German. And why only one German? They say he is referring back to Kasserine Pass where he did shoot a German. So they believe he visualized the German again at St. Raphael and is making that up."

"He's already been through so much, maybe he did visualize one," said Oliver.

"That means if I bring up his past, it might prove that he really *did* shoot Private Thompson on purpose, and we would be playing right into the prosecution's hands. I don't see how any of this is connected or even helps us," said Weinstein.

"I hadn't thought of that. Maybe Andre *does* have an ongoing grudge or hatred that might have caused him to lash out in retribution after all of these years," Oliver pondered.

"Well, you're the lawyer. I guess I thought you needed this information in order to defend the case. I can see I haven't thought this completely through yet. It looks like I'm hurting his case."

"No, you aren't. You're just pointing out things that the prosecution could raise and it's better to deal with them now rather than in trial. I appreciate your ideas," said Weinstein.

They got up and Weinstein walked Oliver out of the office.

"So you didn't tell me. What is your angle on this story? Why are you covering this? There are so many battles going on now, and we are advancing into Germany. Why are you focused on this one case at the moment?" asked Weinstein as they walked to the exit of JAG.

"They are both from Alabama. My paper is in Birmingham. We like to cover stories about our people," said Oliver.

"I see the connection now," nodded Weinstein.

"I met both Williams and Thompson briefly on the ship from London to Africa back in '42. I casually interviewed them and didn't take many notes. I wish now I had taken more time to visit with them."

"Thanks for coming in. You saved me a trip to St. Raphael. I don't think the priest or the nun could be compelled to testify, and they sure wouldn't be helpful in the case, so I think I'll pass on calling them."

Andre had no grudge against Booker. His dreams were being misreported as if they were evidence suggesting a connection between the accidental shooting of Booker, the wrist band incident with Mary, and the childhood fire at Andre's home. Neither youthful memory had anything to do with Andre's misfire. But the appearance of some kind of link between these incidents was clouding the case.

CHAPTER 29

TWO DAYS AFTER Booker signed the statement for Capt. Thomas, Colonel Martins received a report that would change the face of the entire investigation.

Private Thompson was dead.

The hospital confirmed that an infection had overtaken Booker's body and the medics were unable to stop its progression. Colonel Martins called Captains Thomas and Weinstein to his office. "I've learned that Private Thompson died in the hospital a few days ago. Where are we on the investigation of that, Capt. Thomas?" asked the colonel.

"Sir, before the soldier died he provided a statement that said that he was shot by his buddy, Private Andre Williams."

"Deliberately?" asked the colonel.

"Sir, that's not clear. He said that Williams was shooting at Germans. He said that the bullet hit him in the back, but he didn't think Williams meant to injure him."

"Did the private render aid to Thompson?" asked the colonel.

"Yes, sir," said Thomas.

"That sounds like an accident to me," said the colonel.

"That's what I think, sir," said Weinstein. "There shouldn't be any charges brought against him. There is no evidence that he intended to shoot his friend. He even says that he saw Germans in the woods."

"Except that, Colonel, there were no Germans there. And Private Williams walked up to him after the shooting and mentioned a girl named Mary — an old friend from school and the eighth grade," said Thomas.

"The eighth grade? What does that have to do with the shooting?" asked the colonel. "He shot him over a girlfriend in the eighth grade? That's ridiculous. Tell me you have something more than that."

"He didn't do that, Colonel. He said that he was making light conversation to keep Private Thompson awake so they talked about their childhood. Private Williams often said things that were brought up from the past," said Weinstein. "He was just relaying an event in the eighth grade to keep Booker awake. He thought it would make Private Thompson laugh."

"How long have these two been on active duty?" asked the colonel.

"Sir, they enlisted in November of 1941 and were trained at Fort Bragg and sent to Africa with the 9th Infantry Division. They saw their first combat in October of 1942. They served at Kasserine Pass and other battles in Africa. They were transferred to the 3d Infantry Division and fought in Sicily and in the Italian Campaign, and then they were assigned to *Operation Dragoon.* They were on the LST

281 that was attacked at St. Raphael. That was the only ship attacked by the Germans," said Weinstein.

"Thank you, Captain, for that briefing," said Colonel Martins. "I think this is a mistake. We can handle this administratively. There's a lot of battle fatigue going on. In World War I they called it 'shell shock,' but in this war the term circulating is 'anxiety neurosis.' General Patton slapped two soldiers in Sicily for having similar problems with anxiety. JAG has been researching a myriad of complaints regarding battle fatigue and it turns out that fifty percent of these neurosis cases are recoverable, with the men capable of returning to their units."

"I've never heard of that," said Thomas.

"There's usually a reason for what is going on both physically and emotionally with a soldier — you can't simply say it's just 'nerves.' The first soldier that Patton slapped actually had a temperature of 102 degrees and a possible case of malaria. The second soldier had signs of dehydration and a medic ordered him evacuated. The soldier refused evacuation and was sent anyway. Patton walks in the hospital, where the soldier didn't want to be. These things can't be lightly dismissed. There is always a reason for something. Did the soldier show any signs of fatigue or ask to be evacuated prior to their reassignment to *Operation Dragoon*?"

"No, sir. There was no request made and no report of any issues of concern by his command," said Weinstein.

"Let's proceed for now. If he is cleared, then we can send him back to the front."

"I know Private Williams wants this over with so he can get back to the war," said Weinstein.

"I'm sure this will all will work out and Williams will return to duty. There's space becoming available in the Ministry of Justice here in Paris. If we can get him cleared, then we don't have to send him back to the states. He can return to his platoon, and we don't lose an asset," said Col. Martins.

CHAPTER 30

BUT THINGS DID not work out as Weinstein anticipated. Capt. Thomas believed that more was involved than just a misfire of Private Williams's weapon, and he thought Andre's story about the shooting was contrived. He sought to bring charges against Private Williams.

Colonel Roger McDowell was assigned president as the senior ranking officer for the case *The United States v Williams;* he was joined by five commissioned officers that served as the convening authority. The court-martial was convened under the 1928 Manual for Courts-Martial. McDowell was an experienced black JAG officer and had only two more years left before retirement. He was athletic and healthy.

Capt. Thomas was appointed Trial Judge Advocate and possessed a charge sheet for Private Williams and the other parties in court. Thomas sat at a desk on the right; Capt. Weinstein, Defense Counsel, was positioned on the left along with the defendant, Private Williams. Oliver and Cub found seats in the courtroom where they could observe the trial. Oliver still did not know if he would actually cover and report the story, but his interest was piqued. Tatiana decided that if the story was good enough for the *Birmingham Defender*, the *African-American Statesman* would cover it as well.

Capt. Thomas said to Williams, "Private Williams, would you please stand? I am going to put the charge sheet to you and arrange you under charge one and ask you respectfully whether you plead guilty or not guilty.

"On August 22, 1944, you unlawfully discharged your weapon without the intent to kill or inflict great bodily harm and unlawfully killed Private Booker Thompson by culpable negligence in violation of Article 119(b) of the Uniform Code of Military Justice," said Capt. Thomas. "How do you plead?"

Private Williams: "Not guilty."

CHAPTER 31

The pretrial began one month later within the new temporary administration offices that the Allies were given by the provisional government in Paris. Oliver, Cub, and Tatiana were present.

Colonel McDowell began the proceeding: "The first motion is to dismiss this case. Capt. Weinstein, it is your motion, so please proceed."

"Sir, in the heat of battle I believe that a soldier should be given the benefit of the doubt. There's no evidence that Private Williams was culpably negligent in causing the death of Private Thompson. In fact, these were childhood friends that went back for many years. The entire case is based on self-defense. Private Williams was defending Private Thompson and others from the enemy. In Kasserine Pass he killed a German soldier in Africa to protect his friend. It was unfortunate that Private Thompson was shot during his defense in this incident. This is an accident and an accident is not culpable criminal negligent behavior. We ask that the charges be dismissed."

"Capt. Thomas, what is your response?"

"Sir, the evidence shows that immediately after Private Thompson was injured by the bullet, which came from the defendant's weapon, the defendant approached Private Thompson and said this reminded him of something that occurred in the eighth grade with their friend, Mary. Apparently Private Thompson tied his girlfriend to a tree on the school grounds. And this incident at the tree caused the defendant to snap and shoot Private Thompson. He says that he saw Germans, but we checked their stories and there were no Germans in the nearby area."

"Captain, how old was the private when he was in the eighth grade?" asked Col. McDowell.

"He was fourteen, sir."

"What year was that?"

"That would be in 1938, sir."

"This is 1944. This private is twenty years old now and has been at war for how long?" asked McDowell.

"Over two years, sir."

"Ok. Are you are telling us that this incident is the result of something that happened in the eighth grade, when the defendant was fourteen, before he was even in the army?"

"No, sir. We are basing the case on something that the defendant said to Private Thompson immediately after the shooting; that statement refers to his intent when he discharged his weapon."

"Let me check the file. Does the defendant plead insanity?" asked McDowell.

"No, sir, the defendant is not insane and we do not make that defense," answered Weinstein.

"What evidence do you have to rely on, Capt. Thomas?" asked the colonel.

"We have the statement of Private Thompson," said Thomas.

"And how did you get a statement from the deceased Private Thompson?"

"He talked to me — a few of the other officers, that is — in the hospital before he died."

"And that is hearsay," said McDowell.

"We believe that it's a dying declaration, sir."

"Really?" queried McDowell.

"Yes, sir, we have the case of *U.S.A. vs. Perolla*, where a dying declaration was made at the hospital within forty-eight hours of death and was admitted. This statement was made within less time than that," said Thomas.

"Captain Weinstein?" asked the colonel.

"Sir, we object to the dying declaration as a complete violation of due process and our ability to cross-examine the deceased. It's not a dying declaration, but a witness statement given to Captain Thomas by Private Thompson. That would make Captain Thomas a witness in the case and the statement would be hearsay and speculation on the part of the deceased as to Private Williams's intent at the time he discharged his weapon. The court should dismiss the charges and return the defendant to active duty."

"Ok. We really don't know what was meant by the statement. I think, in the interest of justice and for right now, I will let the prosecution proceed with its case. I'm denying the motion to dismiss. The trial will begin two weeks from today."

CHAPTER 32

Col. Martins called Capt. Weinstein and Capt. Thomas into his office prior to the trial. He wanted to talk with them about concerns over this case.

"I know you men have been working hard on this case, but we have a war going on. We have black soldiers fighting across Europe with the Tuskegee Airmen in Africa, Sicily, Italy, and France and the Buffalo Soldiers in Italy. And now the 761st tank battalion is headed to Germany. This story has several media-types, who keep showing up at Public Affairs, asking questions, attending hearings, and one even went to St. Raphael and interviewed a few witnesses. We were not able to do that. I think they are asking too many questions about this case. I'm concerned that this is not a good case to bring to trial, since the evidence seems to me to look like self-defense and is so tenuous that I'm surprised it wasn't dismissed. Besides, these men grew up together, and there isn't any way that one of them tried to deliberately harm the other. We need to bring a quick resolution to this. Capt. Thomas, what has the prosecution offered the defense?"

"An administrative discharge and for the private to be sent home. He's already been in the war for over two years, sir," said Thomas.

"What does the defense say to that?" said Martins.

"Colonel, the private has been serving honorably for the past two years and he deserves to end his career in a good way — and not with anything less than an honorable discharge. I think the incident was an accident myself, meaning he should be sent back to his platoon," said Weinstein.

"I think both of you need to go and talk this over," said Col. Martins.

"Yes, sir," said Thomas.

"Yes, sir," repeated Weinstein.

Capt. Weinstein retired to his cubicle office, followed by Capt. Thomas.

"Do you want to talk it over?" asked Thomas, standing at the edge of Weinstein's cubicle.

"Why not?" said Weinstein.

"So what did you think of the Colonel's suggestion?" asked Thomas.

"Your settlement leaves him with a war record he doesn't deserve," Weinstein responded.

"He wants to go home, doesn't he? This is one way to do it," said Thomas.

"He doesn't need to be discharged. Just transfer him back to the states so he can serve out his enlistment. He hasn't done anything wrong," said Weinstein.

"His weapon killed another U.S. soldier," said Thomas.

"He accidentally injured a U.S. soldier defending the soldier and two women during *Operation Dragoon.* The soldier died later of a hospital infection. He didn't kill anyone. Friendly fire happens," snapped Weinstein.

"Yes, but he didn't have orders to shoot anyone. He was acting on his own initiative."

"He killed a German at Kasserine Pass defending his battle buddy," said Weinstein.

"And good for him for that," said Thomas.

"Weren't they bombed right before his weapon went off? That sounds like an accident to me," said Weinstein. "An accident is not criminal."

"There's more to this story that you are ignoring. I don't believe this story he's telling. It seems contrived. There's something unreal and cooked up about it with all these childhood incidents he talked about right after the shooting. Then there's this religion thing; goodness, don't get me started," said Thomas.

"The what?"

"You know, the stuff at the church he went to afterwards," said Thomas.

Weinstein said nothing in response.

Thomas looked at Weinstein's desk and saw a picture of Weinstein and his wife. "Nice picture you have there."

"Thank you."

"You keep a clean desk."

"I do," said Weinstein.

Thomas walked around Weinstein's cubicle and started looking at the books on the bookshelf above his desk.

"Are you going to go through all of my books?" asked Weinstein.

"Not all of them. They're government property, aren't they?" asked Thomas, putting the book back on the shelf and then removing another. "'*The Life of Andrew Johnson*' — and why are you reading that? This is not an impeachment case. Are you looking for an acquittal?"

"A client gave that to me. I'm holding it for him," said Weinstein.

"I see. And who is this client of yours who likes to read about Andrew Johnson?"

"Actually, it belongs to Private Williams," said Weinstein.

"The private is reading *that* book?" asked Thomas.

"Yes, he is. Any problem with that?" asked Weinstein.

"Hmmph," Thomas said. "So he likes to read. Maybe he will be a leader someday."

There was a pause. Weinstein did not respond. Thomas grabbed another book off the shelf.

"Jesse, you really should settle this case with me," said Thomas, flipping through the book.

"Why are you taking such an interest in this case?" asked Weinstein.

Thomas put the book back and grabbed another one to peruse. "I'm not. It's just work. I have many cases," he said, sorting through the pages. He put the book back and grabbed another one. "This is just one of many," said Thomas in a matter of fact tone.

"What is it about his story that you don't believe?" asked Weinstein.

"His story? You just said it. It's a story. That's exactly why I don't believe it," said Thomas, closing the book and then grabbing another. "It sounds hokey."

"Hokey? And what does 'hokey' mean to you?" asked Weinstein.

"Doesn't it sound strange to you? This case looks like a grudge to me," said Thomas. The cover made a small popping sound as he closed the book. Thomas looked at Weinstein. "We only filed one charge against him. We probably didn't charge him with enough. I'm leaving now." Thomas walked out of Weinstein's cubicle.

"He doesn't deserve to be charged with anything. He needs to be sent back to the front," called Weinstein, slightly raising his voice.

"Fat chance of that," said Thomas, returning to the cubicle.

"Why not?" asked Weinstein.

"I think this case could really blow up in your face if you don't watch it," said Thomas.

"You don't think he was defending Private Thompson?" asked Weinstein.

"I don't. Do you? I don't believe any of his story. Do you believe it? Of course you don't," said Thomas.

"I *do* believe it," said Weinstein.

"And all that religion stuff? And this dreaming of his?" asked Thomas.

"What was that?" said Weinstein.

"You should know. You're his lawyer," said Thomas.

"What do you mean?" said Weinstein.

"Where did he go on his first day after he was recruited?" asked Thomas.

"I don't know," said Weinstein.

"Well, then I suggest you go get your guitar and ...," said Thomas without finishing his sentence.

"What are you talking about?" asked Weinstein.

"Nothing. To each his own. Well, what I mean is ... he needs a reality check," said Thomas.

"My client needs a *reality check*?" replied Weinstein sarcastically.

"Yes," said Thomas.

"He doesn't need a reality check. He's just different."

"He's different alright," said Thomas.

"You think that you know him because you grew up in the same area. You are treating him differently than you would anyone else," said Weinstein.

"I'm treating him differently than anyone else?" said Thomas.

"Yes, you are," said Weinstein.

"And who is this 'anyone else'?" asked Thomas.

"You know what I mean," said Weinstein.

"No, I don't. I'm not treating him differently than I would anyone else," said Thomas. "I will give you this — he is different."

"Come on. You can tell that this is a case of self-defense and defense of third parties."

"Maybe. We will see," said Thomas.

"He *is* different. Everyone is different. We are not all the same. The military is full of men and women that are different, from all parts of the country — this country is not just a single part, but many parts," said Weinstein.

"And what does *that* mean?" asked Thomas.

"It means that we are all different. I'm different from you. You are different from me. You think he is weak. That's why you are going after him," said Weinstein.

"I haven't said anything about that," said Thomas.

"But that's what you think," said Weinstein.

"It is true — he is weak," said Thomas.

"He's not weak. Have you seen what he's been through the last two years?" asked Weinstein.

Thomas said nothing.

"The way I see it is that the people that you think are weak are all the more necessary. The people who you consider less honorable are to be surrounded with greater honor; and our people who are less presentable are to be treated with greater propriety."

"What in the world are you talking about? Greater propriety? I've never heard that," said Thomas.

"You should know that," said Weinstein.

"Know what?" asked Thomas.

"Nothing," said Weinstein.

"Ok. I think we've exhausted this. Before I leave, I want to know — are you going to put Private Williams on the witness stand?" asked Thomas.

"Wait and see. I just might. He has nothing to hide," said Weinstein.

"I hope you do put him on the witness stand," said Thomas.

"Why is that?"

"You never know. Maybe I can get him to sing," said Thomas. He gave a lurking smile to Weinstein. Daring Weinstein. "Ok. We aren't getting anywhere with this. At least we tried. See you later." Thomas walked out of the cubicle.

"Yes, see you later. Maybe we can work this out another time. The point is to get to the truth," said Weinstein after getting up and watching Thomas walk down the hall.

"Maybe we can," said Thomas, turning around to look at Weinstein while walking away. "*In your dreams*," he concluded in a voice so low that Weinstein could not hear.

Thomas was a prepared lawyer. He knew a lot more about Andre and Booker than Weinstein did.

But neither lawyer knew what the other was trying to communicate.

CHAPTER 33

On February 4, 1945, Colonel Dixon summoned Tatiana to his office.

"Remember last year when I told you to find out about Major Charity Adams?"

"Yes, sir," she said.

"Did you find out anything?"

"Yes, sir," she said. "She joined the WAAC in 1942 and was working in training at Fort Des Moines. She was in the states, so I couldn't do much with her being back there."

"Understood. Well, she was reassigned in December 1944 to Birmingham, England. I've heard that she is about to be appointed commanding officer and battalion commander of the first battalion of the African American women with the 6,888th Central Postal Division. They moved it to Rouen, France."

"That's where I came in to France," said Tatiana.

"I remember. Now they are coming to Paris," said Col. Dixon.

"Really. I would like to interview her."

"You can. Here is where you can find her. I already told her you would be calling." Dixon handed her a piece of paper with the address of the hotel.

"Thank you, Colonel!"

Tatiana researched Maj. Adams to prepare for the interview. She learned that the 6,888th Central Postal Directory Battalion was an all-black unit with 850 African American women. Its job was to route the mail from English warehouses to millions of members of the armed forces.

Major Adams was among thirty-nine black women in the corps' first training class in Fort Des Moines, Iowa, becoming one of its first black officers.

Rushing to the hotel where Maj. Adams was staying, Tatiana knocked on the door.

Maj. Adams answered.

"Hello, I'm Tatiana Phillips with the *African-American Statesman*. I'm covering the war here. Col. Dixon said that I could find you here," she said.

"Yes, I talked with him about your coming. It is nice to you meet you. Aren't you the first black female reporter to cover World War II?"

"I am," said Tatiana.

"Please come in. You will have to excuse me, but I have to get ready to meet a general for dinner tonight."

"Of course. So tell me, where were you born?"

"I was born in Kittrell, North Carolina, but I grew up in Columbia, South Carolina."

"Where did you go to high school?"

"I graduated from Booker T. Washington High School and was valedictorian," she said.

"That's fantastic!" said Tatiana. "What about college?"

"Wilberforce University."

"Where is that?"

"Ohio."

"And what year?"

"1938."

"What did you study in college?"

"I majored in math and physics."

"You *are* smart. When did you join the army?"

"I joined the Women's Army Auxiliary Corps in 1942. I was trained at the WAAC Training Center at Fort Des Moines, Iowa. There were 39 in the first class. It was the Third Platoon, First Company, First WAAC Training Center. All of us were different; different personalities, different family backgrounds, and different vocations."

"That does make for an interesting mix."

"One thing that we had in common was that we had all volunteered to join the military. In spite of everything, or because of it all, we were made into soldiers."

"When did you get to Paris?"

"A few days ago. After we arrived in London, I had to make my first trip to Birmingham to the WAC headquarters. We visited the King Edward School where we would be stationed. That was to give us an idea of the amount of work we needed to perform before the troops arrived. I've done nothing but draw floor plans, assign floor space, work space, barracks spaces, offices, you name it — all in one building."

"How long are you here in Paris?"

"We were to leave tonight to go back to London, but we received an invitation for dinner from Lt. Gen. John C. H. Lee, Commanding General, Communications Zone, European Theater."

"That's for tonight?"

"Yes. Yesterday we met with General Benjamin O. Davis, the only Negro general in the entire United States military," said Maj. Adams.

"Really?" said Tatiana.

"Yes, the entire United States. I have to leave now. I can talk with you further tomorrow."

"Thank you," said Tatiana.

Major Adams and Captain Abbie Noel Campbell reported to the Hotel George V to meet the general. A total of twelve accompanied the general to dinner, including four WAAC officers. During the course of the dinner the general asked Maj. Adams, "Adams, can your troops march?"

"Yes, sir. They are the best marching troops you will ever see." She thought to herself, *I will have to prove my words or eat them later.*

PART 5

The Trial

CHAPTER 1

On the morning of the trial's opening, Oliver and Cub were the first civilians in the courtroom. The reporters selected seats within the defense counsel area, where Capt. Weinstein was already at work sorting through his files. Tatiana came later and sat next to her friends in an empty chair.

"Good morning, Tatiana. How are you doing today?" said Oliver, smiling.

"Hello, boys. I'm exhausted after writing and submitting last night's stories."

"Did you decide to cover this story, too?" asked Oliver.

"Yes, I'm curious to see where this case goes," she said.

Oliver leaned forward, touching the attorney's shoulder. "Are you ready?" Oliver asked Weinstein.

"As ready as I can be," responded the captain.

"How are you doing, Private?" asked Oliver.

"I'm ready to get this over with," sighed Andre.

"Good luck," said Cub.

Capt. Thomas stood and began his statement to the court:

"Mr. President, before we commence there are one or two things I need to say to you. Now, I know that you are duly certified and have read the court-martial guide for court members. Please keep its contents constantly in mind during this court-martial in your duties and obligations as contained in it. I'll summarize some of the more important points at this stage."

At that point, Thomas looked over and noticed Oliver and Cub sitting directly behind Weinstein and Private Williams.

"Sir, we object to the defense allowing these news journalists to sit behind the counsel table. The journalists are supposed to be covering the trial, but it appears here that they are assisting the defense in this case. That is outrageous."

Weinstein rose to respond, but the court wouldn't allow him to speak.

"Sit down, Captain. The journalists will have to stay separated from the counsel area and find seats with the rest of the public. They are not experts or witnesses and have no reason to be sitting there," said McDowell.

"Thank you, sir."

Oliver decided to leave the courtroom; he felt awkward after McDowell's admonition and his own mistake of not moving back to public seating. "They don't need both of us here. Just tell me what happens tonight. I'll come tomorrow," Oliver said to Cub. Tatiana smiled at him as he left.

The trial continued:

"You can make your opening statement."

"Thank you, sir," said Capt. Thomas. "Members of the jury, we intend to prove that Private Williams is in violation of Article 119(b) of the Uniform Code of Military Justice, without the intent to kill or inflict great bodily harm unlawfully kills a human being – (1) by culpable negligence is guilty of involuntary manslaughter and shall be punished as a court-martial may direct. On August 22, 1944, Private Williams, by culpable negligence, discharged his weapon in a manner that caused the death of Private Booker Thompson," said Thomas.

Weinstein rose and said, "The defense will waive its opening statement until the presentation of its case."

CHAPTER 2

OLIVER WAS IN the bar at the Scribe Hotel working on a story when Cub and Tatiana walked in the door, sliding into the booth beside him. "So how did it go today?" Oliver asked.

"Captain Thomas called his first witness to prove the cause of death. He was a medical expert who tied the cause of death to the bullet wound," said Cub.

The bartender arrived to collect their orders. "Café pour moi," said Cub to the bartender.

"Café pour moi aussi," said Tatiana.

"So he didn't die from the hospital infection?" asked Oliver.

"No," said Cub.

"Thomas pointed out to the judge that the hospital infection resulted from the wound's exposure to the infecting agents on the ground," said Tatiana.

"He went through a long examination with a medical doctor about how the hospital was unable to stabilize the infection," said Cub. "He made one conclusion on top of the other. He said that the infection entered the bloodstream of Thompson, and so in essence, the shooting caused his death."

"What did Weinstein do about that?" asked Oliver.

"He cross-examined the witness and implied that Private Thompson would have recovered from the bullet wound, and it was the infection that caused the death."

"How did that sound in court?" asked Oliver.

"Sounded fine to me," said Tatiana.

"What happened next?"

"Thomas called a forensic expert to the stand," said Cub. "He tied the bullet in Private Thompson's back to Private Williams's weapon."

"Did he connect Williams's gun to Thompson's wound?" said Oliver.

"There was some confusion on the serial number. I think they went back and forth on that issue trying to settle some kind of discrepancy on that but they did show that the bullet came from Private William's gun as I remember," said Tatiana.

"Captain Thomas had another witness testify to the statements that Thompson made in the hospital," said Cub.

"The declaration." said Tatiana. "They referred to it as a 'dying declaration' during the trial. I thought Weinstein was going to come unglued when McDowell allowed that to be admitted in evidence."

"So with the medical officer determining the cause of death to be the bullet wound, that was the case," said Cub.

"Was that the end of it?" asked Oliver.

"No," said Tatiana, "Weinstein called for acquittal after the prosecution rested. He said Thompson's statement did not implicate Williams. He said something about it being just a childhood recollection, and it was therefore not what they call a declaration, a dying declaration; that's what he called it. He said that Thompson could not have declared what Williams's intent was, even if he was dying, and that it was speculation."

"He said that Williams's weapon was not discharged to cause harm to Private Thompson, but to defend him," said Cub.

"Did McDowell grant the motion?" asked Oliver.

"No, he denied it," said Tatiana.

"I wondered how it was going to turn out," said Oliver.

"I think this has been enough of this particular case for the day. I'm going to see if I can cover de Gaulle tomorrow, so don't expect me at the trial," said Tatiana. "Oliver, where will you be tomorrow?"

"I'm not sure," he said.

"Ok. See you … tomorrow?" yawned Tatiana. She picked up her belongings and headed back to her hotel room. She looked back at Oliver.

"Might as well go," said Cub to Oliver. "You don't need to explain anything to me. If I had someone like her looking at me like that, I wouldn't sit here talking to me either."

Oliver said nothing, but jumped up and followed Tatiana out the door. Cub smiled and pulled out his notes from the trial.

CHAPTER 3

Col. Martins decided to drop in to Capt. Thomas's cubicle. He wasn't going to try to influence Capt. Thomas; he would ask questions and listen.

"How is the trial of the young private?" he asked.

"Fine, Colonel. I was able to get in my evidence. I'm sure Capt. Weinstein will do the same."

"So you two didn't work anything out?"

"No, sir. We didn't come to an agreement on anything."

"This case doesn't sound like a good one to me and besides, this soldier has endured quite a lot over the last few years."

"Yes, he has, Colonel. And I respect that," said Thomas.

"So what's the problem?" asked Colonel Martins.

"The problem, sir?" asked Thomas.

"Why didn't you and Weinstein work something out?"

"I guess we see things differently on this case, sir."

"Is there anything that I need to know about?"

"Not that I'm aware, sir. He is a good officer. I'm sure he will defend his client well."

"I wasn't referring to Capt. Weinstein."

"You weren't, sir?"

"I was not. I wanted to know what it was about this case that led it to trial instead of resolution. It looks like straight self-defense to me."

"It's the facts, sir. I don't believe the private's story and in my judgment this case needs to be tried. Something about this story doesn't check out."

"And what is that?" asked Col. Martins.

"I can see his story insofar as shooting his weapon and defending Private Thompson, sir. But the part that disturbs me is the fact that he went up to Thompson afterwards and mentioned something about his home being burned down when he was a kid. I did some checking and found out that Private Williams's home burned down and his entire family died in the fire. The other private was in the house at the time of the tragedy. I think Private Williams had a grudge against Private Thompson. And I believe that there might have been more to this shooting than just self-defense."

"You think Williams shot him for that?"

"I don't know sir," said Thomas.

"That's a mighty powerful statement to make. Do you have something to go on in court other than a hunch? And why would that come up now, almost fifteen years later?"

"I don't know, sir," said Thomas.

"Well, you better know before putting a soldier on trial based on a hunch, particularly one who has served honorably as this soldier has," said Col. Martins.

"I think there is something else to this case, and in my judgment I have to go forward with it. I can't let this go, sir."

"Alright. I respect that. You are following your conscience. But are you looking at this case objectively or do you have a grudge against the private?"

"I don't have a grudge against the private, sir," said Thomas.

"Good. Carry on," said Martins as he walked away.

"*Except he sings*," said Thomas quietly to himself.

Col. Martins did not hear him.

CHAPTER 4

Tatiana did not attend the trial the next day. Instead, she covered Churchill flying to Paris to meet with de Gaulle:

> *Churchill was received with thousands of Parisians cheering. The crowd was yelling for him like he had never heard before.*

Tatiana was unable to attend the reception, but stood instead in a galley area designated for reporters to observe and cover the event. At the official reception for Churchill, de Gaulle stood up and spoke to the attendees in French.

De Gaulle said:

> *"It is true that we would not have seen the liberation, if our old and gallant ally England and all the British dominions under precisely the impulsion and inspiration of those we are honouring today, had not deployed the extraordinary determination to win and that magnificent courage, which saved the freedom of the world. There is no*

French man or woman, who is not touched to the depths of their hearts and souls by this."

Each day Tatiana worked to find stories with a connection to Chicago in order to convince her father of the relevance of her stay. She was afraid her father might call her back home. She wasn't ready to leave yet — she didn't know where things might go with Oliver. She knew he was interested, and she knew that *she* was interested — but where might that interest lead?

CHAPTER 5

OLIVER DECIDED TO attend trial the following day, but Cub did not. There was too much going on in the fight to Germany for all three of them to attend at the same time.

"Are you ready to proceed, Captain Weinstein?" asked Colonel McDowell.

"Yes, sir. I call Private Andre Williams to the stand."

Andre took the witness stand. He wanted to admit to the judge that he shot Booker, get this over with, and move on. He didn't mean to shoot Booker. The incident happened so fast that he couldn't remember any more.

Oliver was surprised. He thought after his discussion with Weinstein that there was no possibility that he would call Andre to the stand. Now Oliver was *very* interested. He would hear from the private first hand, as would everyone else.

Capt. Thomas swore him in: "Do you promise to tell the truth, the whole truth, and nothing but the truth, so help you God?"

"I do," said Andre.

Capt. Weinstein began his examination.

"Would you state your name for the record?" asked Weinstein.

"Private Andre Williams."

"When were you assigned to North Africa?"

"In June 1942, after basic training."

"Private, how old are you now?"

"Twenty, sir."

"Twenty? You were seventeen when you joined?"

"Yes, sir."

"Where did you serve after your time in Africa?"

"I was in Oran and at Kasserine Pass, Sicily, and Italy."

"Did you come to France with Operation Dragoon?"

"Yes, sir."

"Were you with the LST that was attacked?"

"Yes, sir. I was not originally assigned to that ship, but they transferred Booker — Private Thompson, that is — and me to it. I think they used any ship they could find to transport us to France."

"Thank you, Private, for your service."

"Yes, sir."

"Now, what happened after the ship was bombed?"

"Sir, all hell broke loose on the ship when the bomb hit. We got out of the ship and swam to the shore. At least, those who made it did."

"What were your orders when you were on the beach?"

"We were to go ashore and await the next advance, sir."

"Did you do that?"

"Yes sir. We were spread out and had to climb the cliffs from the beach to take St. Raphael."

"What happened next?"

"We were attacked, and our company fought for a number of days, sir."

"How many days fighting?"

"Probably four or five, sir."

"Six to be exact," said Weinstein.

Capt. Thomas said nothing. He was not going to impugn the service of the young soldier.

"What happened after that?"

"Private Thompson and I were in a wooded area closer to the town. We got separated temporarily from our company, sir. We tried to make it back to the others. On the way through the woods we ran across a home."

"Booker, Private Thompson that is, went into the home and came out followed by two women?" asked Weinstein.

"Objection, leading, sir," said Thomas.

"Sustained."

"Was the home bombed?" asked Weinstein.

"Yes, sir."

"Did the bomb hit the home while you were there?"

"Yes, sir."

"How were the women behaving?" asked Weinstein.

"They were crazy, sir."

"What did you do?"

"I saw them and decided to …"

Weinstein interrupted him before he could answer. “Let me ask you this. Was it possible that another bombing raid was coming?”

“Yes, sir.”

“Objection, sir, he is interrupting the witness, leading him, and speculating with his client,” said Thomas.

“Sustained,” said Col. McDowell.

“Let me ask it another way. Was your ship destroyed in the attack?”

“Yes, sir.”

“Objection, sir. Asked and answered,” said Thomas.

“Objection overruled. He asked if his ship was attacked, not if it was destroyed.”

“Had bombings continued to occur, since the attack on your ship?” asked Weinstein.

“Yes, sir.”

“At the time, in your mind, did you believe that the bombings would continue?”

“Yes, sir.”

“Did you have a weapon with you, Private?”

“Yes, sir.”

“Did you fire the weapon?”

“Yes, sir.”

“Were you intending to fire your weapon at Private Thompson?”

“No, sir.”

“Why did you fire your weapon, Private Williams?”

"I thought I saw a German soldier for a moment, and I was shooting at him when a bomb blast knocked off my aim, sir."

"Was there a German soldier there?"

"I thought I saw Germans, sir."

"But did you confirm there were any?"

"I didn't see any after the shot, sir."

"Did you have any intent to harm Private Thompson?

"Of course not, sir."

"Were there any more bombing attacks later?"

"Yes, sir."

"And what happened after that?"

"I fell into a sink hole after the second blast, sir. When I woke up, the women and Private Thompson had disappeared."

"Are you aware that the prosecution stated that a bullet from your weapon hit Private Thompson in the back?"

"Yes, sir."

"Were you intending to shoot Private Thompson?"

"Objection. Asked and answered," said Captain Thomas.

"Overruled."

"Private Williams, did you intend to cause bodily injury to Private Thompson?"

"No, sir."

"Private Williams, was the discharge of your weapon accidental?"

"Objection sir, that is a legal conclusion," said Thomas.

"Sustained."

"Did you accidentally discharge your weapon?" asked Weinstein.

"Same objection, sir," said Thomas.

McDowell thought a moment about the objection and said, "Overruled. I will let him answer that."

"Well, I was aiming to shoot Germans but the blast caused my weapon to move, and I didn't have good aim when I shot my weapon. I know how to shoot. If I was trying to kill someone, it wouldn't be that hard to do," explained Andre.

"What happened next?" probed Weinstein.

"Sir, as I said earlier — when I came to — Private Thompson and the women were gone. I made it out to the street, and a car came down the road. There was French Resistance around. A Frenchman in a car helped me. I had been shot in my leg earlier from the battle, and I was bleeding and in a lot of pain."

"Then what happened?"

"He gave me a ride. He drove me up the street for just a little way, and then there were shots from Germans, sir."

"What happened next?" asked Weinstein.

"He was killed and the car stopped. I slipped out the passenger side of the car and made it back to the woods, crawling on the ground. There were other shots fired. The Germans came and looked around, and after they left I made it back to the car," said Andre.

"The Frenchman was killed, you said?" asked Weinstein.

"Yes, the Germans killed him, sir."

"What did you do next?"

"I got in the driver's side and moved him to the passenger side and drove the car up aways. I saw a church and I went inside. I was injured in my leg, and I thought I could get help there, sir."

"What happened next?" asked Weinstein.

"I remember talking with them at the church, and the next thing I remember was the Vichy police taking me away, sir."

"Pass the witness," said Weinstein.

"Gentlemen, it is 1700. We are adjourning for the day and will resume on Monday," said McDowell.

Weinstein decided not to have Andre explain his statements in the dying declaration of Booker.

CHAPTER 6

On Monday morning, Capt. Thomas was prepared for his cross-examination. The room was icy cold and tension filled the air. This was the moment that he had been waiting for.

Oliver, Cub, and Tatiana arrived early that day. They were ready for the trial to be over and would not miss the final cross-examination. If the story could be over today, they could transmit the report and move on to something else.

"Sir, I passed the witness last Friday, but I had other questions to ask my client. I ask permission to reopen and ask a few more questions," said Weinstein.

Capt. Weinstein wished to have Andre address his statements to Booker about the incident with Mary and his brother's attempt to clear the home and rescue his family during the fire.

"Denied. You had all weekend to prepare, and that would give you an advantage over the prosecution. You could have asked the questions last week."

Capt. Thomas began:

"Is it true that you and Private Thompson grew up together in Alabama?"

"Yes, sir."

"Where? What city, that is?"

"Mountain Springs, Alabama, sir."

"You played together as kids?" asked Thomas.

"Yes, sir."

"What did you play?"

"Objection, relevance," argued Weinstein.

"Overruled."

"Sports, hunting, anything outside, sir."

"Where did you go to school, Private Williams?"

"I went to St. Matthias School, sir"

"That's not really true, is it?" said Thomas.

Weinstein rose to object: "Sir, none of this is relevant to the charges. I fail to see where he is going with this."

"Goes to credibility, sir," responded Thomas.

"Objection overruled."

"Tell me again the school you went to?"

"St. Matthias Catholic School, sir."

"And where is this school?" asked Thomas.

"Mountain Springs, Alabama, sir."

"Are you sure?" asked Thomas.

"Yes, sir."

"Private, I had your military records pulled, and they say that you had two years at a Negro public school in Haley County, Alabama."

Andre said nothing. He reached for the water from the cup on the witness stand; he took a drink and responded. "I *thought* I went to school there, sir."

"What do you mean you *thought* you went to school there? Is that what you said, Private? You thought you went *where* to school?" asked Thomas.

"At the Catholic school, yes sir," said Andre.

"You thought that you went to school at the Catholic school. Is that what you said?" asked Thomas.

"Yes, sir," said Andre.

"Private, these records say that you attended two years of high school. They don't say which high school."

Weinstein stood up and said, "Sir, none of this is relevant."

"That is your objection? None of this is relevant?" asked McDowell.

"Objection, relevance," corrected Weinstein.

"That's better. Capt. Thomas, what is the relevance of where Private Williams went to school?"

"Sir, Private Thompson's declaration referenced Private Williams's comment about an incident with a young lady named Mary during the eighth grade. I'm probing to find out *where* he went to school in the eighth grade. I think it is important for members of the court to know the name of that school. It goes to credibility."

"Okay I will let him testify to that. I'm beginning to see why that is relevant," said McDowell.

"Sir," said Weinstein, referring to Colonel McDowell's comment. McDowell looked at Weinstein and said nothing.

"Private, why is there no mention of you attending that school in your military records?" asked Thomas.

"I don't remember what I wrote down on my enlistment application, but I definitely went to school there, sir," said Andre.

"You never were a student there."

"Yes, I was," said Andre.

"*Sir*, Private."

"Yes, sir."

"Name one of your teachers," said Thomas.

"Sister Camille was one of them. Father Sanders was one of them too, sir."

"There is a Father Sanders?" asked Thomas.

"He's dead now."

"Who was the headmaster?"

"Father Webster was the headmaster," said Andre.

"Who were some of the students at the school?"

Andre had to think for a moment and then said, "Mary and Sherry were two of them." Andre was recalling his dream and not reality. He realized he was glad that the captain didn't ask him to name any more students. What if he had said that Booker was a student? How could he explain that? Why did he say what he did? He couldn't believe what he was saying. It was as if he couldn't help himself.

Capt. Thomas walked back to his desk and opened an envelope, pulling out some photographs.

"Sir, I would like for the court reporter to mark these as Prosecution Exhibits 27, 28, and 29. Private, I am handing you Exhibit 27. What is Exhibit 27?"

"It's a photograph, sir." Andre looked down at the photograph of a white priest.

"Yes, it is a photograph, Private. Now my question to you, Private, is whose picture is that in the photograph?"

"I don't know," said Andre.

"Private, I am handing you Exhibit 28. Whose picture is in the photograph?"

Andre looked at the photograph of a white nun in his hands. "I don't know."

"Private, I am now handing you Exhibit 29. Whose picture is in the photograph?"

Exhibit 29 was a photograph of a white priest. "I don't know."

"You say you don't know who the people are in these pictures?"

"No, sir, I don't."

"Private, you told me earlier that you knew a Father Webster and a Father Sanders."

"Yes, I do."

"Private, would you look again at Exhibit 27?"

"Yes, sir." Andre looked at the photo.

"Now turn over the photograph. Would you read the name typewritten on the back of the photograph, please?"

"Yes, sir." Andre turned the photograph over. "It says Father Stephen Webster."

"Father Stephen Webster. Didn't you say that he was the headmaster of the Catholic Day School?"

"Yes, sir."

"And didn't you say that you knew him?"

"I did know him, sir."

"But Private, this is a photograph of Father Stephen Webster. You say you know him, but how can that be, if you say you don't recognize the man in the photograph?"

Capt. Weinstein rose to object, "Objection, sir, to the prosecution reading from a photograph not in evidence. That is hearsay."

"Overruled. You waived that by not objecting to your client reading the name prior to the photograph being offered. It wasn't authenticated, but he read from the photograph before you objected, so the name is in evidence. I haven't ruled on whether the photograph is admissible."

"Thank you, sir," nodded Thomas.

"Capt. Thomas, don't thank the court for its rulings. I rule on evidence. That is my job. Whether I admit or deny evidence is a ruling; it is not an indication for or against any side in this case. It is not an indication that you are winning the case, or that Capt. Weinstein is *not* winning the case," said McDowell. "There is no need to thank the court for doing its job."

"Yes, sir," said Thomas. "Private, you say that you knew the headmaster of the school and that his name was Father Stephen Webster. But the man in this photograph is not the Father Stephen Webster that you knew?"

"Yes. I do not know that man in the photograph," said Andre.

"What did the Father that you knew look like?"

"He was tall, black, with some grey in his hair, sir."

Capt. Thomas was annoyed by the answer; he felt that Private Williams was avoiding the obvious intent of his question. He asked: "Private, was Father Webster a white man or a black man?"

Andre paused and said, "He was black man."

Andre did it again. Under pressure, he blocked out the trial and his grief over being tried for shooting Booker; he began to forget what he was saying. The only way to protect himself from the onslaught was to slip into his dream.

Noise from murmurs of the observers in the courtroom grew, while the court members and attorneys stood stunned and silent. Thomas was amazed and stared at Andre in surprise. He turned to look at Weinstein, who appeared frozen like a statue, his eyes wide.

Tatiana was frantically scribbling notes. She had never heard such bizarre testimony in her entire life. *Why couldn't Private Williams admit the obvious*? she thought.

Oliver stopped taking notes. He wasn't writing anything else about this case. Cub was stunned and grief-stricken, watching Skees disintegrate on the witness stand. *Is this the same boy I knew in Mountain Springs?* he thought to himself.

"I assume that you do not know who the photographs are in Exhibits 28 and 29, either. Would you look at them and read the names on the back?"

"Objection, sir, to the witness reading the names on the back of the photographs that have not been authenticated," retorted Weinstein.

"Sustained," said McDowell.

Capt. Thomas approached the witness stand. "Let me see Exhibits 28 and 29, please." Thomas read from the back of Exhibit 28, "It says 'Sister Camille' on the back. Private, do you know a Sister Camille?"

"I do, sir."

"Is this a photograph in Exhibit 28 of the Sister Camille that you knew?"

"No, sir."

"Do you know who this is in Exhibit 28?" Andre shook his head no.

"Private, is Sister Camille a white nun or a black nun?" asked Thomas.

"She is a black nun. The first nun — the first black nun that I ever knew, sir," said Andre.

"As for Exhibit 29, is this Father Michael Sanders?"

"No, sir."

"I assume he is a black priest?"

"Yes, sir."

"And so this photograph of a white priest whose name also happens to be Father Michael Sanders as printed on the back of this photograph, is not the black Father Michael Sanders that you knew at the school that you went to?"

"It is not, sir."

"Private, what was the name of the Catholic church that was associated with the school you attended?"

"The name, sir?"

"Yes, Private, the name of the church that was located on the same grounds as the school that you say you attended. What was the name of the church?"

"St. Matthias, sir."

"St. Matthias. Is that what you said, Private?"

"Yes, sir."

"Who was St. Matthias, Private?"

"He was the thirteenth apostle, sir. He was not chosen by Jesus, but according to the Book of Acts, the apostles voted him to replace Judas."

"Thank you Private, for that," said Thomas.

Oliver came to the conclusion that Andre was slipping back and forth between his reality and his dreams, unaware where he was at times. Andre was grasping his religion for the security that he did not have growing up. He was watching Thomas destroy him on the witness stand, and it was Thomas's intent to make Andre appear a total liar. Thomas was converting Andre's complete self-defense and defense of third party into an intentional murder charge — a crime for which he was not even charged. Oliver could see that Andre was using a self-protective mechanism to survive the immeasurable pressure that Thomas was, and would continue, heaping on him.

The cross-examination went on.

"Private, I have documents that show that the school that you say you went to is an all-white Catholic school on a 300-acre former ranch. It goes by the name of St. Peter's, not St. Matthias. You never went to that school. You walked up there and played on the school grounds. You would see the students in class and look in the windows. The priests and nuns told me that you were asked to leave many times, as the grounds were private property."

"Objection, sir, to the witness statements as hearsay and to facts not in evidence. The court members should be instructed to disregard the statement."

"Sustained."

Capt. Thomas continued:

"Isn't that true, Private Williams? You went up to the school grounds many times and were told to leave because the other kids were complaining that you were using the campus grounds and library when you did not go to school there?"

"That's not true, sir," said Andre.

"Not true you say, Private?" said Thomas.

"No, sir," said Andre.

"Do you know a Sherry Hardeman?"

"Yes, sir."

"Did you go to school with her?"

"Yes, sir."

"At the Catholic school?"

"Yes, sir."

"Did you tie her to a tree?"

"No, I did not, sir."

"Did someone tie her to a tree?"

"Do we really need to talk about this?" Andre asked, looking at Weinstein.

Capt. Weinstein rose to object but before he could say anything, McDowell stepped in.

"Just answer the question, Private," McDowell instructed him. "Did someone tie her to a tree, Private Williams?"

Weinstein sat down.

"No, not Sherry. But Booker tied his girlfriend Mary to a tree as a joke," explained Andre.

"Why did he do that?" asked Thomas.

"I think they were arguing, and he got carried away. She was quite a pistol anyway, and it got out of control, sir."

"Who brought the wrist bands to the school?" Andre said nothing. "You brought the wrist bands to the school, didn't you, Private Williams?" Thomas raised his voice while walking around the courtroom.

Andre waited and admitted, "No, sir. I bought them and brought them home but I gave them to Booker later, and he brought them to school."

"The wrist bands were used to tie his girlfriend Mary to a tree. So you *are* a troublemaker, aren't you, Private? You gave Private Thompson the wrist bands and had no idea where that would lead."

"No, sir. I bought them because I thought Sherry and I were going to go steady. You give one to your girlfriend but I never did that and didn't want them anymore. I gave them to Booker Thompson, not Private Thompson," said Andre.

"Objection. Argumentative."

"Sustained, but the private is correct. His testimony is that he gave the wrist bands to Booker Thompson, not Private Thompson," said McDowell.

Capt. Thomas was ready now. The time had come. He was attacking Andre based on his credibility, instead of focusing on the facts of the actual shooting of his weapon during a time of a military campaign and the circumstances surrounding the event.

"Private, isn't it true that when you saw Booker — Private Thompson, that is — when you saw him and the women move toward the tree, it reminded you of Booker Thompson tying his girlfriend to a tree with the wrist bands that you provided to him? And then you snapped and shot Private Thompson?"

"No, sir, I just mentioned that story to him afterwards to keep him talking. I didn't want him to go to sleep. It had nothing to do with me shooting the weapon. I didn't snap. I thought I saw Germans," said Andre.

"You saw a German or visualized Germans? Is that what you said?

"I saw a German, sir."

"Did you shoot him?"

"I shot at him," said Andre.

"Did you kill him?"

"No, sir."

"And why not?" asked Capt. Thomas.

"My aim was off because we were bombed at the same time. I didn't see him afterwards, but they were there when I left the woods."

"So you saw more than one German and you shot at one of them. Did you think that your fellow army soldier, good friend, and childhood buddy was going to harm the women? Is that why you shot at him?"

"I *didn't* shoot at him. I shot at the Germans. I would never shoot to hurt him, sir."

"But you shot your weapon."

"Yes, sir. I shot and the bullet hit him by accident," said Andre.

"You say your shot was an accident. If it was an accident, why did you flee to a church instead of reporting back to your platoon?"

"Objection, sir, to the mischaracterization," said Weinstein.

"Overruled."

"I didn't flee. I was seeking medical help after being wounded, and I thought I could find some help at the church."

"Medical help ... or mental help?" asked Thomas.

"Objection, sir, to the abusive nature of that question. I ask the Judge Advocate be reprimanded for his prosecutorial misconduct," said Weinstein angrily.

"I withdraw the question," said Thomas as he returned to his seat and sat for a few moments, looking through his notes. He stood up and said, "But let me ask you this question. Private, isn't it true that when you went to the church, you asked to go to confession?"

Andre paused. "What, sir?"

"You heard me, Private. Did you go to the Catholic church and try to go to confession?"

Andre thought for a moment. After a period of time he was forced to admit his response to Captain Thomas's question.

"Yes, sir."

"Private, isn't it true that you are not Catholic?" asked Thomas.

"What, sir?" said Andre, caught off guard. He was stunned. He suddenly realized that he was not really Catholic.

"You heard me," said Weinstein. "Private, have you ever been baptized in the Catholic church?"

Andre could barely speak. He said nothing.

"Private, I asked you a question. Are you Catholic?"

Andre said nothing.

"Sir, I request an instruction that the witness answer my question."

"Private, answer the captain's question," ordered McDowell.

"No, sir. I've never been baptized," said Andre.

"You mean you've never been baptized in the Catholic church?"

"Yes, sir. I've never been baptized in the Catholic church."

"Private, isn't it strange that you shot your friend in the back and fled to a Catholic church, where you tried to confess — even though you are not Catholic?"

"Ok. I'm going to put a stop to this. We are taking a thirty-minute break and will resume at 1530," said McDowell.

CHAPTER 7

Weinstein was deflated, as were Oliver, Cub, and Tatiana, who were watching the disturbing revelations. Thomas made it appear as if Private Williams was lying on the stand, and his lying actually pointed to evidence that Private Williams had snapped when he shot Private Thompson to create culpable criminal negligence. This was not a crime of passion or involuntary manslaughter. This was an accident and the conversations that Andre and Booker had after the shooting were being tortured and twisted into something else entirely. Thomas was making it appear as if Andre shot Booker intentionally.

Oliver decided this should never be reported to the press. Cub was as stunned as the rest of them. He felt that he knew Skees — but he really didn't know that much about him after all, particularly regarding his religion.

"Skees lived with a friend and the friend's uncle," said Cub to Oliver and Tatiana during the break. "He didn't go to a Catholic school. I know the school he's talking about. That school was for rich white folks. I don't know why he is saying he went to school there. It sure is a different Skees than I knew six years ago."

"There isn't anything wrong with him. He's been at war for more than two years and accidentally shot his best friend. *That's* what is wrong with him," said Oliver.

"I'm sorry, but that doesn't excuse what happened," said Tatiana.

"It doesn't?" said Oliver.

"No. It doesn't," said Tatiana.

"How are you going to cover this story for your paper?" Oliver asked Tatiana.

"What do you mean, how am I going to cover the story for my paper? Like I would any story," said Tatiana, unsure of the question.

"But this isn't like any other story. This is war," said Oliver.

"It is war, but how does that change things? He has to be held accountable. Can't you tell something isn't right here?" said Tatiana. "I mean — this is war; you are right. But this case is getting bogged down about where the solider went to school and to church. It's like no case I've ever reported before. They barely talked about his war service over the past two years. That's just my observation."

"Well, we can debate this later. Come on, Cub," said Oliver.

As they walked away Oliver said, "Can you believe she wants to write this like any other story?"

"Well, I'm not sure what I would do," said Cub hesitantly as they walked away. Cub was concerned. What would Nelms do with such a story? Should all stories be written? When do you choose to cover a story, and when do you decline? How do you make that call? *They were reporters, and they would not make that call*, Cub thought to himself. He was experiencing a newspaper editor's dilemma.

Oliver and Cub approached the restroom. Entering the restroom, a wall divided the restroom from the rest of the facility. As they began to enter around the left side of the wall, they heard Capt. Weinstein's and Capt. Thomas's voices in the restroom. Oliver stopped and motioned Cub to be quiet, his finger on his lips, as they listened.

Thomas and Weinstein were alone in the restroom. Weinstein was bewildered as to his next move. Thomas taunted, "So you couldn't plead this one out, could you? You had to take this case to trial."

"I don't know what kind of game you're playing out there, but this is no game," chided Weinstein.

"This *was* no game; this was an assassination of Private Thompson," retorted Thomas.

"You know John, you are one piece of work," said Weinstein, shaking his head and walking over to the sink to wash his hands.

"Whoa there, Captain. Why don't you cool your jets? I'm only doing my job," said Thomas.

"Oh, so doing your job means destroying the private on the witness stand?" asked Weinstein. "Be careful what you ask for. What are you trying to do? Behead my client?"

"What do you mean, behead your client? Is making him answer questions destroying him or beheading him, as you say? Where did you come up with that? I'm just asking questions. You can't destroy someone by asking questions. Everybody can see that something isn't right out there with him. These are questions that need to be answered. He needs to answer. He has to be held accountable," said Thomas.

"Don't you understand that he made a mistake and has had a hard time admitting it? Isn't that something you can understand, of all people?"

"And what's *that* supposed to mean?" asked Thomas.

"You know what I mean. Actually, it doesn't mean anything other than what I just said. Some people make mistakes and have a hard time admitting them. They don't have the integrity to admit they were wrong. They run from their choices and they blame them on someone else, excusing their own behavior and never holding themselves accountable. They use their power to abuse others and to subordinate them. They use them for everything they can get out of them and then abandon them for their own personal gain," said Weinstein.

"What does *that* mean? What are you referring to?" asked Thomas.

"You know what I'm referring to," answered Weinstein, drying his hands with a towel and throwing it in the wastebasket.

"No, I don't. What are you talking about?" asked Thomas.

"You have trouble with paying bar dues, Captain?" said Weinstein.

"What?" said Thomas.

"You know what," said Weinstein.

"No, I don't," said Thomas.

"You were suspended for not paying your dues and accounting annually to the state bar in New York. Then you blamed it on everything else except diligence in paying your bar dues, like every other lawyer manages to do. I suppose you blamed it on getting sick or saying something like 'I was serving in World War II.' You are lucky the State Bar didn't make you retake the bar exam. Tell me Thomas, how does someone forget to pay their bar dues?" asked Weinstein.

Capt. Weinstein played the card he had considered but wished he would never have to play. He said things he wished he had never said. This would mean terrible trouble ahead for him or for his client by impugning Thomas and his troubles with the New York State Bar. He knew Thomas didn't want members of the bar to know about the issue, but he took his chances. He was going to hit Thomas with all he had to keep him from going after Williams again in the courtroom.

"How did you find out about that?" asked Thomas.

"Right. The question is, how did I *not* hear about it? Something like that gets around JAG. Tell me, how does someone forget to pay their bar dues?"

Weinstein pulled a second towel from the dispenser to dry his hands and continued.

"You know, John, the day I became a lawyer I was proud of it. I wanted everyone to know I was a lawyer. In fact, I didn't know what lawyers did. I didn't know where the courthouse was; I didn't know much of anything about attorneys, except that I knew I wanted to be one. The day I passed the bar examination was the one of the proudest moments of my career. But you, you forgot to do something as simple as pay your bar dues. My, my, how judgmental you can be."

"You sorry piece of …" Thomas pushed Weinstein against the tiled wall. Weinstein swung at Thomas, missing his target. Thomas ducked and grabbed Weinstein from behind.

"Whoa, there," Oliver said, stepping around the wall and grabbing Weinstein by the arm. Cub went to the other side and grabbed Thomas, separating the two lawyers.

"I'm going to destroy your boy when I get back in that courtroom. You've made it personal now," yelled Thomas. "I was a member of two bar associations and forgot to pay the bar dues after I left that state. You make it sound like I was disbarred or something."

"You won't get away with it," shouted Weinstein.

"Get away with what? I haven't done anything wrong. He has to answer questions," said Thomas. He pulled his arm away from Cub, straightening his jacket. "You two need to leave — this is between Captain Weinstein and me," Thomas sneered at the reporters.

"All right. All right," said Oliver, raising a hand.

"And don't print anything in your paper about this," threatened Thomas.

"I wouldn't dream of it," said Oliver, now raising both hands up as if he were being held at gun point. "Let's go," he said to Cub. They exited the restroom and made their way back to the courtroom.

"Jesus Christ," said Cub. "I guess Nelms knew what he was talking about when he told me that sometimes we have to do whatever it takes to get the story."

"He's right," said Oliver.

"And he said that if you keep your nose to the grindstone, you might become horribly disfigured. I guess that's what's going on in there."

Oliver smiled. "Very funny, Cub."

Back in the restroom, the attorneys continued to argue.

"You don't seem to understand, do you? No, you will never understand," said Weinstein.

"I know what I have to do is to get to the truth. No matter how hard that might be to do sometimes, you have to do what it takes to get to the truth. You had to take this case to trial. You couldn't plead it, and you put your client on the witness stand. How stupid was *that*? He probably would have been a war hero, but not after this. This is going to destroy him. Who knows what else is going to happen to him when this makes it into print," said Thomas.

"You've lost your mind," said Weinstein.

"I'm going to have his head on a platter," said Thomas.

There was a pause.

"You are a prosecutor. Your job is to seek justice," said Weinstein.

Capt. Thomas said nothing.

Weinstein continued, "You're right. What's done is done. But there was not a good plea offer. He had to go to trial."

Thomas washed his hands in the sink. After drying his hands, he fixed his uniform and looked into the mirror. "We only talked about this once. You never even negotiated."

"Negotiate with what? You care more about the win than justice being served."

"Right," said Thomas, as he looked in the mirror, still straightening his uniform.

"Do you recognize yourself?" asked Weinstein.

"Very funny," retorted Thomas. He took one last look and turned to leave.

Back in the courtroom, Tatiana attempted to make sense of the morning's notes. Cub and Oliver sat down next to her, their suits disheveled.

"What happened to *you* boys?" she asked.

"Thomas and Weinstein had it out in the bathroom, and we had to break them apart."

"*What*?" she asked.

"Yes, it's true. Thomas and Weinstein got into a fight, and Cub and I pulled them apart," said Oliver.

"You've got to be kidding?" she laughed.

"I'm not kidding. Don't write that down! They told me not to write anything about what happened in there," said Oliver.

"Not to me, they didn't," said Tatiana, making note of the fight in her journal.

"Please don't do that, Tatiana. I don't want to get into trouble with these guys," begged Oliver.

She smiled at him, a twinkle in her eye.

CHAPTER 8

"Look, I'm sorry about this. I should not have fought with you, physically or verbally. It's just that this case is a hard one," apologized Weinstein.

"It's a hard one alright," agreed Thomas.

"I'm sorry I punched at you. Well, tried to punch you. And I'm sorry I brought up your issue with the New York State Bar. That was a dirty blow," said Weinstein.

"Sure was," agreed Thomas.

"Look, I don't want this to go anywhere. You have to think about what you are doing here," said Weinstein.

"Think about what?" said Thomas.

"You said you wanted to decapitate him? Did you hear that?"

"Forget it," said Thomas.

"Ok. Let's forget all that was said here. I don't want anything remembered," said Weinstein.

Thomas stared at the opposing counsel. "Me neither," he finally said. "It stays here. But what happens out there, happens. Colonel Martins said to try to make a deal on this case and not bring it to trial, but you did. Now I have to finish it. But I'll tell you what I *will* do. If your client will take a dishonorable discharge and a year in confinement, we can end this now."

"Dishonorable discharge?" asked Weinstein.

"Yes, and a year in confinement."

"Not on your life. You must be crazy," said Weinstein.

"Let's go try the case then," said Thomas.

"Isn't there something else we can do?" asked Weinstein.

"Not that I'm aware of. You wanted a fight. Looks like you got one," replied Thomas, leaving the restroom.

Weinstein stayed behind in the restroom and looked into the mirror. Worried that he had botched his client's defense, he said out loud to himself in anguish, "*What have I done?*"

Capt. Thomas walked back into the courtroom, Capt. Weinstein a few steps behind. Tatiana, Cub, and Oliver sat in anticipation, waiting. They wouldn't miss what was next for the world.

"We are back in session, now. Captain Thomas, you may resume your examination," said Colonel McDowell.

"Private Williams, did you and Private Thompson ever play at your house when you were a young boy?"

"Yes."

"Do you recall the fire at your home?"

The courtroom was silent as all eyes turned to Andre. The young soldier sat in anguish. Although he didn't say a word, his breathing became quick and shallow.

"Does that question bother you, Private?"

"No, sir."

"So what about it, Private? Do you remember the fire in your home?"

"I barely remember it. I was only six years old, sir."

Capt. Thomas led Private Williams through the day of the fire, step by step, leading up to the devastating finale.

On the stand, Andre began to remember. He remembered his brothers and sisters playing in the house. It was his birthday, and he had been allowed to invite a friend over to celebrate — he had chosen Booker.

The boys went up to play in the attic.

"You and Booker went up into the attic, you say?"

"Yes, sir."

"Who lit the candles in the attic?" asked Thomas.

"What, sir?"

"You heard me. Who lit the candles in the attic?"

Under stress from Thomas's examination, Williams's memory flashed back to the recesses of his mind, trying to remember reality and not one of his dreams. He saw Booker in the attic.

"I've killed Booker two times. I won the war," said a young Andre.

"No, you didn't. I killed you three times," said Booker.

"No. I killed you."

He visualized a hand, unsuccessfully attempting to light a match and laying the unlit match down near a pile of old, worn out clothes. The hand struck another match, which also refused to light successfully. The second unlit match was set down next to the first match. Then a third. Maybe the matches were just old or wet. No one looked back at the matches that were set aside. But whose hand was striking the match? Was that his hand? Was it Booker's hand? Andre couldn't remember, because he had chosen to erase the fire from his memory.

"Did someone light a match?" repeated Thomas.

"Yes, sir. Or, they struck a match. There was a hand."

"Whose was it?"

Andre said nothing.

"Did someone light a candle?"

"I think so, sir."

"Who lit the candle?"

Andre wouldn't, couldn't answer.

Instead of raising his voice, Thomas became quiet and approached the witness stand.

"Private Williams, you said there was a hand. Did the hand light a candle? You said there was a hand. I heard you say that."

Andre said nothing.

"Don't look at the window when I'm asking you a question, Private. Are you looking for a window, Private? Look at me when I'm asking you a question," said Thomas.

"Yes, sir," said Williams, looking back at Capt. Thomas.

"Where did he put the match? Private Williams, who lit the candle?" said Thomas.

Andre continued to say nothing. He lifted his head. "Booker was there."

"What do you mean, 'Booker was there,' Private?"

"Booker was in the attic, sir."

"Did Booker — Private Booker Thompson — light any of the candles in the attic?" Thomas began to raise his voice.

"Objection to the reference of Private Booker Thompson lighting a candle when he was six years old," said Weinstein.

"Sustained," said McDowell.

Tears began to pool in Andre's eyes, and still he would say nothing.

After pacing around the courtroom for a few moments, Capt. Thomas walked up to the witness stand and said, "Private. Did Booker Thompson light any of the candles in the attic?"

Andre looked up.

"Private, did Booker light the matches in the attic?"

Andre said nothing.

"Sir, I request an instruction that the witness answer my question."

"Private Thompson, I'm ordering you to answer Captain Thomas's questions." ordered Colonel McDowell.

Nothing.

The prosecutor walked up to Andre and the witness stand. He inched closer to him and asked, "Private Williams, when you were six years old, did Booker Thompson light any of the matches in the attic?"

"Same objection," said Weinstein.

"Sustained."

Andre's eyes were closed, trying to find the memory so deep in his mind.

Andre saw Booker in the attic again:

"I killed you. You are dead. You stink, Booker," said Andre.
"I don't stink. You stink," said Booker.

His voice cracked. "I saw candles and I remember a hand. I saw someone's hand," said Andre.

"Then what happened?" said Thomas.

"I remember being outside, going to graze the horses with my brother."

"What happened next?"

"I remember being on the horse. I looked back at the house; I saw flames coming from the roof."

"What did you do?"

"I was on the horse. I couldn't do anything. My brother got off his horse and ran into the house to get everyone out."

Andre covered his face with his hands.

"Your entire family died in the fire, didn't they?"

"Yes, sir" he sobbed.

"I need a break to talk to counsel in this case. Other members of the panel, you are welcome to join us," McDowell interrupted.

Captains Weinstein and Thomas exited the room with Colonel McDowell, followed by the other court members. Private Williams was left alone on the witness stand.

"I wonder what that was about?" whispered Cub.

"This seems really strange. I'll bet the colonel puts a halt to this trial," said Oliver.

"How can he? He can't just halt the trial, can he?" asked Tatiana.

"I mean, maybe they need a break; clearly the soldier has had enough. Whatever he is going through right now is worse than all the battles he has fought over the last few years," said Oliver, understanding.

CHAPTER 9

Colonel McDowell walked into an adjoining room and pulled a package of cigarettes out from his coat pocket. He lit a cigarette and blew the smoke out while Weinstein and Thomas stood in front of his desk, watching. The room was quiet as the three contemplated the dramatic scene they had just witnessed.

"Okay Captain Thomas, you destroyed the private on the witness stand. Captain Weinstein did not object, but I have to ask. What is the relevance of the fire at age six, to the shooting of Private Thompson, to the charge he is defending?"

"Sir, the army has charged Private Williams with culpable negligence of killing Private Thompson. The defense says that they were friends and purports that Williams would never have shot Thompson on purpose. I think the issue was not that he snapped when he fired his weapon when he saw the women at the trees. He later told Private Thompson that being near the trees reminded him of the incident when he remembered then Booker Thompson tying his girlfriend to a tree in the eighth grade. I believe what really happened was that the defendant resented Private Thompson for many years, because he thought that Private Thompson accidentally burned down his home and killed his entire family. That has to be why he mentioned it after the shooting. This looks like a grudge he has been carrying with him his entire life. I believe that is why he shot Private Thompson. This is a murder case, and I think the private has been dreaming up a lot of excuses and diverting our attention with this story of the wrist bands and the tale that he saw a German like he did at Kasserine Pass. I think the evidence points to an intentional action on his part, and what better place to stage an assassination than to shoot him and then claim that the victim is a war hero?"

"That is outrageous, sir!" said Weinstein.

"It's true!" said Thomas.

Capt. Thomas had created the worst possible explanation. Weinstein knew that he would never trust Thomas again.

"Not so fast, Captain. You haven't charged him with murder. You had the dying declaration. If you thought that suggested an intentional killing, you could have specified that before now. This is prejudicial to the defendant, because you are implying an offense that is not charged," said McDowell. "Captain Weinstein, why didn't you object to the relevance of the issue of the fire going back to the age of six years old?"

"Well Colonel, I couldn't, because it was part of the dying declaration," said Weinstein. "I figured that there was nothing else I could do once it was admitted."

McDowell began to ponder. He realized how devastating the admission of the dying declaration was to the defense.

Weinstein was white as a sheet; he knew he had made a mistake by putting Andre on the witness stand. He realized that he had actually taken Oliver's advice from the first day, when he had already told Oliver the reasons why he *wasn't* going to put Andre on the witness stand. He could have rested his case and saved Andre the ordeal of the trial and challenged the legal sufficiency of the evidence on appeal if he were convicted.

Weinstein began to rebound and think logically. "Sir, he fired his weapon at Germans he thought he saw, and we should believe that. His aim was off due to the bombing that occurred at the same time. He actually did confirm Germans coming out of the woods after he recovered and left the scene. Everything he is saying is true, and it points to self-defense and defense of Private Thompson and the French women, who would have been the first to be harmed had he not acted in their defense. Sir, we object to this line of testimony," said Weinstein.

"That's your objection? That you object to this line of testimony? I think you waived that when you put your client on the stand," said McDowell.

"Sir, by letting that worthless dying declaration in evidence, you forced us to put our client on the witness stand — and now he is using our client to prove his own case," said Weinstein to the colonel.

"That is the chance you took when you went to trial instead of pleading it out. He fought in the war. He doesn't deserve to be on trial for this incident, as if it were an intentional killing, and that is exactly what the prosecution is doing by characterizing it that way. The defendant is twenty years old and faces the possibility of having his entire career destroyed with the outcome of this trial. These are the issues you have think about as a defense counsel when you put a client on the witness stand. I would not have put this man on the stand. These are real people, real lives on trial. Not only does it hurt them, it hurts the entire military as a whole," said McDowell. The colonel paused. "But, in the interest of justice, I'm going to allow this line of testimony."

"Yes, sir," said Weinstein.

"I've noticed you've got three reporters out there. What do you suppose that means?" asked the colonel.

No one responded.

"By the way, what happened to you two during the break? Both of you appear a little different. Can you explain that to me?"

"Nothing, sir," said Weinstein sheepishly.

McDowell looked at Thomas. "Nothing, sir," he repeated.

"That's what I thought," said McDowell. "Return to your counsel tables."

CHAPTER 10

Colonel McDowell told the members of the court, "We are back in session. The defense may continue their examination."

"Thank you, sir. We pass the witness."

Weinstein stood up and said, "Private Williams, you are an expert with a rifle, are you not?"

"Yes, sir. I'd like to think so."

"Where did you learn to shoot?"

"We shot a lot growing up. Everything we ate, we hunted. That was the way it was."

"Were shooting and target practice difficult in boot camp?"

"No, sir."

"Did you in fact shoot a German in Kasserine Pass to defend Private Thompson?"

"Yes, sir."

"You believed that you saw a German in the woods prior to shooting your weapon?"

"Yes, sir."

"Did the bombing affect your shot?"

"Yes, it did."

"Why is that?"

"The bomb affected my aim, and I slipped when the bomb hit nearby."

"Pass the witness."

CHAPTER 11

After the trial Tatiana, Cub, and Oliver walked back to the hotel.

"That was pretty devastating," said Tatiana.

"How are you going to report the story?" said Oliver.

"That question again? I'm going to report it like I would report any story. The soldier's story seems strange to me. I'll report it as a strange story," said Tatiana.

"You can't report this like it's just a strange story or as if it's just another criminal trial on the courthouse beat. This is a war story, and it could have a devastating effect when it is read back in the states. We should all agree not to write anything about this story."

"I can't do that," argued Tatiana.

"Do you know what it's like to be in a war zone?" asked Oliver.

"You know the answer to that. No, I don't," said Tatiana, annoyed.

"Do you know what it's like to be under fire?"

"Asked and answered. You know the answer to that, too. But what are you saying? That I need to report the story some other way? The story is going to be censored by the army anyway. Are you asking me to write it or slant it in a certain direction? I can't do that as a journalist."

"You need to understand what is going on with him. Unless you've been there, you'll never understand that," said Oliver.

"No, I will never understand what he went through in combat. And in this case it's not about what this soldier went through during combat during this war, but instead about what happened to him during the eighth grade or when he was six years old when his house burned down; whichever it is. I can't seem to follow it anyway, since it jumps from wrist bands to a house fire, and this seems like a pretty bizarre case if you ask me. I wonder what all that testimony about what happened in the eighth grade and the fire in his home has to do with fighting World War II. I only need to understand my role as a journalist. I think you have been here too long and are identifying with the soldier. You've lost your objectivity," said Tatiana.

"What about the black soldier?" asked Oliver.

"What *about* the black soldier?" asked Tatiana.

"This is going to make them all look bad," said Oliver.

"It's not going to make *anyone* look bad. This just has to do with this *one* soldier. The war produces all kinds of people. This is just another one of many," said Tatiana.

"She's right," said Cub. "Remember the two soldiers that Patton slapped in Italy?"

"Sicily," corrected Oliver.

"Sicily, then. It is the same thing. Private Williams, Skees that is, has been fighting for years. No wonder he is in the condition he is in," said Cub.

"Oliver, this condition is not just limited to the soldiers. Have you heard about Ernie Pyle?" asked Tatiana.

"No. I haven't," said Oliver.

"He went home to New Mexico because he lost track of the point of the war, according to what he wrote in one of his columns. He wrote that if he were here another two weeks he would have been hospitalized with war neurosis. This is something that all soldiers and even reporters are dealing with," Tatiana said sympathetically, trying to agree with Oliver. "I don't think it changes who we are and how we are to report the story."

"We will have to agree to disagree on this," Oliver said.

The disagreement over the Private Williams story meant the end of Oliver's and Tatiana's relationship. There would be no compromise. Oliver did not approve of Tatiana's view of the case and he didn't want the story covered. He came to believe that there were some stories that did not deserve to be reported in the press.

CHAPTER 12

ALTHOUGH OLIVER DIDN'T want to cover the story, Cub decided to report the account. Nelms selected the title, "Shooting Tied to Childhood Fire."

> *The prosecution reached back to the childhood memories of Private Williams regarding a house fire that killed his family when the soldier was six years old. Prosecutors contend that these memories are evidence that his shooting of Private Thompson was more than negligence. The prosecution contradicted the soldier's testimony that he attended St. Matthias Catholic Day School in Mountain Springs, Alabama, with evidence proving that he instead attended Haley County Negro Public School. The soldier stated that he attended the Catholic school and was taught by a Sister Camille, Father Webster, and Father Sanders, whom he characterized as a black nun and black priests. However, Williams was unable to recognize the photographs of educators that were admitted in evidence. The photographs presented during the trial and depicting the*

true teachers were of a white nun and two white priests with the same names.

Tatiana reported the story in a similar manner, but included the fight between the prosecutor and defense counsel. However, military censors cut that from her article.

CHAPTER 13

The story in Birmingham generated interest at St. Peter's, where Father Webster read the story and was amazed to see his, Father Sanders's, and Sister Camille's names in print relating to a court-martial held in Paris.

Father Webster called Nelms at the newspaper to inquire of the young soldier and ask that Williams be informed that the school was praying for him.

"We are praying for the soldier," said Father Webster over the phone.

"Thank you, Father," said Nelms. "I will let our people know that in France. This story is generating a lot of interest. It is not one I enjoy reporting."

"I understand," said Father Webster.

Father Webster summoned Father Sanders and Sister Camille to his office, although he did not plan to mention the article to either one of them.

"Hello, Father and Sister. How are the students today?"

"Mine are fine. They are preparing for a math exam," said Father Sanders.

"And yours, Sister Camille?"

"Just fine, Father."

"Sister, did you ever hear back from the editor of the newspaper that recently visited the grounds? Did he ever attend Mass?"

"I haven't seen him since his visit."

"Neither have I," said Father Webster. "Father Sanders, do you ever remember teaching a student by the name of Andre Williams?"

"No Father, I do not. I've never heard of him."

"I didn't think that you had." Father Webster paused, reconsidering his decision not to discuss the newspaper report. "I wanted to mention to you that both of your names were noted in an article in the *Birmingham Defender* today."

"Really?" said Father Sanders.

"What about?" asked Sister Camille.

"It seems that there is a young soldier serving in France who believes that he went to school here. His name is Private Andre Williams, and he is from Mountain Springs. I know that he did not go to school here, because we do not have black students in the school. But that is about to change. Sister, have you ever heard of the young Private Andre Williams?"

Sister Camille was quiet for a few seconds and said nothing.

"I was afraid of that," said Father Webster.

"He was the boy from the fire fourteen years ago!" exclaimed Sister Camille, on the verge of tears. There was a pause. Wiping the tears from her eyes, she continued.

"Remember the last service in the old chapel? Your last homily, and we all drove over to rescue the boys from the fire?"

"I do."

"He's the same boy," said Sister Camille.

"Amazing," said Father Sanders.

"He's been trying to get back up here his entire life. We have to help him, Father," said Sister Camille.

Father Webster was amazed. He didn't realize the connection.

"That was the black boy we brought here for a few days before his friend's aunt took him back?"

"Yes," said Sister Camille, wiping away the tears.

"And he is the same boy we told not come up to the grounds a few times?" asked Father Webster.

"Yes, Father," said Sister Camille.

"I had no idea," said Father Webster.

"I was teaching him privately during those years. I told him he was a student here," said Sister Camille.

"My God," said Father Webster.

"I noticed him peering in my classroom a few times. I remember seeing him one day when I had the children move the chairs up so we could clean the floors," said Father Sanders.

"Well then, it looks as if the young Private Andre has gotten himself in trouble in Paris, and he might need our help. Perhaps this is our time to step in," said Father Webster.

CHAPTER 14

Oliver, Cub, and Tatiana still had a job to do. They visited Major Lee and obtained press releases on other stories.

Oliver reported on the Tuskegee Airmen, the African American P-51 Mustang Fighter Bomber Group from Italy. They were members of the 15th U.S. Army Air Force and part of the Mediterranean Allied Air Force. Staff Sergeant Alfred D. Norris, the crew chief of the fighter group, was from Alabama.

Tatiana discovered a story about an African American Combat Patrol in September of 1944 that had advanced three miles north of Lucca, Italy, the furthermost point occupied by American troops, and made an attack. She even procured a photograph of a soldier with a bazooka, firing at a German machine gun nest some 300 yards away.

Cub commenced a story about members of the African American Mortar Company of the 92nd Division who, in November 1944, fired nonstop on the Germans near Massa, Italy. The company was credited with knocking out several machine gun nests.

Maj. Lee offered Cub a story about Brigadier General Davis's inspection of African American troops in France. Lee showed him a photo of the general watching a signal corps crew erect poles during his inspection.

"Did you also know his son is a graduate of West Point and commands the Tuskegee Airmen?" asked Lee.

"Yes, in fact I covered the Brig when he was in Kansas. This will make a great story to send back home," said Cub.

CHAPTER 15

THE NEXT MORNING, Capt. Weinstein gave his summation after Capt. Thomas gave his own short summation. Thomas planned to save his best argument for the rebuttal. Cub, Tatiana, and Oliver were present, sitting in the same seats they selected on the first day of the trial.

"Members of the court, it's hard for me to believe that this case was brought to trial. Private Williams fired his weapon in defending Private Thompson and the two women from a German attack. He said he saw a German, and there were in fact Germans in the area, because he encountered them after he came out of the woods. His aim was off due to a bombing attack while firing at the Germans, and his bullet hit Private Thompson by mistake. These things happen. They are tragic mistakes and no one wants these things to occur. When you go into battle to defend your country, you know this could occur and an American might get shot by a bullet intended for the enemy. You have to remember that Private Williams saved Private Thompson's life at Kasserine Pass, when he did in fact kill a German. The only difference in this case was that there was a bombing that caused his aim to be off. This was an accident. Private Thompson and Private Williams were good friends that go back many years. The men grew up together and practiced with weapons all their lives. Private Williams is a hero who enlisted in the army, trained, and came around the world to fight for his country. It's unfortunate that this incident occurred, but we have many soldiers fighting in Europe. We have no business wasting our time on a case like this."

"Objection, sir. Once again, defense counsel is impugning the integrity the United States Army and this court. I ask that the court reprimand him for his misconduct," said Thomas.

"Sustained, but we are not reprimanding him. Counsel, confine your arguments to the facts of the case," said McDowell.

Capt. Thomas began his final remarks. He was war-torn and weary himself.

"Private Williams reports that he saw a German like he did in Kasserine Pass, but admits he did not see any Germans immediately after the shooting. We don't know if he is making that up or really believed it, which would explain why he pointed his weapon. He says that he went to check on Private Thompson and he mentioned Mary, a friend from the eighth grade with whom Private Thompson had used wrist bands to tie her hands to a tree as a joke. Who thinks of a young girl during a time like that? No one does, except this private. And that leads us to stumbling across the fact that Williams went to a Negro Public School, but *he* says that he went to a wealthy private Catholic school for black students by the name of St. Matthias. It is clear that this is a fictitious name, because the school is actually called St. Peter's and it is an exclusive private school for white students.

"This is troubling to me because it shows that he was not truthful in his application with the military, and I don't understand why he would lie about something as simple as that. It shows that he is not telling the truth with regard to the shooting. I don't know what the point was regarding the incident with the girl at the tree that he discussed with Private Thompson after the shooting. He mentioned something about his home burning down when he was six years old. I don't know why he mentioned that either. Sometimes the truth stares you in the face. If you simply ask people what is going on with them, you will be amazed at how much you will learn when you listen.

"These incidents are small clues that you can piece together. The private school education was a lie. The wrist band incident and the house fire shows that Private Williams held a grudge against Private Thompson for many years. Why else would he bring it up after the shooting incident? It shows that there was really something deeper going on with him.

"Here is what I believe happened, based on the evidence presented today: I think that Private Williams believed that Private Thompson burned down his house, killing his entire family, and he has been carrying a grudge about this for his entire life."

Weinstein was outraged. He rose. "Objection, sir! There is no evidence that Private Williams had a grudge against

Private Thompson and shot his weapon for that reason. I ask that court members be instructed to disregard that statement. I move for a mistrial."

"Overruled. Mistrial denied. The court members will recall the testimony," said McDowell calmly, as if nothing had occurred. The courtroom sat silent as they watched Capt. Thomas.

Thomas folded his hands together and stood for a moment. He was tired, and the trial had taken a toll on him.

"And now in a short period of time, the case will be handed to you. You're going to go back into that deliberation room with that presumption of innocence; that presumption of innocence that the defendant has been cloaked with, while we have been trying this case — that presumption, when you go back in the room right behind you, is going to vanish when you start deliberating. And that's when the presumption of guilt is going to take over you and ..."

Weinstein was taking notes from Thomas's closing and looked over at Private Williams. He couldn't believe what he had just heard. Thomas had just dropped a gift in his lap and he didn't realize it. He turned to Andre and said in a low tone, "Did he just say what I think he said?" He then turned around and saw Tatiana, Oliver, and Cub looking at him. Weinstein opened his mouth and looked around to see if anyone caught what Thomas had said.

Andre said nothing.

Weinstein rose. "Objection, sir! That's misconduct. There is no presumption of guilt. I move for a mistrial," he argued.

Colonel McDowell asked, "Captain Thomas, did you intend to say that there was a presumption of guilt?"

"No, sir," said Thomas, "I'm sorry. I didn't mean presumption of guilt, I meant presumption of innocence. Private Williams has nothing to prove, and it is our obligation to prove the case beyond a reasonable doubt."

McDowell responded, "Ok, with that correction, that's proper rebuttal. Go ahead. You are all right."

Weinstein continued, "But, sir, presumption of guilt can never be proper."

"Overruled," said McDowell.

Thomas continued, unfazed by his slip up:

"But I believe that the facts and the evidence of this case are that Private Williams discharged his weapon and caused harm to a fellow United States soldier. It was no accident. An accident happens if you do not intend the action that you are engaging in or the result of those actions. For example, what if his weapon discharged without Williams pulling the trigger? That would be an accident. But in this case, he aimed and pointed and shot his weapon. That's not an accident. That shows that he intended to shoot his weapon, and he admits that he did not see a German immediately after the shooting. The question here is whether he caused the death of Private Thompson by intending to engage in the conduct of shooting his weapon with culpable criminal negligence. Here he admits that he did intend to engage in the conduct because he pointed and then discharged the weapon. If he was defending Private Thompson from a German attack, why did he walk over to Private Thompson and mention something about his girlfriend and 'the eighth grade all over again'? And, why did he bring up the burning of his home when he was six years old? That doesn't sound like he shot his weapon accidentally because of some alleged Germans in the background, but because of something else.

"In fact, I think the evidence shows that the bombing actually occurred *after* he shot his weapon. And the reason I believe this is because, had the bombing occurred at the moment he made the shot, he would have fallen into a sink hole as he testified occurred afterwards. But we already know that, immediately after the shooting, Williams approached Private Thompson and mentioned something about the 'eighth grade' and his girlfriend and they continued to talk for a while. Was that *after* he climbed out of the sink hole? He must have taken the first shot, walked up to Private Thompson, and then mentioned the 'eighth grade'. He is confusing the facts to cover his crime. I believe that the evidence shows that he either snapped, remembering the 'eighth grade,' or that he shot Private Thompson out of revenge for accidentally burning down his parents' home and killing his family. No, members of the court martial, this was an assassination of Private Thompson."

"Objection, sir. Once again, that is more prosecutorial misconduct by this abusive Judge Advocate. Private Williams is not charged with assassinating anyone. I move again for a mistrial and the court immediately reprimand Captain Thomas," said Weinstein.

"Objection overruled. The members of the jury are instructed to disregard the comment of the Judge Advocate. The prosecution shall confine itself with arguing the charges that are actually brought in this case."

"Yes, sir," Thomas continued: "The bottom line is that Private Williams is not telling the truth. You should find him guilty of culpable negligence in causing the death of Private Thompson."

Colonel McDowell instructed the court members: "It is my duty at this time to instruct you on the law that applies in this case. Also, I'm sure you're all aware of this, but let me just tell you this, before we begin. There is no such thing as a presumption of guilt in a criminal case. All defendants in a criminal case are presumed to be innocent unless or until such time as the evidence establishes their guilt."

The court members retired.

The public had not ever seen such a display of rhetoric going on among the lawyers. The court members decided to retire for the day and take up the verdict in the morning.

CHAPTER 16

Cub's story began:

> *Defense counsel Capt. Jesse Weinstein told court members that Private Williams could not possibly have been criminally negligent in causing the death of his best friend. He told court members that in times of war, the soldier should be given the benefit of the doubt, and that this case hould have never been brought before the court in the first place.*

Tatiana viewed the trial as any other story. Although sympathetic to Andre, she couldn't understand why she should change her version of the story simply because this was wartime reporting.

Tatiana's article ran:

> *Prosecutors portrayed Private Williams as a pathological liar, who could not distinguish reality from fact and deserved to be punished for the negligent shooting of his weapon at Private Thompson. Private Thompson later died following treatment.*

CHAPTER 17

THE NEXT DAY, the court members returned to announce the verdict.

"On Count One: Culpable negligence in causing the death of Private Thompson, the court finds the defendant: Guilty."

"Thank you for your service; you are now excused. Do the counsel have any questions?" asked Col. McDowell.

"No, sir," said Capt. Thomas.

"No, sir," said Capt. Weinstein.

"Okay, Private Williams is remanded to the custody of the army, awaiting sentencing."

Afterwards, Oliver pulled Weinstein aside and said, "I think you did the best you could."

"Thank you, but there's something wrong about this conviction. Anyone can see that. I'm particularly concerned about the closing argument of Capt. Thomas, not to mention all the other tenuous evidence presented. I can't believe this case was even brought to trial. Let's see how the sentencing goes, but I think we have grounds for appeal."

"How long will that take?" asked Andre.

"Several months, but I know we can't spare sending anyone home. Maybe Col. Martins can get us an expedited appeal. I will have to come up with something," said Weinstein.

"Sorry, Skees," said Cub.

"That's ok," said Andre.

"Private, I'm Tatiana Phillips. I hope this works out in the end for you."

"Thank you," said Andre.

Cub, Tatiana, and Oliver left.

Weinstein and Andre remained. The military police let them talk before taking Andre away.

"What do you think?" asked Andre.

"The whole case is a disaster. It should have never been brought in the first place. Anyone can tell that this is a case of self-defense and defense of third person during a time of war, and that Thompson's death was an accident. There was no dying declaration. That should not have been admitted in evidence. Then Thomas implied that this was a murder case when you were charged with culpable negligence. That has to be error. Then his pathetic closing argument, where he says you assassinated Private Thompson, and then totally misplaced the burden of proof. There is no such thing as a 'presumption of guilt' that will take over when the members deliberate this case. And then accusing you of an assassination? How could someone in their right mind make such a charge? I hope the Board of Review reverses this conviction and tells Capt. Thomas to re-take the New York bar exam again. He got off lightly," answered Weinstein.

"What was that, sir?" asked Andre.

"Nothing," said Weinstein.

"Something about an exam, sir?" said Andre.

"It's nothing. I should not have said that and particularly not to you. I should have never impugned the integrity of an army officer," said Weinstein. "For all we know, he was acting in good faith and in the best interest of the army. Like me, he doesn't have much trial experience. I guess he had problems with the case and the issue of your statements about what happened back in the eighth grade and with your home. I think he really believed that you had some motive to shoot Private Thompson."

"I didn't," said Andre.

"I know you didn't. Try not to think about it right now," said Weinstein.

"I didn't do a very good on the stand, did I?" asked Andre.

"You didn't have to; Capt. Thomas with his arrogant ego was too busy listening to himself and making mistakes right and left. This is one case he will regret bringing to trial. No other prosecutor but him would have done that to you," said Weinstein.

Weinstein caught himself again discussing Thomas with the enlisted soldier. "I'm sorry, I didn't mean to say that either," said Weinstein. "Forget what I said. Don't do things like that yourself."

"Yes, sir."

Andre stared and said nothing for a few moments. Weinstein packed his papers and files into his briefcase.

"I don't know why I said some of the things I did up there," said Andre.

"Eventually you will gain control over your mind and subconscious — that's what I'm told. Don't worry about it. Leave the rest to me," said Weinstein as he closed his briefcase and sealed the button. "But those photographs of the nuns and priests ..."

"What about them?" said Andre.

"Did you really think they were black? I did have trouble with that part of your testimony. Why did you say that?" asked Weinstein.

"I don't know," said Andre.

"My guess is that you wanted to go to that religious school, so you dreamed it up and began to confuse it with reality under pressure," said Weinstein. "Let's go."

As the two began to leave, Weinstein looked up and saw the American flag hanging in the back of the courtroom. Then he turned around and looked at the desk, podium, and makeshift courtroom for the Allies in the Ministry of Justice Department of the French government.

"Kind of interesting, seeing the American flag hanging up on the wall in Paris," said Weinstein. "If it weren't for the French, there would be no United States."

Andre nodded.

"Wait a minute," said Weinstein. "Come with me."

Weinstein walked back and went behind the court, looking out the window. Andre followed him.

"See him there?" said Weinstein.

"Who?" asked Andre.

"Capt. Thomas," said Weinstein. "On the sidewalk. Probably on a walk right now." Andre and Weinstein could see the Eiffel Tower in the background.

Weinstein started to laugh. "My gosh. I would have never guessed it."

"What, sir?" said Andre.

Weinstein began to laugh, harder and harder.

"What?" said Andre to Weinstein, as he continued to laugh.

After calming down, the lawyer said, "I know. This hurts. This isn't funny. I'm not laughing because it's funny. It's not funny. I don't mean it to be funny. But don't you see it?"

"See what"? asked Andre.

"It's clear now. It's the only thing that makes sense."

"What sir?" asked Andre.

"He never intended for there to be guilty verdict. He was probably surprised by it himself. That's why he's out for a walk. Mulling this over. He made those mistakes on purpose."

Andre and Weinstein looked out the window as Thomas walked towards the Eiffel Tower.

"He convicted an innocent man," said Weinstein. "He wanted the truth all along. That's why he pursued the case and deliberately made those mistakes — to make sure there would be no conviction or to make certain it would be reversed. That's what the reporter Oliver Smith suggested all along. Thomas wanted to know the truth himself."

"What do you mean?" asked Andre.

"He put you on trial to get to what really happened back in 1930," said Weinstein.

"You mean the fire at my home, sir?"

"Yes."

"How would you ever prove that was the only reason he put me on trial?" asked Andre.

"I guess the same way you prove who caused the fire at your home. You need evidence. He was going to pound it out of you on the witness stand. But he could only do that if you actually knew what happened."

Andre said nothing. He looked out the window. Thomas was walking further away towards the Eiffel Tower.

"Maybe he's looking for his window to the future," said Andre.

"What?" said Weinstein.

"Nothing, sir. I was just thinking," said Andre.

"Well, you go ahead and think and dream or whatever you do in your spare time. You will have lots of it for a while," said Weinstein, watching Thomas in the distance.

Williams and Weinstein turned to walk out of the courtroom.

"I don't know why I said those things during the trial. Sometimes I say things I want to believe instead of what really happened. Saying what I want to believe is a lot easier than telling the cold reality of the truth," said Andre.

"The truth sometimes isn't black or white, and the last thing we wanted in this case was for the prosecution to imply there was some kind of private war between you and Private Thompson," said Weinstein.

Then the lawyer stopped and asked: "If you really thought those nuns and priests were black, then should you have pled insanity?"

"I'm not insane," said Andre.

"I know you are not," said Weinstein. "And JAG would not have prosecuted you if they thought you were. Come on, let's go. We still have a conviction to overturn. Even though some of the testimony was strange up there, the real issue is the handling of your weapon, and as far as I'm concerned it was self-defense and defense of Private Thompson and the French women. I don't know what the Board of Review will do. I'm going to get you back into the field and on to Germany. It can't end like this. You should be commended for your service."

Weinstein and Andre continued to walk outside the room and exited the building. They could see Capt. Thomas walking towards the Eiffel Tower as they were about to depart. Weinstein said, "You know, Private, these dreams that you have? I hope they are really leading to something good for you. I hope they are not some sort of pursuit of what they call a *lost horizon*."

"A lost what, sir?" asked Andre.

"'*Lost Horizon*,' by James Hilton."

"Never heard of it, sir."

"It's just an unusual book written during the depression. President Roosevelt likes it, so people are reading it. He keeps naming everything '*Shangra La*'," explained

Weinstein. "That reminds me, I need to get that book about Andrew Johnson back to you."

"Yes, sir."

"Let's go."

Capt. Thomas kept walking until he reached the Eiffel Tower. He raised his head and looked up to the top of the monument. The public was meandering about, visiting the site. "*What did I do?*" he said to himself out loud. He had deliberately gone after Private Williams to shock him into reality. In doing so, he intentionally tried to harm Williams by proving a crime that did not exist in order to shake the truth out of him. But Thomas truly believed that Williams *was* guilty of something higher than culpable negligence. He thought Williams's story was questionable. If he could shock Private Williams into reality by attacking him, then his attack would be justified. His means justified the ends. His means was to imply there was more to the death of Thompson than just an accident. The end was to bring the young Andre Williams back into reality, but by intentionally causing mistakes that would ensure that Williams would not be convicted. It would be a secret that Thomas would have to carry with him the rest of his life. He would have to keep his methods to himself and reveal them to no one. He had succeeded in convicting Williams, but he realized that he could not use the judicial system against Andre to get to the truth if he did not know the truth. Williams would be better off for it in the long run, he thought. Thomas's duty was to seek justice; not convict.

CHAPTER 18

In late April of 1945, Oliver, Cub, and Tatiana went to Public Affairs for the morning briefing by Col. Dixon. Major Lee saw the journalists and asked them to come back to his office.

"Oliver, look at this," said Lee, handing him a photograph. "I thought you might like to see this one. It might cheer you up. I know you took the soldier's verdict hard."

"Any word on his appeal?" asked Oliver.

"No, but I heard they are expediting an appeal. Maybe it will be reversed and he will be able to return to the front. I think the war is coming to an end," said Lee.

"Let's hope so," said Oliver.

"I wanted you to see these citations we have been working on. Col. Dixon wants them perfect before they are sent up the chain and to Washington. Don't tell the other war correspondents — they will be mad if they find out I shared something like this with just you and not them. You know how war correspondents can be," said Lee.

"I do. It can be difficult at times but I know they have been here and everywhere, doing what they can to get the story. You know, I want to thank you for helping us get through this assignment in Paris. I think you were invaluable in helping us get around London and France, not to mention the press releases. I still remember our dining in outside of Paris," said Oliver.

"Think nothing of it. I was just doing my job. The credit goes to all these men and women fighting this war over here. Black, white, brown, whatever. Here, take a look at the photograph. I think you'll see that there is something greater than Major Jonah Lee here."

Oliver looked at the picture and laughed.

The photograph showed two black soldiers with bombs they were planning to deliver to Hitler taken on Easter of March 10, 1945. One of the soldiers was standing and holding a bomb that read "Happy Easter Adolph." The other soldier had two bombs in a basket with a sign that read "Easter Eggs for Hitler."

"Who *are* those guys?" asked Oliver.

Cub walked over and looked at the photograph.

"What the heck?" said Cub.

Tatiana laughed at the picture. "Now *that's* funny," she said.

Lee looked on the back of the photograph. It was marked *William E. Thomas and Joseph Jackson.* No unit was mentioned.

"I can track them down, if you want to interview them," said Lee.

"Sure do. Some mother back in the states is surely going to be proud," said Cub.

Lee left and came back with some other citations that would be awarded. "I thought you might want to see these," said Lee, handing stacks of press releases to Oliver.

Oliver read the first one: "**Lt. Vernon J. Baker**. And the citation reads:

> *"For extraordinary heroism in action on 5 and 6 April 1945, while serving in Italy, Second Lieutenant Vernon J. Baker, Company C, 370th Infantry, 92nd Infantry Division, demonstrated outstanding courage and leadership in destroying enemy installations, personnel, and equipment during his company's attack against a strongly entrenched enemy in mountainous terrain. When his company was stopped by the concentration of fire from several machine gun emplacements, he crawled to one position and destroyed it killing three Germans."*

"I'm familiar with him," said Cub. "He was in Italy in June 1944 with the Buffalo Soldiers and was wounded in the arm and hospitalized, joining his unit later. He led an assault through the German army to the Castle Aghinoff and destroyed the machine gun, bunkers, and observation posts."

"This one is for **Staff Sergeant Edward A. Carter, Jr.**," said Cub. According to the paper work, he was from Los Angeles and the son of missionaries who moved to Shanghai, China. In 1932, he joined the Chinese Nationalist Army and had to leave because he was 15 years old. He left for Europe and joined the Abraham Lincoln Brigade, an American volunteer unit, and fought with the Spanish Loyalists against Franco during the Spanish Civil War. He was a member of the Seventh Army Infantry Company Number 1 (Provisional), 56th Armored Infantry Battalion, 12th Armored Division near Speyer, Germany.

> *"For extraordinary heroism in action on 23 March 1945, while serving in Germany when the tank on which he was riding received heavy bazooka and small arms fire. Sgt. Carter voluntarily attempted to lead a three-man group across an open field. Within a short time, two of his men were killed and the third seriously wounded."*

"This one is for **First Lieutenant John R. Fox**," said Oliver.

> *"For extraordinary heroism against an armed enemy in Italy on 26 December 1944, while serving as a member of the 366th Infantry Regiment, 92nd Infantry Division."*

"This is for **First Class Willy F. James, Jr.**," said Cub.

> *"For extraordinary heroism in action on 7 April 1945, near Lippoldsberg, Germany. As lead scout during a maneuver to secure and expand a vital bridgehead, Private First Class James was the first to draw enemy fire. He was pinned down for over an hour, during which time he observed enemy positions in detail. Returning*

to his platoon, he assisted in working out a new plan of maneuver. He then led a squad in the assault, accurately designating targets as he advanced, until he was killed by enemy machine gun fire while going to the aid of his fatally wounded platoon leader. Private First Class James' fearless, self-assigned actions, coupled with his diligent devotion to duty exemplified the finest traditions of the Armed Forces."

"And here's the citation for **Staff Sergeant Ruben Rivers**," said Oliver. He read:

"For Staff Sergeant Ruben Rivers' extraordinary heroism in action during the 15 – 19 November 1944, in France though severely wounded in the leg, Sgt. Rivers refused medical treatment and evacuation, took command of another tank, and advanced with his company the next day."

"Your turn, Tatiana," said Lee as he handed her the citation. Tatiana read:

"CPT Charles L. Thomas, *Citation: For extraordinary heroism in action on 14 December 1944, in France. While riding in the lead vehicle of a task force organized to storm and capture of a village in France, First Captain Thomas's armored scout car was subjected to intense enemy artillery, self-propelled gun, and small arms fire."*

"Look at this one," said Cub. "This is for **Private George Watson** from Birmingham, Alabama. I'm going to have to look up his family when I get back to the paper."

"I will too," said Oliver. "What does it say?"

> "**Private George Watson,** *Citation: For extraordinary heroism in action on 8 March 1943. Private Watson was on board the USAT Jacob near Porloch, New Guinea, when he was attacked and hit by enemy bombers. When the ship was abandoned, Private Watson, instead of seeking to save himself, remained in the water assisting several soldiers, who could not swim to reach the safety of the raft. This heroic action, which subsequently cost him his life, resulted in the saving of several of his comrades. Weakened by his exertions, he was dragged down by the suction of the sinking ship and was drowned. Private Watson's extraordinarily valorous actions, daring leadership, and self-sacrificing devotion to his fellowman exemplify the finest traditions of the military service."*

"According to the paperwork here, he is the first black soldier to receive the Distinguished Service Cross during World War II. He was 28 years old and drafted to the 29th Quartermaster Regiment. He was trained at Fort Benning, Georgia," said Cub.

CHAPTER 19

Andre received a probated sentence of six months. But by April 20, 1945, the Board of Review issued its opinion, reversing Williams's conviction entirely and finding no evidence of criminal behavior, ordering him restored to active duty. Williams served no sentence because there was never a valid conviction. His military record was cleared of any conviction; the war was still being fought so Andre could return to the field in Germany immediately or return home. He chose to go to Germany. The end of the war was at hand.

Nelms reported the reversal in the newspaper the next day as "*Soldier's Conviction Overturned.*" The local readers were intrigued with the story. Father Webster followed the story and reported the news to Father Sanders and Sister Camille, who were greatly relieved with the change of verdict.

After the Board Court returned with the opinion, Weinstein read a copy at his desk and called Oliver at his hotel to read it over the phone.

"Williams's conviction was overturned!" he shouted.

"What? So soon?" asked a very surprised Oliver.

"Yes. Brigadier General Martins asked that they review it immediately, and it only took a few weeks. There wasn't much for the court to examine." said Weinstein.

"He's a Brig now?" asked Oliver.

"Yes. Everyone knew it was just a matter of time before he got his star," said Weinstein.

"Listen to this," Weinstein said, reading from the decision:

1. The record of the trial in the case of the soldier named above has been examined by the Board of Review.
2. Accused was tried upon the following charges and specifications.

CHARGE 1: Culpable Negligence in Causing the Death of Private Thompson in Violation of 119(b) of Article of War.

Decision: Guilty

"I'm going to skip over the specifications. It's too long and goes into all the conflicting testimony in the evidence. Here is the rest of it. Paragraph 3," said Weinstein, as he read parts of the opinion to Oliver.

"The opinion read:

3. The court was legally constituted and had jurisdiction of the person and offense. The Board of Review

is of the opinion that the record is legally insufficient to support the finding of guilty and the sentence is vacated and set aside.

4. The defendant contended that: (1) the evidence is legally insufficient to support a conviction; and (2) that the army prosecutor committed prosecutorial misconduct on multiple occasions throughout the trial.
5. We hold that the conviction is not supported by legally sufficient evidence and reverse as to ground 1. We find the dying declaration of Private Thompson to be inadmissible because it was not made at a time that the declarant's death was imminent or spoken without hope of recovery and in the shadow of impending death. The statement was merely something repeated that was allegedly subsequently said after the original incident and caused harm at trial. The statement was speculative and was not subject to cross-examination and constituted legally insufficient evidence of the state of mind of the defendant at the time of the shooting. It was impossible for the deceased to have known the state of mind of the defendant or what the defendant intended by the statement regarding the wrist bands during the eighth grade and the incident of the fire at the defendant's home when he was six years old. Such statements had no connection to the defendant discharging his weapon. We find the defendant's recall

of a childhood memory legally insufficient evidence to support the intent of the defendant at the time of his discharge of the weapon.

6. There is no evidence that the shooting was the result of culpable criminal negligence. The evidence shows that the defendant reported seeing the German enemy and he fired his weapon in response to what he saw at the time. His sight was off due to an attack that took place at that moment. While he may or may not have been mistaken in seeing the German soldier, he did report Germans in the immediate area afterwards and was in fact injured by an attack and the driver of the vehicle, a French resistance fighter, was killed during his escape. A reasonable person would conclude that there were in fact Germans in the immediate area at the time of his initial shot in defending the deceased and the French women, and therefore his shot was made in self-defense and defense of third parties. The court finds no evidence of a criminal offense. The court reverses and renders the conviction.
7. Although the court reverses and renders as to ground 1, the court will also address ground 2. We may not consider all of the prosecutorial misconduct alleged in the defendant's briefing because we find that one of them in particular is sufficient basis to also warrant reversal of the conviction of the defendant. We write separately as to this issue

even though ground 1 is dispositive because we are compelled to address the improper arguments made of the prosecution that would have, standing alone, was error and required a new trial, but for our rendition under ground 1. Ground 2 centers on a statement allegedly made by the Judge Advocate during the trial when he said:

> *"In a short period of time, the case will be handed to you. You're going to go back into that deliberation room and that presumption of innocence ... And that's when the presumption of guilt is going to take over you [interrupted by objection]..."*

8. Private Williams's counsel responded to the statement with a flurry of objections, all which the president overruled. The Judge Advocate attempted to correct his misstatement of the law and admitted error.
9. Williams's counsel argued that the Judge Advocate, by his "presumption of guilt" comment, impermissibly shifted the burden of proof to the defendant. The Army concedes that the argument was improper but argues that it was harmless and cured by the JAG prosecutor's correction.
10. Soldiers have a constitutional right to the presumption of innocence and to have the government prove guilt beyond a reasonable doubt. The right to a fair trial is a fundamental liberty of the 14th amendment. The presumption of innocence although not

articulated in the constitution, is a basic component of a fair trial under our system of criminal justice. It is the duty of the government to establish guilt beyond a reasonable doubt.

11. This notion, basic in our law and rightly one of the boasts of a free society, is a requirement in a safeguard of due process of law in historic, procedural content of quote due process. If we view what happened in this case as constitutional error, we must reverse unless the error was harmless beyond a reasonable doubt.
12. In our view the statement by the JAG prosecutor was a constitutional error and would have warranted reversal and remand. Since ground 1 is conclusive, we reverse the conviction because there is no evidence to support any crime of any nature.
13. The court commends Private Williams for his service to his country during a time of war. The defendant is to be restored to active duty without further delay."

"That is great," said Oliver. "I need to come over and get a copy of the opinion."

"Come get it," said Weinstein.

After the decision, Thomas went to congratulate Weinstein in his cubicle office.

"The court was pretty clear in its opinion," said Weinstein.

"You are right on that. Looking back, I really didn't want to prosecute this case. If Private Williams hadn't mentioned something about the eighth grade and the fire at his home, then nothing would have come from this. Something didn't seem right about the case," said Thomas. Secretly Thomas was relieved over the reversal and glad that it happened so quickly. "I was amazed at how fast the conviction came back."

"Understood. I know my client had weaknesses, but he would not have shot his weapon to get back at Private Thompson for something that happened years ago. Those visions or dreams of his were unusual. No one is completely neurotic nor one hundred percent emotionally stable. After what those guys went through, I'm amazed they are still able to function," said Weinstein.

"Agreed," said Thomas.

"Say, what are you going to do after this war is over?" asked Weinstein.

"I still have a year to go, but I hope to come back to Justice. I want to be a judge after seeing how this one played out," said Thomas.

Weinstein wanted to tell him to make sure his bar dues were paid, but he chose to use a bit of discretion and said nothing on that topic. "With your record during the war, you should have no problem being appointed. I hear there are some U.S. Magistrate positions open."

"What do you want to do?" asked Thomas.

"I hear there's a need for bankruptcy attorneys handling the big Chapter X corporate reorganizations. I doubt I can work those cases from my hometown. I might have to leave to go to Chicago to find a firm, or maybe move to a Washington firm to do that," said Weinstein.

"Bankruptcy? Sounds timely to me, with all that's going on. Who would have thought there was money to be made in bankruptcy? Only a lawyer would think of that!" said Thomas.

"Thanks," laughed Weinstein.

CHAPTER 20

THE REPORTERS WENT back to work. Cub wrote a story about the 99th Fighter Squadron of the Tuskegee Airmen and an operation over Sicily and Germany in March 1945. Forty-three P-51 Mustangs led by Col. Benjamin O. Davis escorted B-17 bombers over 1,600 miles into Germany and back to bomb the Daimler-Benz tank factory in Berlin.

His research showed that more than 900 pilots were trained from 1941 through 1945. Of these, 355 were deployed overseas and 84 lost their lives in combat or accidents. They were credited with over 1,578 combat missions and 179 bomber escort missions, destroying 112 enemy aircraft in the air and 150 on the ground, 950 rail cars, trucks, and other motor vehicles, one destroyer, and 40 boats and barges.

The squadrons and fighter groups were awarded three Distinguished Unit Citations, one Silver Star, 96 Distinguished Flying Crosses, 14 Bronze Stars, 744 Air Medals, and 8 Purple Hearts.

CHAPTER 21

ANDRE WAS MORE than relieved when he heard of the ruling. He was sent to the 9th Infantry to fight until the end the war so that he could reach Berlin. After reporting to a regiment in Cherbourg, the regiment came within three miles of the German lines. Oliver followed him and watched Private Williams as he prepared for battle; Andre looked back at the reporter and Oliver winked. Private Williams gave him a thumbs up. They really didn't know each other and spent no real time together, but in war, participants identify with fellow soldiers and those who share the same experiences.

Oliver noted heavy gunfire and German attacks of spattering mushroom bursts of flak as the Allied planes dove over their lines. Oliver also found the first black 155-mm Howitzer outfit in France. He recorded:

> *It was one of the best groups of artillerymen in the army, white or colored. These hard-working gunners will tell you frankly that they know they are good. Their officers told me that they are good. White infantrymen, who won't budge unless these guys are laying down a barrage,*

say that they are good, and German prisoners ask to see our automated artillery that comes so fast and so accurate.

Late in the afternoon, I was taken to a cleverly concealed gun of one battery engaged in shelling a target miles away by First Sgt. John Clay, of Louise, Mississippi.

As we arrived, S/Sgt. W.G. Gaiter, of Seaside Heights, N.J., had a field phone in his hand and said quietly "fire mission," and all twelve men jumped to alert. "Base deflection so and so," said Gaiter, and the men automatically twisted dials causing the big gun to swerve to the described position. "Load with charge so and so and fire," Gaiter snapped.

At Cherbourg, the greatest gathering of colored war correspondents in history could be seen. There were Randy Dixon, Courier; Edward Toles, Defender; Roi Ottley, Rudolph Dunbar, Allen Morrison, Stars and Stripes; Ollie Stewart, Defender. We visited Nazi subterranean forts, which still smelled of slaughter. Nearby was the supposed launching ramp for pilotless planes the Germans had sent over southern England. It is almost unbelievable in size and ingenuity.

In the Cherbourgh area there are actually more colored troops than white. No one hesitates to give full credit to our lads for the prominent part they have played in France.[45]

CHAPTER 22

Oliver, Tatiana, and Cub learned that Ernie Pyle was killed in the South Pacific on April 18, 1945. He went to cover the war in the Pacific after taking some time off in New Mexico. They were saddened by the news. His death was no different from the death of any soldier on the field. Once in war together, they were connected for life.

Pyle and Lt. Col. Joseph B. Coolidge, the commanding officer of the 305th Infantry Regiment, were traveling by jeep on Iejima, northwest of Okinawa, when they took enemy fire. Pyle took cover in a ditch. He raised his head to look around and a bullet hit him in the left temple. Eleanor Roosevelt paid tribute to him in her newspaper column, *My Day*: "I shall never forget how much I enjoyed meeting him here in the White House last year," she wrote, "and how much I admired this frail and modest man, who could endure hardships because he loved his job and our men."

Maj. Lee reported to Oliver that Allies found Lt. Alexander Jefferson and others at Stalag VIIA. Patton's 14th Armored Division liberated them.

"There were twelve Tuskegee Airmen there. They should all be heading back to the states soon," Lee told Oliver.

By May 1945, the Allies marched on all sides of Germany to crush the Nazis and reach Berlin. Hitler committed suicide, and prior to his death named his successor. The war in Europe would end.

Bill Downs reported on the capitulation of Hamburg on May 3, 1945, delivering a first-hand account of the state of Berlin. He gave an eyewitness account of the German unconditional surrender to Field Marshal Bernard Montgomery in a carpeted tent at Montgomery's headquarters on the Timeloberg Hill at Wendisch Evern. Montgomery sat at the head of the table draped with an army blanket. He called on each German delegate to sign the instrument of surrender. The surrender was filmed by the British Pathe News and recorded for broadcast on radio by the BBC, with commentary by the Australian war correspondent Chester Wilmot.

Downs covered the signing:

> *"When Monty entered the tent, the Germans snapped to attention like puppets. He put on his spectacles, took up the papers and said: 'I will now read the terms of surrender.' The Germans sat like statues, not a flicker of any kind of motion on their faces. Solemnly, but with a note of triumph in his voice, Monty read the terms of surrender. And then, one by one, the Germans signed."*

The 761st reached Styr, Austria, on May 5, 1945, where they lined up along a bridge preparing for the surrender ceremonies. A jeep waving a starred blue flag drove between their lines. General Patton, with his pearl-handled pistols, stood up and the troops of the 761st Tank Battalion stood at attention and saluted. He saluted back sharply and continued on.

The 761st Tank Battalion was in combat a continuous 183 days, participated in four major Allied campaigns in six countries, and inflicted more than 130,000 casualties on the enemy. Eight enlisted men were given battlefield commissions. Three hundred ninety-one received decorations. They were awarded 7 Silver Stars, 56 Bronze Stars for Valor (clusters on three of them), and 246 Purple Hearts (clusters on eight). Three officers and 31 enlisted men were killed in action, and 22 officers and 180 enlisted men were wounded.

CHAPTER 23

THE WAR ENDED in Europe and Andre processed out in December 1945 at Fort Bragg, along with many others who were given awards at a formal ceremony. None of the others with him had such a harrowing experience as Andre. The army gave Williams a bus ticket back to Mountain Springs. During the ride, someone in the bus kept playing the new Lionel Hampton song *"Hey! Ba-Ba-ReBop,"* over and over again. Andre would start his life over when he got back to Mountain Springs.

Once in town, Andre saw the Second Street Barbershop. There were Alvin and Louis inside, cutting hair. And there was Cousin Carl — he remembered Shorty calling the white man "Cousin Carl" and smiled. He saw another shoeshine man in Shorty's place, but still he visualized Shorty at the front window, shining shoes like he did when Andre was fourteen, holding up the brush in his hand for customers to see him. Shorty appeared and looked out the window, raising his brush. Andre smiled. He knew Shorty was not there. There was Betty Lou's Grill next door and Famous Hamburgers, with the smoke coming out of the open window and customers enjoying their meals on the open seating. The smell of onions made its way into the bus.

"Gosh, that smell. It's still there," he said.

There was the same man with the blue umbrella saying, "Prepare for the coming of Jesus Christ." The bus went another block and there sat the lady in the wheelchair, ringing her bell while her voice squeaked across town. He was surprised that her voice didn't stop the wheels of the bus. He knew she had aged, but she didn't look any older. No one could get any older than she already was. He could hear her singing and begging for money, ringing her bell. Andre smiled. Nothing changes in Mountain Springs.

Andre went to see his parents' property, where they lived the life of sharecroppers; they never actually owned the property. They lived in an extra home behind the main home in the front, a home that the owners provided for the workers.

The owner saw Andre walking up in his uniform.

"You need help?" he asked.

"I was looking for the old house that used to be out back. I used to live here with my parents."

"There isn't a home back there."

"I'm talking about around 1930 — there was a house back there."

"The one that burned down years ago? That old shack? People wondered why that house burned down. I was told that from the last owners who sold me the property."

"My family died in the home."

"Sorry to hear that," said the old white man.

He walked with Andre to the spot where the house used to be.

"This is where it happened. I thought I started the fire. We were in the attic with matches, lighting cake candles after cutting up and eating my birthday cake. I was just a kid. My other sisters and brother were inside. There wasn't any way I could take the blame for that. It was an accident. I'm sorry everyone was killed in the fire. I'm going to rebuild this home and stay and work the property."

The old man looked at Andre as if he were crazy and walked back to his house.

Andre crossed over the property and walked up the hill. There was St. Peter's. He traipsed through the woods, stickers tearing his ribbons as he made his way through the thicket. There was the tree where Sister Camille would meet with him. There were the Stations of the Cross along the pebbled walkway path that was surrounded by olive trees. He walked up to the Mother Mary statue, freshly painted white and blue and her face tan.

He looked at the chair and remembered seeing Sister Camille sitting at the bench, waving at him. She was the first nun he had ever seen.

He walked the grounds and up to the windows, looking in at the classes. There was Father Sanders, still teaching math. He had only died in his dream. He didn't see any chairs being moved and he certainly didn't say, "*Horse feathers*!"

Andre smiled. He went into the cathedral that was now over fifteen years old and sat on a pew for a while to think. Finally, he stood up and walked back to his uncle's home.

Arriving at the familiar doorstep, he knocked. George answered the door.

"I'm back. Can I stay here?"

George hugged him and said nothing.

Sherry was excited when he came to see her in his uniform. She was his window to the future, whatever that might be. He had found true love. Now he would have to decide what to do next in his life.

CHAPTER 24

Oliver's last story in Europe was published in February 1946 after he went to Rome and was granted the first private audience by an American black correspondent by Pope Pius XII. He covered the Ceremony of Consistory at St. Peter's Cathedral.

Tatiana departed the same month for Chicago. Covering Private Williams's trial in Paris sparked her interest in the Port Chicago Mutiny, where forty-seven of fifty sailors were released in January 1946 after their convictions; three were still serving time in prison. Tatiana wanted to revisit that story.

She said her goodbyes to Oliver before he left for Rome. She was in love with Oliver and she convinced her father to let her remain after the war, waiting for him. She dreamed about Oliver, looking out the window of her airplane heading to Chicago. But they parted ways abruptly after the trial of Private Williams and kept a professional distance after that, with each suspecting there were words left unsaid.

Her proud father, Andrew Phillips, and his wife Ethyl were there to meet her at the airport.

Oliver returned to Birmingham the next month in March 1946. It was not the same in Paris without Tatiana. He began his daily grind of reporting, just like he did when he joined the paper. It was Oliver and Nelms again, just like old times. Nelms was getting older and still a curmudgeon at times. Cub was in Europe and finally took Oliver's place. Now Oliver found himself editing stories that Cub sent home from Europe.

Oliver had plenty to do, wrapping up his four-year stint overseas. He still planned to return to Paris. He knew Nelms wouldn't like losing two reporters again. He would have to bring Cub back.

CHAPTER 25

After settling in Birmingham, Oliver traveled to Mountain Springs to revisit the life of Andre and Booker for a story one year after the war. Oliver found Andre working at the same gas station with George. Andre was excited to see him. He showed Oliver around Mountain Springs and he took him downtown. He wanted him to see the Bargain Barn, Second Street Barbershop, Betty Lou's Grill, Famous Hamburgers, and Zero Pawnshop; he wanted Oliver to smell the onions and hear the old lady in the wheelchair. Sure enough, there were the onions, the lady in the wheelchair singing, and the man with the blue umbrella. He took him to see where his home used to be. Oliver convinced Andre to visit him at the newspaper in Birmingham the following week. Andre agreed to come, and Oliver gave Andre bus fare for the trip.

Oliver visited the majestic grounds of St. Peter's, finally meeting Father Webster, Father Sanders, and Sister Camille. They were all alive and well. He explained the court-martial of Andre, the circumstances of Booker's death, and the fire at Andre's home. They had read multiple articles about the trial and soldiers and were grateful to Oliver for the details he provided. He asked that they meet him at the newspaper in one week, where they could meet Andre and discuss the story. He told them that he planned to talk with Ed Nelms about giving Andre a job at the newspaper. Oliver wanted to know if Andre could attend the school and receive the education his mother always wanted.

Andre, wearing his uniform and medals, brought Sherry with him to meet Oliver at the *Birmingham Defender*, promising Sherry that he would take her around downtown Birmingham afterwards. He wanted to see Booker's grave marker as well.

"Nice medals. Bronze Star, Purple Heart, Army Good Conduct Medal, American Defense Service Medal, European African Middle Eastern Campaign Medal, World War II Victory Medal, and Combat Infantryman Badge," said Oliver.

"Thank you. I still have some more coming," said Andre. "I haven't worn the uniform since I came back. I decided to put it back on."

"Hello. Oliver Smith," the reporter said to Sherry.

"Sherry Hardeman," she smiled, extending her hand to him.

"Andre showed me your picture in Africa."

"He did?" Sherry said looking at Andre. "You didn't tell me that."

"You've recovered from the trial and service?" asked Oliver.

"Best I can, I suppose," said Andre.

Oliver inquired: "How is Booker's uncle? How did he take the loss of Booker?"

"He wanted him to come back, of course. He didn't follow the story that closely. We don't talk about it," said Andre.

"What are you going to do now?" asked Oliver.

"Work at the gas station, I guess for now."

"You have the G.I. Bill. You should go to college."

"I know. I will."

"I've been telling him the same thing," said Sherry.

"Andre, how about coming to the newspaper. I can get you a job here. We did it for Cub. You could be a journalist. With your experience overseas, we are going to need another foreign correspondent someday."

"In my dream, Father Webster told me that the word would take me somewhere. I never thought it would be as a journalist," said Andre.

Oliver looked Andre in the eye. "We all have the power to change. You can open yourself up to new possibilities. You could put this issue of the fire and Booker behind you." He paused. "I always wondered about this. Did you ever think Booker started the fire? That thought never crossed your mind?"

"Yes, but I could never figure out if I did it or he did it. We just blocked it out of our minds and didn't talk about it.

I remember seeing a hand light a candle in the attic and put the matches down near the old clothes. That's all that I could remember. I couldn't take the blame, so I blocked it out of my mind and had to escape. I guess I always resented him."

Oliver, always the investigator, continued to probe. "How did you know the names of the people at the school if you had never met them?"

Sherry looked at Andre, confused. Andre had not told her what happened at the trial in Paris.

"I met with Sister Camille many times. And there were brochures with the staff's names. Sometimes Booker and I would come up and look around when they were having some kind of event. Sister Camille told me about Father Webster and Father Sanders. After a while, if you go to church, you know who people are."

"Why did you say they were black during the trial when they were white?" Oliver asked.

Sherry was truly curious now.

Oliver looked at him. "You don't have to answer that." He paused. "You seem pretty educated and knowledgeable for your age without formal schooling."

Andre answered his question. "I don't know. Sometimes I visualize these things and then I confuse the two."

"Probably stress," said Oliver. "You know, since I've been writing for the paper, I've found that sometimes there is no truth. There are just facts and opinions. Some good opinions and some bad opinions. Then when I'm writing, I hear some internal voice tugging at me and that internal voice is the one that I end up listening to. That voice that no one pays attention to."

"That's not the truth. That's women's intuition," said Sherry.

They all laughed.

"So you know Sister Camille and Father Webster and Father Sanders?" asked Oliver.

"I know Sister Camille. She taught me a lot. She gave me assignments and books to read. She told me I was a student of hers, so I thought I could say I went to school at St. Peter's and it was the truth."

"Or a fact," said Oliver. "It was the truth. She taught you. I can see how you could say you were her student and therefore a student of the school. So where did you come up with the name St. Matthias, instead of St. Peter's?"

"That was just a dream. Another stupid dream. Sister Camille taught me all the apostles and one day I asked what happened after Judas died. She said that the others elected Matthias to replace him. I never forgot that name."

"Amazing." The buzzer to Oliver's office rang. It was his secretary.

"Mr. Oliver, Father Webster and the staff from St. Peter's are here to see you."

"They are here? Andre, can you step into the next room? There are some people I want you to meet."

"Did she say 'St. Peter's'?"

"Yes."

Andre's eyes widened. Oliver did not tell Andre what he was doing. He arranged for the characters in Andre's dream to be present in the same room.

Andre was speechless. Father Webster, Father Sanders, Sister Camille, Sister Aude, and Sister Laurie were there. They were white in reality and black in his dream. If they only knew how he had perceived them in his dream. He was now in reality. Sister Camille immediately walked forward to hug Andre.

The thought of Booker romancing Mary and singing at the dance at St. Matthias in his dream were funny to him now. Booker never wore anything other than overalls; he hardly took a bath when they were young and his fingernails were never clean. The idea of him dancing like a professional was even funnier. "Booker stinks," his Sister LaVonda said. He remembered that. He couldn't imagine Booker singing publicly to the students at the dance, especially one of the songs that Andre had written. Booker hated all music. It was funny to Andre that he could place Booker in his dream, have him sing and dance and do things that Booker hated and would never do.

Father Sanders had never died. His part of Andre's imaginary story was amusing to him. No students had abused him, as Andre imagined.

"You have quite an imagination, young man," Father Sanders said, offering his hand. "Father Sanders is my name."

Andre smiled. "I know you."

"You do? Did I really say, 'Horse feathers'?"

Andre laughed. But he felt awkward that his private moments were on public display.

"Andre, these people are here to help you in your civilian life," said Oliver.

"As a matter of fact," said Father Webster, "the school has started a college program and you have free tuition to attend St. Peter's College after you complete your high school equivalency."

"And you could work part-time at the newspaper," said Oliver.

Three years at war and Andre still had emotions. He looked much older than his now twenty-two years; he could have passed for thirty years old. He did not know how he would ever get out of the mess with Booker. But now, he was forgiven.

"You know, I have the G.I. bill so it doesn't have to be free," said Andre.

"That's right," said Father Webster. "I had forgotten about that. We will offer another position at the school for a worthy recipient."

Father Webster walked over to Andre and said to him, "Andre, I want you to think about this. Before you were ever born, God knew that you were going to be born and had a plan for your life."

"How can that be?" said Andre.

"You know what? I'm glad that I don't have to understand everything God says and does. I just have to *believe* what he says," said Father Webster.

Andre smiled.

The door opened and Nelms and Tatiana Phillips entered the room. Nelms walked with a limp — his seventy-six years were showing.

"I'm not drunk, just old," Nelms explained, walking to the seat at the head of the table. Father Webster got up and pulled the seat out for Tatiana as she sat down across the table from Oliver.

Nelms sat down and turned to Oliver. "So you have decided to go to France, and now Cub wants to stay over there, too. I think it's time for Cub to come home. You'll be the first permanent foreign correspondent for the *Birmingham Defender* in Europe."

"Thank you," said Oliver.

"Oliver, look who came to visit us today from our friendly competition from the *African-American Statesman* in Chicago. Have you met Tatiana Phillips?"

"Yes, Tatiana and I spent a lot of time together in Europe," Oliver smiled.

"Yeah, I knew that. Her father is the editor the *African-American Statesman*. You should know that," said Nelms. He had forgotten about Oliver's meeting with Andrew Phillips in 1941.

"Really, I didn't know that," said Oliver coyly. "How is your father?"

"He's fine. Thank you for asking," said Tatiana.

"Tatiana Phillips," the journalist introduced herself as she offered her hand to Father Webster.

"Father Stephen Webster."

"Father Michael Sanders."

"Sister Camille."

"Sister Aude."

"Sister Laurie."

"Andre, you will be fine. What are you going to do now?" asked Sister Camille.

"Looks like I have some decisions to make." He looked at Sherry and she smiled. "I think we will go listen to the cotton grow."

Sherry looked at him and asked, "Can you hear the cotton grow?"

"Only in your dreams," said Andre.

CHAPTER 26

After everyone left the room, Tatiana and Oliver remained alone. Oliver looked at Tatiana and said, "I thought I would never see you again."

"I didn't either, but I had to come back."

"And why is that?" asked Oliver. "I thought you were going back to Chicago to be editor of the newspaper."

"No. I came back for you."

"You came back for me?" said Oliver. "And why would you come back for me? I'm headed back to Paris."

"I came back because I love you ... *with my face uplifted toward the eternal snows of the nearby Atlas peaks*," said Tatiana, tears in her eyes.

"You love me? I love you too," admitted Oliver.

The two embraced and remained quiet for several minutes as Oliver became comfortable, remembering Tatiana in his arms again.

"What are we going to do about that?"

She laughed. "Yes, what *are* we going to do about that?"

"I think you need to meet my mother. I'm sure she's going to want you to stay in Birmingham. I want to go to Paris. You want to go to Chicago. How will we figure this out?"

"I have no idea," said Tatiana.

Oliver took Tatiana to his parents' home and rang the bell. Maryellen came to the front door and saw them standing on the doorstep, grinning from ear to ear.

"Oh Oliver, what have we here?" she said. "Bruce, come here! Oliver is home and look who he has with him!"

CHAPTER 27

ANDRE AND SHERRY were married at the First African Baptist Church. The entire St. Peter's staff attended the ceremony. By that time, Uncle George had risen to pastor in the Baptist church and performed the ceremony. Being new to the ministry, George zealously enjoyed his new position. Before the marriage vows were taken, George gave a ten-minute sermon about how couples should be more "childlike" instead of "childish"; a young boy on the front pew fell asleep before the vows even began and fell to his side, his body stretched across the pew. George forgot that he was to perform a wedding and instead gave an awkward sermon; the attendees wondered what the content had to do with the wedding. Father Sanders' eyebrows rose with the unusual lecture. Sisters Camille and Aude smiled, not trying to suggest anything; the other Catholic members glanced at each other, saying nothing. The rest of the church members looked amused, while Andre and Sherry looked at each other and grinned. They planned to have their wedding convalidated (recognized by the Catholic church) next year at St. Peter's after receiving confirmation at Easter.

The newlyweds found an apartment near the newspaper in downtown Birmingham so Andre could walk to work. Andre began his new job at the *Birmingham Defender*, following in the footsteps of Shorty Miller. *I wonder if Mr. Nelms will give me a nickname?* he thought to himself. As he unpacked his belongings, he discovered several pictures and sat down to look at them. They were of he and Booker together at boot camp. And there was the photograph at Kasserine Pass. He smiled. He sat on the bed and lay down, looking at the ceiling.

He started thinking about Aunt Clara and wondered what had become of her. What happened to her during those years after the fire?

Then he heard footsteps coming up the stairs.

"Andre?" someone called. He heard a knock on the door and sat up. "Andre. It's me, Clara. Booker's Aunt Clara."

"Clara?" he said, opening the door. He had not seen her in years.

"Is it really you? It *is* my precious boy. How you have grown!" exclaimed Clara.

"Is that you, Clara? It's been so long. I honestly don't remember the last time I saw you," said Andre. He couldn't believe that she was here. How strange that he had just been thinking about her.

"I heard from George that you were here. I was heading down to Jackson and decided to come to find you. It is me, still here, alive in the flesh. Oh, my precious nephew. I brought you some things."

She hugged him.

"Thank you. Do you want to sit down?"

"Yes."

"My gosh. I haven't seen you in such a long time, I hardly recognize you. I can't offer you anything much. I have some coffee brewing. I was going to stay up late and read a few books that the newspaper folks gave me."

He poured Clara a cup of coffee and she sat down at the small breakfast table. Andre noticed her purse on the floor. It seemed familiar, somehow.

"I came because I wanted you to know that I understand what you went through over there."

"What do you mean?" he asked.

"I mean the trial and all and what happened to Booker."

"Yes. It still hurts. I want to get past it."

"I want to show you some things that I found at my home." She pulled a paper folder from her purse. "Look at this. It is a picture of your parents when they were married. I bet you hadn't seen this before."

Andre smiled. "No. I hadn't."

"I don't know why it never occurred to me that you hadn't seen any of these. But I was going through some things and I found these pictures. I put them up there to keep them safe. Lord knows I had to keep them from Booker. He always liked going into the attic and getting into all kinds of things up there."

"Yes, he did," said Andre.

"Here is a photo of your brothers and sisters. I bet you had never seen that one."

"No. I hadn't."

"And here is one of you. And look, here is one of your family, all five of you one Sunday. Pastor Jones found this one. He said it was Easter and your father had you kids get up and sing "My Shepherd Will Supply My Need" for the entire church. My, how those were good times. You were one singing family. Those times were so grand."

"I don't remember it. I remember singing it in the house one time," said Andre.

"That was the day of the fire. You were so young. I bet you can hardly remember. And look, here is a photo of you and Booker."

"Really? It *is* him. I can see the resemblance."

"Oh, my precious Booker. He was like a son to me. You know I wanted to keep both of you boys with me but I had too many things going on and you know George, he would have none of it. After you two got older you were too much for me."

"I wondered why he took us to his house," said Andre.

"It was a bad time for me back then. George would have nothing to do with me. I was doing all kinds of crazy things. I was reading the Old Testament, trying out Voodoo down in Jackson, calling on the spirits in the attic. In fact, George caught me doing Voodoo in the attic with Booker once. He threatened to take Booker away from me after that. I convinced him to let me keep you boys a while longer, but I couldn't control either one of you anymore."

"You did that kind of stuff?"

Something about the word "Voodoo" jogged Andre's memory. He knew he had heard about that somewhere.

"Oh, I don't like to talk about it. I even went up to the church to confess."

"To confess?" said Andre. "Are you Catholic?"

"Not really, I just went up to the church. I don't know if that makes you Catholic, if you go to a Mass or not. Your mother was the Catholic, or at least she wanted to be. She had a plan to join the church so that you kids could go to school there. Your father would have none of it. She used to take you kids up there to that church when you were young, but she didn't tell your father what she was up to."

"I think I remember that," he said.

"She did. And she took me up there too, sometimes."

Clara began to cry. She paused and said, "Booker's gone and I know it. I know there is nothing that God can do to bring Booker back. He is with God now. He is in God's hands. God bless Booker. Oh, Booker."

She began to cry as she looked at his photo. Andre didn't know what to say.

"I want you to know that I forgive you for what happened over there with Booker."

"Thank you," said Andre.

"I know that God has forgiven you, too," said Clara.

"Thank you."

"I want you to forgive yourself, too."

"I will."

Andre got up to pour himself a cup of coffee. He wondered what Clara meant. He turned and asked her, "When you say you want me to forgive myself, what are you referring to?"

"You know."

"What do you mean, 'you know'?" he asked.

"You've been dealing with it all your life. It's time to let it go."

"Let go of what?" asked a curious Andre.

"The fire," said Clara.

"The what? Why do you bring that up?"

"The fire at your parents' home. I was there that day. I came to pick up Booker after I brought him over to play earlier that day. It was such a fun day with you kids singing and playing; the fire came out of nowhere, like it just zapped the whole house."

"I know. I erased it from my mind. I never think of it."

He continued to look at her, holding his cup of coffee, trying to remember if Clara was at the house on the day of the fire.

Clara looked at him and said, "I know you meant no harm being up there in the attic with Booker. You were just kids. Booker was just playing and didn't know anything about your attic. You two went up in the attic and started playing with those birthday candles. I still remember Booker crying afterwards."

Andre said nothing, trying to remember.

"Don't you know?" she said.

"Know what?" said Andre.

"I know you didn't mean to start that fire up there with the candles. No one blames you," she said.

Andre glanced and looked at Aunt Clara's hand. He looked at her and his eyes widened. He remembered the hand of the woman placing candles at the Shrine of Mother Mary years ago. Now he realized — that's why she came over and put her face in front of him and stared at him. The red fingernails. The gold ring with the eight-pointed star and the Voodoo in Jackson. It was the same hand in the attic. That's why George took him and Booker away from her. She said they were too much for her, but there must have been another reason. He realized that he had never given George much credit.

Then it came to him. It was Clara's hand that he saw in the attic lighting the candles on the day of the fire. Now he finally remembered. Clara was at the house to pick up Booker, and she followed Booker and him into the attic. Clara lit the candles in the attic that day. Andre looked at her and his eyes widened. He finally realized who caused the fire, but he said nothing. There was no one to blame. She must have suffered a lifetime of guilt and found her own way of dealing with the fire. Andre wished that Capt. Thomas had known of Clara and the true reason for the fire, then he could have avoided the trial in Paris. The judicial system could not pound the truth out of someone if that person didn't know the actual truth. Truth was based on all available facts and was a matter of perspective. Good judgment requires knowing all the facts, not extracting it out of someone who is unaware of the facts.

The undesired and cold reality of truth had picked back up and would move on. Andre had faced reality.

CHAPTER 28

Clara left and Andre dressed in his uniform. He decided to revisit Booker's grave marker at the Veterans Cemetery in Birmingham. Although the grave marker was there, Booker's body was actually buried in France. Andre searched the grounds until he found Booker's marker; he fell to his knees, filled with remorse. He would seek forgiveness yet again for Booker's shooting. Andre lifted his head and spoke to his old friend:

"My friend, I'm sorry. I don't know what I can say now to you. All I can think about is how I wish I could go back and change that one split second. If I could go back in time and change that decision, none of this would have happened. I want you to forgive me for what I did."

Andre stood up and saluted Booker's grave. Private Andre Williams began to walk out of the cemetery, dignified, with his head held high.

As he walked through the cemetery, Andre was amazed at the number of soldiers who found their final resting place in this spot. Row upon row of headstones, dated from both World Wars and before, stood across the property.

Andre strolled around the corner of the cemetery. A man wearing a coat and tie appeared near the edge of the sidewalk. The man looked at Andre as if he knew him, but his face was not familiar. He was not a soldier. He raised his right hand and gave a military salute to Andre as he mouthed the words, "Thank you."

Andre noticed another man next to the stranger, standing at attention, saluting. And then another appeared. And then Andre began to recognize some of the faces he had seen so many times in the newspaper or newsreels. There were Oliver, Tatiana, Cub, and Ed Nelms. Then Edward R. Murrow and Eric Sevareid; then May Craig, Howard K. Smith, Ernie Pyle, Ernest Hemingway, Mary Welsh, Andy Rooney, Helen Kirkpatrick, and Martha Gellhorn. As Andre continued to walk past the men and women honoring him with salutes, he realized that he knew none of them.

Where are they coming from? he thought to himself.

And then there were Josephine Baker, Marlene Dietrich, Walter Cronkite, and on and on.

Then Col. Dixon, Col. McDowell, Capt. Weinstein, Capt. Thomas, and LTC Bates.

Seven black soldiers in a row saluted Andre as he walked by. They were First Lieutenant Vernon J. Baker, Staff Sergeant Edward A. Carter, Jr., First Lieutenant John R. Fox, Private First Class Willy F. James, Jr., Staff Sergeant Ruben Rivers, Captain Charles L. Thomas, and Private George Watson, the only black Medal of Honor recipients during World War II.

The line continued down the sidewalk, men and women journalists and soldiers honoring Private Williams.

General Patton saluted him as he walked by. Then finally Eleanor Roosevelt and President Franklin Roosevelt appeared, waiting at the end of the line to shake his hand. The president stood with his hand outstretched, thanking him. He was standing. There was no wheelchair.

Andre straightened his back and stood tall. As he walked through the gates of the cemetery, he turned back for one last look at those who stood in his honor.

They were gone. Andre had dreamed yet again, awakening heroes of World War II.

Acknowledgements

Dear Readers:

I hope you enjoyed this book and reading about the exploits of Andre and Booker. This book began in 2014 when learned of Ollie Stewart and his role serving as a journalist covering World War II in the European theater.

I became interested in Ollie Stewart and began to craft this story around the fictional characters Andre and Booker, merging them into a story about Oliver Smith and creating the characters Cub Miller and Tatiana Phillips.

Actual press reports written by Ollie Stewart during World War II are used in this book and are designated with italics. These writings and more can be found at: http://members.tripod.com/black_and_hispanic/blackhistory/invation_of_france.htm (accessed February 15, 2016). Further references to additional italicized quotes and writings by Stewart and other historical figures may be found within the

Notes section, which follows the acknowledgment portion of this book.

The character Tatiana Phillips was inspired by Elizabeth M. Phillips, the first black female journalist to cover World War II. She took ill in London and did not make the trip to France. Her writing, *3,000 Miles to a Hospital*, also provided inspiration for this novel and (as of February 2016) can be found at: http://black_and_hispanic.tripod.com/blackhistory/elezibath_phillips.htm.

Harry McAlpin was the first black reporter to attend a White House Press conference in 1944. His name was changed to "Henry McClain," attending the White House Conference in 1941. This is fictional, but the recording of that press conference by May Craig did occur. The conclusion of that conversation, as President Roosevelt announces the War Information Office, is fictional.

The scene with Tatiana Phillips following a day in the life and talking with Eleanor Roosevelt is fictional. Mrs. Roosevelt's dialogue comes from her White House writings, although she did visit the destinations on the same days depicted in this book.

The character Alexander MacGowan is based on Alexander Gault McGowan. McGowan was born in England and worked for the *The Sun* of New York; he was the oldest journalist to serve in World War II. His relationship with Oliver Smith is fictional.

The description of St. Peter's church is inspired by the Shrine of the Most Blessed Sacrament in Hanceville, Alabama. The chapel described at the beginning is the chapel in Irondale, Alabama, as part of the Eternal Word Television Network (EWTN).

The downtown scene in Mountain Springs is a depiction of Fort Worth, Texas in 1969. The "Bargain Barn" was the "Bargain Box," located at the corner of First and Main Street. "Betty Lou's Grill" was "Betty's Grill," where members of the jury and judges did frequent during lunch breaks. A pawn shop was located next door to the First Street Barbershop, and next door to that was "Famous Hamburgers," with hamburgers and onions that began cooking as described at 10:30 a.m. — and of course the onion smell that permeated throughout the downtown area. A lady in a wheelchair did sing on the corner and sold pencils. The characters of Louis, Alvin, and Shorty Miller were based on real people who worked at First Street Barbershop in downtown Fort Worth.

Thanks to the license agreement with the estate of Josephine Baker for her depiction in the book. Josephine Baker™ is a trademark of the Estate of Josephine Baker, licensed by CMG Worldwide. www.CMGWorldwide.com.

Ollie Stewart did interview Josephine Baker in Casablanca in 1943. The dialogue in this book between Oliver Smith and Josephine Baker is fictional. A portion of Ms. Baker's interview comes from

Josephine: The Hungry Heart, by Jean-Claude Baker and Chris Chase (New York: Cooper Square Press, 2001), p. 258. She was not at the hotel described in the book and did not perform "Don't Touch Me Tomato" at the hotel in Casablanca.

Ernie Pyle and Ollie Stewart did sail on the same ship from London to Oran in 1942 as depicted in this book; the men actually knew each other. Pyle references Stewart in his writing, but the conversations and relationship between Smith and Pyle are fictional. Many of the scenes depicted in Africa are real representations of the African Campaign, taken from the writings of Ernie Pyle. Alexander MacGowan's dialogue in the ship's cabin with Oliver Smith is inspired by the teachings of Dr. Wayne Dyer.

The scenes depicted in the book of Oliver Smith's travels in Africa come from the following writings: *Ernie Pyle's War: America's Eyewitness to World War II* by James Tobin (Free Press, 2006), *Ernie's War: The Best of Ernie Pyle's World War II Dispatches* by David Nichols (Random House, 1986), and *Here Is Your War: Story of G.I. Joe* by Ernie Pyle (University of Nebraska Press, 2004).

Thanks to Simon & Schuster and the heirs of Ernest Hemingway and Simon & Schuster for permission to portray Ernest Hemingway in this book.

The depiction of Ernest Hemingway before the Inspector General proceeding comes from the book *Hemingway*, by Kenneth Lynn, Harvard University Press (1995). The examination of Hemingway is fictional, but is based on the writing.

The scene depicting the incident in Rambouillet between Ernest Hemingway and Bruce Grant is taken from the book *My War* by Andy Rooney (New York: PublicAffairs, 2002).

Thanks to the heirs and Estate of Marlene Dietrich and Peter Riva, the grandson of Ms. Dietrich, for permission to portray her in this book.

The depiction of the scene between Ernest Hemingway and Marlene Dietrich has fictional dialogue. According to the book by Mary Welsh Hemingway, *How It Was*, New York: Ballentine Books (1976), Marlene Dietrich did visit Ernest Hemingway while in Paris. And Ernest Hemingway did sing on many occasions as reported in her book, while Mary Welsh sang alto.

The story of the capture of Alexander Jefferson comes from the book *Red Tail Captured, Red Tail Free: The Memoirs of a Tuskegee Airman and POW*, by Alexander Jefferson (New York: Fordham University Press, 2005).

The sections of the book depicting the 761st Tank Battalion are derived from the book *Patton's Panthers: The African American 761st Tank Battalion in*

World War II, by Charles Sasser, published by Pocket Books (2004) under a license agreement with Simon & Schuster.

The interview by Tatiana Phillips with LTC Paul Bates is fictional.

Tatiana Phillips's interview of Major Charity Adams is also fictional, but the source material comes from her book *One Woman's Army: A Black Officer Remembers the WAC* by Charity Adams Early, Texas A&M Press (1989). Thanks to Stanley Early and Judith Early the son and daughter for assistance in the portrayal of their mother Major Charity Adams. Further information about Major Adams can be viewed at https://www.youtube.com/watch?v=G2_0HZMv2dA.

The court-martial depicted in this book is fictional.

Other sources for the book include: *Black Warriors: The Buffalo Soldiers of World War II: Memories of the Only Negro Infantry Division to Fight in Europe* by Ivan J. Houston (IUniverse, 2009); *The Face of War* by Martha Gellhorn (Atlantic Monthly Press, 1994); *Operation Dragoon: The Allied Invasion of the South of France* by William Breuer (Presidio Press, 1987); *The Black Panthers: A Story of Race, War, and Courage* by Gina M. DiNicolo (Westholme Publishing, 2014); *The Tuskegee Airmen: An Illustrated History: 1939-1949* by Joseph Caver, Jerome Ennels, and Daniel

Haulman (NewSouth Books, 2011); *A Woman at War: Marlene Dietrich Remembered* edited by J. David Riva (Wayne State University Press, 2006); "The Afro-American's World War II Correspondents: Feuilletonism as Social Action" by Antero Pietila and Stacy Spaulding (Literary Journalism Studies, Volume 5, No. 2, Fall 2013); *Lee Miller: A Life* by Carolyn Burke (University of Chicago Press, 2005); *Soldier of the Press: Covering the Front in Europe and North Africa, 1936 – 1943* by Henry T. Gorrell (The Curators of the University of Missouri, 2009); *Where The Action Was: Women War Correspondents in World War II* by Penny Colman (Crown Publishers, 2002); and *Reporting World War II: American Journalism 1938 – 1946* (Library of America, 2001).

Perry Cockerell
April 2016

Notes

Part 1: "Andre and Booker"

Chapters 1 and 5

Songs: **"Believe In Me" (Chapter 1)**
and **"It's Not That Easy" (Chapter 5)**

Words and Music by Todd Harry Rundgren

Song: **"Believe In Me"**
By Todd Harry Rundgren

Part 2: "The Press"

Chapter 3

1. "May Craig, Maine's Tough-as-a-Lobster Newswoman," New England Historical Society, http://www.newenglandhistoricalsociety.com/may-craig-maines-tough-lobster-newswoman/ (accessed February 15, 2016).

Chapter 4

2. Eric Durr, "Harlem Guardsmen Made Black History," New York State Division of Military and Naval Affairs, http://dmna.ny.gov/news/?id=1207935768 (Feb 13, 2008).

Chapter 6

3. Bob Ray Sanders, columnist for the *Fort Worth Star-Telegram*, Dallas Press Club Excellence in Journalism Award Ceremony, May 21, 2015.

4. Quote attributed to Blackie Sherrod, columnist and sportswriter for the *Dallas Morning News*

Chapter 8

5. Ollie Stewart, "Invasion of France," http://members.tripod.com/black_and_hispanic/blackhistory/invation_of_france. htm (accessed February 15, 2016).

6. Ernie Pyle, *Here is Your War: Story of G.I. Joe* (Lincoln: University of Nebraska Press, 2004).

Chapter 9

7. Paraphrased from Dr. Wayne Dyer.
8. Paraphrased from Dr. Wayne Dyer.

Chapter 10

9. Ernie Pyle, *Here is Your War: Story of G.I. Joe* (Lincoln: University of Nebraska Press, 2004), 4.

Chapter 12

10. Ernie Pyle, *Here is Your War: Story of G.I. Joe* (Lincoln: University of Nebraska Press, 2004).
11. Ibid.
12. Ibid.

Chapter 14

13. Ernie Pyle, *Here is Your War: Story of G.I. Joe* (Lincoln: University of Nebraska Press, 2004).
14. Ibid.

Chapter 15

15. Jean-Claude Baker and Chris Chase, *Josephine: The Hungry Heart* (New York: Cooper Square Press, 2001), 258.
16. Matthew Pratt Guterl, *Josephine Baker and the Rainbow Tribe* (Cambridge: Belknap Press, 2014) and Jean-Claude

Baker and Chris Chase, *Josephine: The Hungry Heart* (New York: Cooper Square Press, 2001), 258.

Chapter 19

17. 1943 “My Day” Newspaper Columns by Eleanor Roosevelt, George Washington University, https://www.gwu.edu/~erpapers/myday/displaydoc.cfm?_y=1943&_f=md056394 (accessed February 15, 2016).

Chapter 24

18. Charles W. Sasser, *Patton’s Panthers: The African American 761st Tank Battalion in World War II*, (New York: Simon & Schuster/Gallery Books, 2005).

19. Ibid.

Chapter 26

20. Walter Cronkite, *A Reporter’s Life*, (New York: Ballantine Books, 1997).

Chapter 28

21. Art Carter, “The Miraculous Jump,” http://members.tripod.com/black_and_hispanic/blackhistory/invation_of_france.htm (accessed February 15, 2016).

22. Art Carter, “When Peace Comes, Joe Wants Conn,” http://members.tripod.com/black_and_hispanic/blackhistory/invation_of_france.htm (accessed February 15, 2016).

Part Three: The Liberation of France

Chapter 7

23. Michael Reynolds, *Hemingway: The Paris Years* (New York City: W.W. Norton & Company, 1989).

24. Lyse Doucet, "Two Women Reporters Determined to Cover World War II," *BBC News*, June 5, 2014. http://www.bbc.com/news/magazine-27677889

25. Ibid.

26. Andy Rooney, *My War* (New York: PublicAffairs, 2002).

27. Ollie Stewart, "Invasion of France," http://members.tripod.com/black_and_hispanic/blackhistory/invasion_of_france.htm (accessed February 15, 2016).

Chapter 10

28. Andy Rooney, *My War* (New York: PublicAffairs, 2002).

Chapter 11

29. Lyse Doucet, "Two Women Reporters Determined to Cover World War II," *BBC News*, June 5, 2014. http://www.bbc.com/news/magazine-27677889

Chapter 12

30. Charles W. Sasser, *Patton's Panthers: The African American 761st Tank Battalion in World War II* (New York: Simon & Schuster/Gallery Books, 2005).

31. Ibid.
32. Ibid.

Chapter 13

33. Alexander Jefferson, *Red Tail Captured, Red Tail Free: The Memoirs of a Tuskegee Airman and POW* (New York: Fordham University Press, 2005).
34. Ibid.

Part 4: "The Dream"

Chapter 2

Song: **"Believe In Me"**
Words and Music by Todd Harry Rundgren

Song: **"Believe In Me"**
By Todd Harry Rundgren

Chapter 5

35. David Nichols, ed., *Ernie's War: The Best of Ernie Pyle's World War II Dispatches* (New York: Random House, 1986).

36. Ollie Stewart, "Invasion of France," http://members.tripod.com/black_and_hispanic/blackhistory/invation_of_france.htm (accessed February 15, 2016).

Chapter 6

37. Mary Welsh Hemingway, *How it Was* (New York: Ballantine Books, 1977).

38. Hemingway letters to Marlene Dietrich.

39. Marlene Dietrich quote.

40. Interview of Marlene Dietrich, Copenhagen (1971).

41. Based on speech by Gregory Peck at Tony Awards in 1968 for Marlene Dietrich.

42. Mary Welsh Hemingway, *How it Was* (New York: Ballantine Books, 1977).

Chapter 7

43. "Airdrop at Arnhem," *Twenthieth Century Documentary Interview with Walter Cronkite.* CBS Network, January 20, 1963. http://billdownscbs.blogspot.com/2014/07/1944-downs-and-cronkite-in-low-countries.html. (accessed February 15, 2016).

Chapter 14

44. Kenneth Lynn, *Hemingway* (Cambridge: Harvard University Press, 1995).

Chapter 24

Song: **"You Are My Window"**
Words and Music by Todd Harry Rundgren

Part 5: The Trial

Chapter 21

45. Ollie Stewart, "Invasion of France," http://members.tripod.com/black_and_hispanic/blackhistory/invation_of_france.htm (accessed February 15, 2016).

CPSIA information can be obtained
at www.ICGtesting.com
Printed in the USA
LVHW052253180219
607900LV00014B/675